The SACRED PLACE

Also by Daniel Black

They Tell Me of a Home

The SACRED PLACE

Daniel Black

St. Martin's Press ✹ New York

To Emmett Till:
Your life forced us to rise
and change the world.

This is a work of fiction. All of the characters, organizations, and events portrayed in this novel are either products of the author's imagination or are used fictitiously.

www.stmartins.com

Design by Maggie Goodman

Library of Congress Cataloging-in-Publication Data

Black, Daniel.
    The sacred place / Daniel Black.—1st ed.
        p. cm.
    ISBN-13: 978-0-312-35971-3
    ISBN-10: 0-312-35971-3
    1. African American teenage boys—Crimes against—Mississippi—Fiction.
    2. Mississippi—Race relations—Fiction. 3. Racism—Mississippi—Fiction.
    I. Title.

PS3602.L267S23 2007
813'.6—dc22

                                                                    2006050974

First Edition: February 2007

10 9 8 7 6 5 4 3 2 1

Acknowledgments

To my elders: Your wisdom permeates these pages. Be proud of what you've taught.

To the Lebechi: Your support made this effort possible. Thank you for funding so meticulously that I could write.

To Akinyele, Kokumo, Akobundu, Makata, Ajani, and Rasidi: Walking with you has been a sheer joy! Might this novel stand as evidence of the fruit of hard work. I thank you for letting me lean on you when my own strength began to falter. You are my sons and daughters forever.

To my friends who read this novel in its embryonic state: Thank you for your criticisms, your encouragement, your belief in my literary abilities, and your reminder to me that I have a gift.

One

"COME ON, CLEMENT!" HIS COUSINS DEMANDED. "YOU AIN'T got no business in dat store! Granddaddy kill you if he find out you went in there all by yo'self!"

Clement smiled at the thought of his own defiance, trying to imagine what eighty-year-old Jeremiah Johnson could possibly do to him, with one bad leg and two failing eyes. Of course a whoopin' would hurt, he considered, but the pain was always temporal. All he wanted was a soda pop, and he didn't understand why he couldn't simply waltz into the General Store and get one. That's what white folks did when they wanted something; why should he be afraid to do the same?

"Clement!" the others screamed more vehemently as he approached the old wooden screen door. Sarah Jane's tears were more than her mouth could speak. At twelve, she knew never to be found alone with white folk because her grandmother's threat to whip her good was not to be taken lightly. Stories of Black kids who disappeared after being last seen with whites was enough to keep her at least fifty feet from any of them, so Clement's audacity frightened her and rendered her mute. Only her tears expressed her fear that he was making a fatal mistake. The boys, Ray Ray and Chop, simply shook their heads, and murmured, "City boys. They think they know everything."

Hoping not to witness a tragedy, the three walked home in the ninety-degree heat and mumbled silent prayers that Granddaddy wouldn't beat Clement too badly. After all, he was new to the place and didn't understand the rules of Black Southern life. Chicago had groomed him for fourteen years prior to his arrival in Money, Mississippi, and left him believing that a resident of the Windy City could survive anywhere. Indeed, the day Jeremiah Johnson retrieved him from the Greenwood train station, Clement boasted of insight beyond anything his cousins could imagine. He spoke of prostitutes, pimps, and kids who roamed the streets long after the night-light appeared. The brand-new twenty-dollar bill he excavated from his front pocket elicited praise and envy from sharecropping children who had never seen anything beyond a five. Clement was the teacher who, with feigned exasperation, shared stories about Chicago Negroes who owned houses and never worked for white folks.

"Whwhwhwhat d-d-d-dey d-do thththen?" Chop stammered incredulously. Silence was his usual mode, but the notion that Negroes somewhere didn't submit their labor to whites unleashed an otherwise restrained tongue. At eight, his self-esteem, like rain on a rooftop, was falling in more directions than he could catch. His stuttering kept folks—both his own and others—from planting seeds of intelligence in him, having concluded already that he would make a marvelous field hand one day. His mother had allowed him to wear his one good pair of overalls to meet his citified cousin, who laughed at the only hole she had failed to patch.

"They work for theyselves, fool!" Clement proclaimed, although everyone knew these weren't his folks. "They own they own businesses, and they hire Black folks just like they white."

"Wow," Chop mumbled. Everybody he knew picked cotton, washed white folks' clothes, or worked on the railroad in Greenwood.

"That ain't all. Some of 'em even marries white, too. And they live together like it ain't nothin'!" Clement continued.

"You hush up dat kinda talk 'round here boy," Jeremiah Johnson interrupted. "You ain't in Chicago no mo. Yous in Mississippi. And round here, coloreds stay wit coloreds and whites stay wit whites. And dat's de way it is."

Chop lamented Granddaddy's imposition and planned mentally what he would ask Clement later. He wanted to know more about city life and how he could, one day, live in a house he owned all by himself. Chop refused to stop hoping for the day when Granddaddy— or any Black daddy—could work without giving all his money away.

Clement entered the General Store with an entitlement unknown to Mississippi Negroes in 1955. He didn't even knock. He just opened the door, walked in, and started looking around for the soda pop machine.

"Help ya?" Catherine Cuthbert's soft soprano voice asked reluctantly.

Staring her in the eye, Clement returned, "Sure. Where you keep your soda pops?"

"In the big barrel over there," she drawled, and nodded. Never had a Negro boy looked directly at her without flinching. She knew he couldn't be from Money or anywhere in Mississippi for that matter.

Clement proceeded, humming snippets of Fats Domino's "Ain't That a Shame," and retrieved a root beer. Setting it on the countertop, he reached into his right trouser pocket and placed a nickel next to the soda bottle.

"You put that nickel in my hand!" she demanded.

Clement frowned, surprised. "Excuse me?"

Catherine Cuthbert's hazel eyes narrowed. "I said, put that nickel in my hand—boy!"

Clement's brow puckered at the insult. "There it is! You pick it up!" he sneered, opening the soda and beginning to drink.

"I said hand me that nickel, nigger boy!" Her outstretched hand trembled with expectation as her face transformed from cotton to crimson.

"I already paid you, lady! If you too lazy to pick up the nickel, that's your problem, not mine," Clement belted, and turned to exit.

"You'll never get away with disrespecting me like that!" she screamed.

"I already did!" Clement chuckled and skipped away. Who did she think she was anyway, he wondered. "Slavery been over," he shouted over his shoulder, sipping the root beer like it was a spoil of war.

Catherine Cuthbert watched him with a vengeance she could not articulate. Never had a colored boy disobeyed her command, and absolutely never had one attempted to speak to her as an equal. "He just laid that nickel down and expected me to pick it up," she whispered repeatedly to herself, inciting an internal rage that produced rivers of sweat beads meandering down her rose red forehead. Pacing in fury, she vowed to reclaim her purity from a nigger boy who dared think he could speak to her any kind of way.

Catching up with the others, Clement told them what had happened.

"Is you crazy?" Sarah Jane yelled. "Don't you know dat white folks kill colored boys over dat kinda stuff?" Her father had rendered his life one windy, October evening a few years prior after some whites had raped and mutilated his wife. Knowing no other recourse, he killed them. By nightfall, his long legs added to the extensions hanging from the big oak tree on Chapman's place. Sarah Jane couldn't explain all the details without wailing uncontrollably, but she tried. "You cain't come down to Mississippi, Clement, and ack like you still up Norf!" She swung mightily and hit him in the shoulder.

"What's wrong with you, girl?" Clement's bulging eyes showed that he didn't comprehend the depth of Sarah Jane's objection.

"No, what's wrong wit you!" she bellowed in his face. "You think you ain't colored like de rest o' us? You think dat jes 'cause you from Chicago, you ain't got to bow to white folks?"

"I ain't got to bow to nobody," Clement said proudly. "My momma told me dat I was jes as good as anybody else, and dat she would whip me if she ever caught me bowing my head to white folks."

Sarah Jane swung her arms as though a spirit possessed and said, "Aunt Possum didn't mean fo you to come down here and sass white folks 'til you git yoself kilt!" She fell to the ground helplessly and released the heavy sobs she had been trying to confine.

"Don't cry, Sarah Jane," Ray Ray begged, embarrassed. "Everythang gon be all right."

"No, it ain't!" she screamed. "You know white folks don't 'low no colored peoples to talk to dem like dat!"

"Well, they don't know me," Clement boasted. "Anyway, I didn't do nothin' wrong. I just went in the store, bought me a soda pop, and paid for it."

Sarah Jane tried not to imagine Clement pleading for his life before a merciless white mob, but each time he spoke, the image became clearer. "Why didn't you hand the woman the nickel, Clement?" she huffed.

"'Cause I didn't have to! All I had to do was pay her, and that's what I did. I ain't no slave! She cain't talk to me like I ain't nothin'!" Clement had hoped his cousins would celebrate his boldness; instead their reprimand infuriated him. "I ain't scared o' white folks! Y'all might be, but I ain't!"

As though she hadn't heard him, Sarah Jane said, "I hope to God this don't come to nothin'." She stood and brushed off her cotton sack dress. "You didn't have no business bein' rude to Miss Cuthbert like dat, Clement. You coulda jes put de money in her hand"—she acted out the motion slowly—"and left."

"Okay, okay. Let's jes fugit about it," Ray Ray intervened before allowing himself to envision a wounded Clement. Ray Ray was fourteen, too, only a month older than Clement, but at least five inches taller. His overalls, which were always too short and too tight, made him look bound and constrained. Most girls considered him the cutest boy in Money though, with his enviable, flawless, caramel brown complexion and hair that curled at the sight of water. He never said much, afraid of saying the wrong thing, and he hated nothing more than tension. Or maybe looking after his younger brother Chop. Ray Ray named him that after watching him devour a pork chop—bone and all—at six months. Their parents had named him Hope, but once Ray Ray started calling him Chop, his birth name faded into myth. At the moment, Ray Ray simply wanted everybody to stop talking so his nerves could settle.

They walked home in silence. Occasionally, Sarah Jane shook her head sadly as she remembered, but she decided to pray now instead of argue. Chop wanted to hear more of Clement's Chicago stories, but as the youngest of the bunch he had learned early when simply to shut up and follow. He watched Ray Ray kick the same stone for almost a mile, amazed at his brother's concentration and precision. Some days, he wanted to hug him and tell him he was the greatest big brother in the whole wide world, but fear of rejection kept him from ever doing it. Plus, his stuttering probably wouldn't have let him get the words out right.

Clement wondered what the summer would bring. He had visited before, but now he wouldn't go home until the end of August. What do colored country kids do when they don't go to school? he wondered. What he knew for sure was that he wasn't going to genuflect to white folks all summer. It seemed demeaning to him, the "yessir" and "no ma'am" Southern culture required of Black folks. How would the world ever become equal if only colored people showed respect? No, that couldn't be right, and he promised himself he wouldn't do it. White folks needed to see what a Black person looked like who re-

fused to degrade himself on their behalf, and Clement concluded that
he was the one to show them.

The house the Johnsons lived in offered very little room to four
grandchildren and four adults. It contained a kitchen, living room,
and two bedrooms, and a small wash area where one could stand and
clean himself. Old man Chapman allowed the Johnsons to live in the
house since they worked his crops. It was the least he could do, he
said. Yes, it needed a little *mending*—that's how he described it—but
it beat living outdoors. "Barely," Miss Mary had mumbled. Still, she
tried her best to beautify a dilapidated structure by placing plants
and handcrafted afghans everywhere she could. The house was always immaculate, and Miss Mary's warm smile kept people coming.
She was a rather burly woman whose ability to construct a full meal
from nothing but flour and potatoes was miraculous. There was always something to eat, even when the cupboards were bare, so Miss
Mary never complained about adverse circumstances. "De Good
Lawd gon provide!" she always said, lifting her thick arms in praise.

Jeremiah had asked, years ago, if he could paint the house, but
Chapman told him to spend his energy raising crops. "You ain't got
time for no foolishness like that, boy!" Chapman scolded. So the dull,
gray planks remained weather-exposed as the Johnsons vowed never
to emulate Chapman's bigotry.

Jeremiah and Mary married in the spring of 1900, the day after
Mary buried her mother. They moved to Chapman's shack a week
later and had been there ever since. The winter before their occu-
pancy, it functioned as the hay barn and toolshed although a badly
leaking roof caused Chapman to build a new barn, thus allowing the
newlyweds to move into the old one. "The rain ain't so bad," Chapman encouraged, spitting tobacco on the tip of Jeremiah's brogans.
"Six or seven buckets here or there oughta take care of it." The poor
Black couple made the best of it. Jeremiah patched all the holes he

could find, anxious to give his pregnant wife a modicum of comfort, and Mary milled about making pretty yellow curtains for glassless windows. Both had dreamed of leaving Mississippi, but poverty and self-doubt bound them permanently to the Delta. However, the land, the Tallahatchie River, the jonquils, the brown squirrels, and the Friday night fish fries were all cultural relics that they cherished. Actually, the only thing they hated about Ole Sippi, as they called it, was the ubiquity of racist white folks.

The couple was determined to retain at least some agency although they owned nothing and possessed little power. The barn shack held memories of Thanksgiving dinners complete with wild turkey and dressing, corn on the cob, collard greens, and chitlins. Miss Mary was famous, before arthritis intervened, for cleaning a hundred pounds of hog guts at a time as she hummed church songs in the deepest alto a woman could sustain. She'd place them in a large black caldron in the front yard and boil them slowly throughout the night. Next day, folks walked two and three miles to partake of what Miss Mary called her delicacy. "Goddamn!" menfolk exclaimed as their wives smiled in envy. "Dese thangs make a man hurt hisself!" By nightfall, the caldron, plates, and forks had been washed and put away, and chitlin lovers were forced to endure until the next Thanksgiving.

The first child was a girl, Clement's mother, whom they called Possum. Her name was Mamie, but when she came out, the midwife announced, "You got yo'self a pretty li'l girl, Miss Mary! Eyes narrow like a l'il ole possum!" so that's what folks called her. She never knew her birth name until the day she started school.

"Each of you stand and introduce yourselves," the teacher insisted.

"Billy Joe Harris," one confident, curly-headed boy began.

"Catherine Sneed," a chubby Black girl followed.

Miss Mary's firstborn rose, and declared, "Possum."

"Beg pardon?" the teacher prodded.

"Possum," she pronounced slowly and more loudly. Other children bellowed.

"Silence!" the teacher demanded. And like the turbulent wind and waves upon Jesus' command, the children calmed instantly. "That is not your name, young lady!"

"Yes, ma'am, it is," she whimpered, afraid to defy yet knowing no other name by which she had ever been called.

"Your name is not Possum, young lady. It may be what others call you, but that could not possibly be your rightful name."

Having no other name to offer, Possum assured her she would inquire at home about the matter, and when she did, her parents laughed gleefully and told her her name was Mamie Johnson. "I don't like dat name," she frowned in return and consequently told the schoolteacher her real name was, in fact, Possum. Unwilling to admit differently, she stood in the corner three weeks until the teacher relented and accepted Possum as her legitimate identity. She would continue this tradition of contentiousness until, at age sixteen, she escaped to Chicago and promised never to pick another cotton bole as long as she lived.

Miss Mary noticed the slow waltz of the children in the distance and knew something wasn't right.

"What's de matter, chile?" she asked Sarah Jane, who dragged onto the front porch lazily. "You been fightin'? Why yo clothes so dirty?"

She looked at Ray Ray, and said, "Somebody better start talkin' 'round hyeah 'fo I get after y'all!"

Not wanting to expose Clement, Sarah Jane lied, "I fell."

"How you fall, girl?"

Sarah Jane hesitated. "When we wuz . . . um . . . crossin' de pond bank, I slipped and fell. Ray Ray had to help me up."

Miss Mary looked to Ray Ray. "Her foot musta slipped on a rock or somethin', Grandma. I don't know how it happened. All I know is I heard her cryin' like somebody wuz killin' her, so I ran to help her out. She okay though." Ray Ray walked into the house, praying his explanation would satisfy a skeptical grandmother.

"Oh I see," she said. "I'm glad y'all takes care o'one another. That's real sweet." Of course she didn't believe them, but Sarah Jane was glad simply for the moment to be over. She had never lied to Miss Mary, and she hoped doing so now would be worth the outcome.

Sarah Jane's father was the second child, a shy, quiet youngster who never bothered anybody. Named Jeremiah, Jr., folks called him Jerry when they called him at all. Sometimes days would pass before he'd utter a single word, and that was usually to his dog Pete. From a distance, his father watched him hold hourly conversations with Pete, crying and laughing as the dog seemingly did the same. Jerry's navy blue-black complexion put off most colored folks, so Pete became his best (and sometimes his only) friend. Miss Mary reminded the boy constantly of his beauty, comparing his complexion to the midnight sky. Her exultations made Jerry smile and forgive others' inability to see God in him. With large, puppy-dog eyes, a soft nature, and eyelashes longer than any woman's, he caused many to wonder why such gorgeous features were cloaked under layers of diabolical blackness. Most rejected him as awkward-looking and smiled condescendingly. Seldom speaking in return, he was often thought impertinent and disrespectful.

"What's wrong wit dat boy, Miss Mary?" folks asked.

She would smile softly, and return, "Nothin'. He jes know when other folks is full o' shit."

Of course no one dared proceed, for Miss Mary was known to fight like a pinned bull to protect her children. "He be all right," she assured people defensively.

Jerry proved to be the smartest boy the Black school in Money ever graduated. At five, he already knew his times tables and could outread most of the fifteen-year-olds. The high yellow teacher searched Jerry's exams desperately for errors, believing it impossible that a jet-black, poor country boy could be that smart, yet, finding few errors, she scribbled "A" on his papers in disgust and disdain.

When called forth to read, he would simply stand and speak with an authority unknown to children—or adults for that matter—in rural Mississippi. The eloquence of his tongue, the confidence flowing from his demeanor, and the pride with which he held his shoulders made him at once the envy and the admiration of children who never imagined God to grant anybody Black such academic prowess. Jerry never thought of himself as different or gifted though. Actually, he was often depressed that his schoolwork was subpar, in his estimation, and troubled that others considered it so meticulous.

After school, he never fellowshipped with other children, preferring to saunter through the woods with Pete and admire the brown, yellow, and golden leaves in the fall and gather wildflowers in the spring. Jeremiah thought something might be wrong with the boy, maybe that he needed a good whoopin' or the love of Jesus Christ in his heart. But Miss Mary warned him not to lay a hand on Jerry or something bad would surely befall him. Jerry was a spirit child, she said, who had to be given space to be himself. "He don't bother nobody, and ain't nobody gon bother him," she proclaimed. Jeremiah walked away, shaking his head.

Late one April evening, a cottonmouth moccasin found its way into the barn-shack house and scared Miss Mary speechless. Hoping not to expose her utter fear of snakes, she froze, statuesque, and tried to remain calm. It was twelve-year-old Jerry who discovered his mother in the living room, staring at something that wouldn't let her go. Following her gaze, he saw the three-inch-thick, black snake coiled in the middle of the floor as though claiming territory.

"Don't move, baby," Miss Mary cried.

Jerry approached the poisonous creature bravely and reached his small hand toward its head.

"No!" his mother yelled, too afraid to rescue him.

But Jerry proceeded, glancing at Miss Mary to assure her he was in no danger. Suddenly, the snake began to slither up his arm and curl around his neck. "It tickles," he laughed heartily, and walked out the front door.

Miss Mary followed in angst and wonder. She wanted to protest, planning the whoopin' he was going to receive later, but in the moment, she was more intrigued than angry. Jerry led her to his scared place in the woods—a clearing deep in the middle of Old Man Chapman's land—and whispered, "This is the Kingdom of God."

"Be careful, son," was the best she could intone since Jerry provided no preamble for what was about to transpire.

He uncoiled the snake from his neck and torso and gently placed it upon the earth. As it slithered away casually, Jerry said, "He won't hurt you, Momma. He just got lost." Miss Mary's pretty mocha face was as pale as gardenia blossoms. She turned and ran home, weeping and gnashing her teeth, trying to convince herself she hadn't seen what she had seen.

"Now you stay put," Jerry said in the direction of the snake. "Folks'll hurt you if you get outta place." He waved good-bye, then tried to ascertain how he'd explain this to his mother. Finding nothing to say, he decided to let God lead him.

Miss Mary was sitting on the porch reading her Bible when Jerry returned.

"It ain't nothin', Momma," he mumbled, and sat on the lowest step just below her thick, flat feet.

"It *is* somethin'," she declared. "You got yo'self a gift, boy. I don't know what de Lawd want wit chu, but He preparin' you for somethin'." She resumed reading and praying for understanding.

In 1940, Jerry earned the first scholarship given to a Black boy from Money, Mississippi. He had never heard the word "Tougaloo" before, although the college was barely two hours away. The day before he left, his father advised, "Study hard, son, and make sho you mind dem teachas. A educated colored man git far in de world today." He wanted to grab Jerry and hold him, yet Southern propriety insisted that he pat his son on the shoulder instead, hoping his touch alone conveyed the sentiment of his heart. Miss Mary, on the other hand, cried freely. A week before his departure, she dreamed about Jerry encountering a group of racist white men on the day of his college graduation. They took his mortarboard cap and stomped upon it.

"You dat smart nigga from Money, ain't cha?" they jeered.

Jerry stared at them, unafraid.

"Ain't you gon say nothin', nigger boy? Use some of dem big college words so we can see what you done learned."

Again, Jerry held his peace, waiting to see just how far these bigots would go. Attempting to walk away, he was overwhelmed with punches and kicks until, balled on the ground in a fetal position, he whimpered like Pete when Old Man Chapman ran over him.

Miss Mary awakened and spent the rest of the night pleading with God to cover her baby with the blood of Jesus and to save him from hurt, harm, or danger.

At Tougaloo, Jerry prospered. His stellar academic performance— 3.8 first semester—made him a faculty favorite. The B came from Dr. Moore, a professor who swore Jerry stole the final exam for Biology 101 because no one had ever scored so perfectly on any of his tests. Unable to convince him otherwise, Jerry took the B as confirmation of his mother's belief that, wherever you go, "somebody ain't gon like you." Other professors adored him. They bought him books, fed him, and encouraged his dream of becoming Money's first Black doctor. However, upon graduation, Jerry returned to Money because Miss Mary's health was deteriorating. She begged him to accept the scholarship to Howard University School of Medicine, but Jerry ignored her, spending his leisure time in The Sacred Place and doing everything possible to assist her healing.

Billie Faye Moore started coming by often, hoping to take up with Jerry whom she had loved since childhood. Jerry liked her, too, but he had never thought about loving her.

"I know you diff'rent, Jerry Johnson, and dat's what I likes 'bout you," Billie Faye told him one summer evening after his return. She had come by to check on Miss Mary, she said, but while she was there, she had a few choice words for Jerry, too.

"You can ignore me if you want to, Mr. Jerry Johnson, but ain't nobody never gone love you de way I do." Billie Faye was known for being outspoken, bold, and absolutely unconcerned with what other folks thought. Still, people claimed she was the sweetest person de Good Lawd ever made. Her three hundred pounds did not hamper her self-confidence and, in fact, she carried her weight like one might a lethal weapon. Large, rounded hips and 44G breasts complemented each other and functioned as armor for a rather delicate soul. Her perfectly round face boasted deep dimples and fat cheeks that shivered when she spoke, and her hair was always cut in a short afro. She often stood arms akimbo, even when laughing, and that very stance is what Jerry admired so deeply. He never told her that she would be exactly the type of woman he wanted—if he ever wanted one at all.

"You can sit here and act like you don't hear me if you want to, but I'm gon keep lovin' you 'til you come to yo senses." Billie Faye switched down the front steps.

"Wait," Jerry murmured intensely.

Billie Faye smiled, turned around, and said, "It's about time, fool. I wunnit gon' wait foreva."

They sat on the porch and held hands as Billie Faye talked long into the night. Jerry never said anything, responding only with grunts and moans to assure his girlfriend that he was listening. And he was.

By morning, he told his mother that he wanted to marry Billie Faye Moore.

"Oh I likes her!" Miss Mary confirmed from her sickbed. Three days later, she was back to her old self again.

When he told Jeremiah, his father teased, "Now dat's a lotta woman, boy!"

The wedding occurred late September in The Sacred Place. Because of its location, people left their wagons along the road and followed Jeremiah through the yellowing forest until they reached the clearing.

"Shit! Dis look like heaven!" Tiny Dawson heralded. Children broke free of their parents and scattered across the opening while adults marveled at the beauty of the place. "De grass is so green!" somebody whispered. "And look at de jonquils! They done withered everywhere else!" another woman noted.

Jerry stood tall in the center of the land, with outstretched arms like a one-member welcoming committee. Dressed in his good overalls and a white shirt, he smiled to see people coming from every direction to witness his wedding. He didn't know that, after that day, people would frequent The Sacred Place as though each had found it, but he was glad to share paradise with whomever needed one.

A few came only to see if Jerry was really going to do it, and when Billie Faye emerged from the woods, draped in an off-white gown trimmed in lace, Jerry wept like Jesus at Lazarus's tomb, and all wondering ceased. The ceremony was conventional and lasted only about twenty minutes. After the two were pronounced husband and wife, and all the guests had gone, they made love right there in the middle of The Sacred Place. A deer stood nearby, watching the beauty of their sensuality, and birds chirped gleefully in praise. Neither had ever experienced another person's body before, but their spirits told them what to do. At his climax, Jerry jerked and emitted a high-pitched whine that made Billie Faye laugh confidently. Then, he buried his head between her mountainous legs, searching desperately to provide her a similar ecstasy. When it came, she growled deep and long like a wild beast preparing for attack. Jerry laughed this time, and the two lay on their backs, completely exposed to the universe, unashamed.

"What we got here, boys!" The cry startled them out of their leisure.

Billie Faye and Jerry stood quickly, attempting to dress themselves. The white men snatched Billie Faye's dress from her trembling hands.

"We got ourselves a wedding! It's dat smart nigger and his new bride! Look at this wedding dress!" The white men held Billie Faye's gown high in the air and mocked its size.

Jerry kept whispering, "Just stay calm," hoping Billie Faye wouldn't be her usual brazen self. She submitted in hopes of maintaining both their lives.

One of the white men robed himself in Billie Faye's wedding dress and pranced around the open space. "You married yo'self a Black cow, boy! She got 'nough milk in dem jugs to feed every nigger in Money!" He reached out and squeezed Billie Faye's left breast. It wasn't this act that took Jerry over the edge; it was the tears streaming down Billie Faye's cheeks that catapulted him into action. Never having seen her weep before, Jerry knew her fighting spirit was slowly seeping away, and he couldn't allow that. So he leapt at the man in Billie Faye's dress and tore dirty white flesh from his face before anyone realized what happened. The other two men jumped on Jerry's back and tried to separate him from their comrade, but Billie Faye lifted them—simultaneously—and tossed them, like discarded chicken bones, into the air. Regaining posture, they lunged back at her, one of them striking her with a wooden stick he found lying on the ground. She never flinched. Instead, she balled her hand tightly, gritted her teeth, and buried her Black fist inside the white man's mouth. His blood splattered the earth of The Sacred Place, and he lost consciousness. Whether he was dead or alive, Billie Faye did not know. The other white man vanished through the woods.

She turned quickly and saw her husband continuing to beat the Bride of Mockery mercilessly. "Let him go, Jerry!" Billie Faye begged, prying his arm from the man's face, but Jerry was in another place and time. The memory of his ancestors who had experienced similar humiliation and grief visited itself upon his spirit and made him vow to end racial inequity once and for all. Or at least to balance the pain of it.

"I said let him go!" Billie Faye protested again, this time pushing Jerry away from the limp white form. Jerry stood, teary-eyed, quivering. "It's gon be okay," Billie Faye comforted. She grabbed his arm and began running through the woods.

"No, it ain't," he murmured softly. "No, it ain't."

They decided to keep the incident to themselves. No need bringing other folks into it and making it more than it was. They expected retribution, knowing full well that they would never get by with beating two white men within a breath of their lives. But, for some reason, the men didn't return. Sarah Jane was born a year later, on the anniversary of the incident, but still nothing had come of the matter. In fact, years transpired as though nothing had ever happened.

Then, on Sarah Jane's eighth birthday, the men came. They figured that, by then, the couple had convinced themselves that they had won and that whites were losing control of Southern Blacks. Such an illusion was precisely what the men desired in order to render a surprise, syrupy-sweet revenge.

Billie Faye had left the cotton field early that day to bake Sarah Jane's birthday cake. As she bent to retrieve it from the old woodstove, she heard the familiar voices.

"Well, well. Dem titties still big like de wuz years ago. Ain't that somethin'."

Billie Faye jerked around quickly, wondering how the men had entered unnoticed. "Get on outta hyeah, now! I don't want no trouble!" She held the hot, cast-iron skillet in midair.

"Oh, it's gon be some trouble, now, darlin'. You didn't really thank we wunnit comin' back, now did ya?" He grinned broadly, showing a mouthful of discolored teeth. "We jes wanted to give y'all time to fo'get."

"Where's dat husband o' yours?" another one asked.

"Not so fast, not so fast," the first one said slowly, motioning for the other to be patient. "We gon have a little fun first."

Billie Faye knew she couldn't conquer all three of them alone. Fear clouded her judgment and eroded her confidence. Yet she was never one to take things easily. She would hold her ground as long as she could, she determined, hoping that by then someone, by the grace of God, might happen by. That someone never came.

As the men drew closer, her once intrepid spirit began to disintegrate.

"Oh, you ain't scairt, is ya?" one asked as he reached toward Billie Faye's breast.

In a flash, she laid the hot skillet against the right side of his face, causing him to stumble.

The other two screamed variations of "Black nigger bitch" and wrestled Billie Faye to the floor. The Bride of Mockery reached under her dress, tore her panties from her flesh, then smelled his finger. "It's ripe for the pickin', boys!" he announced to the other whose total strength was expended binding her arms. The Bride of Mockery unzipped his pants and maneuvered his way between her stiff, uninviting legs. Both entered her before they left her bruised and bleeding.

When she didn't return to the field, Jerry thought little of it initially. Then, after imagining various scenarios, he saw the white men in his mind's eye, and immediately dropped the cotton sack and began running. The swinging screen door told him he was already too late. "No!" he screamed, and ran faster.

Billie Faye lay naked from the waist down. Jerry collapsed onto the floor beside her, repeating, "No, no, no! God, no!" as he covered her gently with the afghan from the sofa and kissed her lips lightly. Closing his eyes in search of strength he could not find, he cradled her in his arms and rocked soothingly, humming every song he knew until Jeremiah and Miss Mary came home. Then, he relinquished her into their care and sneaked out the back door. With his daddy's shotgun and enough calm in his heart to keep from breaking down along the way, he proceeded across the railroad tracks to the white part of Money. Folks asked him where he was going with that shotgun, but Jerry ignored them, having resolved to complete the mission even if it were his last.

He found the redneck white men drinking beer in front of the General Store. They were jovial and almost inebriated.

"What chu want, boy?" they teased. "We didn't hurt yo wife too badly now, did we?"

Their laughter unleashed Jerry's tears. His fledgling manhood was a gargantuan weight upon his soul, and he promised himself that, before the sun set that day, his soul would be free again.

"What chu doin' wit dat gun, Black boy? You ain't mad, is ya?"

That's when Jerry shot all three men dead. His calm disposition made him proud of himself. He didn't even hear the screaming of white women as their men fell. All he heard, in his head, was the "hurrahs!" of his own people. He had never thought of himself as a hero, but then again his mother always said, "De Lawd moves in mysterious ways." He never questioned whether the death of the men was the will of God, having decided a few moments earlier that the will of God is whatever a man gathers the will to do.

Jerry nodded affirmatively and walked back home with a peace few Black men ever know.

"Where you been, boy?" Jeremiah queried nervously upon Jerry's return.

In solemnity, Jerry murmured, "I killed 'em."

"You what?" Jeremiah cried.

"I killed 'em," he repeated.

"Oh God." Jeremiah wept bitterly. "You cain't just shoot white men!" he hollered. "Is you crazy?"

Jerry had hoped his actions might impress his father, but instead Jeremiah's pitiable response reignited Jerry's fury.

"What kinda men are we, Daddy? Huh?" he asked.

Jeremiah never answered. Miss Mary opened her Bible and read various Psalms aloud. Jerry hung his head and went to Billie Faye, who listened as her husband related proudly how God had finally begun to visit vengeance upon the evil of the world. Whether to cry or celebrate she did not know, but Jerry's joy was untouchable. He had always dreamed of being a man, envisioning himself and his father self-reliant, self-determined, and self-empowered. And now the reality caused him to brim with light and enthusiasm.

"They'll hang you sho, man," Billie Faye whimpered, speaking for the first time since the assault. Her hand caressed Jerry's narrow, slender, black face.

He closed his eyes at her touch and assured her everything would be fine. He had done what he was called to do.

The next day, more white men came.

"Where's dat boy!" they screamed at Jeremiah with shotguns pointed at him from every direction.

"He ain't home."

"Then where is he?"

Jeremiah considered that any moment now could be his last, but surprisingly he was unafraid. Maybe his son's strength had become contagious.

"I don't know," he said, smiling.

"We gon kill him when we find him!"

They left foaming at the mouth, swearing that Jerry's blood would flow before the break of a new day. Yet, their thirst to mutilate Jerry Johnson would forever go unquenched because Jerry hanged himself in the middle of The Sacred Place. Jeremiah found him and called Miss Mary and Billie Faye to come. They took down his lean form and carried him home.

"We got to do somethin' now, Daddy," Billie Faye murmured through her pain. "Them mens is comin' back."

"Not for my boy theys ain't," Jeremiah said. He built an altar of fire in The Sacred Place and laid Jerry's body upon it. Miss Mary sang as the ashes rose, "I'm so glad, trouble don't last always." Trees swayed at the sound of her voice, and Billie Faye stared on in silence. "Oh my Lawd, oh my Lawd, what shall I do?"

Billie Faye died eighteen months later. The image of Jerry's lean body swinging from that tree never left her mind and robbed her of all living desires. Her weight dwindled to barely a hundred pounds. Nothing anyone said reached Billie Faye's soul as she sat mummified in the living room rocking chair. When people, like the Reverend Cash, came to see about her, she never acknowledged them. Her mind was still in The Sacred Place, trying to make sense of a loss incomprehensible. Unable to do so, silence became her mantra, and the fighting spirit that Jerry loved so well tiptoed into oblivion. Sometimes, Miss Mary could get her to swallow chicken broth if she sang simultaneously. Tears would jump from Billie Faye's eyes like water from a geyser, and Miss Mary would wipe them gently as she sang, "Trouble in my way, I have to cry sometimes." She would stare at Miss Mary, trying desperately but failing miserably to articulate the pain and emptiness in her heart. Most days, she just shook her head violently, slinging tears from the edge of her face like one scatters grass seeds, never gaining clarity sufficient to reclaim herself.

On the evening of her demise, Miss Mary was reading the Bible to the grandchildren while Jeremiah cleaned his pipe. All hoped the Word of God might usher Billie Faye back to them. "I can do all things through Christ which strengthenth me," Miss Mary began, and Billie Faye turned to face her. The children gasped at what they thought was a miracle of healing until Billie Faye burbled, "Why didn't Christ come?" Then she wilted into the rocker as though part of its structure, and Sarah Jane wailed for a mother who had relinquished the last bit of fight in her. Sarah Jane decided that day never to love a Black man the way her mother had loved her father, for the price of love was more than she was ever willing to pay. So, after the funeral, she assumed a stoic, stainless-steel posture that she hoped would protect her from hurt and trauma for the rest of her living days.

The youngest of Jeremiah and Mary's children was also a boy whom they named Enoch. All he did as a child, Miss Mary complained lovingly, was laugh. Everything was funny to him, and he had a gift for transforming despair into joy. At birth, Enoch only weighed three pounds although he was carried full term. The midwife examined him and said, "I can't find nothin' wrong with this baby, Miss Mary. It's the funniest thing, but he's 'bout the healthiest baby I've ever seen. He's just so little!" Jeremiah laid rags in a little wooden box, and that's where Enoch slept "nearbout 'til he walked," Miss Mary said with a chuckle. The strangest thing about Enoch was that Miss Mary never knew she was pregnant until her water broke Easter Sunday morning. She was in the choir singing, "Down at the cross, where my Savior died! Down where from cleansing from sin I cried! There to my heart was the blood applied! Glory to His name!" when she felt the gush flow between her legs, and she kept crying, "Glory to His name!" as she stumbled to the floor. Jeremiah ran to her side.

"What's de matta, honey?" he asked desperately.

"I'm havin' a baby," she whispered. "Get me outta hyeah!"

Jeremiah wrapped her right arm around his shoulders and escorted her back home. He kept asking, "How you pregnant?"

"De same way everybody else get pregnant, man!" she screamed between contractions.

"But you don't look pregnant! Yo belly ain't even stuck out! Have you been missin' yo time?"

"No, I ain't!" she screamed again although she shared his confusion.

By the time the midwife arrived, Miss Mary was up cooking supper. The contractions had only lasted twenty minutes or so, and then the baby slid out like a wet beaver. He had a grin on his face almost as wide as the face itself, and Jeremiah told his wife, "We gon call him Enoch 'cause he look like he jes seed de Lawd." Miss Mary agreed, but couldn't help worrying about him because of his inordinately small size. The midwife assured her, "I've never heard a healthier heartbeat, Miss Mary. I wouldn't worry. He grips my finger like an eight-month-old." Jeremiah laid him in the box, and he slept all night like a grown man.

He ate like one, too. By six months, Miss Mary had to wean him because he had sucked her breasts dry. At five, he ate more than anyone in the family and complained incessantly about being hungry. Miss Mary swore the child had worms. In addition to unripe apples, peaches, persimmons, and blackberries, he ate fruit peelings, red clay, and green tomatoes in the spring. Like a wild boar, Enoch uprooted peanuts and potatoes in autumn, often building a small fire and roasting them himself. He was never found without a pocket full of pecans or hickory nuts, which only held him over to suppertime. Everywhere he went he expelled a trail of gas so lethal others cursed him. "You must be full o' dead muskrats, boy!" his father often said. Yet the child's jovial nature caused others to forgive his improprieties and, in fact, to revel in his company. In public, people subconsciously gravitated toward him until they found themselves engulfed in his humor. His mother crowned him the "clown of the century."

"Hey, folks!" was his standard, exuberant greeting. His boisterous voice and abundant energy compelled even the diffident to speak. Most loved him and prophesied that he'd be a preacher one day. A few characterized him as obnoxious and flamboyant, but the rest dismissed these comments as evidence of jealousy.

By age ten, Enoch was the community comedian.

"There was a Black man in heaven," he began at the dinner table one evening. Possum started laughing hysterically. She dropped her fork onto the floor, but when she reached to retrieve it, her limp arm simply vibrated with the rest of her body. Her inability to maintain composure always fueled Enoch's performances. Jerry shook his head silently, but loved Enoch's humor no less. Jeremiah and Miss Mary suppressed their laughter long enough to make sure the tale contained no vulgarities.

Enoch cackled at Possum's dismantled form, causing her to laugh even harder. "This Black man had done walked 'round heaven all day long and got tired, so he axed de Lawd fu some lemonade, and de Lawd said 'Sho!' and gave him a glass o' de sweetest lemonade he had done ever tasted."

Jeremiah, who was giggling now, warned playfully, "Okay, boy. You playin' wit de Lawd."

"No, he ain't, Daddy," Possum intervened to make sure Enoch was allowed to finish the yarn.

"So de Black man finished de lemonade and listened to de heavenly choir sing 'til he got tired o' dat, too. He walked through de flower garden and smelled de roses and honeysuckles and smiled at all de folks he knowed. But then he got tired o' grinnin', too."

"What he do then?" Possum instigated, unable to still her jerking shoulders.

"He axed de Lawd if he could visit hell."

Possum fell out of her chair. Until now, Miss Mary had remained silent, enjoying her son's confidence while simultaneously monitoring his play with blasphemy, but this last line was more than she could bear. "You outta order, boy! You don't use dem kinda words in my house!" Her large eyes gazed at Enoch in absolute reprimand.

"I ain't said nothin' bad, Momma! I was jes talkin' 'bout de place where de devil live."

"Finish de story, boy," Jeremiah said, smiling, overriding his wife's objection.

Miss Mary mumbled, "Dat's what's wrong wit him now. Every time I try to chastise de boy you go in behind me and . . ."

Enoch glanced at Miss Mary to make sure she wasn't too angry, and continued: "Well, anyway, de Lawd frowned and axed de man why in de world he'd want to visit hell, and de man said he jes wanted to see what it was like. So de Lawd let him go."

"You a fool, boy," Jerry cackled gently.

Again, Enoch checked to make sure his mother wasn't fuming, and she bellowed, "You may as well tell it now!" in order to hear the rest of the story.

"When he got to hell, he met a lotta his old friends and saw dat people was partyin' and drinkin' up a storm. Dey had jook joints like Fish's place down in de bottom and blues music was playin' real loud. Well, de Lawd had done tole de man dat he couldn't stay in hell long, and de man asked jes how much time he had. So de Lawd tole him dat he had to be back by sundown."

Jerry was laughing now, and Miss Mary shook her head in feigned disgust.

"He went to de jook joint and startin' drinkin' and partyin' real bad and found a girlfriend and they started—"

"All right, clown! You gettin' too mannish!" Miss Mary forewarned.

"Yes, ma'am," Enoch offered respectfully but continued: "De man wuz dancin' and havin' such a good time dat he fugot 'bout being back in heaven by sundown. In fact, when he went outside, de sun was risin' in de east like it do every day."

Possum had never recovered, and every word Enoch spoke worsened her condition.

"Well, when de man got back to heaven, he 'pologized real sincere to de Lawd, but de Lawd told him dat he couldn't let him back in. De man said, 'Oh no, Lawd, I ain't 'pologizin' 'bout missin' yo curfew' "— Enoch mocked a drunk man's raspy voice—" 'I'm 'pologizin' fu troublin' you. I jes came back to get de rest o' my things!' "

For the first time in Johnson family history, Jerry hollered until his sides ached. Enoch's head collapsed onto the table, and tears ran from Possum's eyes faster than she could wipe them away.

"You fixin' to git a whoopin', boy!" Miss Mary jumped up and exclaimed. "You don't make no mockery o' heaven in my house! And dat joke ain't funny!"

She grabbed Enoch by the collar, dragged him out behind the outhouse, and whooped him senseless. Possum was still on the floor crying when they returned, so Enoch concluded he must have a gift. His stories always left Possum dismantled, and, after a while, he started walking to the outhouse on his own as he shouted the punch line over his shoulder.

"You don't get tired o' Momma beatin' you?" Jerry asked him one day.

"She don't really be mad," Enoch explained lovingly. "Dat's jes what she suppose to do. Sometime she be laughin' as she be beatin' me."

Jerry smiled and thought about how much he loved Enoch. He envied Enoch's ability to speak his mind regardless of what others thought. Jerry wanted that boldness, but instead his was a character too sensitive to weather other people's insults. That's really why he loved Enoch's stories—because his brother told them without fear of the cost.

The funniest one, Jeremiah told his grandkids, was the joke about where preachers bank. Walking onto the front porch after church one Sunday, Enoch began, "There was a preacher one day who didn't have no money."

"All right, boy! We jes came from church. Ain't you got no reverence fu de Lawd's day?" Miss Mary protested.

"Yes, ma'am, I do," Enoch said, "but this one ain't bad, Momma. I promise." Miss Mary continued into the house to prepare Sunday dinner. Jeremiah and the children remained on the porch.

"What happened to de preacher, boy?" Jeremiah whispered, and sat in the old rocker.

"Well, he couldn't figure out why he never had any money, so he approached one of the ladies of the church and asked her how she saved her money."

Like always, Possum's laughter poured from her belly the moment Enoch began the story. She had heard this one before, but that never mattered. It was Enoch's drama she loved.

"De church lady told de preacher dat she keep all her money in her bosom—paper and change. She was a big woman wit real big . . . you know." Enoch cupped his hands in front of his chest to approximate the size of the woman's breasts. "De preacher said, 'I'ma man, so that ain't gon work fu me.' De church lady didn't know what to say. Then all o' sudden de preacher clapped his hands and said, 'I got de answer!' De church lady said, 'What is it?' and de preacher said, 'Can I open an account in yo bank?'"

As Enoch began to stumble in laughter, he felt Miss Mary's right palm sink into the left side of his face. "Momma!" he yelped, surprised to learn that she had been listening the whole time.

"Boy, I'll kill you dead if you eva say some mess like dat again! Do you hear me?"

"But, Momma, it wunnit nasty!" Enoch tried to explain through misty eyes.

"It wuz nasty, fool! You ain't got no business talkin' 'bout dat kinda stuff. You's a child!"

Enoch wanted to protest further, but Jerry's shaking head convinced him to let it go.

After that day, Enoch still told stories, but he learned which ones to tell to which folks. That was how he met and married Ella Mae Pearson. She was standing in the crowd in front of Fish's place one night as Enoch carried on something terrible. After the laughter subsided and the crowd thinned a bit, she told Enoch, "You a crazy fool, man."

He smiled broadly at this red-bone, skinny girl whom he had eyed several times in the past. She was light, but her kinky hair confirmed her blackness, standing on top of her head in coiled belligerence. Its thickness allowed no light to penetrate, and Enoch chuckled that even a torrential downpour never found its way to her scalp. Although she was thin, Ella Mae boasted the perfectly rounded, rotund behind that was Enoch's only requirement in a woman's form.

"Hey there," he shouted.

"You oughta be shame o' yo'self"—she smiled sheepishly—"tellin' lies like dat."

"I ain't told a lie since I been born." He winked.

That conversation evolved into a union two years later. They moved to Memphis, where Enoch cleaned bathrooms at the Peabody Hotel during the day and did stand-up comedy in Black-owned clubs at night, although never making ends meet. When Jerry died, Enoch and Ella Mae decided to return to Money where, if nothing else, they could always eat. Things weren't as bad as the couple expected they would be. They had two boys, Ray Ray and Chop, and decided simply to live without the daughter they had hoped Chop would be. Their aim had been to build their own house on their own land, but Jeremiah's sharecropping debt consumed every dime they made. So the couple settled into the dilapidated shack with Jeremiah and Miss Mary and resolved to make the best with what they had.

Two

THE GRANDCHILDREN SAT DOWN TO LUNCH UNUSUALLY quiet. Miss Mary knew something was wrong, and she knew they had lied. Before pressing the matter, however, she studied their faces, looking for clues as to what could possibly have rendered them so inexplicably mute. Her stares were certainly disturbing, yet the children worked hard to remain quiet. Knowing Miss Mary wasn't one to relinquish her suspicions quickly, they knew it was only a matter of time before one of them surrendered.

"So ain't nobody talkin', huh?" Miss Mary set the sandwich bread and the peanut butter on the table. "I see," she mumbled threateningly.

Sarah Jane opened her mouth to explain the matter, but then bit her bottom lip in an attempt to hold her peace. She knew if she spoke, she'd cry, and her grandmother would understand instantly the gravity of the matter, for that day was the first time Sarah Jane had cried since Billie Faye's Homegoing. The thought of unleashing her emotions like that again made her ill and motivated her to deceive her grandmother as long as she could.

"Ray Ray? You ain't got nothin' to say?" Miss Mary entreated.

"No, ma'am," he returned abruptly. "Ain't nothin' to say. Everything's fine, Grandma. Really." Sarah Jane kicked him under the table, a sign that he should simply be quiet. Ray Ray's anxiety was much too apparent, and his rambling only made Miss Mary more incredulous.

Unable to withstand her gaze, Chop screamed, "It w-w-w-was Cll-llllement, Grandma!" and pointed at his cousin's bulged eyes and agape mouth.

"What about Clement?" she questioned irritably.

Chop tried to remain composed, but it was a lost cause. "Hhhhhe b-b-bought a sssssoda p-p-pop in de sssssstore t-t-today." Chop didn't look at the others, who were planning how and when they would beat him.

"Clement, where you git money from?"

"Momma gave it to me before I left home," he said defensively, hoping Miss Mary's suspicions would be thus satisfied. They were not.

"I thought yo granddaddy tole you not to go in dat sto' unless one o' us wuz wit cha?" She had her hands on her hips and a look in her eyes Clement could not ignore.

"I just wanted a soda pop, Grandma. That's all," Clement sniffled.

"Then what chu cryin' fu? Buyin' a soda pop ain't no crime." Miss Mary searched each face back and forth, knowing there was more to the story.

Sarah Jane breached their contract of silence and whispered, "There's more to it, Grandma, and it ain't good, either."

"What chu talkin' 'bout, girl?"

All three boys hung their heads simultaneously. Sarah Jane wished she could close her eyes and make everything turn into a scary dream, but Miss Mary's anger, hovering over her like clouds before an impending storm, disallowed fantasy.

"I'm talkin' to you, chile!" Miss Mary banged her heavy fist on the table and completely destroyed Sarah Jane's fragile composure.

"Clement disrespected Miss Cuthbert in de store," she breathed heavily. "He didn't mean to, Grandma, but . . ."

"But what? Somebody better start talkin' 'round hyeah fo I git a belt to all y'alls behinds!" she hollered.

Sarah Jane simply relented. "Okay, Grandma. Okay." Her slow tongue exacerbated Miss Mary's anger. "Clement went in de store to buy a soda pop"—her hands moved with her voice—"but Miss Cuthbert—"

"Clement, what did you do?" Miss Mary interrupted. "And I mean I want de truf before I git after you!"

Clement glanced at Sarah Jane, who shrugged her shoulders helplessly. "I went in the store to buy a soda pop, and I laid the nickel down on the counter and walked out," he offered lightly. "That's the whole story. I don't know why everybody makin' such a big deal about it."

Sarah Jane shook her head pitifully, and explained, "Miss Cuthbert told him to pick up de nickel and put it in her hand, but Clement wouldn't do it. She was screamin' after him that he was gon pay for what he did, but Clement ignored her and sassed her back." Sarah Jane hoped the truth would, indeed, set Clement free.

"Lawd Jesus!" Miss Mary murmured. Her slow descent into the kitchen chair frightened the once-impervious children.

Clement felt compelled to explain: "I didn't do nothin' wrong, Grandma. I just told her dat I didn't have to put de nickel in her hand. All I wanted was a soda pop—"

"Close yo goddamn mouth, boy!" Miss Mary yelled. The children froze. They had never heard her curse before. "You ain't got no sense at all! You cain't come down here and act like you in Chicago, boy!"

"But Grandma—"

"I said shut up!" She trembled as she screamed louder. "Don't chu know what happens to Black boys who don't know how to mind? Huh?"

Clement assumed the question rhetorical, but Miss Mary took his silence as insolence.

"I'm talking to you, Mr. Bigshot!" She was angrier than any of them had ever seen her. "Yo momma didn't tell you what happened to yo uncle Jerry and aunt Billie?" Her booming voice destroyed the grandchildren's strength and left Clement feeling like a rabbit in a fox-hole.

Miss Mary suddenly rose from the table and grabbed her straw hat. "Y'all run out to de barn and stay there 'til I come git cha. And I mean stay there!" She exited the front door quickly, clumsily, whereto the children did not know.

They ran to the barn, understanding from Miss Mary's reaction the import of Clement's infraction.

"I told you!" Sarah Jane cried vehemently once they barred the barn door from within. They climbed the ladder to the loft and sat upon square bales of hay.

"I ain't done nothin'!" Clement declared again.

Ray Ray grimaced, and whispered, "Jes be quiet. We gotta wait and see what happens."

Chop wanted to apologize to Clement for exposing him, but he knew nothing he said would appease his cousin's fury. Everyone seemed irritated with him, Chop discovered, because they turned their backs once they sat down in the barn. He simply wanted to explain that his grandma's voice had overwhelmed him and forced his tongue from exile. He never meant to get Clement into any trouble, and he certainly didn't mean to disturb the peace in the Johnson household. But they wouldn't have listened anyway, he told himself, easing his troubled heart. He knew he'd get blamed, whatever the outcome of the situation, and he prepared himself for the possibility of having no playmates for a very long time.

The loud banging on the barn door startled the children who, at first, sat transfixed. Ray Ray strained his terrified eyes to see who had come.

"Children!" Jeremiah's raspy, hoarse voice called loudly.

In relief, they scrambled from the loft and unhinged the door. For several seconds, the children stood before their grandfather and Enoch like criminals awaiting sentencing.

"What happened at de sto' today? And I ain't got time fu no foolishness!" The furrows intersecting on Jeremiah's forehead convinced Ray Ray to tell the truth and to tell it in a hurry.

"Clement went in de store to buy a soda pop, Grandpa—," he began explaining, but Jeremiah cut out the middleman.

"Clement, you tell me what happened since you de one what know. And tell me de truth, boy. I mean it." He was holding Clement by the shoulder with a monstrous grip.

"Okay," Clement mumbled, steadying his nerves. "I went in de store to get a soda pop, and I gave the woman a nickel for it. That's how much it cost, Grandpa, so—"

"I know how much a soda pop cost, boy! It's somethin' you ain't sayin', and I wanna know what it is!" His yelling dissolved Clement's constitution and freed his tears.

"Like I said, I went in de store and bought a soda pop and gave the lady a nickel." Jeremiah's eyes searched the barn frantically, looking for a strong whipping stick. His heavy breathing and quivering hands urged Ray Ray to offer, "But he laid de nickel down on de counter."

"What?" Jeremiah asked, confused.

Clement resolved that he could not win, so he sighed deeply and admitted, "She asked me to put de nickel in her hand, but I laid it on de counter instead and walked out."

"You did what?"

Clement said nothing more.

"Is you crazy, boy?" Jeremiah vented each word a little louder. "You jes walked out de do' like you grown?"

"Why did I have to put de money in her hand, Granddaddy?" Clement cried desperately. "I laid de nickel on de counter."

"'Cause she said so, boy! Dat's why! Don't you know dey'll kill you ova somethin' like dat?"

Sarah Jane noticed, for the first time, the gray hairs sprouting from her grandfather's nose. His huffing caused them to dance sporadically, like a feather at the command of gusty winds. Jeremiah's flat, African nose occupied at least a third of the width of his face and convinced many that he was full-blood African. In his anger, the wrinkles in Jeremiah's face deepened until, filled with sweat, they formed brooks and streams running all over his face. Sarah Jane marveled at her grandfather's ability to smile and comfort one moment and to frighten and intimidate the next.

Enoch touched his father's shoulder, and said, "Let's all just calm down for a minute, Daddy." His words softened Jeremiah's expression and made the old man realize how stern he had been.

"Listen, Clement," Jeremiah whispered with closed eyes, "you got to do what I say. Son, you cain't come down to Mississippi all high-and-mighty. White folks hyeah don't care nothin' 'bout you thinkin' you dey equal. They'll kill you befo' dey admit it." He glanced at the other children endearingly. "Dat's why you shoulda put de money in her hand. No, it ain't right and, no, you didn't have to, but I pray to God we ain't sorry you didn't."

Enoch asked, "What exactly did de woman say, Clement? I mean *exactly*." He searched the boy's eyes.

"I don't remember exactly, but she said I was gonna be sorry." Tears now flooded his puffy cheeks.

"What else did she say?" Enoch pressed. "Try to remember, son!"

Clement pleaded, "I can't. She just kept telling me I was gonna be sorry."

"Oh my God," Enoch murmured to his father. "What we gon do?"

Jeremiah placed his hands on Clement's shoulder again and transformed back into the grandfather the children had always known. "I don't know, but for now, we gon watch and pray. Dat's what we gon do. Now you chillen lissen to me, and lissen real good. Y'all ain't to leave dis house fu no reason. No reason at all! You undastand?"

"Yessir," they said in chorus.

"And you ain't to mention dis to nobody else. You hear me?"

"Yessir."

"And whatsoever you do, if you see a stranger comin', run like hell and get me or your uncle Enoch fast as you can."

"Yessir."

"This goes fu every one o' y'all. Y'all look out fu one anotha and don't spend no time layin' blame. What's done is done, and we got to deal wit it. We's a family, and we gon act like a family. Ya hear me?" Jeremiah yelped.

"Yessir," the children affirmed.

"Good. Now. I'ma tell ya one more thang."

Enoch knew what his father was about to say. He, Jerry, and Possum thought they would be the last generation to get The Instructions, as Jeremiah called it, but now Enoch saw that Time had not done what it had promised.

Jeremiah gathered the children closer and spoke softly. "If anything eva happen to yo grandma, yo aunt Ella Mae, or Enoch, or me, y'all run out de back door jes as quick as you can down to de riva next to de big tree where folks fish. Wade in up to ya neck and walk about a mile north to de railroad bridge. Git out there and walk due west about anotha mile 'til you see a old broken-down shack. There's a big pecan tree right beside it. Go in there and wait."

"Wait for what?" Sarah Jane asked.

"Don't chu worry about that," Jeremiah said. "Jes git there. Everything else'll be all right. Somebody'll come for ya."

Chop was crying but didn't know why. He sensed urgency in Jeremiah's words as though knowing they would, one day, save his life, but for now he wanted to play and forget them all.

"Ray Ray, you know de most 'bout dis place, so if anythang happen, you make sho to do what I said."

"Yessir," he mumbled.

"Good. Now y'all jes go on back to de house and git yo work done and keep yo mouth shut."

Like mourners in a funeral procession, the children exited the barn, unsure of exactly how to act but certain they weren't as free as they had once been.

On their way back to the field, Enoch told his father, "Dey ain't gon let this go. You know dat, don't chu?"

Without looking at his son, Jeremiah said, "Yeah, I do," and chuckled nervously. He was trying not to imagine what those white folks might do to Clement. "We jes gotta pray," he continued lightly, disguising the burden his heart carried.

Jeremiah and Enoch resumed their places in the cotton field. The heat was stultifying, and the end of the row was nowhere in sight. Enoch's heart was caught between despising the fields and embracing them as heritage and lineage. Grandpa Moses, who folks said was seven feet tall, was brought over as a slave when he was nine and sold somewhere in South Carolina. A year later, Jeremiah told his children, Moses was bought by Elliot Johnson, who was traveling through South Carolina on his way back to Mississippi—a place Moses had never heard of.

"Daddy and five otha slaves was tied to ole man Johnson's wagon and walked all de way to Money, Mississippi," Jeremiah bragged and decried. "And we been hyeah every since."

So every time Enoch picked a cotton bole, he felt his grandfather standing proud and regal next to him in the field, and he knew the land was as much his own as it had once been ole man Johnson's.

"How we git the same name, Daddy?" Enoch asked on his fifth birthday at the dinner table.

"Yo granddaddy decided to take de Johnson name so dat any one o' his chillen what might git sold away would be able to trace dey way back one day. It helped de family stay together and find one another if any of 'em ever got lost."

Enoch swore he'd change his name when he got grown so he and old man Johnson would never be mistaken as kinfolks, but when Chapman bought the land a year later, Enoch dropped the issue altogether.

"Chop dat cotton, son, and save daydreamin' for later," Jeremiah called to Enoch. What would those white folks do? Enoch pondered as he glanced toward the Johnson shack far in the distance. Times had changed, he tried to convince himself. There were some places in America where white and colored kids all went to the same school. And they got along fine. Maybe Money was changing, too. Jeremiah told Enoch that, just a month ago, for no apparent reason, a white man had bought Chop a candy bar in the General Store.

"N-n-n-no thththank ya, sssssir," Chop had said apprehensively.

"I'm just being nice, son. It's okay. I know you're not supposed to take it, but this one's on me. Don't think anything of it."

Chop shook as he mumbled, "I thththanks ya k-k-k-kindly, sssir, b-b-but nnno thththank you."

Just then, Jeremiah turned the corner, and said, "You knows better, boy. I done raised you right." He grabbed Chop by the forearm and jerked him toward the exit.

"It was my fault, mister," the white man explained. "I was trying to offer your boy a candy bar, and he—"

"He don't take thangs he ain't paid for, sir," Jeremiah announced. "I teaches my chillen dat, and dat's how dey live. We'se much obliged all de same."

"But sir, I meant no harm. I certainly didn't intend to go against your teachings. I just wanted to be nice. That's all."

The look of sincerity on the white man's face disturbed Jeremiah.

"Please allow him to accept it, sir. It's the least I can do."

It was the "sir" that made Jeremiah hesitate. He wondered where in the world this white man had come from.

"I'd really like the boy to have it, if you don't mind." He extended the candy bar and waited for a colored man's trust. Jeremiah studied the stranger, examining his impeccable clothes and his neatly manicured fingernails, and, against his better judgment, he allowed Chop to accept the gift.

"We thank you kindly, sir," Jeremiah murmured as he shook the stranger's hand harder than usual.

"No thanks needed. As I said, it's really the *very* least I can do."

Jeremiah frowned at the man's insinuation that he owed them something. Indeed, the stranger's intemperate kindness momentarily disrupted what Jeremiah knew about white folks. Yet once outside, he warned Chop, "This don't mean nothin'. There's always one or two who don't fit the mold."

When Enoch heard of the incident, he took the man's gesture as sign that things really were changing in Mississippi.

"Get to choppin', boy!" Jeremiah corrected again. "Chapman see you idle, and he dock yo pay twenty-five cents."

Enoch abandoned his thoughts and rendered his labor once again to a man who consumed the Johnson family without a care.

Jeremiah tried hard not to think of Jerry, but he couldn't help it. He had never really gotten over his son's suicidal murder, and now with Clement's incorrigible behavior, he was afraid he'd have to revisit the whole ordeal. The smile on Jerry's face was the only redeeming sight the day they found his body swinging. A rough September wind tossed it to and fro meaninglessly, causing its legs to separate violently like a ballerina's leap just before the plié. Miss Mary and Billie Faye cried in each other's trembling arms, while Jeremiah stood alone, staring at one who dared consider himself a man. Pridefully—indeed arrogantly—Jeremiah climbed the old tree and cut the hay-baling twine with his rusty pocketknife. Jerry's body fell to the earth as though exhausted from a long, hard journey.

When the white men arrived, salivating, Jeremiah announced caustically, "He ain't here. He's gone to see the King."

"What king?" they asked.

Now Jeremiah found himself praying for Clement the same prayer he had said for Jerry. Certainly Clement hadn't meant any harm, Jeremiah knew, but the trouble he had started was yet to be seen.

Three

MISS MARY'S SAVORY MEAT LOAF ELICITED NO COMMENTS at the dinner table that Friday evening, and, much to his dismay, Enoch failed to think of a joke sufficiently amusing to distract the family. Sarah Jane toyed with the same green bean until she asked to be excused. The boys glanced at one another, but said nothing. They, too, wanted to escape the presence of the elders and find solitude elsewhere, although, for whatever reason, they believed their request would be immediately denied. So they sat there and forced food down unwelcoming throats. Only Jeremiah ate freely, unsure of what tomorrow would bring but certain he needed his strength to face it.

Enoch cleared the table—another anomaly—and asked who wanted peach cobbler. No one answered, so he fixed a bowl for himself alone.

"Momma, I sho do love yo cobblers," he proclaimed after the first bite. Still, no one mumbled a word. "These peaches musta come from . . ." and Enoch relinquished the fight to break ice much too frozen.

After supper, everyone settled into their own space as they privately nurtured fear of white retaliation. Miss Mary took her seat in the living room rocking chair and continued piecing, with tremulous hands, the quilt she had started months earlier. Her usual hum, which normally soothed the entire household, refused to leave the safety of her soul, so she rocked silently and prayed for a peace she could not envision. Ella Mae washed dishes in slow motion and mopped the old wooden floor three times to keep her mind from wandering. Then she went to bed with the sun, without her traditional "good night, y'all" salutation. On the way, she touched Miss Mary's shoulder, like a mourner comforting a mother for her loss, and, once inside her bedroom, Ella Mae remained on her knees for the next half hour.

"To everything there is a season," Jeremiah muttered from Ecclesiastes chapter 3. "And a time to every purpose under the heavens. A time to be born and a time to die. A time to plant and a time to pluck up that which is planted. A time to kill"—he sighed—"and a time to heal. A time to break down, and a time to build up. A time to weep and a time to laugh." His voice dwindled with each verse until his lips moved inaudibly. At the close of the chapter, he set his Bible on the stand next to the aging, dusty brown sofa. Old Man Chapman had given the family that trash, as Miss Mary called it, as a wedding present when his wife's order of custom Italian furniture arrived. Its countless holes didn't bar him from believing he was doing the Johnsons an unprecedented favor. Pride colored his demeanor when he ordered his boys to haul the sofa—and its trail of cotton—into the Johnsons' living room.

"Don't worry, it wunnit no trouble," he repeated, waving his hands frantically. "Y'all oughta git twenty more years outta this here couch. It's really for the children. My wife thinks the world of 'em."

Chapman left before Jeremiah or Miss Mary, against their hearts' true sentiment, could properly thank him. From that day, Miss Mary determined never to sit on the sofa as long as she lived.

Enoch retreated to the edge of the porch, swinging his feet like he, Possum, and Jerry used to do on hot summer nights. Picking his teeth with a broom straw and spitting the contents into oblivion, Enoch searched desperately for the optimism that had governed his thoughts earlier in the cotton field. Somehow, though, every scenario he imagined fed his fear that Clement's disobedience would cost his family dearly. "Why couldn't the boy just hand the woman the money?" he asked the wind, rolling one cigarette after the other. Then he remembered Possum's proud recalcitrance and forgave Clement in his heart.

Miss Mary strolled onto the porch quietly, and said, "Look like we ain't gon git no rain, is we?"

"Naw, guess we ain't," Enoch murmured without turning.

"De Good Lawd gon handle it," she offered. "He got de whole world in His hands."

Miss Mary's tone made Enoch wonder if she really believed what she was saying. The confidence with which she usually spoke was now only a shivering whisper. He turned and saw his mother staring into the cloudless black sky and guessed that she, like he, was reliving the horror of Jerry and Billie Faye in The Sacred Place, and praying that they'd not have to lay another family member to rest. Miss Mary found her hum, finally, and swayed like a young cypress tree in a windstorm as she rubbed her folded arms. Occasionally, her head fell back, shaking from side to side, and her good right foot kept a rhythm both cacophonous and soothing. Enoch wanted to ask his mother if she were all right, but he could tell she did not want to be disturbed. She was negotiating something, it seemed, in a spiritual place he had never gone, and the intensity of her melody suggested that the talks were not going very well. Her persistent tune justified why she had been characterized as the family gatekeeper, the stronghold, the fortress, and Enoch now nurtured a new respect for a mother who must have fought God on his behalf without ever having consulted him.

At her hum's crescendo, Enoch looked heavenward and marveled at the night's resplendent display of stars and moon. This time, he allowed himself to be subsumed in the moment instead of, like usual, trying mightily to avoid it. The light summer breeze, which had been his evening companion, disappeared suddenly when his mother's guttural moaning began, leaving streams of sweat and tears intermingling down her mountainous cheeks. The tears weaved their way to the edge of her chin, then, one by one, leapt into the abyss of the Mississippi night. Enoch noticed a deer standing in the distance, staring at Miss Mary as though recognizing in her hum the bars of a favorite melody. Once, or maybe twice, the animal moved uneasily but never shifted its gaze. Maybe beasts have souls, Enoch entertained, and maybe they, too, would be in eternity.

The exact origin of his tears he couldn't identify, but this time he welcomed them. With a heart far too heavy to carry into another day, Enoch gave thanks for the unannounced cleansing by lifting his arms to the sky and pacing across the loose dirt yard, repeating "Hallelujah!" with each step, until, much to his surprise, his legs took a mind to dance. It was an awkward shuffle at first, primarily because Enoch had never danced in the spirit, but now he had no choice. His feet simply would not be restrained. "Let de Lawd have His way, son!" he heard his mother say, so Enoch submitted to a power greater than himself. His arms joined his feet in uncontrolled movements, swinging wildly like one fighting a swarm of bees. He didn't fully understand what was happening to him, but he lacked the power and the desire to stop it. "Let Him use you!" Miss Mary cried. A cloud of dust rose at his feet and slowly enshrouded his form as he danced circles around the little sycamore tree. "Yes, Lord!" Miss Mary declared. "Yes, yes, yes!" Had he paid attention in church, Enoch would have known that the Holy Ghost always comes in the midst of trouble, but Miss Mary couldn't explain that now. All she could do was beg the

Lord to use him. As a child, he had sworn he didn't even believe in the Holy Ghost and, in fact, had mocked those whose unexplainable antics became the punch line of his jokes. But now he believed. At least he believed in something. Maybe it was Miss Mary he believed in. Maybe she was the Holy Ghost, he pondered, for never, ever, had he been so spiritually overwhelmed that his body assumed a life all its own and declared the beauty thereof before the naked universe. He wondered why he wasn't embarrassed. Maybe somewhere in the power of the dance, in the belly of the Holy Ghost, he found a Self he had not known. Maybe the collective unity of tears, movement, freedom, intelligence, and emotion introduced him to the sustaining power of his people and made him proud to be a descendant of the Black ones the world rejected. Or maybe God was getting him ready for something. He wasn't sure. His only regret was that all his life, he had embraced a worldview that left him wanton, barren, and longing for holism. But now he knew why Black women shouted weekly, and he wondered why Black men didn't. Had he been among his ancestors years ago, they would have celebrated the trance, and everyone— including the men—would have joined in. Miss Mary wanted to tell Enoch that his ecstasy was simply the desire of the cosmos to teach him who he was and to assure he knew the source of his strength. She also wanted to tell him that, in the dance, his spirit was pleading with God to protect the Johnson family from a tragedy that might destroy them this time. She smiled as she watched her son evolve into an elder, a keeper of his people, a temporary resident in a spiritual realm to which he would certainly have to return. Her final prayer was that God wouldn't ever let him forget that he had been there.

When Enoch recovered, he was standing in front of the house, panting.

"What jes happened to me, Momma?" he asked bewildered.

"Dat's between you and de Good Lawd," Miss Mary returned joyfully.

"But I don't do this kinda stuff. I mean, I believe in God and all, but—" He was trembling.

"It ain't got nothin' to do wit you believin', boy. God is real whether you believe or you don't. It jes helps if you do." She sat on the edge of the porch with her feet on the steps.

Enoch shuffled his tired legs and sat next to her. He was glad no one else in the family had seen him.

"I ain't mad 'bout what jes happened, Momma. It jes seem lak, after somethin' like dis, God would do whatever I ask him to. But I guess it don't work like dat, huh?"

"No, it don't, son. God ain't in de pleasin' business," Miss Mary answered. "He don't think like folks do. He gotta plan don't none o' us know nothin' 'bout, and he ain't gon change it jes 'cause we ask him to."

"Then why pray?"

Miss Mary's reticent response came slowly. "'Cause we spose to," she said. "God know what you gon pray befo' you even say it."

Enoch's frustration inflamed. "Then why say it?"

Miss Mary approached the edge of her understanding. "Listen, son. Jes walk wit God. Dat's all I know fu sho. You gotta walk wit God so you know where to git yo strength from. All dem otha thangs you askin' me, I don't know. Yo own mind can be yo worse enemy." She waved away mosquitoes swarming around her partially exposed lower legs.

Enoch still didn't understand what had just happened to him. Self-control was always a virtue he boasted, and for something to overpower him made him wonder what invisible beings lurked around the world waiting to teach humans their limitations. Now he wanted the feeling to return, for there was freedom in that moment he had never experienced. Everything he thought he believed proved, not wrong, but irrelevant as something within him granted him the right to be everything simultaneously. No one would believe him, he knew, but he felt the energy of the deer he had seen earlier. It was not afraid. It loved him, he felt, because, like itself, he was included among God's untainted ones. The stars also bore their nakedness before him proudly, and the mosquitoes swirled about even in the midst of his disruption. How had he missed the beauty of the universe before, he wondered.

"We bes be gittin' some sleep, young man. Mr. Sun be comin' up afta while," Miss Mary said, and entered the house.

"Yes, ma'am," Enoch called behind her. "I'll be jes anotha minute."

Enoch turned, finally, and reexamined the still, purple night. The old peach tree standing to the left of the house appeared lonely most times, but now it stood noble as though clear it was exactly where it was supposed to be. He smiled, and said, "God, I ain't neva been so scared in all my life. I know dem white folks ain't gon let Clement git by wit bein' disobedient, but I'm thinkin' that maybe You can make 'em forgive him. You know he didn't mean no harm, Lawd." Enoch searched the heavens for a sign God was listening. "He was jes bein a chile, that's all." He stood on the second level of the front steps. "I ain't neva been one to pray much, and I know dat, but I'm askin You, Lawd, to please ease dis situation. Jerry"—Enoch's voice cracked— "was enough to lose. Why colored peoples always de ones losin'?" he posed indignantly. "Every time somethin' happens, why colored people's always de ones goin' to de cemetery? Lawd, You likes colored peoples, don't chu? Momma swear by You. She say anythang somebody ask in Yo name, You'll do it. Well, I'm askin', Lawd, please don't let hurt, harm, or danger come to my nephew. Or dis family. We done suffered enough."

A shooting star leapt across the sky, and Enoch nodded his appreciation for the sign. "Momma said Daddy named me Enoch after a man in de Bible who walked so close to You dat he didn't have to die. Well, I know me and You ain't dat close, but Lawd, if I had one wish, I would ask for safety for dis hyeah family. At least do it for Momma. She de one who really believe." He was talking louder now, having gathered confidence from somewhere in the night. Yet realizing that God wasn't going to respond verbally, Enoch took a deep breath, and said, "It's all in Yo hands, Lawd. Yo will be done."

He entered the house, blew out the last coal oil lamp burning on the kitchen table and, reluctantly, went to bed.

By 10:00 P.M., everyone was asleep except Sarah Jane. She lay on the battered brown sofa, thinking of her mother the night Jerry "left." That's how Miss Mary had described it. She told relatives and friends that Jerry didn't kill himself; rather, he was simply going home to handle his Father's business. Sarah Jane didn't understand then. The pride with which her grandmother made the assertion, however, comforted her otherwise troubled heart. She remembered Billie Faye in the rocking chair, staring into space, oblivious to the world in which the rest of them lived, and she wanted nothing more earnestly than to escort her mother back into the land of the living. Words, though, had proven ineffectual in reaching Billie Faye. The silhouette of the rocker often frightened Sarah Jane at night, for she swore, on several occasions, she saw her mother sitting there smiling at her. After the first time, she began to look for her. Folks said she was crazy. Even Chop, who believed almost anything, didn't believe her. But Sarah Jane peered hard every night through the pitch-black space between herself and the chair until her mother arrived, extending a warm smile that always made her feel better. Sometimes she didn't come, but most times she did. Once, Billie Faye even reached her hands toward Sarah Jane, who closed her eyes and relaxed in the comfort of her mother's touch. Goose bumps stood at attention all over her body as Billie Faye rubbed her soothingly, leaving Sarah Jane doubtless that this was indeed her mother.

"Girl, you crazy," the boys told her. "Dead people don't visit the living.

"Yes they do!" Sarah Jane insisted. "Grandma said so. Momma comes to see me at night, and sometimes she rubs my back just like she used to when I was little."

"Dead people can't do that," Ray Ray admonished.

"Yes they can!" she proclaimed. "They can do whatever they want to. Plus, I know it was Momma 'cause she was wearing the wedding ring Daddy gave her."

Ray Ray gasped. The night Jerry died, Ray Ray found the ring Jerry had given Billie Faye on their wedding day. She must have taken it off for fear of losing it or something because there it was on the floor next to their bed. Its sparkle caught Ray Ray's eye as he swept, and he picked it up with the intention of returning it to the couple when they came home. However, when he found out about Jerry, he forgot about the ring. When Billie Faye died, he remembered it and, at the wake, slid it on the third finger of her right hand. It was a secret he had prepared to take to his grave.

"Which finger was it on?" Ray Ray inquired suddenly, hoping she couldn't remember.

Sarah Jane pondered. "Um . . . the third one, I think."

"Oh my God," he mumbled.

"What?"

"Nothin'."

He wondered if his aunt would come to him, too, but then, on second thought, he hoped she wouldn't. Stories of haints and ghosts always disturbed his peace, leaving him wide-awake while others slept. No, he didn't want to see Aunt Billie, at least not until he was a spirit, too. He couldn't imagine what he'd say to her anyway.

Sarah Jane waited for her mother that night. Fatigue crept upon her, but she tried hard not to surrender her eyelids for fear that Billie Faye might come and she would miss her. Yet, at some point, she fell asleep, for she was awakened by loud banging on the front door.

"Where dat nigger boy?" the redneck voice bellowed.

Before Sarah Jane could collect herself, Jeremiah was standing in the living room pointing a shotgun at the door. "Get in de back room, girl! Hurry!" he yelled.

"We come afta dat smart nigga, Jeremiah. It ain't got to be no trouble. We jes wanna talk to him," the same voice declared.

"I don't know who you talkin' 'bout," Jeremiah lied loudly. "All my chillen sleep and ain't none o' 'em done nothin', so I speck you betta be goin' on home." Enoch was standing slightly behind his father now, hiding another loaded rifle. Miss Mary and Ella Mae held one another tightly, a few feet behind their men, as they prayed the intruders would go away. At the back door, the children waited for directions from their elders, prepared to run if they needed to.

"Jeremiah, don't make this ugly, boy!" one of the men proclaimed as he kicked the door forcefully.

"Go on 'way from hyeah! We don't want no trouble! We's Christian people what don't b'lieve in killin', but if you make me, I'll blow yo goddamn head off!" Jeremiah cocked the shotgun and motioned for his son to do likewise. The women covered their mouths and quivered.

"I'm gon ask you one mo time, boy! Give us dat smart nigga who don't know how to treat a white lady. We jes wanna ask him a few questions." They were banging on the door with the butts of their guns. Any minute now, that old door was going to fall, Jeremiah knew, but what he didn't know was exactly what he'd do then.

"I'll come out an' talk to you myself," Jeremiah volunteered. "Whatever any o' my kids know, I already know, so you can talk to me." His shimmering voice frightened the entire family.

"No, Daddy!" Enoch urged through clinched teeth. "I'll go," and he took a bold step forward.

Jeremiah grabbed Enoch's arm. "Git back behind me, boy! I done buried one son, and I'll be goddamn if I'm 'bout to bury de otha one. Not today!"

"We don't want you, old man, we want de boy! We promise not to hurt him. Now send him out to us, or we comin' in after him!"

There had to be at least four or five of them, Jeremiah estimated, from the chorus of their multiple voices.

"What we gon do, Daddy?" Enoch whimpered.

Fear cloaked the old man like a tailored suit, but he refused to let the men prove him a coward.

"Don't come in here!" he exclaimed. "I don't wanna hurt nobody, but I sho will."

With another brutal kick, the front door relinquished its hinges and fell helplessly. The lanterns, which two of the men carried, exposed the familiar faces of four young white men, eager to avenge Catherine Cuthbert's virtue.

Jeremiah shot first, wounding one of them in the arm. Gunshot sounds transformed the Johnson living room into a virtual battlefield. Miss Mary cried, "Run, children, run!" when she saw her husband crumble in agony. The bullet lodged in Enoch's right shoulder didn't keep him from killing the other three while the wounded one escaped. He felt honored to complete what his father had begun.

"Oh my Lawd!" Miss Mary declared woefully once the commotion ended. A porch full of dead white men was a problem she had never encountered.

She knelt and touched Jeremiah as though he were fragile glass.

"I'm all right, honey," he said, but didn't move. "Get me up off dis flo'."

Miss Mary and Ella Mae lifted the old man and sat him in the rocker. Enoch was taken to the kitchen table.

"Lawd have murcy," Miss Mary mumbled as she walked onto the porch and tiptoed between the dead bodies.

"What we gon do?" Ella Mae cried.

"Jes stay calm," Miss Mary admonished nervously. "We gon figure somethin' out."

For an instant, the women studied each other's faces, unable to imagine how the family would survive this horror.

"It's gon be all right," Miss Mary said as she and Ella Mae began tending their husbands' wounds. "Y'all know we jes killed de sheriff's brothers, don't chu?"

Enoch and Ella Mae nodded.

"We know," Jeremiah murmured. "But they wunnit 'bout to kill nobody up in here. Not if I could help it." Miss Mary massaged his side in order to locate the bullet. "Ow!" he cried.

"It ain't bad, thank de Lawd. I feel it right here." She touched his flesh a few inches below his left armpit. He winced in pain. "I can cut it out," she said and moved to place a knife on top of the stove.

"Better get two," Ella Mae said.

"Is it bad?" Miss Mary asked.

"Naw. Just barely penetrated his arm. He'll be fine." She rubbed Enoch's head. "Y'all some lucky men."

"Ain't got nothin' to do wit luck, baby," Miss Mary said, shaking her head. "God settin' somethin' up. Y'all know who comin' now, don't chu? And don't neva thank he ain't comin'."

"We ain't gon worry 'bout dat right now," Jeremiah huffed with his eyes closed. "Yeah, Billy comin', and others, too, probably, but we'll have to be ready for them jes like we wuz ready for his brothers."

The women went to work on their respective husbands, slicing just enough flesh to extract the bullets. Trying not to scream, Enoch held onto the kitchen table and moaned while Jeremiah squeezed the handle of the rocker.

Once their wounds were cleaned and bandaged, Jeremiah said, "Now y'all listen to me, and listen good. We gotta stick together. Ain't no two ways 'bout it. We did what we had to, and if I had to do it ova again, I'd do de same thang." He was trying hard to maintain his confidence, but it was slipping fast. "Ella Mae, you go for de chillen and hur'up 'bout it. Bring 'em back hyeah and we'll decide what to do next. Take de light and de gun." Tears hurried down her yellow face, leaving red streaks behind, but they did not deter her.

"We gotta get dese bodies outta hyeah, son," Jeremiah groaned as he lifted his frame from the chair. "Momma, tie dis rag 'round me again tight as you can get it."

Miss Mary obeyed and Enoch asked, "What we gon do wit 'em, Daddy?" He hadn't heard that childhood voice in years.

"I ain't sho, son, but they cain't stay in hyeah. We'll put 'em in de wagon and I'll think o' somethin' by then."

One good arm wasn't very good alone, but Enoch managed to drag the first body off the porch. Miss Mary helped him load it onto the wagon.

"De Lawd gon do somethin', son. I feel it," she huffed. "Git ready.

I'm tellin' you, I feel it." With closed eyes, she reached toward heaven, sensing something very real though obviously intangible. "This ain't gon be like de otha times."

Enoch didn't have time to press for clarity. His most immediate concern was the disposal of the bodies. Miss Mary, whose physical strength now exceeded his, assisted in loading the others, tossing corpses vindictively, like one releasing putrid garbage bags into a Dumpster. She was acting rather callously, Enoch thought, for one who had always preached kindness and compassion, even for her enemies. It wasn't that she hated white people, for Miss Mary would have been horrified had anyone believed she carried such trash in her heart. Rather, Enoch concluded that she was simply finishing the grieving for Jerry that the demands of cotton crops each year had inhibited. Whatever the source of her obstinacy, she kept repeating, "It's gon be diff'rent dis time. I'm tellin' you, boy. It's gon be diff'rent this time," until a smile of certainty beamed across her face.

"Mary, baby, you git dis flo cleaned up. Don't leave one drop o' blood nowhere," Jeremiah instructed, after Enoch confirmed that the bodies were loaded and ready to go. "Now, let's do somethin' wit this worthless white flesh."

Enoch handed Jeremiah his hat. "Git dat ole tarp we use to cover de hay when it rain and put it over—"

"I already did, Daddy," Enoch said.

"Then let's go."

Stepping off the front porch cautiously, Jeremiah yelled over his shoulder, "Tell Ella Mae to put dem chillen back up in de barn loft 'til I git back." He knew Miss Mary would do exactly as he had instructed.

When their grandmother told them to run, the children fled swiftly into the thick, dark night. Chop moved faster than he ever thought he could, assisted tremendously by a big brother pulling him along. In fear, the four moved stealthily among the high moody grass until they reached the bank of the turbulent Tallahatchie River.

"Jes follow me," Ray Ray whispered anxiously as he waded into the viridescent current. Sarah Jane was holding his right hand with her left as though gripping a skillet of hot grease. Her attempt to maintain bravery was crumbling with every step she took, yet she had no choice but to follow. The clear, hot, windless night only intensified matters as nature held its breath to see if the children would make it. The reflection of the moon on the river's surface provided just enough light for Ray Ray to see his way and to determine that, so far, everyone was all right.

"I'm sssssscared," Chop murmured, sitting aupon Clement's shoulders.

"Be quiet, boy," Ray Ray mumbled virulently. "We gon be all right."

Chop tried to hold his tears, but in their mutiny, the salty ones marched proudly down his small cheeks and fell upon Clement's bushy afro.

"I got chu, Chop," Clement assured quietly when Chop's hold around his neck became unbearable. Clement loosened Chop's grip a bit and squeezed the latter's small hand comfortingly.

"Okay," Chop repeated, more to himself than to Clement.

"Stop!" Sarah Jane cried next. The water had reached her chest, and all of her resolve was gone. "I can't go no farther!" Her and Ray Ray's hand had become one tight fist of fear.

"It's okay, Sarah Jane," Clement breathed soothingly. "We ain't gon let you drown."

By "we" Sarah Jane knew he meant him and Ray Ray since Chop was absolutely dysfunctional.

"You jes gotta trust us," Clement pleaded.

"But I cain't swim!" she admitted sadly.

"Don't worry about it," Ray Ray said. "I ain't gon let nothin' happen to you." Her shadow reminded him of the story of Jesus and John in the River Jordan. "You gon be fine. Trust me."

Sarah Jane didn't remember Ray Ray being so nurturing, so loving, so protecting, but she saw that, when called upon, he could rise to the occasion.

"We gon make it, Sarah Jane. Hold on to my shoulders, and if the water gets too deep, I'll carry you."

Ray Ray took another step forward and lost his balance. His head submerged beneath the river, and Sarah Jane knew she'd never see her grandparents again. Yet, instantly, Ray Ray resurfaced, and said, "There's a deep hole right behind me, so step this way."

He led her gently to the left as the water rose to her neck. Sarah Jane sighed. "Come on. Easy, easy," Ray Ray said.

Clement and Chop followed obediently. Both wondered what they'd do when the water reached Clement's neck. The chattering of Chop's teeth kept Clement's nerves on edge, and Sarah Jane's floating form ruined their confidence.

"It's 'bout to get deep now, y'all," Ray Ray warned. "But we gon be all right. Jes stay real close together."

Only their heads were visible now. The children took deep breaths simultaneously, then Ray Ray prepared to lead them into five feet of rushing, dark water.

"Clement, you grab Sarah Jane's shoulder, and Chop you hold on real tight. We cain't let go o' one another 'cause the water is movin' too fast fu me to save you. Jes don't let go!"

And with that, Ray Ray stepped boldly into the deep. He had to lean his head all the way back in order to keep his face above water. Clement was on his toes, barely touching bottom, while Sarah Jane was floating between the two. Chop hadn't meant to leave fingernail prints in Clement's neck, but he was far too scared to be considerate.

"Jes come on," Ray Ray coached, and slithered through the swarthy river.

The children looked like a band of runaway slaves, eager to touch freedom's soil. They were determined to survive, not only for themselves, but also for a family that had just risked everything to assure their future. At one point, Sarah Jane swore she saw a snake. Something raised its small head a few feet away, but then disappeared, so she thanked God and kept the sighting to herself. She was just scared and seeing things, she noted, for had she truly believed a snake was in the water, she would have relinquished Ray Ray's shoulders and given up the ghost.

Chop looked across the glistening river and wondered, if he fell, could he walk on the water like Miss Mary said Jesus had done. Doubting himself, he gripped Clement's eye sockets hard enough to gouge the balls out, having determined that he wasn't going to die at five if he could help it.

"Easy, easy," Ray Ray muttered to the rushing waters. "We gon make it. We gotta make it."

The best Ray Ray could do was to take microscopic steps since he carried the weight—and the fear—of all four of them. The inconsiderate river flowed past them carelessly, like a buffalo stampede, totally unconcerned about anything in its path.

"I cain't see!" Clement screamed to Chop.

Ray Ray stopped. He swiveled his head to see what was wrong with Clement and discovered Chop's fingers buried in Clement's eyes. "We ain't gon let you drown, boy!" he stated passionately. "Now move yo fingers so Clement can see."

Chop was too afraid to move anything. He was willing to take whatever punishment ensued later if it meant he had survived.

"Chop!" Ray Ray roared.

"Just go on," Clement conceded in frustration. "I got Sarah Jane's shoulders."

Ray Ray moved the group another inch forward. Suddenly, he felt Sarah Jane release hold of him.

"Sarah Jane!" he hollered, reaching for her hand.

"Ray!" she cried, and reached back rapidly.

Their hands clasped just in time for Sarah Jane not to be swept away by the swift current. Ray Ray's heart pounded against his narrow, flat chest.

"You all right, girl?" he inquired.

She nodded frantically. Chop was so glad Sarah Jane had survived that he sobbed as though she hadn't.

"Hook back up, y'all," Ray Ray instructed. "We almost there."

The children moved two or three feet forward and felt the river-bank rise beneath their feet.

"It's okay now," Ray Ray announced meekly. The children stepped onto the bank. "We made it."

Clement lowered Chop, who then apologized, "Ssssssssorry 'b-b-bout yo eyes."

"You didn't do nothin' wrong, Chop. You did fine." Clement smiled and patted Chop's small head.

Sarah Jane collapsed upon the earth, relieved. Never had she faced anything so frightening, especially with no grown-ups around. She thanked God for her cousins because now she knew that if they could cross a river in the middle of the night, with only a bright full moon to guide their way, they could survive anything.

"Come on, y'all," Ray Ray called after catching his breath. "We gotta git to de ole shack."

Once again, the children held hands and bounced like rabbits across the field until they found the shack by the pecan tree. Inside, they made a womb of themselves, with Chop huddled in the middle, and they waited.

Four

Y OU RRRRRRECKON THTHTHTHEY C-C-COMIN' FOR US?" CHOP whispered to Sarah Jane, who was in no mood to entertain doubt.

"They comin', boy!" she responded thickly, sorry her nerves had caused her to be so callous. "They comin'."

The old shack had once been the home of Bull Black—that was the man's name—and his seventeen children. He got the name because he wrestled an old, black brimmer bull for five dollars and won. He was always stout, Jeremiah said, and when his older brothers challenged him, at thirteen, to tame the old breeding bull, he laughed, and said, "Where's yo money?"

"I was standing right there," Jeremiah bragged, "'cause Bull was my best friend and we used to play together every chance we could. I tried to talk him out of doin' it 'cause dat ole cow was mean and ornery, but Bull was the most bullheaded somebody de Good Lawd ever made."

The children laughed along with their grandfather, whose favorite pastime was reminiscing about the old days. As he spoke, his chest swelled.

"So Bull told me to hold his glasses—he never could see—while he handled that old cow."

"Stop lyin', man!" Miss Mary instigated. "Bull was jes as sweet as he could be. He ain't neva fought no cow, and you know it!"

"You wunnit there! I wunnit stuttin you yet," Jeremiah teased as he filled his pipe with tobacco. "You was still skinny and ugly. You didn't get pretty 'til de next summer."

Roaring gleefully, the children looked at their grandmother to make sure her feelings weren't hurt. The wave of her hand and sucking of her teeth confirmed that she was simply doing her part to make the story funnier.

"Like I was sayin', Bull stepped over into the corral and jumped on dat bull's back and they went to tusslin'. De bull throwed Bull at first, but he got up and jumped right back on him 'til he wrestled him to de ground." Jeremiah gazed at the children in wonder. "Bull was strong as a ox. He wunnit but thirteen years ole, but he was whippin' dat bull's black ass."

"All right, man!" Miss Mary admonished. "We don't talk like dat 'round no chillen." Jeremiah sighed his consent and continued the story.

"Bull grabbed dat bull by de horns and twisted his head"— Jeremiah stood to demonstrate his friend's exact movements—"and dat old bull bellowed out a holla dat scared all of us. He fell on his back like this." Jeremiah fainted into the rocker like a dead man. "But de bull wasn't dead. He was just unconscious."

"De lies you tell gon send you straight to hell, man," Miss Mary said as she rose to check on dinner.

"Dat bull was unconscious!" Jeremiah screamed heartily. "It was layin' on de ground breathin' real hard, but it wasn't movin'. We thought he was dead at first, but after a few minutes he rolled ova and stood up and walked away." Jeremiah lit his pipe and nodded confidently. "Dat's right!"

"D-d-d-did Mr. B-b-bull get ththe ffffive d-d-d-dollars?" Chop asked enthusiastically.

"Naw." Jeremiah feigned disappointment. Then he smiled, and said, "They gave him ten."

The house shook with laughter. Even Miss Mary, who usually frowned at her husband's stories, chuckled along.

"What happened to Mr. Bull, Granddaddy?" Sarah Jane asked.

"He growed up to be the stoutest little man anybody ever met. The muscles in his arm was bigger than yo grandma's thighs."

"All right, fool!" Miss Mary hollered.

Jeremiah smiled playfully and continued: "He married a girl named Isadore and they had seventeen kids. They lived in the old shack down by the river, sharecroppin' like everybody else did back then."

"Where ththththey at n-n-now?"

Jeremiah and Miss Mary caught each other's eye, and the children knew something had gone wrong.

"They moved," Jeremiah said quickly.

"No, they didn't, man. Ain't no use in you lyin' to dem chillen. If you gon tell de story, tell it right. They old enough to know."

"Alrighty," Jeremiah sighed. "They killed 'em."

Ray Ray's brow furrowed. "Who killed 'em, Granddaddy?"

"White folks," Enoch interrupted. "They always killin' colored people. Dat's why I can't stand—"

"All right, boy. Dat's enough o' dat," Jeremiah cooed before things got out of hand.

"I bet it was white folks, wasn't it, Daddy?"

"Yeah, it was. Don't nobody know exactly what happened though. Different folks said different things, but it was white folks for sho." Jeremiah looked at Miss Mary to see if he should go on, and since she didn't stop him, he proceeded: "They say Bull had challenged a white boy to a arm wrestle. A whole crowd o' folks gathered to see who was the strongest man in Money, and Bull beat dat white boy so bad he broke his arm. He wasn't tryin to break his arm; dat's jes how strong he was. Well, de white boy left, promisin' Bull he was gon pay for showin' out. Didn't nobody think too much about it though. They said the white boy was jes mad cause Bull had beat him so bad. Kinda like how mad white folks wuz when Jack Johnson beat Jim Jeffries in nineteen ten."

"Who was Jack Johnson, Granddaddy?" Sarah Jane asked.

"Who was Jack Johnson?" Jeremiah returned in surprise. "You chillen don't know nothin' 'bout y'all's history. Jack Johnson was the first Black heavyweight champion boxer in de world. He fought a white boy everybody said wuz gone beat him, but he outsmarted dat cracker and knocked his ass out in the fifteenth round. White folks been mad ever since." He paused.

"Anyway, Black folk threw a party dat night to celebrate Bull's victory, and it was so loud the white folks miles away could hear us. Dat's what really got 'em mad, I think. We was rubbin' it in. Really, we was jes havin' a good time. We didn't need to rub nothin' in 'cause colored folks already knowed we was stronger than white folks. Hell, we did all the work." Jeremiah looked at his grandchildren seriously. "But a few days later, Nub Harris came runnin' by our house 'bout six o'clock in de mornin' screamin, 'de done killed 'em all!' We didn't know what he was talkin' 'bout, but Daddy told me to hurry and throw some clothes on so we could find out what had done happened.

"We hitched up de ole mule and buggy and rode ova to Bull's place, and Lawd have mercy." Jeremiah hesitated.

"What was it Granddaddy?" Sarah Jane alone was bold enough to ask.

"They had done hung de whole family, each person from a different tree."

The children's gasps sent chills over Jeremiah's weathered, black skin. "Dat's right. Seventeen bodies hangin' from seventeen different trees."

"But I thought you said Mr. Bull had seventeen kids?" Ray Ray inquired confused. "There should have been nineteen bodies—"

"The oldest two boys got away somehow, they said. Folks don't know where they went and ain't nobody heard from 'em since then. That was thirty years ago or more."

"Did you see the bodies, Granddaddy?" Sarah Jane's curiosity was unbridled.

"Couldn't help but see 'em. I was in de wagon wit Daddy, and he made me look at every single one of 'em. I guess he was teachin' me a lesson."

"What lesson?" she pressed on.

"Neva play wit white folks 'cause they don't play fair."

Now Sarah Jane wished Clement had heard the story and maybe he, too, would have learned the lesson. Oh well, she thought, as they sat huddled together in Mr. Bull's old shack. Cobwebs decorated the wooden walls, and the house was empty except for an old straw-bottom chair and a rusty woodstove. Folks said the house was haunted so that's why it remained empty. But Jeremiah told his grandkids not to listen to other folks. Bull had been his best friend, and the house would protect them if they were ever in trouble.

Engulfed in darkness, the children sat and waited for further instructions. A mouse scurried across Sarah Jane's leg, and she emitted a high, quick yelp before Ray Ray could say, "Be quiet! Nobody's spose to know we here."

Explaining about the mouse was useless, Sarah Jane knew, so she nodded silently and recomposed herself. Looking across the empty room, she imagined the activity it once held as a home to nineteen people. How much food did a mother have to prepare to feed that many, she wondered in awe, and where in the world did everybody sleep? "It could be fun, I guess," she murmured, and shrugged her shoulders.

Clement squirmed a bit and whispered, "Sorry, y'all, I didn't mean to get everybody in trouble."

"Jes be quiet, man," Ray Ray reiterated. "We gon be all right. Ain't nothin' we can do 'bout it now. Jes be quiet and wait." Ray Ray's nerves were frazzled.

"I'ma jes turn myself in," Clement said matter-of-factly and shuffled to break away from the huddle.

Sarah Jane grabbed his arm with surprising strength. "You ain't goin' nowhere, Clement. Granddaddy told us what to do, and dat's what we gon do."

Clement's resolve weakened. "All right," he offered, and sighed deeply before resuming his place among his cousins.

"Jes be quiet," Ray Ray repeated fiercely.

Chop wanted to ask how much longer they would have to wait, but his big brother's tone convinced him to keep his wonderings private. Crossing that river was the scariest thing he had ever done, so whatever awaited them in the future they could survive, Chop concluded. He knew Clement felt bad, but because he had carried him across the river, Chop had totally exonerated him in his heart. He wanted to apologize again for squeezing Clement's neck so hard, but fear of Ray Ray's anger made Chop hold his tongue.

Ray Ray now wished he were the youngest. He knew that everyone's safety was his responsibility, and he would have to answer to his father and grandfather if anything happened to any of them. That's why, every ten seconds or so, he rose from the huddle and peered through a broken window, hoping to see Granddaddy or Ella Mae or somebody familiar.

As though instinctively, Sarah Jane began to hum faintly, "Couldn't hear nobody pray, couldn't hear nobody pray! I was way down yonder by myself, and I couldn't hear nobody pray." She knew the melody because her grandfather sang the song daily, forcing his family to endure what they called the voice of a bullfrog. But now the song served a function greater than anything she would ever have believed. Sarah Jane didn't even understand what the words meant. Not until now. Neither did Ray Ray, but he allowed the murmuring because it reminded him of home and kept the brooding silence from driving him mad. If he could just hear Miss Mary call his name, he thought, he would never ask God for another thing. "I was way down yonder by myself . . . ," Ray Ray mumbled audibly. Then he chuckled. He now knew that, in order to understand the song, you had to know something about trouble.

"Y'all pray," he suddenly told the others. "Say it out loud, but say it softly."

None of them had mastered the art of praying, but now was not the time to be shy. Clement bowed, and whined: "I'm sorry, Lord, for all of this. I didn't mean to bring trouble. I was jes getting a soda—" His voice cracked, and Sarah Jane rubbed his hand. "Don't let nothing happen to my folks," he resumed. "I was jes comin' down here for the summer to play with my cousins, Lord. It wasn't spose to be like this." He paused again. "Lord, watch over my grandma and grandpa, Uncle Enoch and Aunt Ella Mae, Ray Ray, Sarah Jane, and Chop. Amen."

"Amen," Ray Ray and Sarah Jane muttered.

Then Chop offered with a nervous sincerity, "I-I-I d-don't know hhhow t-to pray, Llllawd, 'c-c-cause I-I-I ain't neva prrrrayed out lllloud f-f-for a whole b-b-b-bunch o' p-p-people befo, b-b-but please d-d-d-don't lllllet n-n-obody hurt us 'c-c-c-cause wwwwe ain't d-d-done n-n-nothin' wrong." He took a deep breath as Sarah Jane encouraged him on. "Clement d-didn't mmmean to c-c-c-cause no trrrrrouble, Lawd. He wwwwas j-jes b-b-bein' mannish, Lawd, b-b-but he's my fffffavorite c-c-c-cousin. And Lawd, I-I knnnows d-d-dat white p-people c-c-can be rrrrreal mmmmmean ssssssometime, b-b-but mmmake them nnnicer 'c-c-cause I-I-I d-don't wanna d-d-die t-t-today. Amen."

The other three looked at him in awe. "That was real good, Chop," Ray Ray affirmed. "Real good."

It was Sarah Jane's turn. She didn't know what she wanted to say, but she certainly knew the power of prayer. Bowing her head humbly, she began, "Matchless King"—she got that phrase from her grandmother—"we come before You now as empty vessels before an ever-flowing fountain. Jes like You hung the stars in space and set the sun in the sky, look after us now. We ain't always done what we should, but we strivin' every day to be more like You."

The boys enjoyed the familiarity of their grandmother's words. Sarah Jane even sounded like Miss Mary, Clement thought.

"Thank You for my mother and father, who already in heaven, and for my cousins who helped me across the river tonight. I'm scared right now, God, and I don't want nothin' to happen to none o' us. Please keep Your shield of protection around us. Don't let hurt, harm, or danger come our way. Forgive Clement for what he did and don't let nobody bother him."

She glanced up to see if Clement was paying attention, only to find him staring directly at her. She felt compelled to continue.

"Grandma always says You'll fix it if we jes ask. Well, Lawd, I'm askin' You right now to fix this situation and let us get back home safe and sound."

"Amen," the boys chimed.

". . . and while You fixin' thangs, Lawd, don't let us have hatred in our hearts. I know what white folks keep doin' to colored people, but don't let us get like them. Amen."

Standing watch at the window, Ray Ray affirmed Sarah Jane's prayer with a quick, soft grunt.

"You don't see nobody yet?" Clement asked, simply to hear his own voice.

"Not yet," Ray Ray said. He looked at the full moon and wished for the ability to fly away.

"Some glad mornin', when this life is over, I'll fly away!" Miss Mary sang valiantly every morning. She would throw her head back dramatically and declare her flight plans as a threat to the natural order of things. Ray Ray loved how his grandmother sang, wondering if her conviction would one day grant her wings to fly away. Sometimes he smiled as he listened, almost laughing at Miss Mary declaring her hope in things normally impossible. But what if, one morning, she jes flew away? he pondered. What if God gave her wings jes because she believed and never stopped hoping? The more Ray Ray thought about it, the more sense it made.

Then, simultaneously, he and Sarah Jane began to hum the hymn.

Their heads jerked to stare at each other, but their souls never lost harmony. "I'll fly away, Oh glory, I'll fly away. When I die, hallelujah by and by. I'll fly away." Chop cried and Clement rocked in thanks for hearing the song in another time and place. Sarah Jane whispered the second verse in the call and response tradition: "Just a few more weary days and then—"

Ray Ray answered in another key, "I'll fly away."

"To a home where joy shall never end—"

Ray Ray smiled and mumbled, "I'll fly away."

And together they finished the chorus: "I'll fly away, Oh glory, I'll fly away." Their heads swayed to the rhythm. "When I die, hallelujah by and by. I'll fly away."

In the distance, Ray Ray saw the yellow print of Ella Mae's old housedress.

"They're here!" he whispered intensely, and the others jumped with delight.

Ella Mae motioned for them to remain still and quiet. Once she approached, her silence exposed that all was not well. Ella Mae's panting revealed more about her internal woes than her poor physical condition.

"Momma, it sho is good to see you!" Ray Ray reached for the hug he needed desperately, but Ella Mae refused him.

"Listen to me, children." She was still panting. "This family's in a lotta hot water. We got a long road ahead of us, and I ain't sho what's 'bout to happen. What I am sho about is dat we got to stick together. Don't care what happen, we got to stick together. Y'all understand me?"

"Yes ma'am," the children returned.

"D-d-did D-d-daddy and Grrranddaddy k-k-kill those wwwhite mmmen?"

Ella Mae wasn't sure just how much she should tell, but since the children were in the middle of the ordeal, she thought they should know. "Yes, they did. One got away, but the others were killed."

Sarah Jane clasped her mouth while Clement hung his head in

shame. "I woulda put de nickel in her hand, Auntie, if I knew it was gone be like this."

"I told you to go back in there and—" Sarah Jane fell silent before her temper exploded.

"We ain't got no time fu that right now, y'all," Ella Mae corrected. "We got to get outta here and stick together. Clement"—Ella Mae put her right arm around his shoulder lovingly—"this ain't yo fault. If it wasn't you, it woulda been some otha Black boy or Ray Ray or anybody. This is 'bout us as colored folks. And that's how we gon fight—standin' together as colored folks. So stop blamin' yo'self, you hear me?"

Clement nodded, unable to speak. Sarah Jane rolled her eyes.

"Look here, young lady!" Ella Mae snapped. "Ain't nobody perfect, includin' you! Git off dat high horse o' yours and get clear dat we standin' together as a family. Yes, Clement made a mistake, but so have all of us. But that don't mean he ain't in de family no mo! Once you in dis family, you in it forever. And if you in it, you fight for it! It don't make no difference if you agree or not. Anybody come against dis family got to fight de whole family. We stands as one. You understand me, girl?"

Sarah Jane hesitated but offered a weak, "Yes, ma'am." She looked at Clement's water-streaked face, and said passionately, "I ain't really mad at Clement, Auntie. I'm jes scared."

Clement grabbed her in his arms and, together, they wept until Ella Mae said, "Let's go."

Like Harriet Tubman leading anxious slaves to free territory, Ella Mae tiptoed quickly around the side of Bull Black's old shack, with the children mimicking her careful steps. She stopped, peered deeply across the dark, empty field, and without announcement hoisted her dress above her knees as she led the way back to the river. The children crossed again, this time in a shallower place, each one borrowing enough of Ella Mae's confidence to do it with relative ease. Anxious but cautious, they moved through the woods easily, hoping the night brought no more surprises.

Five

WHERE WE GOIN', DADDY?" ENOCH ASKED WHEN JERE-
miah directed him to turn the worn, weathered wagon
down a narrow, weeded lane. "Jes do what I tell you,
son," Jeremiah whimpered. He hadn't meant to be short, but the pain
in his side left him little room for sensitivity.

They rode on in awkward silence. Enoch kept looking behind him,
afraid that, at any moment, those bodies might rise and mock him
and Jeremiah for thinking themselves empowered enough to destroy
white life. He just wanted to dump them somewhere and bring the
matter to closure. Yet his father's face carried a slight smirk that, if
Enoch hadn't known better, he would have read as pleasure. He
didn't understand it. From the moment they left home, Jeremiah
chuckled along the way, sometimes loud enough to startle Enoch and
confuse what he thought should have been Jeremiah's dismay con-

cerning everything. Staring at his father yielded no clarity since Jeremiah's eyes bespoke absolutely nothing. No regret. No confusion. Nothing. Enoch didn't ask Jeremiah about his strange disposition, for, in truth, the son sensed that something in the world—or at least in Money—was shifting before his very eyes. He had never seen his father relaxed in the midst of chaos, so maybe now, he thought, he'd learn the secret of Black survival in the racist white South.

"Right over there," Jeremiah said, pointing the flashlight toward a thick grove of cypress trees in the distance.

Enoch winced in agony as he manipulated the reins and directed the mules to the appointed spot. Bringing the wagon to a halt, he sat perfectly still, waiting on instructions from a man who seemed to have perfect peace.

"We'll throw 'em out right here, boy," Jeremiah announced lightly, and descended from the wagon.

"Ain't we gon bury 'em or at least cover 'em up?" Enoch asked while struggling to remove the tarpaulin.

"Hell naw, we ain't gon bury 'em! We ain't wastin' no goddamn energy on these worthless crackers! Shit!" Jeremiah's bandages, like a corset, bound his midsection so tightly he could hardly move, yet he did what he could to help unload the bodies. "I'm tired o' kissin' white folks' asses, and I'll be damned if I do it when they dead."

Enoch studied his father's expression and concluded that he had simply snapped. Jeremiah Johnson had never been vindictive, and Enoch never would have guessed that they would simply discard the bodies like dirty dishwater. After having followed instructions obediently, he hoped his father might volunteer an explanation of what they were doing and why.

Jeremiah turned off the flashlight, leaving them in utter darkness. "You know where we went wrong, boy?" He sighed deeply, leaning on the side of the wagon. Enoch thought the question rhetorical although the long pause made him unsure. He played it safe and said nothing.

"We shoulda showed these white folk years ago that they couldn't kill us and get away with it. That's where we went wrong, boy. Right there." He lifted his head toward the sky as though thanking God for the revelation.

"When we came outta slavery, we shoulda came out whippin' ass."

Enoch groaned.

"That's right!" Jeremiah declared. "When white folks started lynchin' our boys and rapin' our girls, and we wuz free? We was spose to do more than pray. See, prayer don't mean nothin' to somebody who don't respect God noway. And you see God ain't gon do nothin' you ain't willin' to do first. I done learned that. That's why God ain't moved on colored folks' behalf like we want Him to! 'Cause colored folks ain't moved on colored folks' behalf like we spose to! We been teachin' these crackers that they can come in our houses and take our chillen and we ain't gon do nothin' 'bout it. That's why they keep comin'! They done learned that God ain't gon stop 'em if we ain't. We sit around like scared li'l chickens waitin' on momma hen to come and protect us. But we got to grow up sometime. And today I'm a grown-ass man who done decided that ain't no white man—or any other man—gon harm my family without feelin' the wrath of me! Now maybe they'll kill me, too, but I'll die in peace knowin' that my children was proud of me."

Jeremiah's tone had changed from lightheartedness to vehemence. Enoch had a feeling this was more guilt concerning Jerry than fear for Clement.

As though reading his mind, Jeremiah continued with, "That's the only regret I done had to live wit my whole life—feelin' like I didn't fight for my boy the way I shoulda. I was spose to go over there—not Jerry—and kill dem peckawoods years ago. He was spose to watch his daddy stand up for him, come what may, so he'd know how to be a man when his turn came. But I was too scared, Enoch. I didn't want nothin' to happen to the rest o' y'all, so I held my peace. But white folks didn't respect my silence. That's why these crackers came to de house tonight—'cause they thought I wunnit gon do nothin'. Just like last time."

Jeremiah cackled at the profundity of his own words. "But we surprised they asses, didn't we boy?" He laughed loud and long, while Enoch watched him transform into a self-assured colored man. Then his expression changed abruptly. "This ain't gon be easy, boy. These white folks 'round here 'bout to be fightin' mad 'bout Black folks protectin' theyselves." He turned on the flashlight and looked at Enoch. "But that's okay 'cause I'm mad, too. Shit, they can't be madder than me!"

Enoch understood his father's speech as an announcement of something to come.

"Get ready for this one, boy! When they find these bodies they gon come after us like Pharaoh's army!" Jeremiah said, then Enoch helped him back onto the wagon. "This gon be a doozy!"

"Billy!" Cecil Love screamed from the road, clutching his bleeding left arm with the palm of his right hand. "Billy! They killed yo' brothers!" he panted loudly. Getting no response, he yelled at full lung capacity, "Billy!"

Rosalind heard the last cry and nudged her sleeping husband. "Sweetheart, wake up. Somethin's wrong. Somebody's screamin' for you out in the yard."

"Huh?" Billy mumbled, disoriented.

"Billy!" Cecil called again.

"What the fuck?" Billy said, rubbing his eyes. "Who is that screamin' my goddamn name in the middle of the night?"

Rosalind gathered her robe about her shoulders and went to the window. "I can't tell, honey, but it sounds like Cecil. Whoever it is, he's holdin' his arm like he's hurt."

"Shit," Billy said, and reached for his trousers on the floor. "This better be serious, or I'ma kick some mutherfucker's ass."

Smoothing out his frazzled hair, Rosalind said, "Just go see what it's about, honey. Don't get worked up before you know."

"Billy Cuthbert!" Cecil screamed again just as Billy opened the front door.

"What! Asshole! Why are you yellin' in the middle of the fuckin' night when decent folk—" The sight of Cecil's blood dripping onto his front steps caught his attention. His voice softened. "What the hell happened?"

Cecil sighed. "They killed yo' brothers. I got away."

"What are you talkin' about, Cecil?" Billy began to shiver. "Who shot you?"

"The niggers who live on Chapman's place. They killed yo' brothers and tried to kill me, too, but I got away." He was still huffing.

"They killed my brothers? Who killed my fuckin' brothers, Cecil?"

"Like I said, some o' Chapman's niggers. Mary's kin. We went there to get that boy who sassed Catherine today in the store, and those niggers just shot us in cold blood."

"Who sassed Catherine? What the hell are you talkin' about?"

Cecil grimaced as he shifted his arm slightly. "Catherine told Alvin that some nigger boy from up North came in the store today and sassed her somethin' awful. She said she was bein' real nice to him, but he bought a pop and just threw the money at her. He's one o' Mary's grandkids, she said. At least he was with them earlier, so we was goin' over there tonight to straighten him out, and that's when the boy's daddy and uncle, I guess, started shootin'. They killed Alvin, Mark, and Jay."

Billy's hands quivered. "Why the fuck did y'all go over there without me?" he screeched.

"We couldn't find you!" Cecil whined. "We come by here, but Ros said she didn't know where you was."

"I'll kill those fuckin' bastards!" he screamed, and buried his right fist in his left. "You get to Doc Gunderman 'fore you bleed to death, boy. I'll take this from here."

Cecil nodded and stumbled away. He wanted to watch Billy put Jeremiah and Enoch back in their places, but his dripping blood convinced him to save his own life before he watched others lose theirs.

"What was that about?" Rosalind asked, watching Billy retrieve his rifle from the wall and load it.

"Don't concern you," he murmured. "Just take care o' the girls. I'll be back in a while."

"It does concern me, Billy Ray. Anytime you get like this, somethin' bad happens."

Billy ignored her.

Rosalind folded her arms in disgust. "Then I'm comin' with you."

"No you ain't!" he shouted. "This is sheriff's business. It ain't your concern. I'll be back in a while," he repeated, patronizingly.

"Don't go by yourself, Billy Ray! You ain't thinkin' straight, and you likely to do somethin' you sorry for."

"I ain't gon do nothin' I'm sorry for!" he bellowed. "I'm gon do somethin' what shoulda been done a long time ago. I don't need no help, and I don't want no help."

Rosalind shook her head. "I think you do, honey," she pleaded. "You too mad to think right now."

"I'm just fine," Billy Ray whispered. He rose from the kitchen chair. "I gotta go."

"Billy!" she cried after him although to no avail.

Her mother had warned her it would come to this. When, fifteen years ago, she first announced her crush on Billy Ray Cuthbert, her mother's silence startled her.

"Don't you think he's 'bout the cutest boy 'round, Momma?" she asked, expecting an immediate affirmation. Her mother said nothing. "What is it Momma?"

Through pursed lips, her mother said, "He's headed for trouble, Rosalind."

"What chu mean?"

"Cain't you see nothin', girl?" her mother said sadly. "He and dem rogue brothers o' his don't do nothin' but stay in trouble."

"Ah, they're just young, Momma. They'll grow out of it."

"Sweetheart, Billy's twenty years old."

"I know, but you know how boys is. They just foolish and like to have fun."

The mother knew her words were in vain, but she had to try. "Rosalind, don't be a blind fool. I didn't raise you to have you give yourself to some no-good hoodlum like Billy Ray Cuthbert. He don't respect nothin' and nobody but hisself."

"Aw, come on, Momma! He ain't like that at all." She danced around the room with him as her imaginary partner. "I think he just likes to have fun, like most boys his age. And he's cute as pie!"

Her mother cackled. "Cute don't mean kind, girl. I hope you don't learn that the hard way."

She did. Only weeks after they married, Billy called her a fuckin' bitch the night she denied him sex. His words pierced her heart and made her wonder what, in God's name, she had gotten herself into. However, determined to prove her mother wrong, she dismissed the verbal abuse as overwhelming fatigue and counted the incident exceptional. When, a month later, he hit her, she was still more committed to the dream of him than to the truth.

"So you gon let him kill you before you wake up?" her mother asked when she saw the bruised cheek.

"What do you mean, Mother? You think Billy Ray did this?" She touched her face and flinched. "I bumped into a door when—"

"Stop it, Rosalind! Don't be too proud to say you wuz wrong. Ain't nothin' wrong with bein' wrong, girl, once you discover it. But, whatsoever you do"—she was more intense than Rosalind had ever seen her—"don't try to make it right. That'll kill you."

Rosalind couldn't maintain the charade. She dropped onto her mother's living room floor and wept in sorrow. "Momma, what have I done? What have I done?"

Her mother held her close, and said, "Look, honey. You ain't got to pay for a dumb mistake the rest of yo' life. You can always come back here. This is home."

Yet determined not to be the gossip of Money's white citizenry,

Rosalind returned to Billy and decided to be a better wife. Anytime he wanted her she submitted, even when she was too tired to participate, and when the girls came, she named one Billie Jean and the other Rayina. Billy was pleased. That is, until Rosalind started cooking food whose names he couldn't pronounce.

"What is this shit?" he asked one evening, frowning at the meal she had worked hours to prepare.

"It's chicken cacciatore, honey. Just try it. I think you'll like it."

"Well, I don't, and I ain't eatin' this crap." He turned from the table and left Rosalind sitting at the other end. Seconds later, he returned.

"Cook me somethin' decent, woman."

The look in his eyes frightened Rosalind, but by then she had had enough. "Just give it a try, honey. You never know what you like until—"

"Don't tell me what I fuckin' like! I been workin' hard all day and gotta come home to a meal I don't even want?"

Rosalind heard her mother's voice in her head. "Then if you don't want this, you'll have to fix yourself something else."

He moved toward the kitchen, then suddenly swiveled and struck her in the mouth. "Who the fuck are you talkin' to? I said fix me somethin' to eat and, goddamnit, that's what I expect you to do. I don't pay de bills 'round here for nothin'."

Rosalind didn't move. Her tongue felt around the inside of her mouth for any loosened teeth.

"I said, fix me somethin' to eat, bitch!" Billy yanked her from the chair and pushed her toward the kitchen.

"Okay, okay," Rosalind cried. "Whatever you want. Just don't hit me. I'll fix whatever you want."

"Good. That's more like it," he said, and sat at the head of the table. "And make it snappy."

She would have left him that night if she hadn't been pregnant. But, as a child, she promised herself that her children would have a father, their real father—unlike she had—so she discarded all her cookbooks and served fried chicken, fish, or pork chops every evening for the next fourteen years. Once her mother died, and Billy became sheriff, she knew she'd be with him until she died. Or until he killed her.

Not knowing what else to do, she returned to bed. Lying awake, she thought about how much she hated Cecil Love. Some folks thought he was one of the Cuthbert brothers, but actually he was their first cousin. Their mothers were sisters, and since Cecil was an only child, Billy and his brothers made him an honorary Cuthbert. He was about as ignorant as the others, Rosalind noted, so his presence among them made perfect sense. She marveled that all the boys had lived so long.

Billy drove toward Chapman's place with the rifle in his lap. Everything he saw looked red. Trees, the moon, squirrels . . . everything. He considered stopping to invite others along for the ride, but not this time. He wanted the full joy of putting colored folks back in their place. He wanted the credit for every Black life destroyed and the pleasure of doing it. Niggers killin' whites—who would ever have thought it? Billy pondered. Somebody had to restore order around Money, Mississippi, and as sheriff it was his job to oblige, especially since, now, niggers had taken every brother he ever had. Had it been daylight, Black folks in the field would have marveled at the sheriff, flying down the road like a crazy man, and they would have wondered what in the world he was rushing to. The trail of thick dust might have made them believe he was trying to enter another place and time, that maybe he had left something undone in another life that, now, he desperately needed to complete. Yet, in the dark, his law enforcement vehicle moved swiftly like a phantom, which, at any moment, might vanish into the night.

Sweeping the porch with hot water and ammonia, Miss Mary saw the bouncing headlights the same instant she heard Ella Mae and the children enter through the back door.

"Take the children to the barn, Ella Mae!" she hollered through the front screen. "And stay there with 'em. Somebody comin'."

By the quick patter of footsteps she knew they had heard her, and although afraid, she braced herself to stand alone. "Lawd have mercy!" she mouthed and grabbed Jeremiah's shotgun. Having never killed anything, she didn't want to start now, but she prayed for the strength to do so if necessary.

Billy slammed the car door shut, and Miss Mary concluded that he, too, must be alone.

"Who killed my fuckin' brothers?" he screamed from the yard. Getting no response, he yelled, "Mary, don't make me come in there!" Then he marched onto the porch and flung the screen door open.

The coal oil lamp next to the ragged sofa illumined an empty room. Billy looked around quickly, and shouted, again, "Who killed my fuckin' brothers? I know you niggers is 'round here somewhere. And when I find you, I'ma kill every one o' you fuckin' bastards!" He turned.

"Not if we kill you first," he heard the familiar voice say.

Billy stiffened. He glanced around again, but saw no one.

"You ain't got no business talkin' like dat 'round my house, Sheriff Cuthbert. I near 'bout raised you myself," Miss Mary declared, staring at the angry white man from her view next to the peach tree. She had exited through the back when she heard Billy approaching the front. "Don't act like you done fugot! You ain't plumb crazy!" She knew she was taking the risk of a lifetime, but, in the moment, it seemed her only option.

Billy Ray hadn't forgotten. "I didn't come here after you, Mary!" he shouted into the night. "I come after whoever killed my brothers."

Miss Mary paused to gather her senses. Already in dangerous territory, she decided to go further. "I killed 'em!" she screamed boldly. "They busted my do' down, seekin' to take one o' my chillen, and I wunnit givin' up another one."

Seeing Billy return to the porch, Miss Mary eased toward the back of the house.

"You knows me, Sheriff. I near 'bout raise you!" she declared again. "You know I wouldn't kill fu no reason at all."

"I ain't here fu you, Mary!" he repeated louder, hoping she'd show her face and close her mouth.

"Then go on home 'cause ain't nobody else here but me. If you wants to talk, we can do dat afta you calm down, but I don't intend to be killed by somebody I nursed back to life, colored or white."

Billy was sure, moments ago, he would have killed anybody Black he encountered, but now his certainty, at least concerning Miss Mary, was weakening.

"I slept on de floor next to yo' bed when you wuz so sick yo' folks thought you wuz gon die," Miss Mary yelped. "I went to *my* God"—she poked her chest in the dark—"fu you. Every time you coughed, I poured a li'l chicken broth in yo' mouth to give you a li'l strength. De doctor said you wunnit gon make it through de night, and I asked yo' momma if I could stay 'cause you wuz like one o' my own."

Billy's rage mounted. "I said, I didn't come for you, Mary!" He shot into the sky. "I come for whoever killed my brothers, and I know it wunnit you."

Miss Mary shot, too. The loud bang frazzled her momentarily, but she maintained composure. "You don't know nothin'!" she said, and walked to the left side of the house as Billy walked to the right. "Don't act like you don't remember all dem meals I cooked and how I kept a cool rag on yo' momma's head fu two weeks befo' she passed. Don't act like you don't remember, Sheriff!" Miss Mary's adrenaline was flowing like the Tallahatchie.

"It was Enoch and that old man, wunnit it!" he asked from the other side of the house, trying to ignore her.

"NO!" she answered much too quickly. "I told you it was me, and de only reason I shot was 'cause they broke my do' down." She paused. "I near 'bout raised all you boys, 'cept Cecil. You know dat! I spent mo' time in yo' house than I did in my own for damn near twenty years. I didn't leave yo' momma 'til y'all got grown, and when she got sick, I went to see 'bout her every day. Didn't miss a day!"

"Stop playin' games with me, goddamnit!" he shouted. "If we gon talk, come on out and let's talk."

Miss Mary knew better. "You ain't no good when you mad. I always knowed dat 'bout you. So go on home, and we'll talk afta you git yo'self together."

He looked toward the rear of the house, into thick black nothingness, and decided not to risk it. Miss Mary thanked a sovereign God.

Billy Ray thought of a better plan and walked back to his truck. "Tell yo' menfolk I'll be back," he said. "Oh boy, will I be back. And when I come, you gon' be real sorry, old lady. Real sorry."

"You jes remember what I did fu you and yo' family, Billy Ray Cuthbert!" Miss Mary yelled. "You remember dat befo' you come back here again."

Billy Ray smiled devilishly and cranked the truck. "When I git through wit dis family, you'll never be de same. I promise you dat."

Sheriff Cuthbert left as he had come—fast and reckless. The retaliatory idea he had conceived made him smile. Demons in hell would have gawked at a plan so devastating, so sinister, but Billy promised himself and his dead brothers that he'd do it. He would never let niggers get away with killing whites, especially his own, and this time he promised to teach a lesson they would never forget.

Before he reached the bend in the road, he saw the countless headlights approaching. He had to stop them. They would ruin his plan.

The men parked their trucks on the side of the road and exited like anxious children.

"We heard what happened, Sheriff, so we come to give you a hand!" someone shouted. "Let's slay these bastards once and for all!"

"Yeah!" the mob roared.

Billy Ray counted at least ten lanterns swinging with the desire to kill.

"Just hold on there," Billy Ray cooed. "We ain't gon do it like that this time." He winked.

"Huh?"

"What d'ya mean?"

"Why not?"

"'Cause these colored niggers killed my brothers and they don't deserve to die. I want 'em to hurt for the rest o' their lives."

The men didn't understand.

"You ain't makin' much sense, Sheriff," Larry Greer, the local banker, said. "These niggers gotta die! And they gotta die tonight!"

"No!" Billy shouted. "That ain't enough. If we killed 'em, then what? I wouldn't feel no better 'bout my brothers just cause some worthless niggers is dead. I want more than that!"

"What chu want, then?" someone shouted impatiently.

Billy wasn't ready to reveal his plan, but he had to say something. "I wanna make these niggers hate that they wuz ever born. I want 'em to feel pain so deep inside they can't even reach it. I want 'em to run and tell all the other niggers never, ever to fuck with a white man long as they live!"

Billy's nostrils flared as his teeth chattered.

"That's what I want! And I don't want none o' you"—he looked each man in his eyes—"messin' it up."

"But what chu gon do?" Larry asked.

Billy pondered. "Tell you what. Anybody interested, meet me at my house in the morning 'round nine and I'll explain everything to ya. For now, spread the word that ain't nobody, and I mean nobody, spose to touch none o' Chapman's niggers. Let 'em wonder what we gon do 'til we show 'em. They'll wish they had never seen a white man!"

The men nodded. They didn't know what the sheriff was planning, but they loved the way he was talking.

"So you boys go on home now, and I'll meet you in the morning. I'll talk to Chapman, too. And remember—these niggers is mine!"

Six

MISS MARY STUMBLED TO THE FRONT STEPS AND HUFFED, "Thank ya, Lawd! Thank ya!"

Ella Mae stepped from behind the barn. "You all right, Momma?"

"Yeah, I'm all right, daughter," Miss Mary said. "Jes a li'l wound up, dat's all."

"I was sho scared Billy Ray wuz gon try to hurt you," Ella Mae said, joining her on the steps and leaning Enoch's rifle against the porch. "But if he tried to kill you, he wuz sho gon join his brothers to-night!" she said with more courage now than she had before.

Miss Mary looked astonished. "You saw me, girl?"

"Saw the whole thing!" she boasted. "I wuz standing right there beside de barn wit dat gun pointed at Billy's head the whole time."

Miss Mary's mouth dropped open.

"Aw, Momma, come on! You know I ain't gon let nothin' happen to you. You de only momma I got."

The women embraced warmly. They were proud that, in the absence of their men, they had stood just as tall.

"Girl, I thought I was gon die fah sho!" Miss Mary sighed and lifted her hands.

"Not tonight, you wunnit," Ella Mae assured. "Not if I had anything to do with it."

Miss Mary smiled. "De chillen in de barn loft?"

"Yes ma'am."

"Well, take 'em some dry clothes and tell 'em to wait 'til dey granddaddy get back befo' dey move."

"Yes ma'am."

"And you get some dry clothes, too. You oughta be tired, all dat runnin' you done done tonight."

"I'm all right, Momma," Ella Mae said, and disappeared into the house.

After she attended the children, she returned to the porch, only to find Miss Mary pacing the front yard, conversing with something or someone invisible. Ella Mae watched in wonder.

"... but that ain't what You said, God! That ain't what You said!" Miss Mary screamed.

"   ," God must have said.

"That don't make no difference! You and me had a deal and I intend for You to keep Yo part of it!" Ella Mae couldn't tell if Miss Mary was crying or laughing.

"   ," God must have said.

"Then do what You promised! Be the God You spose to be! It don't make sense for Black folks to keep on sufferin' de way we sufferin' when we serve a mighty God! Now, come on, Lord! You know what to do, and I expect You to do it!" Miss Mary was shaking her head as though trying to rid it of some intangible confusion.

"   ," God must have said.

"And what about the chillen?" Miss Mary asked matter-of-factly.

"   "

"Uh-huh."

"   ?"

"Yes, but—"

"   "

"You right, Lawd. You right." Miss Mary tossed her hands up in surrender.

"   "

"But the night I buried my oldest boy You told me that—"

"   "

"Yes, Lord. I'll do it. But—"

"   "

"Lord, you know I love You? Why You ask me that? Sometimes I don't like Yo ways, but me and You been walkin' sixty years or mo." Miss Mary sounded offended.

Miss Mary's face was lifted toward the sky although her eyes were closed tightly. Finally, she said, "I'll follow You wherever You go, Lord, but trust me on this one. If I'm wrong, You can take my life and I won't say nothin' 'bout it. But, please, Master, think about what I said." Miss Mary opened her eyes.

"Ella Mae," she said, a bit startled. "I didn't know you wuz there." She tried to distract Ella Mae from what she had witnessed. "The chillen okay?"

"They fine. I told 'em to wait there 'til somebody come get 'em."

"Good, good," Miss Mary said, and entered the house with Ella Mae following. "Let's get a fire goin' in dis old stove and get some breakfast together."

Ella Mae was not put off so easily.

"Who was you talkin' to, Momma?"

"Oh chile, don't worry 'bout dat. Every now and then, me and de Good Lawd have it out!" She chuckled heartily.

Ella Mae's eyes bulged.

Miss Mary looked up from the stove, and said, "Aw, girl! Me and God go waaaaay back. We fuss all de time!" She looked at a bewildered daughter-in-law. "Ain't no need in you thinkin' I ain't had no right to talk to God that way. Dat's what you thinkin', ain't it?"

Ella Mae smirked.

"Well, you wrong! God ain't so arrogant that He can't listen to nobody else's opinion. What kinda God would dat be? He gave us minds so we could think just like He can think. That's why God don't talk to most folks. They ain't got nothin' to say. They thank He's spose to do all the talkin'. What kinda friendship is dat?"

Miss Mary didn't wait on Ella Mae's confirmation. She filled the coffee kettle and placed it on the stove, and said, "Coffee be ready in a few minutes." Then she sat in the rocker and began peeling potatoes for fried potatoes and onions.

Ella Mae dismissed the conversation and found a knife and bowl and sat on the floor next to her.

"What we gon do, Momma?" she asked, slicing potatoes carefully.

"I don't know, chile, but somethin' wrong. All de white folks in Money shoulda been out here by now. We ain't even heard from Old Man Chapman." She shook her head. "This is mighty strange."

Ella Mae could tell Miss Mary didn't want to talk, so she didn't force it. Miss Mary started nodding and murmuring "uh-huh" like one in the midst of difficult negotiations.

When the men returned, Jeremiah told Enoch, "Clean out de wagon real good, then check on de womenfolks. I'll go to de barn and see if de chillen in there."

They heard the familiar knock and unlatched the door. After hugging each of them, Jeremiah asked, "Y'all okay?"

"Yessir," they said.

"Good. Good."

Chop asked, "Who d-d-did you k-k-kill, Grrrranddaddy?"

"Shut up, boy!" Ray Ray said, saving Jeremiah the trouble. "That ain't none o' yo' business."

Sarah Jane changed the subject. "I thought I was gonna drown in that river, Granddaddy, but Ray Ray took care of us. You shoulda seen us! We was—"

"Wooo. You chillen be quiet now. I gotta lot on my mind and a lot to tell you. This ain't no playthang, and we sho ain't seen de last o' white folks. Now listen to me good."

Jeremiah sat on a nearby hay bale and motioned for the children to gather around. His whispering reignited the fear Sarah Jane thought the river had washed away.

"This ain't gon be easy, children," the old man began softly. "Me and yo' uncle Enoch done killed three white men, and another one got away."

"B-B-But you was prrrrrotectin' us, Grrrrranddaddy," Chop averred.

"I know it, boy, and I'd do it again, but dem white folks is comin' back for revenge. You gotta know dat. Now stop talkin' and listen to what I'm 'bout to tell y'all."

Ray Ray covered Chop's mouth, then mumbled, "Go 'head, Granddaddy."

"I get a feelin'," Jeremiah began, "dat this gon' get worse before it gets better. If I know white folks like I think I do, they gon try they best to hurt one of us. Or all of us. But we done come this far by faith, so we ain't turnin' 'round now."

The children's hypnotized eyes were glued to their grandfather's.

"Whatever I say do, I intend for you to do it and to do it quickly. We ain't got time for no clownin'. We all in this together. This ain't 'bout Clement either. It's 'bout the Johnson family. It's 'bout colored folks standin' up for theyselves. But white folks is gon try to scare us back into bondage. They pretty good 'bout what they do. We jes gotta be strong and know dat God is on our side, and that God been waitin' on us to fight for ourselves."

Jeremiah looked to see if the children understood what he was saying. Believing they did, he declared, "Now here's what I want y'all to do. We gon go in the house and eat breakfast like we do every other mornin'. Then we gon talk as a family and figure this thang out. But two things you got to remember 'til this situation over with: number one, never, under any circumstances, leave this house. Never!

Fu no reason. No berry pickin', no goin' down to de fishin' hole, nothin'. Make sure somebody can holla yo' name and you hear 'em. You understand me?"

All heads nodded.

"And, number two, don't neva tell nobody what you seen happen in dis house tonight. If somethin' happens, and we get separated, keep yo' mouth shut. Don't try to explain nothin' to nobody. Family business is family business, and we don't go 'round tellin' family business to folks what ain't in our family. Got me?"

"Yessir," the children responded like soldiers preparing for war.

"Good," Jeremiah said. "Now one more thing." He rubbed Clement's head. "This ain't yo' fault, boy. Mississippi been dis way long 'fo you come. Dat's why yo' momma left here. She couldn't stand de way colored folks wuz treated, and with that li'l feisty spirit o' hers, she wouldn'ta ever had no peace. Naw, this ain't yo' fault. We all to blame. Every colored person ever lived here. We wuz spose to stand up fu ourselves, and we ain't done it yet. But we gon do it now."

The children didn't understand. Chop tried to ask what they were going to do, but Ray Ray's hand muffled his voice.

Jeremiah motioned for the children to precede him. "Let's go eat."

Inside, Ella Mae told Enoch about Billy Ray's visit.

"Oh my God!" he murmured. "Y'all coulda been killed."

Miss Mary and Ella Mae winked at one another, and Ella Mae said, "We all right. We did what we had to do."

When Jeremiah entered and heard about the incident, he froze. Images of Miss Mary and Ella Mae lying in their own blood flooded his mind, and he knew that something radical had to be done. Once his heartbeat calmed, he said, "Y'all some powerful women. I'm mighty proud o' you. Wouldn't take nothin' fu you." He proceeded to the table.

Before they said grace, Miss Mary offered, "I knowed dat boy from de day he was born." Everyone stared at her. "And, sho as de sun rise in de east, he comin' back. He's connivin' somethin' right now to make us pay." Miss Mary closed her eyes. "And whatever he plannin' is gon be de worse thang this community ever seen 'cause, if he die doin' it, he gon have de last word. He been dat way all his life."

Jeremiah said, "Well, he better get ready to die."

No one else said anything. Bacon, eggs, and fried potatoes were passed automatically until everything had been devoured. The adults then drank coffee while the children waited stiffly for someone to speak. A mouse caught Chop's eye, but instead of hollering, as was his custom, he studied it. First amazed that his own fear had apparently dissipated, he then became envious of the mouse's carefree existence. Having found a piece of yarn, the mouse played with it, seemingly unaware that, only a few feet away, someone was plotting its destruction. The varmint discovered a crumb and ate it. At one point, Chop's eyes met the mouse's and, for some unknown reason, he felt sympathy instead of wrath. Unlike other times when he wanted someone simply to stomp the thing to death, the meeting of their eyes made him want to protect it, to understand it, even to love it. He began to wonder where it lived, who its momma was, why it would take the risk to expose itself to those who despised it. Really, he wanted to ask the mouse, "Is it fun being a mouse?" but then he thought the question ridiculous. Nobody wants to be a mouse, Chop told himself, yet he couldn't help wondering if being so little might actually be freeing. Then people ignore you, and you can have all the fun and food you want because nobody thinks enough of you to care one way or the other. On the other hand, he thought to be little might be lonely and depressing, too, for then you have to tailor your life to what others think and like. So, in the end, he appreciated the distance between himself and the mouse and, in fact, felt sorry for the unwanted creature. Why did God make them anyway? he asked himself.

"We gon call a town meetin'," Jeremiah said hastily. Miss Mary smiled at the idea. "Enoch, we gon go 'round and ask all de colored peoples who's willin' to meet us in de barn tonight for a very important meetin'. We'd betta not try to fight this one alone. My daddy used to say 'there's strength in numbers,' so we gon see if he's right."

"Children, y'all go on back to de loft and stay quiet 'til we come git chu. Don't make a sound and don't say a word. Momma, you and Ella Mae jes act like ain't nothin' happened. If anybody colored come by, tell 'em 'bout de meetin'. If anybody white come—"

"We know what to do," Miss Mary assured.

"Fine. Then let's say . . . seven tonight."

The women agreed and the menfolks grabbed their hats and left.

Seven

JEREMIAH WALKED IN EXCRUCIATING PAIN. AFTER APPROACH-
ing the third house, he had no choice but to return home and
rest. Enoch pressed on with his throbbing wound, speaking to
half the Black folk in Money before he, too, was compelled to take a
break.

Jeremiah awoke when Enoch returned, and asked, "How far did
you get?"

"I talked to most folks." Enoch sighed and reclined cautiously in
the rocker. "We should get a crowd if they don't get scared. I didn't
get to Mr. Tiny, though."

"Tiny be by here after while," Jeremiah slurred. "You ever knowed
a Saturday he didn't come?"

Enoch cackled.

"I'll tell him then."

"You menfolks hongry?" Ella Mae asked. "I can make y'all a sand-wich or somethin'."

"That sho would be nice, baby," Jeremiah returned. "We'll take it outside. It's too hot in here."

Enoch followed Jeremiah and both men sat on the edge of the porch. Ten minutes later, when Ella Mae offered the sandwiches, Enoch snickered, and said, "Glad I didn't bet against you, Daddy" when he recognized Tiny's size 58 overalls in the distance.

"How ya doin', Tiny!" Jeremiah hollered long before his old friend reached the house. Enoch smiled at Tiny's overweight form, wob-bling like a newborn calf in a windstorm.

"Oh, I guess I'll do, Mi," he returned and hobbled onto the porch. Only those who had known Jeremiah as a child called him Mi. No one else would have dared.

Tiny Dawson and Jeremiah grew up pickin' cotton together, they claimed. Nobody believed them, though, since Tiny's youngest boy was at least ten years older than Jeremiah. Yet since no one could dis-pute it with any authority, the two perpetuated their claim virtually uncontested.

"I thought you said you was gon stop smokin'?" Jeremiah teased, as Tiny wheezed and plopped down onto the empty, rusted, fold-up chair Enoch offered. Enoch stayed on the edge of the porch, where his father had taught him to sit when elders came around, and prepared himself for the drama that always ensued whenever Tiny arrived.

"I ain't neva told you dat, man. Shit. You may as well choose what's gon kill you. Don't chu think?" Tiny filled his pipe and offered it first to Jeremiah, who refused politely. Then he frowned at Enoch.

"What happened to yo' arm, son?"

Enoch turned to his father who shifted uneasily.

"Well, this morning—"

"Don't worry 'bout his arm," Jeremiah taunted, hoping to distract. "You need to concentrate on losin' some o' dat weight." He poked Tiny in his rib cage with his cane. "You been four hundred pounds ever since I knowed you."

Tiny took the bait. "No I ain't! I used to be a li'l bitty fella! You don't remember dat, Mi?"

Enoch couldn't hold his laughter. He thought of Mr. Dawson's sons, all of whom outweighed their father, and his shoulders jerked constantly with mirth.

"You remember how little I was, Mi!" Tiny shouted. "I was smaller than you 'til I had dat stroke back in 'thirty-six. Then I couldn't get 'round like I was used to doin' and—"

"Aw, hush, man," Jeremiah said playfully. Then he assumed a stoic expression. "I got somethin' serious I gotta tell ya, Tiny. I need yo' help."

"What's wrong, Mi?" His voice deepened so suddenly that Enoch looked to make sure someone else hadn't taken his seat.

"Cuthbert boys come by de house dis mornin' lookin' for Clement. Said he disrespected Miss Cuthbert in de store yesterday. De boy told me she asked him to put a nickel in her hands for a soda pop, but he laid it on the counter instead. I don't know no details, but somethin' happened. All I know is dat dem boys wunnit takin' my grandson."

Studying Jeremiah's face, Tiny knew something very serious had happened. "What did you do, Mi?" he asked cautiously.

Jeremiah hung his head. Then, he lifted it and declared proudly, "I killed the sons of bitches. That's what I did. They broke my front do' down, thinkin' they wuz 'bout to take one o' my grandchillen, so I blowed they asses away right smack in the middle of my livin' room."

Tiny Dawson's eyes almost popped out. With trembling hands, he pushed himself up from the old rocker, and burbled, "You did what?"

"That's right! I killed 'em. I had to. Either I was gon kill them or they was gon kill me. And you see me standin' here, don't chu?" He paused. "They shot Enoch in the arm and got me right here"—he touched his side—"but we all right."

Tiny looked at Enoch, hoping the son would deny the words of his father, but Enoch's silent posture confirmed what Tiny feared. "Lawd have mercy Jesus," Tiny mumbled, and fell back into the chair.

Jeremiah tried in vain to ease the news. "It all happened so fast, man. I sent the chillen runnin' out de back do' to Bull's old place, and me and dis boy hyeah did what we had to do. I didn't mean to kill 'em, Tiny, but if I didn't they woulda—"

"I know! I know! I know!" Tiny repeated in frustrated sympathy. His hands waved in the air. "You know they ain't gon let this go!" he said.

"Of course they ain't!" Jeremiah hissed. He calmed a bit, then added, "That's why we got to come together." He looked at Enoch, who grinned in support.

"I'm callin' a meetin' tonight, Tiny, of all de colored people 'round hyeah. We got to come together. White folks been killin' our children too long, and we ain't done nothin'. That's got to stop."

"I 'gree wit chu, Mi," he said, and stared at his lifelong friend, "but I ain't neva heard o' nothin' like this happenin' 'round here."

"'Cause we been too scared! But now I need yo' help."

The silence made Enoch understand, finally, the enormity of the sacrifice he and his father were asking from others. This ain't gon be easy, he told himself.

"What time is de meetin'?" Tiny asked, after taking a deep breath.

"Seven. In de barn. You comin'?"

Tiny closed his eyes for an instant, then opened them wider and relented. "I'll be there. You know I ain't neva been no coward. I might be fat as hell, but I'll stand when I need to."

The old friends chuckled until their nerves settled.

"Good," Jeremiah said. "Now help me spread de word to anybody who ain't heard yet. Don't tell 'em what happened though. I'll say all that tonight. Some colored folks is so scared o' white folks that if they know de truth, they gon run and tell de world befo' I get a chance to say anything."

"Lawd knows dat's de truf!" Tiny agreed.

"Enoch done walked 'round and told most folks. If everybody tell somebody, then we oughta have a pretty good turnout."

"Well, let me get on back to de house and tell de old lady. She'll be wit me." Tiny rose and waddled off the porch in a hurry.

"Thanks, man," Jeremiah said sincerely. "I can always count on you."

Tiny smiled and said over his shoulder, "I shoulda throwed yo' ass away years ago, but somebody gotta fool wit chu! I'll see y'all later."

"See ya," Enoch called, grateful that his father had at least one faithful friend.

Convincing others hadn't been quite so easy. A few wanted to know exactly why colored folks was meetin' and whether white folks knew about it. Enoch laughed, and said, "Forget it" and counted them out.

Most folks, however, agreed to come, especially Aunt Sugar. Hers was the first house they approached. "'Bout damn time!" she said. "I been waitin' on some men 'round here to stand up and be men." Leaning upon a broomstick, she spit a string of tobacco juice into the dirt yard. "We 'bout forty years late, ain't we, Mi?" she said, and resumed sweeping the porch. "Dat's why I ain't neva married. Shit, I ain't met a man wit enough balls fu me!" Enoch hollered, but Aunt Sugar never smiled. "We'll see what happens, boys. I'll be there." She turned and entered her house.

Aunt Sugar's birth name was Margarite Daniels, but nobody ever called her anything but Sugar. Any child who walked by her house was guaranteed a slice of sweet potato pie, lemon pound cake, or a bowl of blackberry cobbler. Why a single woman baked two or three desserts every day was a mystery to the colored citizens of Money but, as she boasted, "I don't neva throw none of it away, do I? Greedy niggas always find dey way over hyeah." Of course no one argued, for there was not a single colored soul who hadn't tasted Aunt Sugar's cooking. The strange thing though was that no one ever saw her cook anything other than sweets. Ever. At church functions, she brought desserts, but never ate anyone else's food. She had no garden, no cows, no hogs, no chickens, and no children to bring her food. She gotta eat somethin', folks thought to themselves.

Chop knew the truth of Aunt Sugar's sustenance. During the summers, he visited her often and she fell in love with his appetite.

"I like chillen like you," she told Chop one day as he devoured the last piece of sweet potato pie. "You eat like you alive."

"I-I-I lllllike to eat, Aunt Sh-Sugar."

"Dat's good, boy," she encouraged. "That means yo' spirit is free."

Chop frowned and mumbled, "Huh?"

Aunt Sugar laughed. "See, the body gets hongry when the spirit is free to roam the earth. Folks who ain't got no appetite got po' spirits. When yo' spirit is free, you get hongry a lot quicker."

Chop didn't fully understand, but Aunt Sugar's words sounded good so he nodded along.

"W-w-why d-d-don't you ever eat?" he asked innocently.

"Who said I don't eat?" Aunt Sugar teased.

"Everybody. Thchtcthey ssssssay you d-d-don't n-never eat nnnnothin', b-b-but you g-g-g-g-g-g-gotta eat sssssssssomethin' or you'd be d-d-dead."

"Maybe I am," she said.

"But if yyyyyou wuz d-d-dead, I c-c-ccouldn't sssssee you." Chop frowned so hard his head began to hurt.

"That ain't necessarily so, son. Some dead folks is still walkin' 'round, and some live folks been dead fu years."

"Huh?"

Aunt Sugar tapped his hand. "Don't you worry 'bout dat none, Mr. Poke Chop. You jes come on and get much o' dat dessert as you want."

"Yyyyyyyesmam," he said gladly. "B-b-but how you lllllive without eatin'?"

Aunt Sugar paused, and said, "By givin'. If you learn to make givin' yo' livin', then you won't need man's food. God'll feed you His-self 'cause He loves a cheerful giver. But you gotta do it 'cause you love it and you gotta love de people you givin' to. Otherwise, you gon have to settle for this crap we grow on earth."

"Yyyyou mean yyyyyou d-d-don't eat n-n-none o' de ffffood we eat?"

"Chile, I ain't ate dat stuff in years. Every time somebody come by and I get to give dem some o' my sweets, I get so full in my soul my appetite jes go away." She flung her arms wide.

"Wwwwwow," Chop marveled.

"I guess dat's why folks call me Sugar, baby. I love bein' sweet, I love makin' sweets, and I love sweet folks. But don't get me wrong. I can be a bear if you make me mad."

Chop didn't know what to say. He had never heard anyone speak poorly of Aunt Sugar, and he certainly couldn't imagine her being mean.

"Th-th-thank you, mmma'am," he said kindly.

"Oh you sho is welcome, Mr. Chop. Anytime!" she sang and embraced him.

Chop's eyes teared. "I-I-I rrrrreally llllllike you, Aunt Sh-Sugar."

"I love you too, baby."

As he walked away, he turned and asked, "W-w-why do you thth-think I sssstutter so bad?"

Aunt Sugar met him in the yard and placed her arm around his shoulder. "Baby, let me tell you somethin'," she said, rubbing his head. "Stutterin' is God tellin' you to be careful what you say, son. See, words can bring life or words can destroy life. God's got somethin' special for you to do. That's why he can't let you spoil your destiny by murderin' things with yo' mouth. You got to keep your tongue clean and your heart pure, young man. God is tellin' you to slow down and think about what you sayin'. Make sure you bringin' life with yo' words and not death. Maybe you gon be a preacher when you grow up," she said.

"I-I-I d-d-don't thththink so. I-I-I d-don't talk ssso g-g-good."

"But I bet you will when you grow up. God's jes gettin' you ready for somethin' right now. He's makin' you think about every word you utter so you know to be careful about what you say. Most folks jes talk to hear theyselves talk. That's why their words ain't got no power. But you, Mr. Poke Chop, you gon be a great man one day."

"Yyyyou rrrreally thththink so, Aunt Sh-Sugar?"

"Is Sugar sweet?" They laughed. "Don't you worry none 'bout yo' talkin'. De Good Lawd knows 'xactly what He's doin'. He's jes gettin' you ready. Dat's all. You jes be ready when de time come."

"Yyyyes, ma'am," Chop mumbled. "I-I-I guess I-I-I b-b-better be g-g-gettin' on home now. Thththank you again ffor thththththth-thththe pie."

"Anytime, sugar. Anytime."

When Jeremiah and Enoch left her house the day of the gathering, Jeremiah said, "You know, boy, Aunt Sugar ain't aged in fifty years. She looked jes like she look now when I was a boy. B'lieve what I tell you."

"Come on, Daddy!" Enoch prodded. "That would make the woman over a hundred years old."

"She waaay over a hundred, boy. 'Bout a hundred and thirty or so would be my guess." Jeremiah knew Enoch wouldn't believe him.

He didn't, but the assertion was still intriguing. "How you know, Daddy?"

"'Cause my daddy said she used to bake cakes and stuff for them, too. And he was born in eighteen sixty-five."

Enoch held his arm and laughed painfully. "What? Daddy, you oughta be shame o' yo'self. You know dat woman ain't dat old!"

"Okay," Jeremiah said indifferently. "You ain't gotta believe it. But what you don't believe would make another world, boy."

"I'm sure it would," Enoch yielded.

After Tiny left, they rested a while, then Enoch rose. "I'ma go tell a few other folks 'bout de meetin' so nobody won't have no excuse fo' not showin' up this evenin'." He brushed the seat of his overalls.

"I'm goin' wit cha," Jeremiah said.

"Don't you think you better rest some more, Daddy?"

"Naw, I feel better now. That wrap was too tight." He stood slowly.

"I sho hope dis work, old man. Lawd have mercy."

"It's gon work," Jeremiah reassured. "It's gotta work."

Eight

WHILE THE MEN WERE AWAY, THE CHILDREN HEARD someone attempting to pry open the barn door. Sarah Jane looked at Ray Ray, who motioned for everyone to be still and quiet. They obeyed, hoping against all odds that the intruder was someone they knew. When the door gave way, they saw the white faces.

It was only a matter of time, Sarah Jane knew, before the white men discovered them in the loft, so, for better or worse, she reached into the center of her soul and yelled, "Help!"

Ella Mae heard her, and screamed, "Momma! The children!" as she ran to the barn with her dress flying wildly in the air. Billy Cuthbert grabbed her from behind when she tumbled through the barn door and covered her mouth with his broad, pink hand. She fought like a caged bobcat, but her strength was dwarfed by one who weighed at least 150 pounds more than she did.

Miss Mary was a different story. The white man who thought his strength sufficient to handle her soon regretted his assumption. His bleeding nose and bruised ribs forced him to believe, against everything he had ever been taught, that *some* women's physical strength exceeds that of most men. Undoubtedly, his ego was more bruised than his body, especially since he learned this lesson at the hands of a seventy-year-old colored woman. Yet had the other men not assisted him, the price of maintaining his ego would surely have been his life. And even when they did, they all received battle scars—swollen eyes, busted lips, marred faces—until Miss Mary's adrenaline was drained dry. Only then did they subdue her, embarrassed that it took all of them to do so.

"Fuckin' bitch," one panted heavily. "Strong as a goddamn ox."

Together, they tied Miss Mary and Ella Mae each to a single wooden post holding up the barn, then gagged them with strips of white cloth. The children watched in absolute horror. Ray Ray almost climbed down to help, but Clement yelled, "No!" and held him back. Sarah Jane cradled Chop in her arms, covering his eyes so he couldn't witness the assault. Her only prayer was that the white men wouldn't hurt her grandmother and aunt, and when they tied them and turned their backs to them, she gave thanks to a God who answered at least some prayers.

Billy Ray snickered. "I knowed it was somethin' in dis barn you wuz protectin'." He looked at Ella Mae. "You didn't think I saw you pointin' that rifle at me last night, did you?"

Ella Mae tried to scream, but couldn't.

"Well, I did." Billy Ray smiled. "That's why I left. I didn't know how many o' you niggers was hidin', dyin' to blow my fuckin' head off if I shot at Mary. But I'm back now!" he roared.

The children peered over the edge of the loft, paralyzed.

"I had to get me a plan," Billy Ray explained. His comrades cackled. "I had to figure out a way to set things back in order 'round here, and I think I got a good idea. Y'all wanna hear it?"

Miss Mary and Ella Mae stared at the children.

With his arm in a sling, Cecil said, "Naw, let's not tell 'em. It would ruin de surprise." He giggled like a toddler.

"Okay," Billy consented. "Which one we gon take?" He nodded toward the loft.

"Let's take 'em all!" Larry Greer suggested.

Billy glanced at Miss Mary's pleading eyes. "Naw, we don't need but one. It won't take but one."

They haggled a moment about which child would best fit the plan, then Billy Ray offered, "Tell ya what. Let's kill two birds wit one stone and get de one who sassed Catherine."

Cecil agreed and hollered up to the loft, "Which one o' you nigger boys was flirtin' with Miss Cuthbert?" The other men stood like bodyguards awaiting instruction. "You'd better tell me, or all you fuckin' nigger children 'bout to die!"

Sarah Jane noted that Cecil's eyes resembled those of the old stray cat that lingered around the house looking for table scraps. She gazed deeply into the hazel green, hoping to soften his monstrous desire, but everywhere she searched inside him she found only emptiness and hatred.

"Either you speak up or we'll just have to hang all of ya," Cecil declared. The children huddled closer together. They had nowhere to run and no one to call. Trying desperately to figure out a plan of survival, they shivered in fear and held their breath while the white men taunted them.

"Okay, here's the deal," Billy said with a smile and a rifle pointed at the middle of Ray Ray's forehead. "I'ma count to three—"

"Nigger children cain't count!" the others jeered.

"Well, they better hope they can 'cause when I count to three if one of 'em ain't down here, I'ma blow all their fuckin' heads off!" Billy looked at the others, who nodded greedily.

"One."

Sarah Jane loosened her hold of Chop, preparing to give her life for her cousins. She would see her mother again, she justified. Plus, Money had already lost enough boys. Every time a child came up missing it was a boy, so Sarah Jane concluded it was simply a girl's time to die. Yet she couldn't move. Her mind was made up, yet her body was unwilling. She was relieved in that moment that her cousins would live because she had the courage to do what her mother and father had done years ago. But, still, her limbs would not obey her mind's resolution.

"Two."

Just pull the trigger, Ray Ray thought. That would end the matter, and everyone could go home and live the way they had always lived. Unlike he had considered before, he wasn't afraid to die in that moment. Actually, his only fear was that his death wouldn't be the end of the matter. He knew white folks well enough to know that one dead Black boy wouldn't satisfy their thirst to destroy Black life; so his hesitation represented only his inability to make the men promise not to bother any of the others once he was gone. And wouldn't his father and grandfather be proud? As the oldest, it was his responsibility, he knew, to protect the others at all costs. He would be the hero of the family and he could die satisfied with that, he told himself.

"Three."

"It's me!" Clement stood and shouted. "I'm the one you lookin' for." His blurry eyes hindered his ability to see his cousins reaching for him.

"No!" Sarah Jane wailed.

"Take me!" Ray Ray heralded repeatedly. "I did it." He lunged toward the ladder, but Clement was already descending it. *"No!"* he screamed uselessly.

Miss Mary and Ella Mae kicked and squirmed like worms on hot coals, but their antics were not enough to save Clement.

Chop had closed his eyes by now. He knew something bad was going to happen, but he didn't know how to stop it. That's the worst feeling in the world, he told himself, to watch destruction unfold and be absolutely unable to prevent it. He prayed the white men might give Clement a good whoopin' and send him back home later.

"Oh, don't worry," Billy Ray said, looking up at the loft as though reverencing heaven. "We ain't gon hurt him. Least not too bad." The others chuckled and grabbed Clement's arms, dragging him out of the barn.

"You women take care, you hear?" they mocked and strolled past Miss Mary and Ella Mae. "We jes gon talk to 'im and see if we can figure out what happened. That's all. Don't worry yo pretty little heads." One patted the crown of Ella Mae's head patronizingly.

"We'll be seein' y'all. Take care," Cecil snickered, as they disappeared.

Ray Ray wasted no time descending the loft and untying his mother while Sarah Jane freed Miss Mary. Chop ran to the barn door to see if he could tell in which direction the men had gone.

"Go find yo' granddaddy!" Miss Mary screamed to Ray Ray. "Hur'rup!"

Before she could finish the command, Ray Ray was sprinting down the dirt road faster than he had ever run. He didn't know where to find the menfolk, but he knew that if he just kept running he'd meet them somewhere.

Ella Mae cried, "Lord have mercy, Momma! What we gon do?" She was rubbing her arms frantically, trying to conceive a plan of action. "You think they gon hurt Clement? Huh, Momma?"

"I don't know what they gon do, chile," Miss Mary said, pacing the barn floor. "But we got to keep our head. And trust in de Lawd." She grabbed Sarah Jane and Chop simultaneously. "Now help me git dese chillen in de house so we can think."

All four held hands, like childhood playmates, and ran into the house, taking their respective places at the kitchen table.

"Git me Jeremiah's shotgun off de wall there," Miss Mary told Ella Mae. "Let 'em try takin' somebody else 'way from my house! We'll have some mo' to bury!"

Miss Mary's clarity and determination strengthened Ella Mae, who retrieved Enoch's gun and convinced herself again that, if necessary, she, too, would kill and God would forgive.

Jeremiah and Enoch were about to approach another sharecropping shack when Enoch heard Ray Ray's faint voice crying, "Daddy! Daddy!" At first, he doubted his paternal instinct, but the next "Daddy!" was too pronounced to be denied. Enoch looked down the winding dirt road and squinted as far as he could see. Ray Ray's long, lanky, swinging arms confirmed that Enoch had heard the voice of his firstborn son.

"Daddy!" Enoch screamed in fear.

Jeremiah turned and Enoch ran to meet Ray Ray.

"What's de matter, boy?" Enoch yelled, gripping Ray Ray's shoulder with his left hand.

Ray Ray had run so hard and fast that, now, he was out of breath. "They took"—he panted—"Clement."

"What? Who?" Jeremiah hollered.

Enoch stomped and screeched, "No!"

"Mr. Billy Ray and some otha white men," Ray Ray huffed. "They busted in the barn and said they'd kill all of us"—breath—"if somebody didn't tell them who disrespected Miss Cuthbert." Ray Ray was half–bent over, with his hands resting on his kneecaps. "Clement gave hisself up."

"Gave hisself up? What chu mean, boy?" Jeremiah inquired.

Ray Ray stood erect, took a deep breath, and explained more cogently. "We wuz up in de loft like you told us to be and de white men busted through the door and Sarah Jane screamed out, and Momma and Grandma come runnin' out to de barn and the men tied them up. Dat's when they looked up in de loft and started threatenin' to kill all of us if somebody didn't tell them somethin'. I was gonna say it was me, but then Clement jumped up and said it wuz him."

Jeremiah and Enoch were confused, frustrated, and enraged. They questioned Ray Ray until he confused himself, then Jeremiah said, "Where did they take him? Did they say?"

"No, sir. They didn't say. But they promised not to hurt him." The words now sounded ridiculous, even to Ray Ray.

"Did they hurt Momma or Ella Mae?" Enoch burbled.

Ray Ray paused, trying diligently to reconstruct the correct sequence of events. He marveled that, although everything had occurred only moments earlier, now he seemed to be recalling details of a time long gone. He was still panting. "Like I said, the white men tied up Momma and Grandma when they come runnin' into de barn."

"I'ma kill dem crackers—"

"It's gon be all right, son," Jeremiah comforted.

Ray Ray went on: "They didn't hurt them though. They jes tied 'em to de post holdin' up de barn and stuffed they mouth with some rags."

"What about Sarah Jane and Chop?" Jeremiah asked.

"They fine," Ray Ray said. "The white men jes wanted Clement. And they wouldn't even o' known which one o' us was Clement if—"

"Don't worry 'bout dat now, son," Jeremiah soothed. "We jes got to find Clement. Come on."

The three generations of Johnson men walked alongside one another, each with a vengeance and purpose all his own. The precision of their steps gave them the look of a battle infantry whose one hope was to taste the blood of the enemy. Because they walked in penetrating silence, each mind was given the opportunity to imagine what might become of the Johnson family and, indeed, colored folks throughout Mississippi.

Jeremiah had dreamed of this day as a child longs for Christmas. He wanted, finally and simply, to count. He had gotten tired of burying colored folks whose names evoked nothing in succeeding generations. Deep in his heart, his only desire was to live out what he believed in. Yet it had taken him more than seventy years to prepare for the mission. Better late than never, he told himself.

Enoch couldn't get Jerry and Billie Faye out of his head. The more he thought of them, the more incensed he became. He had never really forgiven white folks for murdering—as he called it—his brother and sister-in-law. Actually, he never thought he was supposed to. Typically, colored folks just bury the dead and move on, so, until now, Enoch had

not considered that he had the right to fight white folks for their treat-
ment of his people. As he, Jeremiah, and Ray Ray marched on, the desire to scream "Fuck this!" grew stronger in his throat until a cough
overpowered what would have been more verbal defiance than he had
ever manifested. In his frustration, Enoch wanted to hit somebody, to
whip enough white asses to let the world know that Black silence was
over. He suppressed this desire, however, as he thought about his children and the price they'd have to pay once white folks killed him. Only
in that moment did he understand, finally, why it had taken his father
so long to be courageous.

Aunt Possum gon be mad, Ray Ray thought, imagining how everything might transpire. She was rambunctious, folks always said, and
stories about her suggested that she had never been one to take
things easily. She had left Mississippi precisely because she refused to
submit to sharecropping culture, Jeremiah had explained, and now
she would be forced to return. Ray Ray dreaded seeing his aunt under
such adverse circumstances, but now it seemed unavoidable. What
would he tell her? How would he explain that he, the oldest, had let
those white men take his cousin? She would call him a sorry, worthless colored boy, Ray Ray feared, and never would he regain his dignity. Now, even more than before, he wished he had volunteered to go
with the pink, rosy-colored men. He knew the land, the people, and
the places to hide. He could outrun Clement, he assumed, and once he
got away from the men, he'd be back home in a flash. "Damn," he
mumbled inaudibly.

When they reached home, the menfolks marched into the house in
chronological order. Their own shotguns greeted them.

"Enoch!" Ella Mae blurted and ran into his outstretched arms.
"They took Clement! What we gon do?"

"I know, baby, I know," Enoch responded. "Ray Ray told us everything. They didn't hurt you, did they?"

"Naw, we ain't hurt. But we gotta find Clement!" Ella Mae
screamed.

"Jes calm down now, daughter," Jeremiah commanded. "We gotta think this thang through. Everybody sit down." The family gathered at the kitchen table. "I can't tell y'all what's 'bout to happen, but I can tell you it ain't gon be pretty," Jeremiah began. "Colored people 'round hyeah shoulda done somethin' 'bout this years ago, but we wuz too scared. I ain't scert no mo."

Everybody looked at Jeremiah skeptically, but he knew they were on his side.

". . . and you can't be scert neither. We got to fight this battle. We gon win it if we stick together. Some folks ain't gon stand with us 'cause they think they got too much to lose. They think food won't grow out de ground if white folks don't plant it, so I ain't lookin' for 'em to stand. But a lotta other colored people 'round hyeah tired jes like we is o' always buryin' our own folks 'cause white folks don't like somethin' 'bout 'em. I ain't doin' dat no mo!" Jeremiah's shout frightened Sarah Jane and Chop.

"Here's what we ain't gon do. We ain't gon rush over to no white folks place all by ourselves. That's exactly what Billy and dem other white boys wants us to do. They waitin' right now to blow our heads off. Dat's what happened to Elijah and Martha Redfield. You 'member dat, Mary?"

"Un-huh," Miss Mary mumbled.

"Somebody hung their son Joshua, and Elijah and Martha went cross de railroad tracks questionin' white folks, and they shot 'em down in de middle of the road. So, naw, we ain't gon fall in dat trap. We gon outthink 'em this time."

Jeremiah tried hard not to let his emotions lead him. "Now, here's what we gon do. First, we gon pray. God done brung us this far, and we ain't goin' nowhere without Him. Then, Enoch, you and Ray Ray gon snoop 'round and see if you can find out where dey mighta took Clement. We ain't got to be scared now 'cause if they wanted more than one o' us, dey woulda took ya. I can't figure out why they didn't. They must be plannin' somethin' terrible." He paused, looked up, and said, "Lord, please let dat boy be all right."

"Momma, you and Ella Mae guard dis house jes like y'all wuz already doin'. Don't be scert to shoot neither."

Miss Mary's expression assured Jeremiah that her ability to kill was solid. He had never seen her hold a gun, much less shoot it, yet something in her eyes confirmed that the other children would be well protected.

"Sarah Jane, you and Chop gon sit here 'til we meet tonight and mind de womenfolks. If anything happens to 'em, y'all take dem shotguns and blow de head off o' any white man try to bother you. Y'all understand me?"

"Yessir!" Chop declared. He had never been entrusted with such responsibility before, and he promised himself to make his granddaddy proud if given the opportunity.

Sarah Jane nodded although she hoped she wouldn't have to kill. She had seen what happened to colored people who kill white men—regardless of the reason—and now she couldn't imagine that the outcome would be different.

"If otha folks come by, don't tell 'em nothin'. We'll talk about everything tonight at de meetin'." Jeremiah looked at Enoch and nodded toward the door. "You and Ray Ray go 'head on."

They left hurriedly.

"What chu gon do, man?" Miss Mary asked Jeremiah on his way out the door.

"Don't worry 'bout me, Momma. I'll be back by meetin' time."

Nine

JEREMIAH HADN'T GONE TO THE SACRED PLACE IN YEARS. ONCE Billie Faye died he resolved to leave the space to her and Jerry. But the day the white men took Clement, he found himself pressing through the woods in search of something untainted by man's hands. He needed a moment to think things through, and he needed a place where he wouldn't be disturbed. He also needed a space wherein God dwelled so that, as he always put it, "God could tell me where my thinkin' ain't right." So Jeremiah stepped carefully back into The Sacred Place, walking like one on holy ground.

Much to his surprise, it looked exactly the same. He had expected the grass to be scorched by the relentless Mississippi summer sun, but it was so green he bent and touched it to make sure it was real. Jonquils, wild roses, and little white flowers whose name he didn't know decorated The Sacred Place, and the cool breeze made him close his eyes and think, *This has got to be heaven.*

"Wow," Jeremiah murmured, looking around. Maybe the place was even more beautiful now, he thought. When Jerry and Billie Faye married, he remembered green grass, but nothing so verdant that it looked artificial. He remembered flowers, too, but not so many that, everywhere he trod, he discovered a new one. The lone deer, standing idle in the middle of the grass, confirmed the majesty of The Sacred Place, for, even after noticing Jeremiah's presence, it never moved. He walked the circumference of the area, and neither rabbits, opposums, nor squirrels feared him. Back where he began, Jeremiah shook his head at the splendor and glory of The Sacred Place. Perhaps the few times he had visited, after Jerry and Billie Faye married, he had come at the wrong time of year. Or maybe he never came enough. Whatever it was, Jeremiah was saddened that only now he saw what his son must have seen years ago. He felt embarrassed that Jerry had beheld the face of God as a child while, after seventy-odd years, he was still longing for a glimpse.

The tree, which once held Jerry's lifeless form, was broader now and waved its limbs freely with the moderate evening breeze. Even the limb from which Jerry had hanged himself jutted out farther from the tree, like an index finger pointing a traveler in a particular direction. It was larger than the other limbs, as though over the years it had taken an unfair portion of the tree's nutrients. At the place where the limb met the trunk, a nest rested wherein Jeremiah watched a mother bird feed worms to her ravenous chicks. The mother's eyes met his own and made him feel warm and welcome. He wished she would land somewhere close to him and tell him the secrets of The Sacred Place, but, instead, she flapped her wings and soared away in carefree ecstasy.

Jeremiah sat on a nearby stump. He didn't know if his plan was going to work, but with Clement gone, he needed to believe in something.

"I'm sorry, son," he said aloud in his scratchy baritone. "I loved you. You knowed dat, didn't you?" Jeremiah looked around nostalgically.

"Yes, Daddy, I knew."

"What?" he murmured in surprise. "Who wuz dat?" Cold chills ran up Jeremiah's arms like flames in a dry hay barn. He stood quickly, searching to the right and left for the voice he was sure he had heard.

"Jerry?" he asked cautiously, trembling with both fear and anticipation. His eyes were easily quarter size.

"Yes, Daddy?"

"Is d—d—dat you, son?" Jeremiah asked, frightened.

"Yes. I am here."

Jeremiah didn't know what to say or ask. He examined The Sacred Place thoroughly, but saw no one.

"Don't be scared," Jerry sang soothingly.

Jeremiah's breathing calmed a bit, and he resumed his place on the tree stump. His right hand brushed over his salt-and-pepper hair— what was left of it—and he struggled hard not to be afraid.

"I, um, don't know wh—wh—what to say. I thought you wuz dead." Jeremiah's words hadn't come out right, but he didn't know how to fix them.

"I will always be with you, Daddy. Dead don't mean gone," Jerry chuckled.

Jeremiah smiled at the familiar sound of his son's rare laughter. He had come to The Sacred Place for clarity and understanding, and now he delighted in God's method of meeting his needs.

"I woulda come sooner, son, if I had knowed."

"No need to explain. I understand."

He wanted to ask Jerry a million questions, but he settled on, "I guess you know what happened to Clement?"

"Yessir, I know. What y'all gon do?"

"I don't know," Jeremiah confessed in honest exasperation. "I shot some white men who came—"

Jerry interrupted. *"I know. I saw everything. I was real proud of you."*

"Huh?" Jeremiah inquired, confused.

"You did what you thought was right, Daddy. That's what you gotta keep on doin'."

Jeremiah didn't know how to take his son's affirmation, so he simply asked, "What should I do now?"

"That's up to you. You have to decide for yourself. But don't be afraid of what you decide."

"We gon meet tonight in de barn . . . well, you know everything already." Jeremiah waved his hands lightly, remembering to whom he was speaking.

"Yes, I know that. But what are you going to do, Daddy?"

Jeremiah picked up a twig and began to strip it bare with his fingernails. "I don't know."

"Yes, you do know. You're just afraid."

"I'd like to shoot all dem bastards and be done with the whole thing," Jeremiah stated, half-jokingly. "But I guess dat wouldn't be right."

"Why wouldn't it be?"

Jeremiah grimaced. "Well, I jes thought . . . that God or . . . angels . . . or . . . y'all . . . might not like that."

"Daddy, the question you have to answer is what do you believe? That's what we want—for you to live out the truth of what you believe."

"But what I b'lieve right now don't seem . . . holy, son. Dese devils been killin' colored folks for years and ain't nobody said nothin' 'bout it. They don't respect nobody—and I mean *nobody*—and they always want colored folks to kiss they behinds. I'm sick o' dat and I ain't doin' it no mo'." Jeremiah's confidence had returned.

"Good, Daddy. Be clear 'bout what you think and why, and don't be scared to stand on it when the day comes."

"Today is the day, huh?" Jeremiah giggled in awe.

"Yessir, it is."

"I jes want my grandson home and my family safe. Is that too much to ask for?"

"Nothing is too much to ask for if you're willing to make it happen. That's the job of the living—to make the seemingly impossible come to pass. I'll be right next to you, Daddy, every step of the way."

"Then I know what I'm gon do," Jeremiah announced as he rose to leave.

"Fine. Do it good, old man."

"Can I come see you any time I want to, son?" Jeremiah looked into the treetops, hoping for a physical sign of this metaphysical moment.

"I am with you always, Daddy. Even until the end."

Water gathered in Jeremiah's eyes and escaped through routes of wrinkles down his dusty brown cheeks. He walked slowly throughout The Sacred Place, singing both the call and the response to "Father I stretch my hand to Thee, no other help I know." His rich, Black-Baptist-church-deacon voice purged his soul of innumerable and unspeakable fears he once thought to be the inheritance of every Black man. Truth be known, he had convinced himself, for the last seventy years, that his pitiful state was God's doing. He was relieved now to know that it had been his own.

As he sang, he picked flowers and made a bouquet of mauve, white, red, and violet and placed the offering at the base of Jerry's tree.

"I'm ready now, son," he whispered. "Thank you. I'm sorry it took me so long, but I promise not to let you down this time."

Jeremiah didn't need a response. He left The Sacred Place surer than ever of what he was going to do. Jerry's words had convinced him that God was waiting on him to act, and Jerry's voice alone had reminded him of his unfinished business with whites in Money. Now he would bring it all to closure.

Ray Ray followed Enoch to Mr. Pet Moore's house. Mr. Moore had worked in the General Store almost forty years, and Enoch hoped he might have heard something.

Seeing the house in the distance, Ray Ray said, "Mr. Moore don't neva say too much, Daddy."

"Well, we'll see what he say today. You cain't neva tell what a man might say when his heart get troubled. He mighta heard somebody say somethin' 'round de store. We'll see."

Ray Ray could tell, by Enoch's tone, that his father wanted him simply to be quiet until Mr. Moore's inquisition was over.

Enoch removed his straw hat and knocked on the front screen door. He glanced at his son and tried to smile, but the corners of his mouth refused.

"Yes?" Miss Gladys's faint voice called.

"How you doin', ma'am?" Enoch hollered through the screen. He couldn't see anyone, and he dared not open the door without permission.

Seconds later, Gladys Moore appeared, and said, "Pet ain't home, boys." Her usual broad smile was softer, and she seemed preoccupied.

"Oh, okay," Enoch returned politely. "I jes, um, wanted to talk to him 'bout somethin'. Can we wait?"

"Help yo'self, help yo'self," Miss Gladys said kindly. "He be home directly." She turned from the door without inviting them inside.

So Enoch and Ray Ray sat on the edge of the Moores' front porch, with their legs swinging gently. The house was hoisted by cinder blocks, stacked three high, so a man would have to be quite tall before he could sit on the porch and his feet touch the ground. Enoch noticed that Ray Ray's feet hung closer to the earth than his own and that one of the boy's big toes had barged its way through the front of his left shoe.

"You done growed up, boy," Enoch said proudly, shaking his head in disbelief.

Ray Ray didn't know what to say, so he smiled slightly and nodded. As much as he loved his father, their communication had always been a bit awkward.

"I 'member bein' fourteen," Enoch chortled. "I was at least five inches shorter than you, and I neva could get enough to eat."

Ray Ray laughed gratefully. He knew nothing would be funny in the coming days and, in fact, he had a feeling that Mr. Moore's return home would be the beginning of a very difficult time for his family. But if joy came only for a moment, he told himself, he'd take it.

"I had a crush on this girl named Trish. She was fourteen, too. She was de prettiest thang I ever seen. She had long, black hair and curves windin' like de Mississippi River."

"At fourteen?" Ray Ray roared.

"Hell yeah!" Enoch proclaimed. "She had titties like cantaloupes"—Enoch cupped his hands in front of his chest—"and a ass round as a black diamond watermelon!"

Ray Ray fell over in mirth.

"Her daddy told me he'd kill me if he ever caught me at his house, but I snuck over there every chance I got, tryin' to get me a glance at dat rose. Dat's what I called her—my Pretty Rose."

"Did she like you?" Ray Ray panted.

"Hell naw!" Enoch admitted freely and Ray Ray crumbled again. "I wuz jes a po', nappy-headed, country boy who didn't have nothin' but one good pair o' overalls. But I sho liked her." Enoch frowned playfully at Ray Ray. "What's so funny?"

Resuming his upright position, Ray Ray sighed heavily and screamed, "I was jes imaginin' you tryin' to kiss her!"

Enoch laughed along. "Shiiiiiiit, her daddy woulda killed me. I knowed better'n dat!"

"Did you talk to her?"

"I tried to, but she always told me to leave her alone." Enoch snickered as he remembered. "Everywhere she went, I'd follow her like flies follow shit, but she neva did want anythang to do wit me. She wanted yo' uncle Jerry."

"What? I thought people said Uncle Jerry never said much to nobody?"

"He didn't, but she thought he was de cutest Black thang she had eva seen. She told me to stop botherin' her and to tell my brother to come over."

Ray Ray slipped off the front porch hollering. Then he realized his father's feelings might have been bruised, so he reclaimed his seat, and said, "Sorry, Dad."

"Oh, no. I'm fine now. But then? I was so mad at my brother I didn't know what to do. He didn't even want her! All he ever wanted to do was read and walk in de woods. He told me he didn't even think she was all that pretty. Boy, was I mad! She was my girlfriend, I told him, and he wunnit gon talk bad about her. Jerry ignored me and went about his business. But the more she liked him, the madder I got. That's the only time we ever fought."

"What? Who won?" Ray Ray cackled.

Enoch guffawed unashamed. "I ain't neva got no ass whippin' like de one I got dat day, son."

Ray Ray was enjoying his father's memory. For a moment, he wondered why Enoch was telling him this now, but then he decided he didn't care.

"Jerry was comin' back from de Sacred Place one day," Enoch explained. "I told him, shamefaced, that Trish said hello, and he said, 'Tell dat girl to stop botherin' me.' I don't know why, but his words made me so mad I couldn't see nothin' but fire in front o' me."

Ray Ray was trying to suppress his laughter, but his shoulders jerked involuntarily.

"So I jumped on his back and wrestled him to de ground. I started punchin' his head wit my fist and kickin' him like he was some ole stray dog. At first, Jerry just laid there doin' nothin'. Then he said, 'Don't hit me no more, boy', but I wunnit payin' him no mind. In fact, I went to beatin' him even more after he opened his mouth. That's when Jerry threw me off o' him like a ole wild boar and knocked de shit outta me."

Ray Ray's mouth fell open, and his eyelashes batted repeatedly. "Are you serious, Dad?"

"Dat's right!" Enoch affirmed. "Yo' uncle Jerry laid my ass out with one punch. I think I was more shocked than hurt. He was so skinny and quiet that I assumed he didn't have no strength, but when he hit my ass, I fell over like a sawed-down tree. He stood over me, and said, 'Don't neva hit me again. Ever.' And he walked away slowly, like nothin' happened. I was sweatin' and huffin', layin' on de ground in de front yard, but Jerry was cool and calm like always. I hated him even more after that. I probably went three weeks without sayin' anything to him. Sometimes at the dinner table he would look at me, but I refused to open my mouth. I guess I was shamed."

"He didn't speak to you either?"

"Naw. Jerry didn't say too much to nobody. He was always off by hisself readin' somethin'." Enoch smiled. "You talkin' 'bout smart? Boy, yo' uncle could outspell and outread anybody in Money—colored or white. Sometimes they would ask him to read the scripture in Sunday School and, soon as he began, people would freeze perfectly still until he finished. His voice was deep and soothin' like God's. Some o' de old folks would close they eyes, throw they heads back, and sway as he read, mumblin', 'Yeah, uh-huh,' as though Jerry's voice was massagin' their souls. Wow. Dat boy was special."

Ray Ray glanced at his father, and asked, "You loved Uncle Jerry, huh Daddy?"

Enoch smashed the tear with his right index finger before it could leave his eye. "I worshipped my brother. He was really like God to me. He could answer any question I asked him and I never heard him say a foul word about anybody. Even when he shot those white men for rapin' Billie Faye, Momma said he never cursed them. He jes got Daddy's gun and did what he thought was right. I didn't understand him then, but as I got older I started to understand exactly why he did what he did."

Ray Ray saw Mr. Moore coming but he didn't want to interrupt his father's nostalgia.

Enoch picked up a pebble and threw it far as he could. "Jerry was tellin' me dat a man's gotta make de righteousness he wants. It ain't gon fall out de sky. He gotta be willin' to suffer somethin' and sacrifice somethin' if he gon make de world a betta place for hisself and his kids. Somebody might even have to die, but it'll be worth it to comin' generations. It'll even be worth it to him."

A blue jay landed near Ray Ray's feet.

"Jerry told me one night in de bed dat people live forever. They jes change forms. Sometimes you can see 'em, sometimes you cain't. Sometimes dey in the trees, sometimes dey in de animals. But once you get life, he said, you don't neva lose it."

"What about dyin'?" Ray Ray asked.

"Jerry said dyin' was jes God's way o' movin' you from one kinda life to another to see which one you like de best. I told him he wuz crazy, but I knowed he wunnit. He jes started talkin' one night. I still wasn't speakin' to him, on account o' Trish, but he acted like everything was fine. He rolled over and put his arm around me, and I pushed it off in anger. He said, 'Stop, boy. I love you,' and put his arm around me again. I jes laid there this time. The way he said he loved me almost made me cry. He rubbed my head, and said 'You de only brother I got, and I wouldn't trade you for the world.' That's what got me, Ray Ray. Hearing my brother tell me how much I meant to him tore me up inside. I always admired him, but I always thought he didn't like me. After he said that, I melted into Jerry's skinny arms and went to sleep with him rubbing my temples. I'll never forget it long as I live. He was miraculous, son. I wish you and Chop coulda knowed him longer. He wuz crazy 'bout you boys."

Ray Ray beamed broadly. He was thankful for his father's vulnerability and for Enoch's assumption that Ray Ray would appreciate it.

Mr. Moore approached, and Enoch rose, preparing to greet him. "Let me do de talkin'," Enoch said, and Ray Ray gladly acquiesced.

Pet Moore's family was the oldest colored family in Money. Legend had it that his great-grandfather, Tiger Moore, came when slavery first started and worked until he bought his own freedom. Pet always bragged that his great-granddaddy's real name was Ato Lebechi, which meant "the brilliant one who watches God." He was taken from Africa when he was eight, but he never forgot the name the griot gave him. He told his children the story of his capture and made them promise to tell their children forever. And that's exactly what his seven boys and one daughter did. Every chance Pet got, he would retell the story of his family's journey to America and boast about how they were free when most other Black folks were enslaved.

"It couldn't have been dat much difference," Jeremiah told Pet one day defensively, "'cause they raped and killed his daughter, too." Pet fell silent and never mentioned the story to Jeremiah again.

His grandfather, Isadore Moore, the oldest of the seven boys, worked in the fields to make extra money. People said he could pick three hundred pounds of cotton a day and still tend to his own personal crops in the evenings. In fact, old man Johnson needed him so badly that he begged Isadore to pick for him. Folks say that's the only time they ever heard of a white man begging a Black man for anything. According to Jeremiah, old man Johnson agreed to pay Isadore ten dollars a week, which was twice what everybody else got. Plus, Isadore sold the biggest tomatoes, squash, and crowder peas in the county, so he lived a little better than most other colored folk. He and his wife had only two children, a boy and girl, before his wife died, but women around Money testified that Isadore Moore could take care of a house better than any woman they knew. He made curtains, mended socks, knitted gloves, and braided his daughter's hair in cornrows. His daddy taught him that, they said. Actually, he was a little too feminine for most people's taste, but no one could beat his work ethic or argue that Isadore didn't manage his affairs well.

That he never remarried was the source of much gossip in Money, coupled with the fact that his best friend, Authur Thompson, had never been. They often fished together and, after his wife passed, they sat next to each other in church. Seemingly oblivious to others' wonderings, Isadore and Authur never saw the need to defend their virtue. They visited one another daily and sat on each other's porch in bold dismissal of what others thought. Isadore's son, Jonathan—pronounced Joe Nathan—and his daughter Octavia would fight anybody who dared question the integrity of Isadore and Authur's relationship, so most people were careful not to gossip around the children. When the men died on the same day in 1900, colored folks in Money smiled sympathetically to Joe Nathan and Octavia and, behind closed doors, said "old couples do dat sometimes."

The day after his father's death, Joe Nathan started working in the General Store. "He wasn't broke," Jeremiah told Enoch, "he just needed to get his mind off his daddy. The white folks was glad to get him," Jeremiah remembered, "'cause the Moores was 'bout de hardest-workin' people around. But Joe Nathan didn't like workin' fu white folks 'cause he said they didn't have no spirit, so he told his son Pet that he didn't want him working there, but he could if he wanted to. Pet wasn't bothered by white folks' nasty attitudes, so he took de job and been workin' there every sense."

Pet had always been friendly with children, Enoch recalled. In fact, although Pet was a big man—six-seven or more and at least 350 pounds—he was easily the nicest person Enoch had ever met. Anytime he, Jerry, or Possum entered the store, they would leave with at least one piece of peppermint each and a hug that made them tingle all over. He had a stomach that looked like he had swallowed a pumpkin, children used to say, and Mr. Pet could make it move like there was a baby in it. Children would scream and laugh as he entertained them, until one of the Cuthberts admonished, "Pet, I pay you to work—not to play with colored children." The children would leave and return days later to repeat the ritual. Why the Cuthberts didn't fire him no one knew, but Miss Mary conjectured that Miss Cuthbert, like every other woman, "enjoyed the company of a handsome Black man."

"Howdy, Enoch . . . Ray Ray," Pet Moore greeted, breathing heavily. "I done got too old fu this walkin!" Everyone shook hands and Mr. Moore invited Enoch and Ray Ray inside.

"We got any lemonade, honey?" he hollered toward the kitchen. Getting no response, he whispered, "Me and dat woman 'bout to fall out." Enoch and Ray Ray chuckled, knowing that Pet Moore was only joking since he and Miss Gladys had been married at least forty years.

Moments later, she emerged from the kitchen with three glasses of ice-cold, freshly squeezed lemonade.

"Thanks, Miss Gladys," Ray Ray said respectfully.

She winked. "You welcome, baby. You welcome, too, Enoch, but, Pet, next time you come in dat do' you betta speak to somebody befo' you start givin' out orders."

Again, Ray Ray and Enoch snickered.

Pet looked at Ray Ray, and said, "You jes do what I tell you, woman." He reached to slap her on the behind, but Miss Gladys blew him off with her left hand as she disappeared into the kitchen.

"Boy, a woman make a man a straight fool if he ain't mighty careful!" Mr. Pet bantered. "If I could do it all over again, I wouldn't be bothered with dat woman." He smirked. Then he leaned back in his rocker, and said, "What can I do fu you gentlemen?"

Pet Moore searched Enoch and Ray Ray's faces for clues as to the nature of their unannounced visit, but Enoch spoke before Pet guessed anything. "We jes come by to see if . . . um . . . you mighta heard anything . . . strange in de sto' today."

Pet's fake cough gave Enoch hope. The man started rocking faster and reached for his pipe, shoving it into his mouth clumsily. "Anythang like what?" he murmured.

Enoch realized this encounter was going to be harder than he thought. "Like . . . um—" He didn't want to say anything about Clement unless Pet mentioned it first.

"Like what happened to dat boy?" Pet Moore said.

"Yes!" Enoch almost screamed.

"Well, I don't know nothin'," Mr. Moore said rather tight-lipped while lighting his pipe.

"Then how you know they took somebody?" Enoch asked. Mr. Moore couldn't devise a lie before Enoch said, "Please, sir. Tell me what you know. It was Possum's son, Clement, who they took."

Pet Moore's eyes closed painfully. He used to call Possum his daughter because she took care of him and Miss Gladys after their daughter Laura Jean drowned. Every evening she would comb Miss Gladys's hair or cook or read out loud until their depression subsided. Pet got so attached to Possum that he began to sit by the window and wait for her arrival every evening. When Possum moved to Chicago, Miss Gladys told Miss Mary that Pet didn't eat for three days. Miss Gladys had come by the Johnson house, she said, to see if somebody might have an address where Pet could get in touch with Possum. Miss Mary provided as much and, in church a few weeks later, Miss Gladys told her that Pet had "bounced back" after getting a letter from Possum. It purged his soul so completely, she testified, that he ate a whole chicken the day the letter arrived.

"I makes it my business to keep my mouth closed, Enoch. You knows dat 'bout me," Mr. Moore began. "Whatever I hear in de sto', I leaves in de sto'." His face lost all signs of emotion.

"Okay, Mr. Pet. I cain't make you say nothin' you don't want to. Let's go, boy." Enoch and Ray Ray stood as though having rehearsed the motion and moved toward the door. Mr. Pet sat motionless.

Before leaving, Enoch honored his manners above his frustration, saying, "Thank you for your time, Mr. Pet. If you hear anythang, you can tell me—"

"Sheriff and Cecil hidin' him somewhere. They ain't killed him. Not yet. That's all I know. Don't ask me nothin' else. Please." Pet Moore stared into space without looking at his company.

"Please, Mr. Moore," Enoch begged. "Tell me everything. You remember how they did Jerry. Don't let me lose nobody else in my family. We done worked too hard to keep losin' folks, and if it was one o' yo kin, you'd want me—"

"Fine!" Mr. Moore hollered. "I'll tell you what I heard. But if you mention my name, boy—"

"I won't say nothin' to nobody 'bout you, Mr. Pet. I promise." Enoch was antsy with anticipation.

"Sit down." Pet Moore pointed to the same chairs Enoch and Ray Ray had previously occupied. They obeyed quickly.

"I was gettin' some supplies from de supply barn when I overheard Cecil talkin'. He didn't see me, so I hid and waited for him to continue. I knowed what he was sayin' had somethin' to do wit colored folks 'cause he was laughin' and screamin' de word 'niggers' when I walked in." Pet Moore crossed his legs and puffed smoke from his pipe to calm his agitated nerves. "That's why I hid. To see who and what he was talkin' 'bout. Then Cecil started describin' what went on at y'alls house last night. He said you and Jeremiah attacked them and killed Billy's three brothers, but he got away. Then today, him, Billy, and some other white boys come back and took de boy who disrespected Miss Cuthbert. That's how they described him. They said they didn't need but one o' y'all 'cause what they wuz gon do would make de rest o' y'all wish you wuz dead."

Ray Ray looked at Enoch, who, instead of reacting, asked, "Did they say what they did with Clement?"

"No. Not exactly." Mr. Pet paused.

"What chu mean 'not exactly'?"

"I mean they didn't say exactly where they took him."

Enoch's patience was failing. "Did they sorta say where they took him?"

Mr. Pet sighed heavily, and said, "They joked about lynchin' him. But then they said that was too easy. They needed to make an example of him that colored folk would never fugit. I could tell they hadn't done it though 'cause they was describin' various things they might do to him."

"Is that all they said, Mr. Pet?" Enoch pleaded further.

Pet rose from the chair. "Just about," he said, and walked to the front screen door. "They also said the boy was in a safe hiding place for now. They said they wuz gon take their time and"—he shook his head—"separate him, piece by piece. They didn't say where they wuz hidin' him. I'm sorry." Mr. Pet's sympathetic eyes moistened.

"Thank you, Mr. Pet," Enoch said, wiping tears. "I gotta go find him, sir. I gotta." He motioned for Ray Ray to follow.

As they left, Mr. Pet said, "Try de Cuthbert barn. Dat's my best guess." After the screen door slammed, he hollered, "Be careful!"

"We will," Enoch answered.

He and Ray Ray walked away briskly. "We gotta find him, son. We gotta find him," Enoch repeated, like one thinking aloud unaware.

"Where we goin', Daddy?" Ray Ray asked, already knowing the answer.

Enoch ignored the question and walked with a precision Ray Ray could not emulate. He wanted to beg his father to wait, to think before they headed over to the sheriff's place, to give him at least a minute to gather some courage, but Enoch's silent determination was impenetrable. There was no place else to go, Enoch thought, except to save his nephew. This was the chance he had waited for since Jerry's death to restore honor to the Johnson family name, and, regardless of the cost, he was determined to show Ray Ray what kind of man he was.

Ray Ray wished Enoch would get a few other men to come along, just in case something happened. He tried not to imagine what Billy Cuthbert and Cecil Love might do to him and his daddy if they caught them snooping around their barn, but Ray Ray had a feeling the price of such rash behavior might be high. He also knew there was simply no use in mentioning any of this, for Enoch was on a mission from which God above could not have deterred him. So Ray Ray walked quickly, trying to keep pace with a father whose eyes burned with vengeance. A rabbit hopped alongside them, a safe distance away, seemingly curious as to where a colored boy and his father were going so determinedly. The rabbit disappeared and reappeared intermittently, raising its head above the high grass on the side of the dirt road and looking at Ray Ray. Its gaze hypnotized the boy and made him envy the creature's freedom, but then he thought about how much he loved his grandmother's rabbit stew and—

"Jes follow me, boy," Enoch interrupted unknowingly, although never slowing his steps. The sheriff's barn was barely five hundred yards away.

Ray Ray's fear seemed to multiply his father's obstinate determination, for Enoch's steps quickened as Ray Ray tried to hesitate.

Sensing his son's reserve, Enoch said, "Don't worry, boy. We gon be all right," and kept marching. His voice carried more certainty than Ray Ray's heart.

"What if he ain't there, Daddy? I mean, what if they done took him someplace else?" This was all Ray Ray could think to say, but he had to say something to keep from fainting in the center of the road.

"We jes gon check and see. We gon be all right. De Good Lawd's on our side. Ain't dat what Momma say?"

Ray Ray neither affirmed nor denied. He was simply frustrated that he couldn't change his father's mind. For each seed of doubt Ray

Ray tried to plant, Enoch uprooted it with hope and wrath until the boy had no choice but to follow in peace. Ray Ray would have been ashamed of being scared, but he was never afforded the time to think about it. The speed of his father's pace only allowed him opportunity to hope that Clement was in the barn, and they could rescue him without detection.

Dusk was coming on, so Enoch knew the residents would be home soon. He grabbed Ray Ray's arm as they reached the back of the barn, and whispered, "Don't make a sound. We jes gon look and see if we find Clement. If we don't, we'll leave. I got chu, boy. Don't be scared."

Enoch unlatched the big barn door quietly and opened it just wide enough for the two to slither through. Ray Ray hung on his father's arm like a young bride proceeding down a wedding aisle. They began to look around suspiciously.

"Clement!" Enoch whispered emphatically as he tiptoed across the dirty, hay-strewn, wooden barn floor. "Check over there," he told his son, who moved with the stealth of a thief. Ray Ray began to look behind the huge barrels, which probably contained flour, sugar, or corn meal.

"Clement," Ray Ray mumbled. Then he sighed, "Please let us find him, Lawd."

Enoch climbed the ladder to see if Clement were bound in the loft. Shifting piles of hay with his right foot, he hoped to find his nephew buried underneath. Suddenly, the barn door opened.

"Let's go get the rest of 'em!" Cecil urged. "You saw what they did to yo' brothers!"

"Yep, I know," Billy said with a suspicious calm. "I know."

"They jes killed 'em and throwed 'em out in de dirt like they wun-nit nothin'!" Cecil droned. "You de sheriff! You cain't let 'em get by with that, Billy!"

"Oh, they ain't gon get by. Trust me. When we git through wit dat boy, they gon hate they ever seen a Cuthbert."

Billy opened a barrel and began to scoop flour without ever notic-ing the top of Ray Ray's head only inches below. Enoch had slowly and quietly burrowed himself underneath the hay, confident that, wherever Ray Ray was, his fear would keep him still and quiet.

"I still think we should git de rest of 'em," Cecil said. "Then we could make a example o' de whole family."

Billy smiled. "Naw, like I said this mornin', we ain't gon do it like that this time. Dem niggers done got uppity, like they ain't gon bow to white folks no more. They waitin' fur us right now. If they crazy enough to kill my brothers and throw 'em out in de woods, they'll kill us, too. We gotta keep our head and make this one count. If we don't, they gon take over the world." He resealed the barrel.

Cecil wasn't convinced. His wounded arm had only exacerbated his wounded pride. "Couldn't we git jes one more? I mean, if we took the old grandmother, then the men—"

"No!" Billy demanded. He saw Miss Mary in his mind's eye, curled on the floor next to his bed. "We ain't takin' her."

"Why not? I'm tellin' you, the men would fall right into—"

"I said we ain't takin' her!" Billy screamed.

"What's the matter with you, Billy Cuthbert?" Cecil yelled back. "What kinda sheriff are you anyway?"

Billy almost explained that Miss Mary had once been his caregiver, but since Cecil was too young to remember and would certainly find the fact irrelevant, Billy simply said, "Jes follow me on this one, cousin. We don't need but one o' 'em. Believe me. We don't need but one."

"Fine," Cecil surrendered. "But I hope your plan works."

"It's gon work," Billy confirmed. "Oh boy, is it gon work!"

Cecil smiled at the evil in Billy's eyes. He was content now. "I jes cain't understand what's gotten into 'em," Cecil said, leaning on the flour barrel. "We give 'em everything they need and still they want more. Now niggers is havin' voter registration rallies all over this state, upsettin' de peace we've had for hundreds o' years. It's all in de papers! They ain't never satisfied!"

"That's why we gotta handle this situation really delicate, Cecil," Billy said slowly. "We gotta take back our place in society. God made white men to rule over everything and everybody, and sometimes it's a hard job, but it's our destiny. When thangs git out o' order like they is 'round here right now, it's our job to restore order to de world. Dat's why God made Adam first—to have dominion over everything. And you know he's white 'cause his name is Adam."

Cecil's nodding affirmed Billy's logic.

"What kinda God woulda put niggers in charge? They wouldn'ta done nothin' but destroyed de whole world. God is smarter'n that!" Billy nudged Cecil, who nodded more vigorously.

Ray Ray never prayed so hard his entire life. He knew his father was somewhere in the loft, and he begged God not to let those men go up there.

"You think they'll come lookin' fu de boy?" Cecil asked.

"They'll come," Billy assured. "They always do."

Enoch closed his eyes and sent Ray Ray a telepathic message not to move. The boy's legs were cramping beneath him, yet he had no choice but to endure.

"Remember how they said that nigger couple came runnin' all over the white neighborhood, blamin' whites for takin' their boy?" Billy asked.

"Yep," Cecil said.

"Well, remember what they said they did to 'em? That's what we'll do to these niggers when they come, too."

Cecil clapped excitedly.

"And if they don't come, when they find that boy they'll never fugit it."

"I likes that kinda talk!"

The two moved toward the barn door.

"So don't get anxious," Billy warned. "We gotta do this right. Every white person's life in the state of Mississippi is dependin' on it."

"All right, all right," Cecil agreed as they turned.

"Plus, niggers do better when whites rule 'em 'cause..." and Billy's voice faded into the evening.

Enoch waited twenty seconds before he dared move or speak.

Then he uncovered himself, descended the loft quickly, and found Ray Ray shivering behind the barrels.

"We gotta get outta here, boy! Hurry!" he whimpered.

Ray Ray followed Enoch out of the barn and across the field. He never knew his father possessed such speed and, in fact, by the time they reached home, Ray Ray was the exhausted one.

"Daddy!" Enoch huffed in the living room. Ray Ray simply fell out on the couch.

"What's wrong, boy?" Jeremiah jumped from the rocker. "What's done happened?" Miss Mary and Ella Mae froze in the kitchen.

"We went lookin' for Clement"—breath—"in Sheriff Cuthbert's barn." Enoch could hardly speak.

"What?" Jeremiah's anger flamed. "Who told you to go over there?" He looked from Enoch to Ray Ray, who was glad to let his father be the spokesman.

"We went to see Mr. Pet to ask him if he heard anythang in de sto' today." Enoch took two big breaths. "Well, at first he didn't want to tell us anythang, but then he told us that he heard Billy and Cecil talkin' like they had Clement tied up somewhere"—breath—"so we went to see."

"All by yo'self? Is you a fool, boy?" Jeremiah screamed.

"We all right, Daddy. We all right."

"I ain't talkin' 'bout y'all bein' all right! I'm talkin' 'bout you two goin' over there by yo'self. What if they caught y'all? Huh? How wuz y'all gon fight off a gang o' white men by yo'self? Huh?" Jeremiah trembled. No one dared interrupt him. "Ray Ray," he turned and reprimanded him. "You didn't know no better either? You too big and too old fu this kinda foolishness, boy!"

Ray Ray wanted to explain how he tried to slow his father's steps and how he tried to urge Enoch to reconsider, but remembering that most of his hesitation had been internal, Ray Ray sat quiet and humble as his grandfather's wrath confirmed that his fear had indeed been legitimate.

Jeremiah's rampage ended abruptly. The old man returned to the rocker, clearly disheveled and infuriated, but a bit calmer now than before. Tension held everyone at bay as they waited for the family patriarch's permission to speak. He spoke himself. "What did Pet say?"

Enoch fidgeted, trying to figure out what more he could say. Finding nothing, he repeated what he had just said: "He told us that he overheard Billy and Cecil talkin' in de supply barn 'bout how they wuz gon do somethin' unimaginable to Clement."

"Lawd have mercy!" Miss Mary cried out.

Enoch continued: "And Mr. Pet said they said he was bein' kept in a safe place somewhere. They didn't say where, but I thought—"

"You thought?" Jeremiah cut him off. "You didn't think, boy! You definitely didn't think!" He started rocking so hard Ray Ray feared he might topple the chair.

"Daddy, don't be mad," Enoch begged softly. "I was jes tryin'—"

"You! You wuz jes tryin' to what? To see if you could git yo'self and dat boy killed?" Jeremiah stared at Enoch with a piercing disgust.

Enoch's humiliation was more than he could bear. "What did you expect me to do, Daddy?" he hollered.

"I expected you to come back and get me or get somebody jes in case somethin' went wrong. That's what I expected you to do, boy!"

"I ain't no boy, Daddy, and fugive me for not bein' you!" Enoch screamed.

"I ain't neva asked you to be me! All I asked you to do is to use yo' head, and you cain't seem to do that 'cause—"

"I wuz followin' a hunch, man, okay?" Enoch yelled. "I didn't think we had time—"

"You always got time to be safe, boy!" Jeremiah stood.

Enoch shouted, "I ain't no boy!"

"You *my* boy! And long as you live you gon be my boy 'cause you de only one I got left." Jeremiah fell into the chair and wept. He had tried to keep his emotions in order, but the possibility of losing Enoch overwhelmed him.

Enoch fell to his knees in front of the rocker and laid his head in his father's lap. Jeremiah lifted Enoch's head and pulled it into his chest, and the two cried years of pain and love suppressed. Everyone else watched, glad the exchange hadn't gotten violent. Ray Ray's heart warmed at the display between his father and grandfather, and now he knew why he was proud to be a Johnson.

"Listen, son," Jeremiah finally said. "I know you ain't no boy. You's a grown man, and a damn good one. But I cain't lose you. I jes cain't." He began to cry again. "I jes cain't lose no more chillen. I cain't!"

"I'm all right, Daddy," Enoch mumbled through his own tears. "Me and Ray Ray, we all right."

Sarah Jane, Chop, and Ella Mae cried more than the men. Miss Mary sniffled as she watched her family come closer together.

"Come here, boy," Jeremiah called to Ray Ray. He had the only dry face in the house.

Ray Ray stood next to the rocker and waited as Jeremiah blew his nose on a handkerchief. The boy was trying not to cry, but he was losing his grip.

"Enoch, I want you to tell dis boy what he mean to you. Tell him right now," Jeremiah insisted.

"What?" Enoch said, feeling awkward.

"You heard me, son. Dis boy is 'bout to be a man, and you don't know what's 'bout to happen 'round hyeah in de next few days. But one thang fu sho—make him know what he mean to you. Make him know it."

Enoch knew his father was pressing him past the error Jeremiah had made with Jerry, and although he understood his father's urging, speaking the fullness of his heart was something he had never done.

Ray Ray stood alone with downcast eyes. He sympathized with Enoch's naked vulnerability and, really, he wished his grandfather had simply let their assumption of love reign.

Enoch stood and took Ray Ray's hand. He tried to smile to ease the moment, but staring into his son's eyes softened an otherwise tough exterior. "I ... um ..." Enoch's voice shattered. He dropped his head and tears fell onto the living room floor. "The day you wuz born was the happiest day of my life," he began. "Me and yo' momma thought you wuz gon be a girl, and when you come out a boy, I jes started hollerin'. 'I got me a son!' I went around tellin' everybody. Folks thought I was crazy, but I ain't neva been dat happy. You wuz just one day old, and I took you from dat crib and showed you all 'round de county. Yo' momma told me you wuz too young to go out, but I couldn't help it. I wanted everybody to see my beautiful baby boy."

Ray Ray's hold on his tears was about to break.

"I used to watch you go to sleep. I would stare at you and listen to you breathe. It was smooth and easy, and it always calmed me down. I would whisper to you how much I loved you, and I would tell you jokes everybody else had done already heard. Sometimes you would smile in yo' sleep, and I swore you heard and understood me." Enoch embraced Ray Ray and held him close. That's when the boy's trapped tears burst free.

"You mean everything in de world to me, son. Don't chu neva fugit it. Sometimes I ain't good 'bout tellin' you, but I'd give my life for ya. You and yo' brother." Enoch motioned for Chop, who cried openly and unashamedly, to join them. "You my soldier, too, Mr. Pork Chop," he teased lovingly as he included him in the paternal embrace. "You squirmed so much as a baby I thought worms had done took you over."

Everybody laughed.

"De docta said wunnit nothin' wrong you. You jes had a lot o' energy. He said to let you run and play, and you'd be fine. Now look at you!" Enoch scattered Chop's miniature afro. "I wouldn't trade you fu all de money in de world."

"I-I-I wwwouldn't trrrade you nnnneither, Daddy." Chop smiled.

The three lingered in a moment they knew wouldn't come again soon.

Enoch loosened his embrace of the boys, and said, "Sarah Jane, you come here, too."

She went hesitantly, having concluded that this moment was simply for her cousins to enjoy. Thinking of her own parents, she had resolved to bask in her memory of their love for her and to learn how to thrive from that alone. But she admitted to herself, years ago, that a tangible, visible love would be nice.

"You my daughter, now, Sarah Jane, and you de most beautiful little girl I done ever seen." Enoch stroked her plaits nurturingly. "You de only child of my brother, and cain't nobody love nobody like I loved my brother. So now you mine, too."

"D-D-Dis mean Sarah Jane my sssssssssssssssista?" Chop asked.

"Yes, son, dat's what it mean," Enoch chuckled. "She gon be dat forever. Dis is what Jerry and Billie Faye would want, and dis is what we gon do. Now I don't eva intend to take they place, Sarah Jane. You know dat. I jes want you to have what all de rest o' us got—somebody who's livin' to call yo' own. And you got dat right hyeah. I love you jes like you mine 'cause you is mine."

"That's right," Ella Mae reinforced.

"You ain't got to bow yo' head to nobody, thinkin' you ain't got no folks, girl, 'cause me and Ella Mae intend to finish what my brother and Billie Faye started."

Sarah Jane let her tears flow without wiping them. She had hoped something would come one day to bring closure and healing to her heart, but she didn't know it would come from Uncle Enoch.

"Thank you," she mumbled.

"Ain't no thank you, girl," Enoch corrected. "This ain't no favor to you. We's family, and family loves one another, come what may." He was holding her shoulders sternly and looking deeply into her dark brown eyes. "So don't you neva thank me for lovin' you. You understand me?"

Sarah Jane smiled, and said, "Yessir."

"All right then," Enoch concluded with a wink.

Jeremiah stood up proudly, laid his hand on Enoch's shoulder, and declared, "Now! Dat's what I'm talkin' 'bout! A man is spose to keep his family together. You cain't do dat, you ain't no man."

"Amen," Miss Mary chimed. "Now let's eat befo' dis town meetin'."

Ten

EVERYONE MOVED TO THE KITCHEN TABLE AND SAT DOWN quietly. The old clock hanging on the wall read 6:15.

"Where'd you go today, Daddy?" Enoch asked while spooning purple hull peas and ham hock portions onto his plate.

"I jes went for a walk," Jeremiah said, "so I could think thangs through." He stabbed the big, fried chicken breast with his fork and hoped Enoch wouldn't press him further.

"Where'd you walk?" Enoch pried and smacked.

"Just . . . around," he said in annoyance. "I wuz jes tryin' to clear my head. Pass me dat cabbage." He hoped Enoch would be deluded.

"You walked down by the river?"

"No!" Jeremiah roared, paralyzing everyone at the table. His forehead wrinkled, and his trembling, arthritic hands dropped the chicken he was holding.

"What's wrong wit chu, man?" Miss Mary's tender voice inquired.

Sweat trickled down his temples. "Nothin'. I'm sorry. I'm jes . . . nervous about everything, I guess." He resumed eating.

No one believed him, but since no one wanted his wrath, they dropped the matter.

"Y'all hurrup and eat 'cause de meetin' gon start pretty soon," Jeremiah said.

Sarah Jane knew something was troubling her grandfather, but she decided to ask him about it later. Chop seemed oblivious to Jeremiah's emotional distress, devouring chicken wings like a bear at a salmon run. At three, he had determined never to eat chicken again, after watching Miss Mary wring one's neck violently.

"You ain't got to eat it, boy," Miss Mary declared. "Mo fu de rest o' us. But how you gon fly wit no wings?"

The day before, Chop had told his grandmother about a dream he had wherein he flew in the sky like a bird. "I j-j-jes waved my arms in d-d-de air and my b-b-b-body started ffffloatin', Grandma!" he yelled.

"What?" Miss Mary instigated.

"I p-promise!" Chop was jittery with excitement. "I-I-I was lllllike a b-b-bird in de sky. Everything w-w-was llllllittle when I-I-I llll-looked down, and de wwwwworld was ssso pretty."

Miss Mary laughed broadly. "Well, well, Mr. Bird. I speck you better eat some chicken wings so you can be big and strong."

The next day, Chop watched in horror as Miss Mary killed a chicken for dinner.

"You want de wings?" she asked in jest.

"No, mmmmam," Chop refused. "D-d-dat chicken w-w-was cryin' wwwwwhen you b-b-b-b-b-broke his neck."

"But how you gon fly without wings, baby?" Miss Mary asked. "You gotta eat chicken wings so you can grow some of yo' own." She dipped the bird in boiling water and began to remove its feathers.

"For real?" Chop asked skeptically.

"Dat's right!" Miss Mary snickered. "How a man gon fly without wings?"

Chop couldn't argue, so he concluded his grandmother had a point. "Okay," he said slowly. "But only the w-wing 'cause I wanna ffffffffffffly."

"Then go fly, child," Miss Mary chuckled as he walked away.

The evening of the town meeting, Chop ate all the wings he could hold. He had a feeling he might need to fly away quickly—if the white men came again—and he wanted to be prepared. He watched Sarah Jane eat a wing and assumed she, too, knew the secret. Ray Ray always ate the drumstick, and Chop didn't tell him differently because, in Chop's eyes, Ray Ray was big and could fight for himself.

"Who all spose to be comin' to de meetin', Daddy?" Ella Mae asked, wiping chicken grease from her hands.

"I don't know, baby. We gon see."

"You think a lotta folks comin'?" Ella Mae pressed.

Jeremiah's frustration rose again, but he dammed its overflow. "You cain't neva tell 'bout colored folks, honey. We change like de wind." He prayed his answer would dilute her line of questioning or, better, destroy it altogether. He was trying to eat quickly in order to secure a few minutes alone before the meeting. He had a plan in his head, but thinking about it made him cautious. Jerry's support certainly strengthened his courage, but it also made him wonder if, in the end, he would have to fight this battle alone. His family's questions pushed him closer to the edge as he tried furiously to imagine a South purged of racism and hatred. Unable to do so, Jeremiah became agitated with himself for having called the meeting. He looked at the clock—6:40—and shook his head with uncertainty. He couldn't turn back now.

"I'm goin' out to de barn jes in case somebody come early," he said, and rose prematurely from the table.

"But you ain't finished eatin'." Miss Mary frowned.

"I ain't too hungry," he said, exiting the front door. "Y'all come on out in a few minutes."

"I'll come wit chu now, Daddy," Enoch offered, rising from his chair.

"No! I jes wanna think fu a minute by myself. Take yo' time and eat, boy." Jeremiah hobbled off the porch toward the barn. When he opened the barn door, he saw Pet Moore.

"How ya doin', Mi?" Pet said cordially. He pushed himself up from the rusty, iron fold-up chair.

"Doin' fine, Pet," Jeremiah returned surprised. He had no hope Pet Moore would come to the meeting, much less arrive twenty minutes early. Now that he had, he didn't know what to say.

"How's Gladys?"

"Doin' good, Mi. She still fussin', so she must be all right."

The men laughed far past the humor of the statement.

"You didn't think I was comin', Mi, did you?" Pet said as he resumed his seat.

Jeremiah didn't know how to answer the question without insulting him. "To tell you de truth, I guess I didn't, Pet." He unfolded a chair for himself. "You always wuz de one who played thangs safe, so I didn't think—"

"I know, I know," Pet said, freeing Jeremiah from trying to explain. "But this is different. You know how much I love Possum, and this 'bout her boy, so I had to come."

Jeremiah extended his hand. "Thank you, man," he said, and they shook with all their might.

"Don't thank me, Mi. I ain't done nothin' yet, but I sho hopes to."

The men stared at the ground in silence. They had never been particularly close, and now a touch of intimacy felt strange.

"Y'all told Possum yet?"

Jeremiah bit his bottom lip. "Naw."

"I don't blame you. Give it a minute before you make dat girl go crazy. Maybe after tonight, won't be no need to call at all. You cain't neva tell."

"Naw, you cain't, Pet."

Silence forced its way into the conversation again and brought an awkwardness both hoped another's arrival might destroy. They looked in every direction but saw no one.

"I done worked in dat sto' forty years, Mi, and I'm tired o' grinnin' at white folks," Pet volunteered. "Every day, 'how ya doin', ma'am?' or 'nice day, sir, wouldn't you say?'" Pet mocked himself bowing before the white citizens of Money. "And not one time in forty years has any one of 'em asked me how I was doin'. Dat's a dam shame, ain't it?"

Jeremiah nodded.

"Oh well," Pet continued, "dey all de same. I thought workin' in de sto' was gon make dem like me better 'cause I wunnit out in de fields."

"Sh-sh-shit!" Jeremiah hollered. "I know you knowed better'n that."

"Look like I didn't, Mi," Pet admitted freely. "Dat's how dey get us. Daddy didn't know no better either. He used to tell me dat he got mo' respect from white folks 'cause he didn't have to go to de field."

"Get outta hyeah!"

"Dat's what he said. He was foolin' hisself 'cause dem damn white folks treated Daddy like a dog." Pet scoured his face as ugly as he could make it. "They called him 'boy' when they spoke to him at all, and sometime they didn't even pay him."

"What? Why not?"

"'Cause they said de sto' was short on money. Too many colored peoples buying on credit so wasn't no cash."

"That's a goddamn lie!" Jeremiah asserted. "De Cuthberts de richest people this side of the Mason Dixon line. They ain't nothin' but money!"

"I know. Daddy was jes too proud to go to de field. And since he come from folks who never had to, he promised hisself he wunnit goin' to neither. He didn't make but fifty cents a day."

Jeremiah jumped to his feet. "What! You have to be lyin'!"

"Dat's right," Pet confirmed.

"We made a dollar a day choppin' cotton!" he screamed in disbelief.

"Yeah, but y'all was out in de hot sun and Daddy thought that was beneath him. So when I took over his place at de sto', I was surprised at what they told me they was gon pay me."

Jeremiah asked, "You been makin' fifty cents a day for forty years?"

"Hell, naw!" he corrected. "I been makin' seventy-five!"

Both men hollered. Jeremiah couldn't believe what he was hearing, and Pet was glad, finally, to get it off his chest. They calmed and reoccupied their seats.

"I told Gladys this evenin' after Enoch and . . . um . . . uhru . . ."

"Ray Ray."

"Yeah! Ray Ray!" Pet clapped his hands thunderously. "I cain't neva remember dat boy's name to save my life." Pet paused, then went on: "But like I was sayin', I told Gladys this evenin' after yo' boys left dat I wunnit shufflin' 'round dat sto' no mo, keepin' white folks' secrets as they kill colored folks."

"You quit?"

Pet pondered a moment. "I guess I did. I don't know what I'm gon do though. I done got too old to be choppin' cotton and, anyway, I don't know how."

Jeremiah chuckled. Pet didn't.

"It's gon be all right," Jeremiah assured. "You jes watch how de Lawd work dis out. I was talkin' to Jerry this afternoon—"

"Jerry?" Pet frowned. Somehow, Pet's courageous move had freed Jeremiah, too. "Yeah, Jerry. I went down to de clearin' in de middle o' Chapman's place, and Jerry started talkin' to me." Jeremiah looked at Pet, who simply nodded.

"Go 'head," Pet encouraged.

"Well, anyway, I was down there thinkin' 'bout things. When all of a sudden, I hear Jerry talkin' to me."

Just then Pet glanced out of the barn door and bucked his eyes. "Good Gawd! Looka yonda!"

Jeremiah stood slowly and gave his bad eyes time to focus. The approaching crowd looked like thousands of black ants marching. He was sure he had never seen that many colored people in one place in his life.

"You done started some shit now!" Pet said enthusiastically.

"Well I'll be doggone," Jeremiah whimpered. "De Lawd is good!" A smile blossomed on his face.

"I sho hope you got somethin' good to say, Mi, 'cause all dese folks is gon be mighty pissed off if you don't."

"Oh, I got somethin' to say!" Jeremiah proclaimed. "You betta believe I got somethin' to say!" He hollered out for the rest of his family. "Momma, Enoch, Ella Mae . . . y'all come on!"

Watching Jeremiah's excitement grow energized Pet. He had known he was supposed to come to the meeting, and now he knew why. There was something about the crowd of colored people that made him proud. They looked like soldiers, he told himself, marching to a battle they had postponed too long. He wanted to be one of the fighters—not one of the appeasers of the white enemy. He wanted to go to bed proud of his people and how they decided, one day, to stand up for themselves. But more than anything, Pet wanted to be free of the need for white validation. He desired nothing more than to believe in something simply because it was right—not because white folks said.

"Good evenin', everybody," Jeremiah called to the approaching crowd.

"How you doin, Mi?" they returned in chorus.

"Fine, fine." He smiled broadly. "Y'all come on in de barn hyeah, and we'll git dis meetin' goin'." He whispered, "Ray Ray, you stand at de do' and let us know if you see anybody comin'."

"Yessir."

Miss Mary and Enoch, like church ushers, opened the doors and greeted people as they passed.

"Evenin'," Enoch must have said thirty times.

Some folks spoke in return while others nodded. The barn was overflowing with the bulk of Money's colored population. Enoch hadn't guessed that so many people would come. He felt a bit ashamed, now, for doubting his people, but a gathering of such size usually only happened at funerals.

They had long run out of chairs, so as protocol demanded, the elders sat, and the adults and children stood behind them. Miss Mary was the first lady, at least in the Johnson household, and she made sure to touch every hand in the barn. She raved over the babies and teased the children about growing so fast she couldn't keep up. Then her husband rose.

"I'm gon ask my boy hyeah to open us up in prayer." He motioned for Enoch to stand next to him in front of the gathering.

Enoch hadn't planned on praying but he certainly couldn't deny his father's request. He asked everyone to join hands, then improvised the "Lord's Prayer." "Our father, who art in heaven and earth below, hallowed be thy Holy name, they kingdom come, thy will be done, on earth as it is shonuff in heaven. Give us this day and every day our daily bread, and forgive us, Lawd Jesus, our trespasses as we forgive those who trespass against us. And lead us not into temptation, Oh God, but deliver us from evil. For thine is the kingdom and the power and the righteousness and the might and the glory forever. Amen."

"Yes, Lord!"

"Amen!"

"All right now!"

"Hallelujah!"

"You betta say that!"

"Glory!"

"Oh bless His name!"

"I'm tellin' you!"

"Now dat's all right!"

The affirmations stunned Enoch. No wonder preachers love to preach, he thought.

"Now. Let's get down to business," Jeremiah said. The crowd fell silent. "We here to do somethin' ain't neva been done long as I been livin' here." He hesitated a moment, then said, "Bring colored folks together."

"Amen," people agreed.

"De Cuthbert boys came to my house dis mornin' to take my grandson, Clement."

"My Lord!"

"Dat's right. Cecil was wit 'em, and me and my boy shot and killed all of 'em 'cept Cecil."

The enthusiasm died instantly. People began to frown.

"What's de matter?" Jeremiah asked in surprise.

"You killed the Cuthbert boys?" an unidentified voice asked.

"Hell, yeah! I wunnit gon' let them take my kids! Not long as I was standing there! What else was I spose to do?" The people's diffidence left Jeremiah agitated.

Pet Moore rose, and said, "He did jes what he was spose to do."

The crowd hadn't expected Pet to come, much less stand for anything. But he wasn't about to let this opportunity pass.

"Dat's why we hyeah, y'all—to learn how to take care o' our own so white folks can stop killin' us. Mi done buried a son and daughter-in-law, and y'all wanted him to sit back and let them goddamn crackers take some mo' o' his chillen?" Pet surveyed his neighbor's silent faces. "Well, dat's exactly what happened. They come back later and took Clement."

"Oh, Lord," people cried.

"So listen to what de man gotta say, and let's see if we can find dat boy." He sat down and winked at Jeremiah.

"We have to organize ourselves," Jeremiah began again. "We gotta find my grandson, then we gotta keep dem white folks off de rest o' us. You know they comin' back." In his heart, Jeremiah couldn't figure out why they hadn't already.

"Yeah, dey comin', Mi, 'cause you done fooled 'round and killed de sheriff's brothers," someone offered in disbelief.

"See, dat's our problem!" Jeremiah screamed, and pointed in the direction of the voice. "We so scared o' white folks so bad dat we don't eva want to make them upset. But they need to know dat we upset! Killin' our chillen and rapin' our women don't make us upset?" Sweat boiled on Jeremiah's forehead. "Dat's why dey keep comin'— 'cause dey know we ain't gon do nothin' 'bout it."

"And most times we don't," Pet added for emphasis.

"Dat's true," many agreed.

"But it cain't stay true all de time. Everybody got they breakin' point," Jeremiah explained, "and I reached mine today." The urgency in his voice elicited only a few amens, so he talked further as he paced the barn floor. "Don't wait 'til dey come for your chillen befo' you stand up and fight. Maybe mine don't mean dat much to you, but if you imagine Clement as yo' own, then I think you'll understand what I'm talkin' 'bout."

A few more "Amens" came in.

"And then we'll learn how to protect all colored folks 'cause everybody's life mean somethin' to them and they folks. Dat's why I shot dem white boys dis mornin'—so dey folks could know what colored peoples been feelin' for two hundred years or mo'. Dat's de only thing they understand."

"Why didn't you try to talk to 'em first, Mi?" someone asked loudly.

"What?" Jeremiah yelled. "We don talked—"

"'Til we blue in de face!" Pet Moore shouted, struggling to stand again. Something about the person's request to handle things in a more diplomatic manner infuriated Pet. "Shit!" he hollered. "All y'all know I done worked in dat damn sto' fu forty years, and I can tell you firsthand dat white folks ain't got no respect for colored folks. Dey ain't in'ersted in nothin' you got to say and no opinion in yo' head. Dey think we spose to be glad to follow them and dat God made it dat way. So talkin' to them ain't nothin' but a waste o' time."

"Now dat's de truf!" many affirmed.

"And anyway," Pet continued, standing next to Jeremiah like a bridegroom, "what chu gon say if you did talk to 'em? Huh?"

"All right, Docta!" Jeremiah encouraged.

"You gon tell 'em not to come to yo' house botherin' yo' folks no more? And they gon obey you?" Pet laughed in ridicule. "Shit!" he yelled again. "Dey really comin' for you and your folks now 'cause you think y'all equals and you know dey ain't gon have that!"

"Sho you right!" Jeremiah said.

"So stop bein' scared and listen to de man. Hear him all de way out befo you start judgin' what he sayin'."

Jeremiah envied Pet's eloquence and command of the crowd, but with what he was about to say, he welcomed all the help he could get.

"You don't go to a man lookin' fu respect if he done already showed you dat he don't respect you," Jeremiah explained.

"Uh-huh," many mumbled.

"And," Jeremiah emphasized, "you ain't got to disrespect his folks jes 'cause he disrespect yours. But you gotta show him, somehow, dat yo' folks mean somethin' to you, and you ain't gon continue to stand by and let him destroy them. If you do, what kinda example is you givin' yo' chillen? They spose to know how to take care o' families from watchin' us do it—not watchin' us kiss white folks' asses."

"Now you talkin'," Pet said. "Go 'head."

Jeremiah hesitated, then offered, "So here's what I'm proposin' we do." Most people sat still and peered at the old man until, like Moses on the mount of transfiguration, his face transformed. "Each household needs at least one gun." This wasn't far-fetched since most men in rural Money were hunters of one type or another. "And each family needs a hiding place. It's got to be somewhere you can get to quick."

"Is we 'bout to go to war?" a voice asked.

"We already at war and don't know it," Pet returned sharply. "When yo' enemy kill yo' people, you at war. Not knowin' this is why de enemy is guaranteed to win. He countin' on us neva knowin'."

Jeremiah appreciated Pet's expressed support. He never thought Pet would be so brave, but then again every man has his day, he told himself.

"We jes gotta be ready when they come, and believe me, they comin'," Jeremiah said.

"Why don't *you* fight 'em, Mi, since you de one killed 'em," a scared mother asked.

Miss Mary stepped forth suddenly, and said, "We got to fight together, sista! He shot dem men for all of us—not jes the Johnson family!" She was preaching a hedge of protection around her husband. Some of the men in the crowd seemed disturbed that a woman had taken the floor, but Miss Mary wasn't about to relinquish it until she had her say.

"We gotta start thinkin' collective instead o' individual. That's how they get us. When it come time fu us to stand together, we as separate as the fingers on a hand." Miss Mary held up her right hand and spread the fingers. "You can always destroy a person who stands alone, but a strong group o' people gon last a long time 'cause they gon take care o' one another. Dat's how we gotta be, y'all. We gotta stand together." She locked all ten fingers together tightly. "I woulda expected yo' menfolks to do what mine did. And we ain't gon ask fu no forgiveness 'cause ain't nothin' to forgive."

People weren't used to Miss Mary upholding the use of violence; that's why she commanded a listening ear greater than her husband.

"I ain't sayin' killin' is right. But I ain't sayin' it's always wrong neither. What I'm sayin' is dat when dey kill us, dey think dey doin' a favor to white people everywhere. So when we stand up, we gotta understand we doin' de same thang fu colored people. Amen?"

"Amen," the brave responded.

"I wuz proud of my men dis mornin'. They stood up like men oughta stand, and they kept they family together. These chillen wuz proud, too. We all wuz proud. And you oughta be proud."

Miss Mary dazzled the crowd with her charm and drama. Jeremiah's jealousy almost got the best of him when he thought of telling his wife to sit down and shut up, but she evoked from the crowd the enthusiasm needed to get his plan under way, so he remained quiet and grew humility.

"How we gon have any kinda pride in ourselves if every time white folks show up we get scared? That ain't no way to live!" Miss Mary paced the floor and shook her head. "We got jes as much right to live in peace as they do, and if we have to teach them that, then we'll do it. But I think y'all agree wit me on that point. Right now, we gotta find my grandbaby and try to make sure these white folks don't take no mo' colored chillen." She calmed and stepped back behind her husband. "Tell us yo' plan, baby."

Jeremiah didn't have time to sulk, so he said, "I want a committee of men willin' to help me find my grandboy. We gon comb dis county 'til we find where dem white folks took him."

No one volunteered. Then a few brave soldiers stepped forward. "Good," Jeremiah said. "We gon start lookin' soon as dis meetin' over."

"I'll go witcha," a woman's voice declared.

Jeremiah hadn't thought of the possibility of women on the search committee. "Um . . . well . . . maybe—"

"I don't see why not," Miss Mary affirmed loudly. "Anybody wanna help we'll take it. Ain't dat right, sweetie?"

"Uh . . . yeah. Come on," Jeremiah yielded reluctantly and decided he'd talk to his wife later. He then said, "We also need some watchmen who'll spread de word if they see any group of white folks comin' toward colored people's place. Yo' job will be to walk 'round and keep yo' eyes open."

"Now I can do that," several people said.

"Ella Mae, you take de names o' people and what they gon do so we can keep up with what we decide."

"Okay, Daddy," she said, and ran into the house to retrieve a notepad and pen. Upon returning, she announced, "I'm ready."

"All right. Now. I want every man to teach his wife and children twelve or over how to use a gun."

The crowd mumbled its reservations. Once again, Pet Moore came to the rescue. "Y'all betta teach 'em!" he told the men. "What they gon do if somebody come, and you ain't home?"

"That's a good point," a bass voice murmured.

Pet held his peace and waited for Jeremiah to finish what he had begun, clearly unaware of how he and Miss Mary, throughout the night, were continuously trampling on Jeremiah's already-wounded ego.

"I cain't promise none o' y'all what might happen in de next couple o' days, but we gotta be prepared for anything. One missin' child is enough, ain't it?" Jeremiah asked.

"Amen," people chimed although Jeremiah couldn't discern if their affirmation resulted from a newfound sense of unity or from the relief that the missing child wasn't their own.

"We can't let them catch us off guard. Soon as we get—"

"Granddaddy!" Ray Ray whispered loudly through a crack in the barn door. "Somebody white's comin'."

The crowd froze. Jeremiah motioned for Pet, Tiny, and Enoch to join him at the door. "Enoch, you go in de house and get my gun. Go out de back do' and wait. If I whistle, you come runnin' and shootin'. If I don't, jes be cool." He took a deep breath. "Pet, you keep de people calm. We don't want folks to get spooked and panic."

"Yessir," he said, and began to pacify the audience with empty assurances.

Jeremiah's trembling hands exposed the fear he was trying to hide. The only thing he could do was shove them in his pockets like an angry child.

The darkness made it impossible for him to identify the stranger, but, for some reason, he didn't sense danger. The man was practically in his face before he recognized Edgar Rosenthal.

"Evenin'," Jeremiah said cordially.

"Jeremiah." Rosenthal nodded.

Mr. Rosenthal dropped his eyes and bit his lower lip as though already dreading what he was about to say. Jeremiah relaxed his guard and waited.

"I heard about your meeting tonight, Jeremiah, and I'm sure it's pretty darn rude of me to come, but I need to tell you people something."

"Mr. Rosenthal, I've known you 'bout all my life, I guess, and in all that time, you ain't neva done me or mine no harm. But you comin' here tonight looks mighty strange to me," Jeremiah yielded honestly.

"As well it should, Jeremiah, but I knew this day was coming. I never knew when, and I prayed I'd never see it, but I knew it was coming."

Jeremiah didn't know exactly what Rosenthal was talking about, but he believed that if he waited a moment, clarity would arrive.

Rosenthal continued: "Let me get straight to the point."

Amen, Jeremiah thought.

"I've been telling whites around here that coloreds aren't going to tolerate their own annihilation long."

"What?" Jeremiah frowned.

"I knew coloreds were going to fight back at some point. It's the law of nature. Everybody wants to survive. Nobody believed me, but I knew."

"Okay, you right. But what chu come hyeah fu?" Jeremiah hadn't wanted to seem rude, but he didn't know how else to frame his question.

"To tell you that I'm not one of them. I was once, but I'm not now."

"I don't understand what you sayin', Mr. Rosenthal. I don't mean to be mean, but you jes as white as de other white folks 'round hyeah."

"That is certainly true, Jeremiah, but I don't agree with them. Especially on racial matters."

Pet Moore came to the barn door to make sure everything was all right. "You ain't gon believe this," Jeremiah whispered to him. Pet stayed and listened.

"You have every right and reason not to believe me," Rosenthal said, "but I'm really not like other whites around here. I came to see if I could help."

"What?" Jeremiah asked boldly. "You help? Us? We don't need yo' help, Mr. Rosenthal."

The white man smiled kindly, and said, "I do understand. I meant no harm and I hope I haven't offended any of you. That was not my intention in the least." He turned to leave.

"Jes a minute," Pet said abruptly. He whispered to Jeremiah, "I think he might be sincere. I don't know fu sho, but I get a feelin' he's tellin' the truth."

"So what!" Jeremiah offered through clenched teeth. "We can't let no white man convince us dat he's on our side. Is you crazy?"

"I ain't sayin' he's necessarily on our side. What I'm sayin' is dat I think we oughta hear him out. Everybody oughta hear him so everybody can decide fu theyself."

Pet's judgment had been sound thus far, Jeremiah decided, so he resolved to follow him a little further. "Fine. You wanna bring him in and let him talk to de whole crowd?"

"Yeah," Pet said. "Then we can ask them what they think. That's good leadership. It keeps you from carryin' de weight o' all the decisions."

"Fine," Jeremiah said again. The night was turning out to be much more than he had planned or imagined.

When Rosenthal walked through the barn door, the crowd began to murmur. Most of them knew him, in one capacity or another, but none were expecting to see him at the colored people's meeting.

"What is this?" a bold voice asked.

"Hold on, hold on," Pet Moore soothed. "Mr. Rosenthal here got somethin' he wanna say, and I think you wanna hear it."

"Thank you, Pet, Jeremiah," he acknowledged humbly. Then he glanced across the crowd and tried to return kindness to skeptical eyes. "I have no business here really—"

"Amen," Tiny belted.

"Come on, y'all. Ain't no need to disrespect de man," Miss Mary admonished.

"I understand your sentiment completely, and it's quite logical." Rosenthal clasped his seventy-year-old hands and proceeded. "But had I died tonight, my only regret would have been that I didn't come here and finally make peace with colored people."

The crowd relaxed a bit, and Rosenthal seized the moment. He cleared his throat and began, "Fifty years ago, something happened that changed my life forever. I've tried to ignore it, even to forget it altogether, but I can't."

The crowd's curiosity was now greater than its suspicion. Many still shifted nervously, but they held their peace and endured Rosenthal's memory.

"My daddy sent me to Harvard, up in Massachusetts. He had always dreamed of one of his son's boasting the Harvard diploma and coming back south to 'civilize these backward-ass whites' as he always called them. I was the chosen one. I had never been north before, and when I got to Cambridge, I was amazed at the beauty of the place. I suppose I was a bit anxious, too, for I wondered if my academic preparation here in Money was sufficient for eastern college rigor. Well, when classes started, I performed marvelously in everything except literature. I've always been a rather straightforward fellow, and when asked to interpret someone else's meaning in a poem or story, I always wanted to know why people didn't simply ask the author what he meant."

Rosenthal got a few unsolicited amens. This settled his nerves and compelled him to proceed. "Well, one day I was sitting on the yard, as we called it, trying desperately to understand what the hell *Hamlet* was about when a colored fellow approached me and introduced himself.

"'Good afternoon,' he said kindly.

"I was a bit disturbed, I must say, about seeing a colored fellow at Harvard. He was dressed as I was, so I could not relegate him to the janitorial staff. In hindsight, I'm sure I was rude and uninviting, but his persistent kindness peaked my curiosity. So I said, 'Yes?'

"'You're in my lit class,' he said softly, 'and I thought you might want to study together for the next exam.'

"My ignorance at the time was far greater than my kindness. I screamed, 'Hell no!' I am most ashamed, but it's important to represent the event as it occurred. Bear with me, and you'll understand why."

Some were getting restless, and others wondered how any of this was relevant to the issue at hand.

"The next day in class," Rosenthal continued as he excavated a handkerchief from his white shirt pocket and wiped the sweat covering his beet-red face, "our professor asked for a volunteer to explain the overall message of *Hamlet*. Well, of course I dared not raise my hand because I understood exactly nothing about the play and, indeed, I hoped some really brilliant fellow would rise and impart an interpretation that might get me closer to comprehending at least some aspect of the play. That's when the colored fellow rose and began to speak. Everyone turned around in shock, for simply being at Harvard was his privilege, we thought. Speaking in class was stretching that privilege too far. Not until later did I learn that his hand had been raised the entire time our professor was looking around. And since no white boy volunteered, our professor allowed the colored one to have his say. That was a moment in my life I shall never forget. His eloquence, boldness, and mastery of Elizabethan English dwarfed even the professor's.

> "'To be or not to be,' he quoted effortlessly, 'that is the question:
> Whether 'tis nobler in the mind to suffer
> The slings and arrows of outrageous fortune,
> Or to take arms against a sea of troubles,
> And by opposing end them. To die: to sleep;
> No more' and by a sleep to say we end
> The heart-ache, and the thousand natural shocks
> That flesh is heir to, 'tis a consummation
> Devoutly to be wish'd. To die, to sleep;
> To sleep: perchance to dream . . .'

"Then he explained: 'In this soliloquy, Shakespeare asks listeners to ponder the price of freedom. He warns that it carries an expensive bounty, yet seemingly encourages people to seek it nonetheless. "To be or not to be" is actually a question of what one is willing to sacrifice in order to achieve an abundant life. If one is going to "be," then one must be prepared to pay dearly for that conscious existence. If one possesses not the courage to "be," then one must surrender to a premature death of the spirit, which indeed, is worse than death itself. The few whose inner strength demands that they "be"—that they live free—will be remembered as those who took the risk "perchance to dream" . . .'

"When he took his seat, the room remained silent for several minutes. I was stunned, amazed, and angry that a colored boy was smarter than me. I understood more Shakespeare that day than the professor had taught all semester. But now I found myself in a conundrum. I couldn't respect a colored man's intelligence. That went against everything my Southern heritage had bestowed upon me. Yet I had no way to dismiss the sheer brilliance with which he spoke that afternoon.

"'Hey, you,' I called to him as we exited the classroom. 'Where you learn to read and analyze like that?'

"'From my grandfather,' he said proudly. 'He taught himself to read while yet a slave, and his only hope was that one of his children attend Harvard one day. I'm the lucky one, I suppose,' he cackled.

"'You're a smart boy,' I said with intent to insult.

"'No, I'm an intelligent young man,' he corrected, 'who is still willing to help you if you want it.'

"In my conceit, I wanted to deny his offer and refuse him the satisfaction of saying he had tutored a white man, but my poor grades forced me to accept. I had failed our first Shakespeare exam, but after studying with the colored fellow, I got a B on the second. He received an A on both. I should have been grateful, I know, but quite the opposite, I was angry beyond measure. My pride was wounded and my ego damaged, and I needed some way to repair them both. So I gathered a group of white boys from the class and we assaulted the colored fellow one night in the dark."

Miss Mary shook her head while others grunted their disapproval.

"I know I was wrong!" Rosenthal cried. "Every time we hit him, my stomach churned. He kept asking what he had done wrong, and we could never provide an answer. I didn't know any better."

"Yes, you did, Mr. Rosenthal. You *chose* not to do any better," Pet Moore offered indignantly.

Rosenthal's head fell like a guillotined criminal's. "You're right,

Pet," he surrendered. "I could have done better. Even then. But I had no dignity, no honor, no real knowledge. I just wanted that colored fellow to believe I was better than he was."

"Did y'all kill him?" Jeremiah asked.

"Not exactly. We returned to our rooms and went to bed, but my consciousness afforded me no peace. I was shaking under the sheets and tossing restlessly. Then, suddenly, I couldn't stand it any longer. I jumped out of bed, dressed quickly, and ran to his room where I found him barely breathing. Since no one wanted to dwell with a colored fellow, he occupied his room alone. I went there to apologize. I was prepared to confess my ways and to face any repercussions which ensued because of them, but when I entered his room and found him bleeding on the floor, I swore to God that if He let him live I would never mistreat colored people ever again. Through tears I promised God a transformation in me as I carried the young fellow to the campus infirmary. To my surprise, they were as ignorant as I was and refused to help him. My protestations fell on deaf ears. I eventually dismissed them and carried the colored fellow to a nearby hospital, where he was also rejected. Then I knew what to do." Rosenthal sighed heavily, remembering. "I carried the colored fellow three miles to the nearest colored hospital. I was afraid he had died somewhere during the transportation, but the colored doctors said he was alive, and they'd do what they could to sustain him. I collapsed in the waiting room and awakened at dawn. A doctor soon informed me that, sometime during the night, the young colored fellow began to hemorrhage, and they lost him an hour or so before dawn."

"Lawd have murcy!" people murmured in anguish. Most of them had never seen a white man cry, and certainly not about a Black man.

Rosenthal dabbed his tears with a handkerchief. "I swear I'm sorry!" he kept repeating. "I tried to fix it, truly I did, but the damage had already been done." He broke down and wept hard for a good three minutes. Upon recovery, he said, "That's why I'm here tonight. I owe that colored fellow something and, for fifty years, I've not been able to figure out how to pay."

"We don't need yo' guilt, sir," Ella Mae said. She thought of the colored fellow as one of her own boys, and she refused to forgive.

"I'm not offering you my guilt," Rosenthal said. "I'm trying to up-hold a responsibility. I graduated from Harvard partially because of that young colored fellow. He's the reason my family has had a mod-icum of privilege over the years. He sacrificed for me, and I destroyed him. Walking back to my dorm room, I prayed for forgiveness, but God wouldn't grant it. He kept telling me to fix it. *Me.* I kept asking Him to relieve my conscience and to allow me to move on, but the more I prayed, the more intense the pain became in my heart. If the colored fellow had only returned malice when I offered the same, I could have justified my abuse of him. Yet never did he show me any-thing but the highest character.

"I walked the streets of Cambridge a zombie, trying to figure out why God wouldn't release me from my bondage. In the coming weeks, I tried to forget about him, so I graduated the following spring and moved back to Money. But I've had nightmares at least twice a week for fifty years now."

"So now you want to help a colored boy so God can give you peace?" Ella Mae asked sarcastically.

"Ma'am, I dismissed the possibility of peace a very long time ago. I've just been too arrogant or racist to do what I knew was right. I want to do it now"—he paused—"just because it's right. All these years when whites have mistreated most of you in one way or an-other, I remained silent because I was afraid. I didn't want colored people to get power and treat us the way we've treated you.

"Now I'm too old to care about that. Maybe that's the price whites have to pay, I keep telling myself, for destroying every group of peo-ple we've ever encountered. If so, I'll pay it. It may be my last act, but I want to help colored people, for once, because it was a colored boy—excuse me, man—who kept me afloat when I was surely about to drown."

Edgar Rosenthal folded his arms and waited. He knew how

volatile such a moment would be, and for that courage alone, Jeremiah respected him.

"Would you step outside for a moment, please, Mr. Rosenthal?" Jeremiah asked, standing next to him.

"Certainly," Rosenthal said. "I understand if you people don't want my help. I understand perfectly."

Everyone held his peace until the aged white man stepped into the muggy Mississippi night.

Tiny shook his head and declared, "I don't trust him!"

"Me neither," a few others agreed.

"This ain't only about trust though," Pet Moore said and stood. "Do we need him is the question."

"Why we need a white man if white folks de enemy?" Tiny asked.

Pet Moore offered, "Everybody white ain't de enemy. Most of 'em is, dat's fu sho, but I believe God dwells in a few of 'em. Maybe Rosenthal is one."

"What?" Tiny screamed.

"Age has a way of forcing a man to see the truth of himself," Pet Moore claimed. "The older you get, you start realizin' dat ain't nothin' in de world absolute."

"What chu talkin' 'bout, Pet?" Tiny responded hastily.

They were almost face-to-face. "What I'm talkin' 'bout is human bein's, man. You cain't neva put all human bein's in one category, don't care which ones you talkin' 'bout. Like take colored folks for instance. Everybody colored in Sumter County heard 'bout dis meetin' tonight, but everybody colored sho ain't here."

"That's true," the crowd confirmed.

"But who wuz really expectin' everybody colored to show up? Y'all know well as I do dat jes 'cause you colored don't mean you stand fu colored people. It oughta, but it don't."

No one could refute his argument, and everyone could think of at least one colored family that wasn't represented at the meeting.

"So all I'm sayin' is dat when it come time to fight for right, who standin' and who ain't is usually a surprise, at least in a few cases. We all know how white folks is. Dat ain't no secret. But we gotta tell de truf 'bout how colored folks is, too."

"Amen," people chimed.

"Sometime de reason we don't stick together is 'cause we so busy tryin' to be like them and get what they got. We say we cain't stand white folks, but we sho do love the way they live. Now dat don't make a piece of sense, do it?"

Most folks remained silent, so Pet answered his own question. "Naw, dat don't make no sense. If it look like we might get some o' what they got, we do our best not to make them mad or upset so they won't ruin our chance of livin' like them. That's why other folks ain't here tonight. They too scared we gon mess up thangs for them. They don't want nobody to say they wuz fightin' white folks 'cause white folks got exactly what they been tryin' to get all they life. Ain't that funny? The one who hate us is de one we love?"

Again, no one responded.

"Well, dat's why I think we oughta think about takin' Mr. Rosenthal up on his offer. People change sometimes. Not often, but every now and then, a person really does change. Why did Mr. Rosenthal tell us all dat if he wasn't serious?"

"That's right," Miss Mary reinforced. "I can feel when people lyin' and I think he wuz speakin' from his heart. I ain't neva heard no white man say dat a colored man wuz de reason he made it. I think he's serious."

"Well, I don't!" Tiny said on behalf of the insurgents. "I think he heard we wuz meetin' and got scared colored folks wuz 'bout to start killin' white folks, so he came to see if he could find out what we wuz doin'."

"You sayin' Mr. Rosenthal is spyin' on us?" Enoch inquired.

"Dat's exactly what I'm sayin'!" Tiny yelled. "You didn't think white folks wuz gone let colored folks meet in Money without sayin' or doin' somethin', did you?" Tiny was looking at Enoch although addressing the entire crowd. "But de real question is how did he know about de meetin' in de first place?"

People murmured and offered guesses, but, in the end, no one knew for sure.

"Let's ask him," Tiny suggested, "and if he tell de truf, I might believe he's genuine."

"Fine," Pet Moore agreed. "But the man's not on trial, so let Jeremiah ask him and let's be done with this."

They brought Rosenthal back into the barn, subjecting him to the stares and frowns of the doubtful, yet his countenance never altered.

"Mr. Rosenthal," Jeremiah said cautiously, "we wuz wondering how you knowed 'bout de meetin' tonight?"

Rosenthal smiled, and said, "I had a feeling someone would ask me that." He paused. "Your Jerry told me."

Colored folk went berserk. They started declaring Rosenthal an agent of the devil, and Tiny affirmed that either Rosenthal leave or he would.

"I can prove it," he said calmly. "I know precisely why my answer has disturbed you so greatly."

"Then prove it," Tiny challenged.

Rosenthal began, "I often go for long walks in the evenings simply to enjoy a nice summer breeze if I can find one, and today I stumbled upon a clearing in the middle of Chapman's land. It's a beautiful little oasis, almost like a Garden of Eden, right in the midst of the forest."

Everybody knew where Rosenthal meant, but no one was willing to assist his effort to prove that Jerry had relayed the message.

"I was thinking about Sutton, the colored boy at Harvard, wishing I could reverse time and do the right thing, when I heard someone say, 'There is something you can do.' I stumbled in fear and convinced myself that my old age was the reason I was hearing things, but the voice came again louder, and said, 'Don't miss this chance. It'll never come again.' I couldn't deny it this time.

"'Who are you? What do you want?' I asked in utter trepidation.

"'I am Jerry, the son of Jeremiah and Mary Johnson,' he said proudly. Then he explained, 'I know what happened at Harvard. That was a terrible thing you boys did.'

"'I swear I'm sorry,' I screamed in fear of damnation.

"His emollient voice banished my fears when he said, 'There is something you could do right here.'

"'What?' I pleaded.

"'The colored folks are having a meeting tonight,' Jerry said. 'Go and stand with them, come what may. My father could use your help. You have connections and information that will assure their success both in finding my nephew and in gaining the courage, finally, to fight for themselves.'

"'Will your people believe me?' I asked with great uncertainty.

"'If they don't, tell them dead don't mean gone. Then they'll know.'"

"Oh my God!" Jeremiah screeched. "He's tellin' the truth, y'all! Jerry spoke to me earlier this morning and said those very words— dead don't mean gone. I didn't know who would believe me so I kept it to myself. Oh my God!" he repeated.

Miss Mary was both elated and confused. She couldn't understand why Jeremiah hadn't mentioned something so important, yet she was thankful Rosenthal's sincerity was being corroborated.

"Ain't no way he coulda knowed dat," Jeremiah said confidently. "He's tellin' de truf. Believe him."

Even Tiny appeared convinced. He certainly didn't celebrate the revelation, but his quandary had been resolved. There was nothing to do now except welcome him, Tiny thought.

"I am willing to do whatever I can," Rosenthal said again. "I just want to walk the earth as a righteous man for once in my life, and I pray you folks give me the opportunity to do so. I had it once and failed, but now I'm ready."

Pet Moore chuckled. "De Lawd is a funny God, ain't He? He got angels everywhere, willin' to talk to anybody. I'm glad His ways ain't our ways."

"I'm glad, too," Miss Mary said.

A penitent Rosenthal offered, "Then I must be the gladdest of all."

"I say we welcome Mr. Rosenthal," Miss Mary suggested heartily.

"I second that motion," Pet Moore said.

"All right, all right," Tiny murmured. Then he said, "I didn't mean no harm, Mr. Rosenthal. This is just a sensitive issue, and—"

"Please don't apologize, sir. Your skepticism was well warranted."

"Fine. Let's get back down to business," Jeremiah said, offering Edgar Rosenthal a chair.

Rosenthal was still not fully embraced by everyone, and he knew it, but their reservation was a small price to pay, he decided, to a people whom, for fifty years, he had dismissed. His white hair looked ashy against the sea of brown and black faces in the barn that night although most concluded that Rosenthal had undoubtedly been handsome in his day.

Jeremiah was anxious to see just how and when he would prove useful. His submission was a bit unsettling, for they had never witnessed a white man relinquish privilege in hopes of helping colored folks. Miss Mary told Ella Mae that Rosenthal's presence confirmed that "You cain't neva tell 'bout God."

"We need two more committees," Jeremiah announced. "One of those committees I'm callin' a prayer group. The job of the prayer group is to keep us spiritually grounded. Whoever's on dis committee should meet every evenin' and go befo' de Throne o' Grace to make sho we always in de will o' God. If you cain't get no prayer through, don't get on dis committee," Jeremiah half joked.

"Amen," others returned seriously.

Miss Mary made herself the chairperson of the Prayer Posse and seven or eight others included their names. "Billy Joe Henderson," she said, chuckling, "you on dis committee, too."

This was the only announcement all night to be received unanimously. Whether folks loved the Lord or didn't believe in Him at all, they went to church expressly to hear Billy Joe wail. Miss Mary always said that church would be empty were it not for Billy Joe's song and prayer. He had a high tenor voice that drew tears from eyes too weak to hold them, and the pleas he offered to heaven sounded more genuine than any of the other deacons'. "Guide me over, thou great Jehovah! Pilgrim through this barren land!" he chirped and the congregation repeated his lyrics with joy and gladness. Sometimes folks couldn't tell whether he was using natural voice or falsetto, but they didn't care. His runs delighted their souls. That's why most of Money's colored church populace assumed Billy Joe a little closer to heaven than the rest of them.

"Y'all might wanna meet at de church house since it's a central location. Y'all decide when," Jeremiah assigned. "Now de last committee is a real special one. We need people on dis committee who work in white folks' houses. I'm callin' dis de spy committee."

Moans and grunts emitted from the skeptical, and shifting bodies illustrated people's discomfort with the idea.

"Now hold on," Tiny assisted although clearly wary of the notion. "Let Mi explain befo' y'all get all worked up. I'm sho it ain't what you thinkin'."

Jeremiah was tired of tiptoeing around cowardly colored folks, but he pressed on. "I was thinkin' that some' o' y'all who cook and clean and shouffer for white folks could keep yo' ears open jes in case you hear somethin'." Actually Jeremiah wanted something much more intensely surreptitious, but he noticed quickly that folks weren't nearly as courageous as he had hoped.

"I can do that," a few women mumbled.

Jeremiah chuckled at their struggle to remain loyal to white benefactors while trying to stand with colored folks against them. "Fine," he offered, and relinquished the specificities of his original thought. "Mr. Rosenthal, you be on dat committee, too."

"It would be my pleasure," he said boldly. "I'll find out everything I can." A hush fell over the crowd as though people expected him to say more, so he added, "You can trust me. You'll see."

Eleven

THE CROWD LEFT, WHISPERING SOFT SALUTATIONS AS THOUGH suspecting a lurking foe. The search committee sneaked into half the barns in the county before they agreed, long after midnight, to resume the search the next morning.

"Y'all didn't find him?" Miss Mary asked Jeremiah, who undressed in the dark.

"No, ma'am, we didn't. Ain't no tellin' where dey got dat boy," Jeremiah said, defeated.

Miss Mary reached for her husband's hand. His touch was cold, but she was determined to soothe his fretting heart.

"I feel so . . ."

"Shhhhhhh," she hissed comfortingly and pulled Jeremiah onto the bed. "Just lay right here and don't say nothin'." Miss Mary placed

Jeremiah's right hand on her left breast and embraced him fully. "We still got each other, old man. Dat's how we done made it dis far, and dat's how we gon make it on."

Jeremiah stroked the left side of his wife's face, loving the wrinkles and grooves as testimony of the longevity of colored love, and he knew at that moment he wouldn't take anything for the years he and Miss Mary had endured. At one point, years ago, he had hoped she might drop some of the weight that mounted after the birth of each child, but now, staring at her round form, he realized how much more he loved this woman than the one he had married.

"How's yo' wound?" she whispered, touching his side gently.

"Oh, it's fine. Still a little sore, but nothin' to worry about. You fixed me up good, old lady."

He kissed her cheek.

"Jes hold me, old man," she sighed, wrapping her husband's wiry frame in her wide, thick, safe arms.

"Yous all right wit me, old woman," Jeremiah smiled. "I don't know how all dis gon turn out, but I'm sho is glad I got you right next to me."

Miss Mary met his puckered lips with her own.

"We jes gotta keep on believin', old man. I speck I oughta get word to Possum tomorrow. We cain't put it off forever." She looked to Jeremiah for confirmation. He had hoped this decision would remain unnecessary, but he knew Miss Mary was right.

"Dat girl gon have a fit," he whimpered, shaking his head sadly. "She done sent him down here to stay wit us, and I done let—"

"*You* done let?" Miss Mary repeated, sitting up in bed. "I thought we stand together as a family?"

"You know what I mean, honey," Jeremiah said dismissively.

"Naw, I don't." Miss Mary's tone was terse. "Like tonight at de meetin'. Every time I said anything, you looked at me like I wuzn't suppose to say nothin'."

"That ain't what I meant, Mary. You jes seem to be takin' over sometimes and—"

"So I wuzn't spose to have no opinion on nothin'? I wuz spose to jes grin and agree with everything you said?"

"No." Jeremiah joined Miss Mary in the upright position. "But you is spose to be my helpmeet. I'm de husband."

"I know what you is, man!" Miss Mary spoke a little too loudly. "But dat don't mean I'm spose to stop bein' me. I was jes tryin' to help convince other folks dat—"

"I had everything under control, woman. I ain't mad at you sayin' stuff, but maybe you shoulda been quiet a little more often so that—"

"So that what? So people could walk out de barn before they understood anything? That's exactly what wuz 'bout to happen." The same wrinkles Jeremiah loved moments earlier now stood in defiance to his words.

Jeremiah breathed deeply and relaxed onto the feather pillow. "I know. I jes wanted to be de big dog, I guess. I'm sorry."

"Now dat's better." Miss Mary smiled and kissed his cheek. "I ain't neva yo' enemy, man. Neva. Sometimes we don't see eye to eye, but when you start fightin' folks be clear dat I'm on yo' side, even when we disagree."

"I know, baby. You done put up wit me near 'bout fifty years, so believe me I know you wit me. Sometimes I git a li'l beside myself, but I'd give my life fu ya."

Miss Mary cackled. "You done already done dat, fool."

"You have, too, you fine-lookin' colored woman," Jeremiah mumbled in the sexiest voice he could feign.

The two held each other tightly. In their silence, they tried to imagine where Clement was and what Billy might be doing to him. In his mind's eye, Jeremiah saw several white men beating him as the boy's blood splattered their clothes. He was screaming, "I didn't do nothin'!" although to no avail. When Jeremiah heard Clement's arm break, he shivered and erased the thought from his mind. Miss Mary saw Billy force Clement to his knees and make him do things no child should experience. Then they stripped the boy naked. "Dear Jesus," was all she knew to say. Both elders feared, although neither was willing to admit, that Clement might already be gone. They had lived far too long in Mississippi to convince themselves that whites had miraculously evolved. Quite the opposite—white folk had been consistent in terms of Black degradation, and they knew that Clement's youth would only make Billy and the others more anxious to continue the tradition. But, even against the probable, they had to believe. Too many people were risking their lives. Too many were standing with the Johnsons for them not to retain at least a smidgen of hope, Jeremiah told himself, and Miss Mary knew she couldn't lead others in prayer if her faith were weak. So, against the odds, against history, against Sheriff Cuthbert's nature, they had to believe. When sleep came in fretful drifts, the couple maintained their embrace, hoping desperately that, indeed, Sunday would bring the resurrection.

The next morning, the search committee gathered at 6:45 on Jeremiah's front porch. Hungry for a victory, the men sat anxiously as the Johnsons ate biscuits, smothered squirrel, and fried potatoes. Enoch and Jeremiah emerged, praying that Clement would be found before Miss Mary had a chance to notify Possum.

"Let's go, boys," Jeremiah instructed like a lieutenant headed for battle.

Enoch wanted the victory more for his father than himself. Having gathered half the colored population of Money, Jeremiah's reputation depended upon his ability to make such a gathering, ultimately, fruitful. Enoch didn't want his father remembered as one who had a good idea, but in the end, no power to bring it to pass. For the moment, the other men seemed full of hope and expectancy, but each day promised to drain their adrenaline if Clement wasn't found soon.

"Where we gon start lookin', Mi?" they asked.

"We gon check out the barns we missed last night," Jeremiah said. "Then, if we ain't found him, de Good Lawd gon lead us."

Four hours later, at the edge of The Sacred Place, an exhausted Enoch said, "Ain't nowhere else to look, Daddy. We done checked some barns twice and still ain't no sign o' Clement."

Jeremiah stared across the clearing. "What they done to my grandson?" he asked, hoping Jerry might reappear and provide the answer. But Jerry never came.

Several men expressed their sympathy and went home to prepare for church.

"Come on, y'all," Enoch said to those remaining. "We may as well go home, too. Ain't nothin' else we can do out here."

Approaching the shack, Enoch could tell something was wrong. The wind began to blow wildly although there were no rain clouds in sight. The old peach tree in the front yard waved its limbs frantically as though begging the men to stay away.

"Daddy!" Enoch murmured as he began to run.

"Wait, boy!" Jeremiah called after him, but Enoch never heard the warning. The other men followed in triangular fashion like migrating birds.

Enoch slowed when he reached the barn. "Daddy, take two wit chu and y'all go 'round de back o' de house," he whispered quickly, "you otha two stay here. Ricky, you and Willie come wit me."

The latter three heard white voices as they slithered onto the front porch. "Shhh," Enoch motioned with his right index finger over his protruding black and pink lips. They lay still and listened.

"So you fuckin' niggers think you can kill white men and git away with it?" Cecil cackled. "Well, you're wrong!" he screamed.

"Take your time, Cecil," one of his comrades said. "You don't want this to be over too soon. Spoil the fun."

Enoch raised his head just enough to see the three white men bunched together in the Johnson living room. Sarah Jane and Chop were huddled beside Miss Mary and Ella Mae, but Enoch couldn't see Ray Ray anywhere.

"Now," Cecil said, "it's important that you know why we gotta kill ya." He had one eye closed as though searching deeply for understanding. "Y'all jes don't know how to 'preciate good, decent white folks. We let you work our fields, buy in our store, fish in our rivers—" he paused and shook his head sadly "—and you still don't

159

recognize how good we are to ya." He began to pace. "That's why now"—he raised his gun and pointed it toward Sarah Jane's weeping eyes—"you gotta die."

Enoch, Willie, and Ricky burst through the front door and planted their rifles in the white men's backs before they could turn around.

"Praise God," Miss Mary slurred toward heaven.

"Drop your guns!" Enoch demanded. The white men laughed. "I said drop your guns!" he yelled louder.

"No, you drop yours," said the white men who stepped from behind the front door.

"Shit!" Enoch murmured. He, Willie, and Ricky laid their rifles on the floor.

"You didn't think I was stupid enough to come without backup, did ya?" Cecil laughed. "Of course not."

The other white men confiscated the abandoned shotguns and smiled as Cecil continued his speech. "See, that's what I mean. You people can't think. And you want to vote? Why? Don't you see that you'd mess up everything if y'all started makin' decisions about who governs you?"

Enoch didn't hear a word Cecil said. He was calculating how, miraculously, he could free his folks from their seemingly impending doom. There had to be a way, he kept telling himself, but his fury clouded his thinking faculty. As long as Cecil kept talking, he was granted more time to find that solution.

"The Bible says in the beginning God made Adam." Cecil stood directly in front of Enoch and demeaned him. "Now how many colored boys you know named Adam? Huh?"

Just be cool, Enoch told himself. It can't end like this.

"That's how you know the white man was given dominion over everything and everybody. His job is to keep things on earth in order. I don't like it any more than you do, but now I understand why God set it up this way. You people done gone and killed three o' my cousins for absolutely no reason at all. We jes wanted to talk to the boy. That's all. Just wanted to see exactly what he said to Catherine. Nobody was gonna hurt him. But now you done messed up everything. See? Then we white folks are left to clean it up."

From the corner of his eye, Enoch thought he saw something flash past the west window. He tried to remain inconspicuous, but his adrenaline was flowing faster than his mind. He blinked several times, attempting to calm himself, then saw Ray Ray peep his head above the base of the window.

"Oh my God!" Miss Mary groaned.

She must have seen Ray Ray, too, Enoch thought. Then Ray Ray appeared again, this time with his finger over his mouth, urging his parents to remain acquiescent and to endure Cecil patiently. Enoch couldn't ascertain exactly what was going on, but he definitely liked it.

Cecil was too self-absorbed to notice Enoch's nervous excitement. "You can't go around killin' innocent white folks!" he preached. "Everything you have came from us! Your jobs, your homes, your food . . . everything. Don't you see? You're biting the hand that's feeding you. That's why we have to take care of you and teach you right from wrong. If we didn't, you coloreds would fuck up the whole world and nobody, including you, would have anywhere decent to live."

Cecil and the other white men began pushing the Johnson family, along with Ricky and Willie, through the squeaky screen door with rifles pointed at them from every direction. They stepped off the porch slowly, trying to give God time to do something, anything to protect them from what Cecil had in mind.

Midway between the house and the wagon, they heard Jeremiah say, "Wooo there!"

Everybody froze.

"What the hell?" Cecil mumbled.

"I don't know!" his comrades murmured, searching for the source of the voice.

"Ha-ha-ha!" Jeremiah laughed as all eyes, black and white, looked for him.

The white men grabbed the nearest colored victims and pressed the barrel tips of their shotguns against their heads.

"We'll blow their heads off, you old nigger muthafucker!" Cecil said. "So just come out slowly and—"

"Oh I ain't gon worry too much," Jeremiah sassed and appeared from behind the house with his arm around a proud Ray Ray. "'Cause see if you kill my folks, you and all yo' people gon die befo' de sun go down."

By the time Jeremiah finished his statement, colored people appeared like apparitions, armed and ready to fight. Some came from the corner of the old shack, some from the opposite side of the wagon, and several from every side of the barn. The whites were outnumbered at least ten to one.

"You jes cain't neva tell 'bout what a colored man might do to save his family. See, dat's where y'all always go wrong." Jeremiah was the preacher now. "You think you know us, when really you don't know a goddamn thing 'bout colored people. You think de colored man ain't nothin' but a workhorse. He ain't got no feelins, so his heart don't hurt. But one day, and one day real soon, you gon learn dat colored people love they own jes like you do, and we'll fight a bear to protect our younguns. But for now, jes let my people go, and you can go on home in peace. Wouldn't that be nice?"

Jeremiah smiled, showing his few remaining teeth, and winked at Cecil.

"Goddamnit!" Cecil muttered. He hadn't intended to admit failure to Billy—who would surely be furious that Cecil hadn't obeyed him—but now that admission was imminent.

"Now ain't no need in you fellows tryin' to figure out how to kill us all 'cause it's a whole lot more o' us than you. Really, we coulda killed you, but we a God-fearin' people, and we don't get no pleasure out o' destroyin' nobody." Jeremiah hobbled on his cane until he stared Cecil Love in the face. The laughter subsided. "Git away from my house and from my people. I got one aim, and dat's to find my grandson, and unless you 'bout to tell me where he is"—Jeremiah clenched his teeth—"I suggest you git de hell away from here rat now."

Cecil's face flushed bloodred. "You gon pay for this, nigger," he whispered hatefully. "I swear to God . . . you gon pay for this."

Jeremiah grinned. "My granddaddy used to say 'Be careful how you treat others, 'cause dat's exactly how God's gon treat you—one day.' Did yo' granddaddy tell you this, too?"

The frustrated white men drove away angrily. Before the dust could settle, shouting and hand clapping praised the watchmen who had sent word for others to come the moment they spotted Cecil's truck in the distance.

"Daddy, I thought today was gon be my last," Enoch confessed exasperatedly, patting Jeremiah on the shoulder.

"Well, I'm sho glad it wunnit, son!" he giggled. Jeremiah grabbed Miss Mary's hand, and said, "Everybody listen to me for a minute. Don't let yo' guard down jes 'cause we won a li'l victory. White folks is too arrogant to let us think we ever beat them, so you gotta be ready when they come back again. But Lawd knows I'm grateful y'all wuz here today. This what happens when colored folk stand together!"

The crowd smiled.

"H-h-h-how you know d-d-d-dey comin' b-b-b-b-back, Gr-rrrrraandy?" Chop asked.

Jeremiah knelt next to his grandson, but spoke loudly enough for everyone to hear. "It's sorta like what happened when God kicked de devil out o' heaven, son. The devil been mad about it every since. His biggest problem in de first place is dat he thinks he's God, but God keeps showin' him he ain't. So he git madder and madder every time he try to beat God and lose. He cain't accept defeat. Dat's how you know he's comin' back."

Twelve

THE JOHNSONS KNEW THEIR VICTORY DID NOT EQUAL THE end of the war, for Clement was still nowhere to be found. Yet the solidarity of colored citizens gave many hope while a more strategic plan was being formulated.

After church, the family ate dinner in silence. Enoch worried that the earlier display of unity was the exception to the rule of how Black folk stood together in Money, and Miss Mary waited for God to do whatever He had promised. The children, proud and skeptical, theorized that Black folk, for the first time in history, might actually overcome. They dreamed different scenarios of colored liberation although the denouement was the same—coloreds laughing and loving boldly and whites learning to do likewise.

After supper, Jeremiah sent Enoch to tell the watchmen to be especially alert. The whites were coming, he was told to reinforce strongly, and colored folks couldn't afford to be caught off guard.

When Enoch returned, he and the search committee—larger now after people saw its power—crossed the railroad tracks again and continued hunting for Clement. They asked every white person they encountered, "Have you seen him? Were you there?" Most returned slurs and insults, which didn't deter Enoch, but occasionally a sympathetic white eye gave them hope that someone might talk. They never did.

Meanwhile, Miss Mary told Ella Mae, "Girl, let's git dese dishes cleaned up and git on over to town. I guess I betta call Possum and tell her what's done happened." She was scraping leftover food particles into the garbage pail. "Dat girl gon have a fit."

"Don't worry, Momma. Everything gon be all right," Ella Mae reassured.

"I don't know, chile. I don't know. Them white boys left here mighty mad. If they ain't killed him yet—"

"Don't say that, Momma! Clement gon be all right. I jes know he is."

The two cleaned the dishes, wiped the tabletop, and swept the floor while humming lamentations and pleas to a God who, as Miss Mary complained, was mighty quiet lately.

"Come on, Ella Mae." She sighed. "We cain't put it off no longer." The two retrieved their hats and pocketbooks. "Chillen, y'all stick close to yo' granddaddy and mind whatever he say."

"Yes, ma'am." they said.

"Pick up a few menfolk from the search committee down the road," Jeremiah insisted. "Y'all strong, but don't be crazy. You might need a little protectin'."

Ella Mae agreed.

"You jes get some rest, old man," Miss Mary said, "so that wound can finish healin'. We'll be back soon as we can."

They left Sarah Jane and Chop standing at the screen, whispering.

"Wh-wh-what do you ththink ththey d-d-did wit Clllement?"

"I don't know," Sarah Jane returned irritably, toying with the pink ribbon in her hair.

"I b-b-b-bet thththey t-t-took him out in d-d-de wwwoods and b-beat him up," Chop guessed, hoping to inspire Sarah Jane to share her thoughts with him.

"I don't know, and I don't care!" she lied.

Chop missed the hint. "I b-b-bet thththey b-b-beat him rrreal b-b-bad."

"Just shut up, boy! Okay?" Sarah Jane yelled. "I don't wanna talk about it and I don't wanna hear what chu think. Just leave me alone!"

"Sssssorry," Chop slurred.

Sarah Jane huffed. "I didn't mean to scream, Chop. I jes . . ." She felt emotion flood her eyes. "I'm tryin' to think good things, and you're sayin' bad stuff."

"I w-w-uz jes tryin' to thththink what thththey mighta d-d-did," he explained slowly, apologetically.

"I know, Chop," Sarah Jane said. "But you makin' me more nervous. Jes be quiet 'til we hear somethin' else. Okay? Please."

On the way to town, Miss Mary hummed, "Precious Lord, take my hand! Lead me on, let me stand! I am tired, I am weak, I am worn! Through the storm, through the night, lead me on to the light, take my hand, precious Lord and lead me on." Ella Mae rocked to the rhythm, guessing that, as the next family matriarch, she'd better learn all of Miss Mary's survival tactics. Bouncing with the wagon, Ella Mae glanced at her intermittently, knowing she had much growing to do before she could fill Miss Mary's enormous shoes.

"Momma, we sho need God to sho up soon, huh?"

Miss Mary frowned. "Sho up? Girl, God done come and gone!"

"When?" Ella Mae asked. "I ain't seen Him, and Clement still missin', so it seem like to me God ain't come yet."

"Oh He done come!" Miss Mary testified. "You didn't see Him today?" She looked at Ella Mae.

"No, ma'am, I guess I didn't."

"Aw come on, daughter!" Miss Mary chided. "You wuz standin' right next to me."

"Huh?"

"God comes in many different ways, baby," she explained. "When Jeremiah and de watchin' committee showed up and saved us, dat wuz God."

"Don't get me wrong," Ella Mae cautioned, "I'm sho is grateful they came, but when God come, I expect somethin' much bigger'n that."

"Be careful, honey, be careful, be careful," Miss Mary sang. "What happened today wuz big! If God hadn't come, we'd be starin' Him in de face right now! See, God comin' is another way o' sayin' dat people got courage. Really, we don't neva have to ask God to come 'cause He always here. What we got to do is get bold enough to be Him. Dat's when God come!"

"Sound like you sayin' we God?"

"Sho we God! You didn't know dat? God is everythang and everybody, chile. And anybody bold enough can be God. So, you see, God done already come today. De Bible warn dat He comes like a thief in de night. If you ain't careful, you'll miss Him every time!" Miss Mary threw her head back, laughing.

"But if we God, then why don't we change de world?"

"Yea, why don't we!" Miss Mary posed. Then she answered her own question. "Fear. That's why. We too scared to believe dat we got de power to do much o' anythang. I'm talkin' 'specially 'bout colored folks 'cause white folks is clear they God. They think de whole universe belongs to 'em, and they'll kill you over it. Slavery ruined colored peoples. It made us think that they God wuz de only God. But see I'm here to tell you dat anybody can be God if you ain't scared to be."

"But I thought you said God didn't have no color or no race?"

"What color is courage, baby? Anybody can have that. You jes gotta be willin' to live or die for it. And whoever willing to stand when everybody else is too scared is gon look mighty divine."

Ella Mae nodded.

"So get you a new set o' eyes, girl, so you can see God when God come."

Miss Mary resumed singing, introducing Ella Mae to a few songs she had never heard. At one point, she sang, "Low down the chariot, let me ride! Low down the chariot, let me ride! My mother's on the chariot, let me ride!" Ella Mae opened her mouth to ask what the song meant, but Miss Mary's waving right hand suggested she shouldn't. Instead, she hummed along, the best she could, promising herself to ask for explanations later.

Using the telephone at Cuthbert's was, of course, out of the question, so Miss Mary and the others traveled the extra five miles to Bailey's General Store in Greenwood. Mr. Bailey was a kind man, allowing the poor to purchase items on credit whenever necessary, but the woman behind the counter had the nastiest disposition Miss Mary ever encountered. She hated most the way the woman looked at her, as though colored people should thank her for the air they breathe. Regardless of how much kindness Miss Mary extended, the woman always treated her with contempt. She was the only person Miss Mary called "Heffa" and never asked God for forgiveness. Miss Mary hoped she wouldn't be there.

When they arrived, the women tied the mules to the post in front of Bailey's store and the men encircled the wagon like angels protecting the Ark of the Covenant. Miss Mary told them, "We'll be right back."

She grabbed Ella Mae's hand and said, "Come on, chile. Let's get this over with," as she led the way.

When she saw the nasty attendant, she prayed internally, *Lord, give me strength* and said politely, "Excuse me, ma'am."

The woman looked past Miss Mary and asked another white lady standing behind her, "May I help you, ma'am?"

The second woman smiled and stepped around Miss Mary to the counter. "Yes, thank you," she sneered. "I appreciate your kindness and your prompt attention. I need . . ."

Miss Mary asked God to keep her calm and pleasant. The thought of socking both women in the mouth crossed her mind, but she let it go when she remembered why she was there.

After the patron exited the store haughtily, the lady attendant frowned at Miss Mary, and asked rudely, "What do you want?"

"How do you do, ma'am?" Miss Mary returned.

The clerk scowled, and hollered, "Do you want somethin', gal?"

Miss Mary collected herself, and asked, "Is Mr. Bailey here?"

"Naw, he ain't here. And he ain't comin' today."

"Okay," Miss Mary said slowly. "How much do you charge to make a collect call?"

"Fifty cents," she said nastily.

"Fifty cents," Miss Mary screeched. "It's only twenty-five cents at—"

"Then you go there, nigger!" The lady was perfectly content in her belligerence.

Of course she's overcharging me, Miss Mary thought, *but don't make a scene*. "Very well. Here's fifty cents." She held out the money, and the white woman snatched it from her hand.

"Phone's over there." She pointed in no particular direction.

"Thank you." Miss Mary also thanked God He didn't let her whip the white lady's ass like she wanted to.

Walking to the back wall, she retrieved Possum's phone number from her pocketbook. The white woman at the counter never stopped staring. "I paid my money," Miss Mary murmured in disgust.

Turning her back to the skinny, pale lady, Miss Mary dialed the operator with an index finger almost too thick to fit the number hole. She managed, however, and when, after five rings, no one answered, Miss Mary feared she'd have to repeat the process again the next day. Just as she was about to hang up, Possum answered.

"Will you accept a collect call from Mary Johnson?"

"Yes ma'am, I will."

"Hi, baby!" Miss Mary practically screamed.

"Hi, Momma!" Possum said. "Is everything all right? You ain't neva called me on no Sunday. What Clement 'nem up to?"

Miss Mary didn't know where to start. Her long pause heightened Possum's suspicion. "Momma?"

"Uh . . . yes, baby, we all doin' jes fine. How're things with you?"

"Oh, I'm fine. Jes workin' hard everyday. These white folks think a Black woman don't love nothin' more than washin' and ironin' they dirty draws. But it keeps a roof ova my head. How you been?"

"Fine, fine," Miss Mary lied anxiously. "I . . . um . . . jes wanted to check up on you."

"On a Sunday afternoon?"

"You know how I am." Miss Mary chuckled darkly. "Just thought about you so I thought—"

"What's wrong, Momma?" Possum asked seriously.

"Oh, it ain't nothin' to go frettin' over. It's jes that—"

"Momma, tell me!" Possum spoke louder. "Is Clement all right?"

Miss Mary couldn't postpone the truth any longer. "I need to tell you somethin', baby, but hear me out. Don't go gettin' upset befo you hear everything."

"Is my baby dead, Momma?" Possum cried.

"No, no. He ain't dead." Miss Mary prayed she was telling the truth. "Here's what happened . . ."

She relayed the details of the past few days but still avoided telling Possum about Clement. She even bought extra time by retelling Mr. Rosenthal's story.

"Well, I told Clement not to go down there, bowin' and shufflin' like no coon," Possum boasted. "Time out for all that demeaning crap."

"Amen," Miss Mary appeased. "But . . . um . . ."

"But what, Momma? Is everybody okay? I feel like you ain't tellin' me somethin'."

"Well, sweetie . . . see . . . when de white men tied up me and Ella Mae . . . dey took Clement."

Miss Mary closed her eyes in preparation for Possum's wail. "Momma! What chu mean? Did they kill my baby? Where is he?" she yelled.

"Calm down, baby, jes . . . jes calm down." Miss Mary was losing control of the conversation. "We don't know exactly where dey took him, honey. We think he's all right though. Yo' Daddy—"

"Where is my son!" Possum hollered.

"We don't quite know, baby, but we lookin' for him. All de colored people in Money is lookin' for him. You'd be so proud of how de people—"

"Momma!" Possum sobbed. "Have they killed my baby?"

Miss Mary dropped the façade. "We hope not, Possum, but we ain't sho." Her heavy sigh lifted the weight of dread from her heart. "Thangs been real crazy 'round here. Yo' Daddy and brother killed three o' de white men who tried to break into de house. They wuz de sheriff's brothers."

"Killed em? What? Daddy and Enoch killed some white men?" Possum asked, in shock and disbelief.

"They didn't mean to. They wuz jes protectin' us. De men started breakin' de do' down and Jeremiah knowed it was gon be us or them."

"Oh my God!" Possum groaned.

"I know, baby, I know. We wuz tryin' to git Clement back befo' we had to trouble you, but . . . ."

"But what, Momma?" Possum inquired sternly.

". . . but he's still missin'. And, truthfully, we don't know what mighta done happened to him. But, honey, we serve a God who sits high and looks low—"

Possum ignored the religious rhetoric. "I'm on my way, Momma," she said resolutely, and hung up.

There was so much more Miss Mary had wanted to say, but now it all seemed irrelevant. Walking back to the wagon, her strong, sassy strut deteriorated into a limp similar to Billie Faye's toward the end.

That's how Ella Mae knew the conversation hadn't gone well. "It's gon be all right, Momma," she consoled, after Miss Mary turned the wagon and headed for home.

"I didn't want Possum back under these circumstances," Miss Mary lamented.

"Sometimes God works in mysterious ways," Ella Mae reminded her. "Ain't that what you always say?"

Miss Mary nodded. "Un-huh."

On Monday, Edgar Rosenthal entered Cuthbert's General Store without much notice. In his later years, he avoided public places at all costs, having tired of stale exchanges and narrow-minded whites whose place on earth he could not justify. Yet, occasionally, bare cupboards forced him to Cuthbert's and thereby back into public life. His plan was to purchase five pounds of sugar and flour each, and enough tea and coffee to last throughout the summer.

He thought to ask Rosalind about Catherine's whereabouts, or maybe to offer condolences for the Cuthbert loss; instead, he assumed Catherine was consumed with grief and felt relieved to be shielded from her bigotry, if only for a day.

"Anything else I can help you with, Edgar?" Rosalind Cuthbert asked kindly, handing Rosenthal his change.

No one calls me Edgar! Rosenthal almost said, but he murmured, "No, thank you," and turned quickly to leave.

"Shame how they did dat colored boy, wouldn't you say?" she whispered sincerely.

Rosenthal dropped the bags and wasted white powdery substances all over the hardwood floor.

"My Lord, don't worry about it," Rosalind reassured and reached for a broom. "I'm sure it happens all the time. Why, I'm 'bout the clumsiest person you'll ever meet!" She giggled.

"I'll pay for everything," he mumbled in frustration. "Jes give me another five pounds—"

"Oh, don't you worry yourself, Mr. Man," Rosalind called over her shoulder. "We'll have you fixed up here in a jiffy!" She disappeared into the storeroom.

Rosenthal had hardly recovered when she returned and offered him two additional brown paper bags. "Here you go. Good as new!"

He accepted the packages gratefully, and asked, "Now what did you say about the colored boy?" He tried not to appear too interested.

"Oh yes! You ain't heard? Everybody's talkin' 'bout it. I don't know for sure, but Billy said they took care o' him."

"What exactly did they do?" he asked.

"Well, like I said, I don't know for sure, but Billy come home last night laughin' like a hyena and sayin' how sorry Mary and her folks were gonna be for thinkin' they could shoot a white man and get by with it."

"How y'all doin?" several whites greeted as they entered the store.

In her distraction, she turned her attention toward their needs and left Rosenthal to guess what the sheriff and others had done to Clement.

Rosenthal drove home, trying to determine how he might investigate the matter further. In his heart and in recompense for crimes of his past, he wanted nothing more desperately than to deliver the boy home safely, but, somewhere deep within, he sensed that such an opportunity would never come. If he knew anything, he knew white Southerners, and absolutely never did they allow righteousness to override vengeance.

Rosenthal rounded Lover's Lane and saw Larry Greer's three grandsons walking toward him. The sun had baked them burgundy, and their limp hair suggested they had found a waterhole somewhere. Except for wet, baggy, cutoff shorts that clung to their skinny bodies, they would have been completely naked, looking more like paupers than the sons of Money's white elite. Rosenthal thought to ignore them, like one might an insignificant stone or an indistinguishable blade of grass, but he stopped in order not to dishonor the rules of social etiquette which no one in Money—Black or white—found negotiable.

"Howdy, Mr. Rosenthal," the oldest and biggest of the boys greeted.

"Good day, gentlemen," Rosenthal overarticulated, hoping to inspire in the boys at least a value—if not a desire—for good diction. "Looks like we've been swimming."

"Yessir!" they chimed. "We wuz fishin' at first," the big spokesboy explained, "but wunnit nothin' bitin', so we decided to jump on in and cool off a li'l bit." His speech was slow and heavily drawled, as though he had only recently acquired the facility of language. Rosenthal noticed the extraordinary length to which he stretched long vowels sounds.

"It has been rather hot these days if I must say so myself," Rosenthal added pleasantly.

The boys stared at him, wondering if he were going to offer them a ride. When he didn't, they said, "We'll seeya later, Mr. Rosenthal," and commenced, once again, the long walk back to Money's white section of town.

Rosenthal hesitated initially, then waved the boys back to his car. Now they were certain he was about to offer them a ride.

Unsure of exactly how to maintain the façade of disinterest, Rosenthal risked exposure, and asked, "Did you gentlemen happen to hear anything about the colored boy who . . ." Rosenthal wanted to be careful ". . . had the encounter with Mrs. Cuthbert?"

This time, the redheaded boy with freckles yielded, "Yeah!" and the other two nodded wildly. "My granddad and his buddies was drinkin' last night, and they started laughin' 'bout how they beat that nigger boy to a pulp."

Stay calm, Rosenthal told himself. *Just listen.* "What exactly did they say?"

Suddenly, the boys looked suspicious. Rosenthal's interest appeared too desperate, too demanding to be genuine. There was only one way to restore their faith in him.

He chuckled, and said, "I mean . . . everybody likes to hear a good story about . . . a nigger beating."

Immediately the boys relaxed, and the big one continued: "It was funny the way they told it, Mr. Rosenthal. They said they took him out in de woods somewhere near the river and his eyes was big as full moons. He was kickin' and hollerin', Granddaddy said, and that made beatin' him even funner."

Rosenthal felt bile gather in his stomach, but he couldn't bail out now. The joy the boys described was hauntingly familiar.

"They cracked him over the head with a two-by-four," Redhead bellowed. "He squirmed somethin' awful, they said, then they put a noose around his neck."

"They hanged him?" Rosenthal almost yelled.

"Naw, they didn't hang him," Redhead explained. "They jes wanted him to think they would. They said he was cryin' and screamin' all kinds of different names."

Rosenthal asked cautiously, "Did they say what names?"

"Naw. They jes said he was screamin' names. Then they said they let him go."

"What? They released him?" Anticipation colored his question.

The boys laughed. "They released him all right," said Redhead. "He took off runnin', and they counted to ten and played like he was a 'coon in the dark. They had dogs and guns and everything."

In his head, Rosenthal was screaming, "No! No!" How could children glory in such brutality, he wondered.

"He ran like a wild boar hog, Granddaddy said, but they caught him. I forgot who they said did it, but somebody beat his left eye plumb out o' his head. He fell on the ground kickin' and screamin' like a scalded chicken. Can you imagine that, Mr. Rosenthal?"

Had Rosenthal opened his mouth, he would have wept, so he forced a smile and continued listening.

"But that ain't the good part," Redhead continued. Rosenthal braced himself by wiping imaginary sweat from his forehead. "Granddaddy said, before they beat him, the nigger gave all of 'em a good blow job!"

"Dear Lord," Rosenthal mumbled, covering his mouth in shame.

"Yeah, they said they promised to let him go if he'd do it, and so he started suckin' like a newborn babe!" The other two doubled over with laughter. "They said he moaned and groaned as he was suckin', so bustin' a nut was pretty easy—"

"That's enough!" Rosenthal declared.

"Oh, we didn't mean to be disrespectful, Mr. Rosenthal. We apologize." The boys stared at him strangely.

Rosenthal couldn't bear another word. "I . . . um . . . need to get my store goods home." He put the car in gear.

"Nice talkin' to ya, Mr. Rosenthal. You take care now," the big one said.

Rosenthal sped away, leaving a mountain of dust behind. He ignored the tears skiing down his red cheeks, and several times he considered turning around abruptly and telling the boys how wrong they and their grandfather had been. Instead, he retreated into his quiet home, both angry at himself for letting the Greer boys believe he was one of them and thrilled to learn news, however horrible, concerning the colored boy's fate.

Sitting at his kitchen table, he thought of all the chances he had over the years to alter the state of the world or, at least, Money, Mississippi. He wondered if God would condemn him to hell not because of his shortcomings, but because of his refusal to help when he could. Actually, Rosenthal had convinced himself, years prior, that heaven, hell, the devil, and all other such biblical notions were constructs of fear that possessed absolutely no validity at all. He told a friend at Harvard that surely God hadn't written the Bible. If so, he was disappointed.

Suddenly, Rosenthal picked up his car keys and hat. He would have to search diligently, he resolved, but he wanted to see the place where Clement was dismembered. He hadn't figured out exactly why, but something within him compelled him to want to revisit the moment, the place, and the torture, in hopes of . . . something.

Instead of driving down Talley Lane and turning right onto Fish Lake Road—the most direct route to the river—Rosenthal parked at the corner and decided to walk through the woods until he found whatever his spirit was looking for. He waited until no cars were in sight before he exited his own, having grabbed a flashlight from under the front seat. His plan was to return home before dark, but, just in case, he didn't intend to get caught deep in the forest at night without a light.

Go home, he kept telling himself. Yet the trees summoned him onward. Fifteen minutes later, he found himself engulfed in green darkness. From what the boys described, Rosenthal gleaned that the mob of men had taken Clement somewhere near the intersection of Chapman's land and the Tallahatchie River. He began to inspect the earth like a homicide detective, trying desperately not to miss any clues. "What am I looking for?" he murmured, tossing his arms in the air. Nonetheless, he continued, propelled by some external force to discover something his senses told him was out there. After several minutes, Rosenthal's heart and head began to battle for governance over him until, aloud, he said, "Enough" and granted his heart leadership. He wondered what his father would have said about his attempt to help a colored boy, especially one who had supposedly disrespected a white woman. He probably would have warned him not to take his Harvard liberalism too far, Rosenthal conjectured.

After an hour—maybe two—he decided that the search was more guilt than reason. Besides wild ferns and fallen tree limbs, he hadn't found anything that would corroborate the boys' tale, much less indict the perpetrators. Dusk forced him to use the flashlight now as Rosenthal looked around one last time. He scampered hurriedly, sure he had missed something. Finding nothing, he turned to exit and tripped clumsily over a rotten log. "Shit!" bellowed from his throat as he plummeted, facedown, into the soft forest mulch. "Just go home," he chafed in exasperation. Resolving that the whole idea had been erroneous, Rosenthal placed both hands on the earth, in push-up position, preparing to lift himself quickly and go home when suddenly he released a scream loud enough to vibrate the tallest trees, for, on the ground, just below his nose, was a human eye staring boldly up at him. "Oh fuck!" he said as he rose to his feet. His hands trembled too badly to hold the flashlight steady, and his feet shuffled the dance of dismay. "Oh my God! What is this?" he mumbled in horror.

Rosenthal folded his arms and prayed for someone or something to tell him what to do next. He stared at the eye, which studied him from every direction. At times, he could have sworn the eye blinked as though resting comfortably within its original socket, then another time the eye appeared glazed over with tears. Stay calm, he told himself. Everything's going to be fine.

Of course it had to be the colored boy's, Rosenthal deduced, but what was he to do? "Those fuckin' idiots!" he proclaimed to no one, and explored the heavens for a sign of how to proceed. He bent cautiously to examine the eye once again and calmed to note that a colored eye looked like any other. It was mostly white, streaked with dark purple blood vessels and round like a marble. The pupil seemed larger outside of a human head, Rosenthal marked, and the leaf on which the eye rested held a small pool of fluids at once nauseating and unidentifiable. While in squatting position, he wondered if colored people's eyes saw the world differently from white people's eyes. He pondered the possibility that this eye had seen something, in its short tenure, which seventy years of living had never brought before him. Rosenthal smiled involuntarily as he contemplated how much more of the world he might know if he exchanged eyes with someone of a different race. It would be difficult to hate, he reasoned, if people could just exchange eyes for a day—

"Stop it!" he yelled, bringing himself back to reality. "Just go home and forget about this!" Rosenthal's hands gestured like a teacher trying desperately to explain a difficult concept.

He took a deep breath, closed his eyes, and stood in preparation to depart. His feet, however, felt bolted to the earth and his conscience was not inclined to abandon the eye quite so abruptly. As if in obedience to an unseen ruler, he stooped again to study the eye and, this time, it hypnotized him. Somewhere in his head, he heard the cry of thousands of unknown children, begging, weeping, and moaning for things indiscernible, and Rosenthal grabbed his head tightly. "No!" he answered the call, but the voices petitioned him nonetheless, having waited a lifetime for his audience. The eye begged for mercy,

Rosenthal ascertained, although he knew not how to dispense such favor. In its pupil was a longing for love, understanding, hope . . . something foundational to human thriving. "What is it?" he implored on his soul's behalf. "I have nothing to give." The eye ignored his empty confession and, instead, beseeched Rosenthal to nurture and forgive both himself and a world for centuries of transgressions unspoken. "Fine," he relented and, without entertaining why he shouldn't, Rosenthal reached tenderly for the eye and placed it in his left hand. It seemed now to be looking beyond him, far into his ugly past, interrogating him on issues he hadn't thought about in years. He examined the eye with the light from the flashlight, bringing his own eye only inches from the colored boy's. The brown surprised him, since he thought all colored people's eyes were black, and then he noticed that the outer ring of the iris was actually golden. The pupil alone was black, and as Rosenthal lifted the eye even closer, he gasped when he saw his own reflection. Staring now in wonder and confusion, he looked deeper into the pupil and saw that, actually, it wasn't black at all but rather clear and transparent, for, like a mirror, it reflected his image exactly as he knew himself. The closer he examined the eye, the deeper it probed into his soul until his image was reduced to nothing. He noticed that, somewhere, somehow, in the black abyss of the colored boy's translucent eye, he had completely disappeared.

Rosenthal pulled a handkerchief from his pants pocket and wrapped the eye carefully. Afraid of bruising it, he carried it cautiously in his left hand like a child might handle a fragile egg. Night had fallen, and Rosenthal gave thanks for the shield it provided against those who might have discovered him. Although his sight was severely hindered, he found his way in the dark more quickly than he had in the light, only now understanding how his blind grandfather had painted so beautifully.

At home, Rosenthal undressed and lay naked upon his bed with the eye in his right palm. Although there were now three eyes instead of two that beheld him, he felt no shame. The colored boy's eye extolled his nakedness, he convinced himself, and insisted upon vulnerability he had never yielded.

He placed the eye on a nightstand and leaned across the bed to turn on the radio. Soft jazz broke the room's stale silence and helped Rosenthal regain his senses. He then brushed the eye with his fingertip and smiled at it like a long-lost friend returned.

"Hello," he whispered with his mouth close enough to kiss the eye. "I hate the bastards who did this to you. It didn't have to be this way." He rose from the bed and returned with a small, but obviously expensive glass stand, upon which he set the eye.

"Now," he said contentedly. "Fit for a king." Rosenthal rolled over on his back. "I'll return you tomorrow." He couldn't figure it out, but something about the eye was eerily familiar. When it hit him, he cried, "Oh my God! Oh my God!" and lifted himself to a sitting position. "It's you! I knew I'd get another chance one day. I always knew it!" He placed the eye in the joined palms of his hands. "Oh, Sutton! I'm so sorry!" he wailed. "I remember this eye the night we . . . um . . . hurt you." He pressed the eye gently against his flabby chest and drifted back fifty years. "I didn't mean for you to die. I really didn't. And now you've come back." He returned the eye to its throne and sat on the bed's edge in thankful bliss. "But I'm not going to spoil this chance. I'm going to love you and nurture you and treat you royally. I owe you that much."

Again, he reclined and said, "Wow. Who would have thought I'd find you in Mississippi? I'd know your eyes anywhere. I'm sorry I never called you by your proper name, but now I get the chance to. Sutton Griggs, Jr., Sutton Griggs, Jr.," he repeated countless times. "You said it so eloquently that day. That's why I hated you—because you were more articulate than I was. I was white, and I was supposed to be smarter, but you proved me wrong. And I couldn't handle that. So I . . . hurt you." Rosenthal's sobbing came and went quickly. "You will forgive me, won't you? I'll never call you a colored boy again. I promise. I'll call you Sutton or even Mr. Griggs if you like."

He paused. "Then Sutton it is. Like best friends. You can even call me Edgar if you want, but I prefer Rosenthal. It just sounds better you know?"

He glanced at the eye, resting atop its grand Imperium.

"This is great!" He smiled. "Of course you're *really* Jeremiah's grandson, but since I don't know his name, what difference does that make? For all I know, you, Jeremiah, Sutton, and all colored people are probably related. And since you look just like Sutton's eyes looked that night, that's what I'll call you. And now I can redeem myself." He smiled again.

After several minutes, Rosenthal folded his hands behind his head and told Sutton, "I know I'm old and ugly now, but I used to be quite a lover, you know." He closed his eyes to summon the memory of by-gone days of prowess. "I've always liked closeness. There's nothing more beautiful than two human bodies meshed together in search of needs neither can find alone. Wouldn't you agree?"

Rosenthal strained his neck to look at Sutton. Thinking he saw corroboration, he continued, "All my lovers have been white women, but I'd guess that colored people do it pretty much the same. I'll never know now anyway." He rolled onto his left side and stratched his hairy right butt cheek.

"Someone made love to get you, you know? I bet it was beautiful, those caramel brown bodies sweating in the fight to create life. I bet they dreamed of you even before you were conceived. They surely worried about you growing up in a place where people like me usually despise you." He smirked at the thought. "They probably swore they'd protect you from me and promised each other to give you the best life possible. Now, they'll conclude they failed. But it isn't so. Do you think it's so?"

Every time Rosenthal asked a question he looked at Sutton. The eye seemed like a being in itself, he thought, who simply had no mouth or voice with which to speak.

"I'm sorry about our sheriff, Larry Greer, and whoever else did this to you," he said again and picked up Sutton like one would pick a rare, delicate flower. "I used to do it, too. I don't know why. We were taught to hate coloreds and to remind all of you of how won-derfully superior we are. I know it sounds ridiculous, but everything from the Bible to the White House reinforces white beauty and Black ugliness. But I don't think you're ugly." He touched Sutton sensually and shuddered at its rubbery texture. "I think you're beau-tiful. I'll never forget the day you explained the *Hamlet* passage. I was so envious of your insight and your vernacular that I planned how I'd destroy you. But now I have to take care of you. I owe that to your people."

He returned Sutton to his glass throne. "Since you never have to blink or sleep, I guess you'll see everything now." He closed his eyes. "I'm sorry, Sutton. I really am. I can't believe I did that to you. We white men . . . we're all alike. I hate to say it, but it's true. What they did to you I did years ago, so what's the difference?" Rosenthal hesi-tated. "Or maybe the difference is that I've changed while Billy and the others haven't. I hate scum like him—now. Can you believe he's the sheriff? I wish we could take all the racist rednecks and let your people have their way with them. But I guess that would make your people racist black necks!" He chuckled.

Thunder rolled and rain soon fell in sheets while the radio played easy-listening melodies.

"Naw, it's been enough killing in America. No need in coloreds be-coming murderers, too. Y'all are good, nice people. I'd hate for you to ruin your reputation trying to get back at bad folks like me." Rosen-thal closed the bedroom windows.

"I used to play the guitar," he told Sutton, smiling. "When I was a teenager, I thought I'd grow up to be a famous pop musician like Elvis Presley is now. You ever heard of him? I loved the big bands, and I taught myself to play the guitar so I could join one one day. My daddy said it was downright sinful to play the devil's music, but he never stopped me. Momma, on the other hand, loved it. She wanted nothing more than her children's happiness however we chose to get it. So I started writing my own songs and singing them for Momma who ranted and raved about how talented I was. But, in the end—as in the beginning—Daddy's hope for my life prevailed, and I read more than I sang." Rosenthal checked to make sure Sutton was still paying attention.

"That's how I ended up at Harvard. If Dad had known that was where I would learn to question his belief system, he surely would have sent me elsewhere. But Dad wanted the benefit of the name more than the fruit of a Harvard education in me. We never really saw eye to eye anyway, but after I returned from a four-year sojourn up North, we clashed irresolvably. Because he was my father, I acquiesced and acted like other Southern white men who harass colored people for fun. I'm so, so sorry. You will forgive me, won't you?"

Rosenthal sat up with his back against the headboard and his hands buried between his legs.

"I saw what they did to Joshua Redfield. I was there. I shouldn't have been, but I was."

He started crying again.

"This was more than fifty years ago, Sutton, so please forgive me." He blew his nose. "Some of the local boys came by one evening and asked me if I wanted to go for a ride. At first I refused, but boredom compelled me to relent. We drove for miles down Highway 3, then turned off on an obscure dirt road. I asked them where we were going and they said to have a little fun, so I thought the adventure harmless. But when they parked the truck and we got out, they uncovered the colored boy tied up in the truck bed. My eyes must have revealed my horror, for one of them said, 'Aw, Rosenthal. Be a man!' I didn't know what to do, so I went along."

Rosenthal wept heavily. He had consciously avoided this memory since the event, but now, with Sutton's return, he felt the need to confess it.

"Bad thing about it, I knew his parents well. His father, Elijah, was my daddy's chauffeur for years. Little Joshua used to chase squirrels and eat pecans in our front yard until his daddy finished working. That's why I couldn't look at him because he knew me. I asked the men why they had him, and they said he was fucking—that was their word, not mine—some white girl. He was around sixteen then, I believe. He kept shaking his head violently, trying to scream through the rags in his mouth, but it was too late. They tied a rope around his neck and hanged him on a huge oak limb. Then they cut out his genitalia and pinned a note to his clothes that read 'I'M A DICKLESS NIGGER!' It took everything within me to keep from crying, Sutton. I swear it did. Blood poured down his legs and onto the ground as the men drank corn whiskey. I vomited, and they laughed at me. 'Rosenthal's got a weak stomach,' they jeered. When they dropped me off at home, I was trembling so bad I collapsed beneath the pecan tree. The sun rose the next morning before I gathered enough strength to go inside."

Rosenthal buried his face in his hands.

"A few hours later, Elijah was walking the streets, screaming, 'Who did my boy like dat?' His wife Martha marched behind him with a shotgun. When they got to our house, my daddy told Elijah that if the boy was dead couldn't nobody bring him back now, so he might as well come on to work. Elijah ignored him, for the first time in his life, and I remember my daddy telling me, 'Niggers are such ingrates. That's why they never have anything. They're so selfish.' I almost told Daddy everything, but I think I was more scared than Elijah and Martha. Then, of course, he would have asked me how I knew so much, and I would have had no choice but to tell him I was there, and I didn't want anybody to know that, so I didn't say anything. At supper, Daddy told me that Elijah was scaring people, so somebody shot him and Martha before they hurt innocent white people. Of course I knew the truth, but now it was too late to tell it. I realized in that moment that I could have changed the course of history, but I didn't. Elijah had worked for Daddy almost twenty years without ever missing a day, holidays included, but that didn't mean enough for me to tell the truth. I'm so ashamed, Sutton!"

Rosenthal hadn't cried like that in years. His sides ached, and his eyes burned, like one standing too close to a fire.

"I drew the line that day. Really I did. When I saw those boys again, I gave them the meanest look I could muster. They knew I meant business, too." He sniffled and huffed. "So, you see, I've changed. I wouldn't ever do something like that again. Never. Yes, that's the difference between most Southern white men and me. They're still mean, racist bastards. They'll probably always be. Folks like that hardly ever change. But, Sutton, I promise to honor you from now on."

The rain was still pouring.

"We're gonna get drenched tonight," Rosenthal said and slid under the ragged quilt Martha Redfield had pieced as a Christmas gift for the family years ago. One last time, he placed Sutton in his palms, and said, "I feel so connected to you now. I thank God I found you. You're mine." He pressed the eye gently to his bosom and drifted off to sleep.

Thirteen

POSSUM STARED OUT OF THE TRAIN WINDOW AT THE GREEN cotton plants and remembered what she had tried desperately to forget. In Chicago, she hadn't seen a single cotton bole and, consequently, she called the place divine. But now circumstances had insisted that she return to the underworld, as she thought of it, and every mile south forced her to admit that hell is usually closer than we think.

"Wow," Possum mumbled when the train halted in Greenwood. She had prepared herself not to recognize the place, but she marveled that everything looked exactly the same. Some minor difference would have been enough to convince her that a progressive idea had found its way into the Delta, yet the similarity of things confirmed Possum's long-held belief that God had forsaken Mississippi years ago.

Upon exiting the train, she wanted to ask whomever she saw, Black or white, if they had heard anything concerning the whereabouts of her son, but she determined it was wiser to go home and gather details firsthand.

Out of panic, Possum had left Chicago with nothing but the clothes on her back and a worn pocketbook. The thought of Clement being harassed, molested, or assaulted by white men was enough to make her forgo preparations as she pondered simply how to protect her son's life in a place committed to its destruction. All she knew for sure was that she needed to get home, so that's what she did. She would worry about the trivialities of clothes, money, and food later, she told herself.

The four-mile walk wasn't as bad as she had envisioned. Colored folks waved cordially like they always did, and white folks noted one more nigger to tolerate. Jerry and Enoch became very real for her again as she recalled times with the brothers she thought of daily.

"Where yo' thang at?" Enoch asked Possum one lazy Saturday afternoon as they undressed to take a dip in the cool Tallahatchie River.

"She a girl, stupid," Jerry said. "She ain't got no thang."

"Then how she pee pee?" Enoch posed, confused.

"She got a split," Jerry chuckled. "Look. See?"

Enoch put his face directly in front of Possum's private. Thinking it necessary to teach her baby brother about gender difference, Possum spread her legs voluntarily and looked with Enoch at his first encounter with a vagina.

"Ugh! I don't like that," Enoch frowned. "It look funny."

"You'll like it soon enough," Jerry prophesied.

Possum laughed to remember Enoch's innocence. He and his jokes had kept her sane while imprisoned on Chapman's land, and she prayed now that he had learned some new ones. She would need something jovial, she thought, if she were to survive the kidnapping of her only son.

Lying in bed one night, Possum asked Jerry, "What do you think hell is really like?"

"Go to sleep, girl!" he sputtered angrily.

Possum pressed her luck. "But I cain't sleep, Jerry." She was looking at a cluster of stars shining brightly through a hole in the rusted tin roof of the old sharecropper's shack. Enoch had fallen asleep the moment his head hit the feather pillow.

Jerry sighed deeply and told Possum, "Ain't no such thing as hell, girl. Somebody made that up to make us believe what the Bible say."

Possum's eyes bulged in horror. "What? Preachers said that when people sin—"

"Ain't no such thang as sin either," Jerry interrupted, more annoyed than before. "It just depends on how you define right and wrong," he explained.

Possum listened intently, overwhelmed by what she saw as her twelve-year-old brother's extraordinary wisdom.

"Why you think people be fallin' out, cryin', and shoutin' in church every Sunday?" Jerry asked sleepily. Before Possum could answer, he retorted, "Because they're afraid of going to hell. They're begging God please not to send them to hell even though they've been wrong all week long."

"But God ain't dumb enough to believe the shoutin' every week," Possum said.

"Precisely," Jerry confirmed, and lovingly patted his sister's head. "That's how you know the crying and stuff is just performance. Ain't none of it 'bout God for real 'cause if God weighs the heart, there's nothing people need to say or do. All the hollerin' is so that other people will think they holy."

"Oh," Possum murmured.

"Plus, if you really love God, what do you need a hell for? You do the right thing because it's right. Period. Not because you scared to go to hell. Wrong motive."

Possum didn't know what "motive" meant, but she understood what her brother was saying. She didn't sleep that night, thinking about how much sense Jerry had made and why, deep in her heart, she believed him. That's the night she began to see God more like her own mother, who baked pies in the spring and boiled chitlins in the fall for others simply because she wanted to—not because she wanted or needed something back from them. She liked God better this way, for now she didn't fear Him. She simply wanted to be His friend. She wanted to ask Him how He hung the stars in the sky without them falling and how the ocean remained salty although rain is always freshwater.

After that night, Possum decided to tell her parents that they could stop worrying about eternal damnation, but Jerry warned against such an announcement.

"Why not? Possum asked in wonder.

"Because they've believed it so long, their whole lives would fall apart if they learned something different. It's all they have, so let them have it."

"But what if what they have ain't right?"

"It don't make no difference, girl," Jerry asserted. "God judges people on what they believe—not on what's actually true 'cause don't no human being know the full truth that God knows." Jerry glanced to make sure Possum understood. "You're only wrong when you do what you think God don't like, and what God don't like changes from one place and time to another. I was readin' this book on . . ."

Possum had heard more than she could digest. How a simple question about hell had evolved into a lecture on the conceptualization of God she could not explain, yet what she knew for sure was that, somehow, her brother had set her free forever.

When she migrated to Chicago, Possum joined First Baptist Congregational Church, not because she needed a public sanctuary wherein to find God, but because she enjoyed watching others purge their guilt. The performances often made Possum laugh boisterously, although occasionally an intense solo yanked a tear from her usually unyielding eyes.

"Oh, Jerry!" she mumbled, and burst into tears. "What have they done to my boy?" Finding strength in a nearby tree, she leaned upon it and unleashed years of pent-up grief. Hugging the tree as though giving birth to it, Possum repeated Clement's name like a libation, allowing herself the right to mourn the abduction of her only son. Unlike before, she didn't care who witnessed her cleansing, for the pain of Clement's trouble was a weight she needed, finally, to relinquish. Prior to this moment, she had refused to weep or crumble because she wanted to assume vicariously the strength Jerry must have had in order to meet death voluntarily. Yet, collapsed against the tree, the thought of life without Clement swelled in her like an ocean tide, and she admitted that her pseudostrength had simply proven ineffectual. Her emotions gathered power and burst every wall within which Possum had tried to contain them. So she let them go without resistance, glad to be relieved of the burden of their confinement.

Possum sat on the ground and leaned her back against the base of the tree. From her purse she retrieved a ragged lace handkerchief her mother had given her the day she left, and, with it, she wiped both tears and sweat in an effort to recover and complete the journey. She rotated and placed her left hand against the tree and remembered, surprisingly, that her father's rough, work-gnarled hands had felt like the tree bark the last time he caressed her face. "I love you, baby," he had sniffled, and encased Possum's face with his dusty hands. "This ole place ain't so bad," he said. "But jes in case I don't see you again, you 'member that I gave you de best I had." Possum closed her eyes, and Jeremiah's hands rubbed her wet cheeks dry again. Then, studying the outline of the tree's bark more thoroughly, Possum noticed that the small, microscopic lines on her own hand resembled the deep, capillary-like indentations on the tree's bark. "Well, I'll be damn." She smiled. She moved her palms lovingly across the bark, up and down, until what was once rough and unpleasurable became soothing, misunderstood history. As a child, she marveled at the coarseness of her grandfather's hands and couldn't understand why the wrinkles were so deeply embedded. Now, as she looked at the old tree, she understood that age loves to announce its presence. That tree probably had a smooth, silky bark in its youth, she presumed, but after enduring decades of wind, rain, sun, and bitter cold, the old tree boasted a tough, impenetrable outer shell. Stroking the back of one hand with the other, Possum chuckled at the bygone days of her baby-smooth, delicate skin, and happily joined the ranks of those whose wrinkled, coarse hands marked their adulthood. The roughness was sign of survival, she discovered, as she guessed the tree to be at least a hundred, and, for the first time in her life, she was proud of her callused hands.

The heat waves running across the road guaranteed that Possum would be soaking wet by the time she reached home. She walked on nonetheless, fighting a battle with the sun no human had ever won. Occasionally, she fanned herself with her bare hands, only to be frustrated further by the scorching air that confronted her. Possum looked up and realized that home was no closer now than it had been yesterday.

"I saw a man walk on water one time," she recalled her grandfather telling her. "You don't believe it, do you?"

Possum definitely didn't, but she perceived this to be the wrong answer. At twelve, she had learned to distinguish between truth and Southern Black storytelling, but every now and then the boundaries blurred, leaving her unsure of exactly what to believe.

"Well, it's de truf, chile," he continued. He was filling his pipe with tobacco as the family awaited supper.

Possum closed her eyes playfully, and said, "Granddaddy, come on. You ain't seen nobody walk on no water and you know it."

"I knows what I done seen, girl! Is you crazy? I ain't senile!" Granddaddy defended.

He was always telling the children some fantastic tale of the supernatural, swearing every word to be the absolute truth, although no one living could ever substantiate his story.

"Okay, Granddaddy, tell me about it," Possum surrendered.

"No, no, chile," he responded, obviously offended by her demeanor. "If you don't wanna hear it, I sho ain't gon make you."

Granddaddy rocked himself, hoping Possum would beg him so he could share the story with genuine enthusiasm. She took her cue.

"For real, Granddaddy! I wanna hear it. Tell me. Please." Possum actually hated this feigned coaxing, but it seemed the respectful thing to do.

"All right, all right, chile. You ain't gotta beg." Granddaddy lit his pipe and leaned forward, preparing to stand although he never did.

"We had jes finished pickin' two hunnert fifty pounds of cotton," he explained loudly. "It was a Friday evenin' and me and yo' Uncle Brother and some otha boys run off to de river to take a quick dip in de cool evenin' water. Well, we got to de river and started takin' off our clothes when we heard some otha kids swimmin' nearby. We didn't think nothin' of it, 'specially since dey wuz colored, too, but all o' sudden we heard somebody holla"—Granddaddy sat his pipe on the end table, cupped his hands around his mouth, and imitated how the children must have screamed—"'he's drownin'! Help!'" Then he reclaimed his pipe and continued the story.

"Yo' Uncle Brother led de way as we ran to see if we could help. When we got to where de otha chil'ren wuz, two young boys wuz cryin' and carryin' on somethin' terrible. We kept tryin' to ask them what happened and who wuz in de water, but they wuz too traumatized to say anything clearly. We finally made out dat their big brother wuz tryin' to see if he could swim all de way 'cross de river when he got tired and went under de water. We ask them if de boy wuz a good swimmer, and they said he wuz, but he started drownin' for some reason.

"'He all we got,' one of the boys cried pitifully. 'If he drown, we ain't got nobody.'

"Dat's when yo Uncle Brother walked out on de water and rescued him."

"What?" Possum screamed in amazement.

"You heard what I said." Granddaddy paused, looking around the room for anyone who dared challenge the validity of his tale. "Yo' Uncle Brother closed his eyes and whispered somethin' to de Good Lawd 'cause he said amen at the end, then he ran out on dat river jes like it was dry ground."

"Are you serious, Daddy? I never heard this story before," Jeremiah told his father.

"Hell yeah, I'm serious! You thank I'd play 'bout somethin' like dat? I don't play wit God. You might, but I don't." His drama was intense.

"Brother brought de boy back on dry ground, too. He was unconscious so he didn't remember none o' it later, but de rest o' us seed everythang. I'm de only one left of dat crew though."

Of course you are, everyone thought.

"But I'm tellin' you what I saw myself. This ain't no story 'bout what I done heard somebody else say. I seed dis wit my own eyes!" His vehemence made Possum begin to believe him. "At first I didn't believe it myself, but when he came back wit dat boy in his arms I knowed dat he had really walked on de water. I asked him real slow, 'Did you jes git through walkin' on dat water?' and he said, 'I did what I had to.' I asked him, 'Why ain't I eva walked on de water?' and he said, ''Cause you ain't neva needed to. You don't do it jes to be doin' it. You ask God to give you dat kinda power only when yo' own ain't enough. Otherwise, you ain't gon git it.'

"De otha two boys looked like they had done seen a ghost. They didn't say nothin' to Brother when he come back. They jes stared at him, frozen like they wuz under a spell. Brother laid de otha boy's body down real gentle and he raised his hands and started shoutin' and praisin' God for de miracle, I guess. I ain't neva seed Brother shout like dat befo' in my life, and I knowed somethin' had done happened dat I might not neva see again."

Possum interrupted. "Did those other boys ever say anything to Uncle Brother about it?"

"Not really," Granddaddy pondered. "Sometimes we'd see 'em and they'd get real quiet and stare at Brother like he wunnit real, but they never said a mumblin' word to him, far as I know. Now I think about it, didn't none o' us say nothin' to nobody 'bout what happened."

"Why not?" Possum inquired.

"'Cause we knowed nobody would believe us. We didn't even believe what we saw, so we knowed wunnit nobody else. This de first time I ever mentioned it since it happened. But it *did* happen. You believe that."

Granddaddy sat back in the rocker with a self-assurance no one could alter. He examined everyone's faces to see how much they believed him, then he said, "Okay," and relaxed in his own inner peace. "You ain't gotta believe it. De truth don't need no witnesses."

Possum often found herself in relentless silence after hearing her grandfather's tales. He never told normal stories, she used to say, about killin' hogs or stealin' watermelons; instead, he always talked about the supernatural, the illogical, the unbelievable, the impossible, and the boundaries of Possum's little brain simply didn't extend far enough for her to believe most of what he said.

Now, walking down the road as a grown woman, Possum needed to believe in the impossible, for it would take a miracle, she knew, to get Clement back in her arms safely. What exactly had the boy done? she asked herself. Why didn't Daddy beat him and make him act right?

The cute little open-toe shoes, which started aching once she arrived in Greenwood, now swung by their straps in her right hand. Her feet hurt so badly that she wanted nothing more than to lean back and throw the damn things as far as her strength would allow. Because she had no others, though, she decided to tolerate their existence, especially since she might have to wear them again. Whoever had convinced her that heels were attractive was a fool shonuff, she thought, as she tiptoed her way to her old stomping grounds.

The bra had to go, too. It didn't matter much anyway since Possum's breasts had never grown beyond a 34B. However, her small, perky breasts had long been the envy of all her woman friends, most of whose huge breasts, without a bra, sagged like wet potato sacks. She reached behind her back with both hands and unsnapped the hooked brassiere, releasing a sigh of a woman deeply relieved. Folding it into a warped ball, she placed the bra in her pocketbook and wondered—like she had about the shoes—who had convinced women they needed it at all. It had to be a man, she concluded, for surely no

woman would ever have created anything so uncomfortable and con-
straining. When she thought about it further, Possum decided that
much of what women do is for male pleasure and comfort. "You ain't
got no business wit yo' titties hangin' out!" she imagined men telling
a busty woman. "It ain't decent!" But do men know how uncomfortable that damn thing is? she thought angrily. Do they care?

She began venting aloud. "And who created dresses? Certainly nobody who knows about Mississippi mosquitoes!" Possum laughed at
herself. "And what idiot came up with this shit called stockings, especially in the summer?" She frowned at an invisible listener, pointing
her finger and rolling her neck rebelliously, transferring arbitrary
frustrations to a wind that gladly carried them away.

"Hey there!" a voice startled her.

Possum jerked around abruptly, clearly unprepared to entertain
another. At first, she did not recognize the voice or the face.

"Good afternoon, Miss Possum Johnson. I knowed you wuz
comin' soon. I heard 'bout yo' boy."

Possum thought she'd never see Sammy Spears again. "How you
doin'?" She smiled.

"Real good. Real good," he said, still sitting atop the wagon. "Got
me a wife and three daughters, so I ain't done too bad for myself I
guess."

Possum couldn't think of any more small talk, so she bypassed it,
and asked, "You heard anything about my son, Sammy?"

He shook his head. "I ain't heard nothin'. I sho do hope he's all
right though."

"Yeah, me too." Possum tried to smile, but couldn't.

"I went to de meetin' yo' daddy had. He asked colored folks to help
him find yo' boy, and I been askin' 'round, but don't nobody know
nothin'."

"Or ain't nobody talkin'."

"Yeah. You know how that goes."

An awkward silence lingered between the ex-lovers who shared
more history than either desired to remember.

"How old was—is your boy?"

"Fourteen. He be fifteen in a few months."

"Wow. He ain't a kid no more. That's how old I was when I first asked yo' daddy if I could come see you."

Possum smirked, but she wasn't in the mood to walk down memory lane. "How old are your girls?"

"Fifteen, twelve, and eight."

"Is that right?" Possum tried to figure out how to segue out of the conversation without being rude. "Well, I guess I'd better be getting on—"

"It don't look good, Possum. You know how white folks do 'round here. They ain't changed."

She grabbed hold of the wagon to steady herself. "I don't know what I'd do without my son, Sammy."

He descended the wagon and embraced her. Possum immediately recognized his fish-and-motor-oil scent.

"Everybody prayin'," he said with her face pressed into his chest. "Don't get upset 'til you know somethin'. God can do the impossible."

"The question is, will He," Possum said, rubbing tears into her cheeks. "I guess we'll see," she huffed.

"You gotta believe," Sammy said. "You can't think the worst."

"You de one sayin' it don't look good!" she shouted and broke free of his embrace. "That's 'bout the last thing I needed to hear!"

"It's the truth, Possum. But that don't mean stop believin'. You gotta keep yo' faith."

"I'm tryin hard, Sammy, but it's slippin' fast."

"I can only imagine. If it was one o' my girls—"

"I guess I better be gettin' on," Possum interrupted, clear now why she had dumped him. "If you hear anything, you will let me know, won't you?"

"You know I will. Ain't neva been a time you couldn't count on me."

"Thanks," Possum said before Sammy took her to a place she didn't want to revisit. "I'll be seein' you around." Possum turned.

Sammy mounted the wagon. "I really loved you, Possum Johnson. I really did."

"I can't handle that right now, Sammy," Possum said, shaking her head. She refused to face him.

"I understand," Sammy whimpered. "I just needed you to know."

"Why?" Possum regretted asking.

"'Cause I get a feelin' de next few days might be the hardest days o' yo' life, and you might need to hold on to somethin' real."

"Was it real, Sammy?" Possum turned and hollered. "Was it? Or was it always about you?"

"It was real," he answered coolly. "I ain't never felt like that about nobody before or since you."

"Let's just let bygones be bygones," Possum suggested. "Right now, I gotta find my baby."

"I understand," Sammy muttered. "But don't forget what I said. And if you need me, just send word."

"You have a wife, man!"

"I know. But I'd swim de ocean for you." His gaze pierced her heart.

"Go home, Sammy Spears. Just go home. I gotta go, too. Pray for me."

Possum walked away, and Sammy led the mules in the opposite direction. Farther down the road, she passed the pear tree where they shared their first kiss. She remembered how his full, pink-and-brown lips engulfed her more narrow ones and how his strong grip made her feel safe and wanted. His pearly white teeth, which distracted folks away from his extralarge forehead, granted him a smile that, in 1935, made all the girls in Money envious of Possum. The night they made love for the first time, she remembered how his teeth shone in the moonlight and how his guttural laughter eased her apprehension.

Now, the last thing she needed was to consider life with a married man. So, with a slight wave of hand, she dismissed Sammy from her immediate reality and tried hard to hold herself together until she arrived home. Every time she tried to imagine where Clement might be or what some old dirty white men might be doing to him, her chest throbbed, and her breath evaporated. "Everything's gon be all right," she had repeated all the way from the Windy City to the Land of Cotton. Believing it was now the challenge.

Approaching the old house, Possum felt her resolve weaken. Miss Mary was sitting on the front porch shelling peas into her apron when she looked up and saw her only daughter. It was the meeting of their eyes simultaneously that brought Possum to her knees. She breached all internal contracts and emitted a screeching yell that made Miss Mary's skin dance.

"Momma! Momma!" she shouted from a deep, dark place within, and wilted in the front yard.

Miss Mary jumped, spilling peas in every direction, and ran to assist Possum. "It's gon be all right, baby," she comforted, struggling to stand her daughter upright again. "De Good Lawd gon make a way. You watch Him." Possum's piercing cries loosened Miss Mary's otherwise airtight faith.

"What they done done to my baby, Momma? Huh?" Possum mumbled like one fully inebriated. Her head lay limp on her mother's shoulder.

"You jes keep the faith, baby. Everything gon be all right. Clement's jes fine." Miss Mary rubbed the left side of Possum's face soothingly and rocked both of them back and forth, searching the heavens for something else reassuring to say. Finding nothing, she called loudly, "Jeremiah! Children!"

"Momma," Possum pleaded, "where is my baby?" She was clawing Miss Mary's arms. "Is they done killed my baby?"

"No, chile!" Miss Mary whispered. "Now stop talkin' like that. Clement's gon be jes fine. Yo' daddy, brother, and everybody else is lookin' for him, and they gon find him. Mark my word."

Possum didn't hear the assurance in her mother's voice she desperately needed to hear. "Oh God!" She wept bitterly.

"It's gon be all right, Possum," Jeremiah preached, lifting her from the earth. "Don't git beside yo'self now, baby. We gotta keep a straight head so we can think." He threw her right arm across his shoulders and nodded for Enoch to support her on the left.

Chop and Sarah Jane cried from the porch and watched the menfolk drag Possum into the house. Her paralyzed legs hung impotent beneath her torso, and her small, firm breasts pressed forcefully against the contours of her dress. She looked nothing like the children had envisioned. Even in her distress, she was a pretty woman, Sarah Jane noted, unlike the bold, recalcitrant, unruly child everyone had described. As the men carried Possum into the house, Sarah Jane discovered her aunt's narrow waistline, complemented by protruding, rounded hips that produced an hourglass shape like one she hoped to have one day. She wanted to tell her how pretty she was, but it was clearly not the time.

"Get yo' aunt Possum some water," Miss Mary called out. Sarah Jane obeyed instantly, and when she presented Possum the glass, Possum's weak smile evoked her own.

"You must be my Sarah Jane," Possum murmured sweetly.

"Yes ma'am, I am," Sarah Jane said excitedly. It was the *my* she loved most.

"You just as pretty as a purple sunset," Possum complimented. She sat in her father's rocker and tried to recompose herself.

"Thank you, Aunt Possum. You're pretty, too. I been thinkin' 'bout you and tryin' to imagine what you might look like and Uncle Enoch always be tellin' us kids stories 'bout you, him, and Daddy and sometimes I think about Chicago and what it must be like all de way up there 'cause Clement used to tell us—"

"Hush, chile," Miss Mary reprimanded. "Don't talk yo' aunt's head off befo' she git to relax a li'l bit."

Trying hard to refashion a familial atmosphere in the midst of intense chaos and unspoken fear of Clement's demise was more than Sarah Jane could handle alone.

"You, sir, must be Pork Chop," Possum said more lightly.

"W-w-well, no, mmmmam," Chop corrected innocently as he

moved to stand before his aunt. "I-I-I'm Chop, b-b-but I ain't p-p-p-pork chop."

"Yessir," Possum cackled. "And how did you get that name?"

"Everybody say w-w-when I w-w-was lllllittle I ate a wh-h-hole pork chop, b-b-b-b-b-b-bone and all," he explained, then smiled, clearly proud of the achievement.

She patted his head lovingly. "Well, you jes keep on eatin', young man, and you'll get big and strong jes like yo' daddy." Chop embraced Possum like Clement used to. She held him until he pulled away.

"I'm Ray Ray, ma'am."

Possum turned and saw Enoch as a child again. "If you ain't the spittin' image of yo' daddy, boy, my name ain't Possum!" she declared. "Come over hyeah, and hug yo' aintie's neck. You might be big, but you ain't grown."

Ray Ray shuffled across the floor, not wanting to be treated like the other younger ones.

"Just as handsome as you can be! Look at ya!" Possum slapped Ray Ray on the shoulder harder than he had anticipated.

"You mighty purty, Aunt Possum," Ray Ray complimented freely. "Mighty purty."

"Well, thank ya, son. You don't look half-bad yo'self."

After the introductions, Miss Mary said, "Come on to dis table and let's eat."

Ella Mae placed cabbage, fried pork chops, sliced tomatoes and onions, and butter beans on the table, and everyone waited for Possum to sit first. Once she took her seat, the others began to chatter, hoping privately to avoid the topic of Clement, at least until supper was over.

"When God created the world," Enoch began solemnly, "He looked at everything he made and evaluated it."

"Uh-huh," Ella Mae responded, trying not to laugh prematurely. She spilled butter bean pot liquor all over Possum's dress. "I'm sorry, girl," she apologized, and dabbed at the spots with an old dishrag lying on the table. "Yo' brother is a straight fool, chile," she commented.

Possum never smiled.

"He made the stars and the moon, then He stepped back, and said, 'That's good'."

"Yeah!" Ella Mae said far too loudly. The children were snickering by now although their grandmother was giving them the eye. Miss Mary would have stopped Enoch's blasphemy, as she called it, except for her hope that his humor might bring Possum temporary relief.

"Then he made the trees and the flowers, and God stepped back and smelled their fragrance, and said, 'That's good.'"

"Well," Ella Mae moaned, old Baptist-deacon style. Possum wished they would simply be quiet.

"Then God made the oceans and the seas, the lakes and the rivers, and He stepped back and looked at them, and said, 'That's good.'" Enoch's shoulders began to jerk, but he denied their fullest expression in order to tell the remainder of the story.

"Tell it, tell it," Ella Mae encouraged as she discovered that Jeremiah, Miss Mary, and Possum weren't even listening.

"Then God made the beasts of the field and the birds of the air, and God looked at the animals, and said, 'That's good.'"

Ella Mae couldn't fake it any longer. She, too, hung her head and let Enoch proceed alone.

"Then God looked at everything He made, the stars and the moon, the animals and the birds, the oceans and the trees, and He said, 'I'm lonely still. I think I'll make me a man.'"

Enoch determined to finish the story whether the adults listened or not. At least the children were laughing.

"So God scooped down in the bed of the river and gathered a ball of Mississippi Delta mud and shaped it 'til he had formed a strong, muscular Black man. And God looked at de brotha and said—"

"Thththththththththat's g-g-good!" Chop belted.

"That's right!" Enoch said, and continued: "Then God looked at dat good-lookin' brotha, and said, 'Ain't no need in him bein' on dis earth all by hisself. He need a helpmate. So God went back to de river and scooped up some more clay and decided to shape it a li'l different. He put lumps in de chest—"

Miss Mary cleared her throat.

Enoch paused, then said, "He made another figure out of de clay from de riverbed and called this figure woman because that's what Adam said when he saw her—wooooooo man!"

Ray Ray chuckled loudest while Sarah Jane and Chop only smiled.

"That ain't the end of the story," Enoch declared, refusing to admit that what the family needed was not humor.

"So God put the man and woman in a special garden where they didn't have to do nothin' all day but eat and enjoy theyselves. God looked at them together, and said, 'That's good.'

"Then God heard the man and woman huffin' and breathin' loud one day and God came to see what was wrong. When He got to de garden, he saw the man and woman makin' love, and God looked at them, and said—"

"Enoch, that's enough," Miss Mary muttered. "Ain't nothin' funny 'round here today."

Possum reached and touched his shoulder gratefully. Enoch had no choice but to stop.

Miss Mary rose and sat in the rocker. She opened her Bible and read silently. Jeremiah joined her.

Possum followed Enoch to the edge of the front porch. "I know what you wuz tryin' to do, and I'm mighty grateful, but I ain't got nothin' to laugh about right now."

"I know, sis," Enoch said. "I just hoped I could make you smile at least once."

"I'm jes glad you here, li'l brother." She reached for his hand.

After a few seconds, Enoch said, "I wish I coulda protected him, Possum."

"It ain't yo' fault, Enoch. It ain't nobody's fault, I guess. 'Cept these goddamn crackers who don't care 'bout nobody and nothin' but theyselves."

The siblings stared across the open field, unsure of what more needed to be said.

"It's definitely hot," Possum offered to lighten the mood. "I guess Mississippi is 'bout as close to hell as one can get on earth."

"It don't git dis hot up in Chicago?"

"Yeah, it do, but it's a different kinda hot."

"Really?" Enoch asked, confused. "Heat is hot everywhere."

Possum said simply, "Guess you right."

A mosquito lit on Enoch's left arm and died three seconds later. "How's life been treatin' you in de big city, sis?"

"Oh fine."

Enoch stared at her until she told the truth.

"Okay, okay. It's hard as hell, Enoch. I git up 'bout five every mornin' and work 'til 'bout dark."

"What chu do?"

Possum wanted to tell Enoch something that would make him proud of her, something that would justify her decision to abandon Mississippi, but all she had to offer was the truth. "I clean houses some days and otha days I wash white folks' dirty clothes."

Enoch nodded and asked, "They pay you pretty good?"

"No. Negroes in Chicago barely make ends meet, and sometimes de ends don't meet. But, overall, I guess I'm doin' all right for myself."

"You ain't found yo'self no husband?" Enoch nudged playfully.

"Chile, please," Possum grunted. "I'm sick o' smooth-talkin' colored men. They don't want nothin' but a woman to take care o' them, and I sho ain't gon do that. I can barely take care o' me and Cle—" Possum covered her mouth abruptly.

Not knowing what to say, Enoch rubbed her back in circular motions and prayed that she would not crumble again.

Feeling his apprehension, Possum took a deep breath and tried hard to relax. "What these white folks done gone and done to my son, Enoch?"

"I don't know, sis," he admitted helplessly. "I jes don't know." They ceased talking for a long while, then Enoch added, "Everybody colored in Money, and a few white folks, is lookin' for him real hard."

"What happened?" she asked.

Enoch explained everything, even how Rosenthal had volunteered his services. He told Possum about the town meeting and the subsequent commitment everybody made to find Clement, come what may.

"Good, good," Possum repeated solemnly.

"I wish I could promise you Clement's gon be fine, but ain't no need in me lyin' to you. I sho hope he's all right, but ain't no guarantees. All we know to do is keep lookin'."

"Why didn't you make him come outta dat store, Enoch? He woulda minded you. I know he woulda."

"I wunnit even there!"

Possum sighed. "I'm sorry." "I know it ain't yo' fault. I jes want my boy back, that's all."

"I know, sis. Dat's what we all want."

Pet Moore's old '52 Dodge truck came rattling down the dusky road. Enoch and Possum looked up simultaneously.

"Who in the world . . ." Possum mumbled.

Enoch squinted his eyes. "Look like Pet's old pickup, but I cain't make it out. Whoever it is, they flyin' like they goin' to a fire."

Seconds later, Pet Moore hopped from the truck and trotted over to the Johnsons' front porch. When he saw Possum, he grabbed her quickly, squeezing her harder than he had intended.

"Uh . . . Mr. Pet?" Possum burbled in confusion. "Is you all right?" Her face was practically buried under his right armpit.

Pet Moore held her tightly, like one trying desperately to keep water from leaking through trembling hands.

"Daddy! Momma! Ella Mae!" Enoch called. He knew something was terribly wrong.

When the family had gathered on the porch, Pet Moore slowly released Possum, exposing his wet eyes and distressed look.

"I sho is done missed you, young lady," he said in a broken voice.

Possum was totally off guard. "I missed you, too, Mr. Pet. But surely you ain't cryin' cause . . ." Then her eyes bucked in fear. "Oh my God, Momma!" she cried, and reached for someone to grab hold of.

"They found a body in de river dis evening," Pet Moore explained painfully. "Whoever it wuz, he wuz beat so bad cain't nobody recognize him." He paused and added reluctantly, "It's a colored boy's body."

"No!" Possum wailed. Her voice echoed in the nearby woods. "It ain't my boy! God *no!"* Miss Mary and Enoch held her hands as the agony twisted her body into contortions. "Momma! My baby!"

"Jes hold on," Miss Mary counseled. "It probably ain't even Clement. Don't git bent all out o' shape 'fo we know somethin'. We gotta keep on believin' 'til we find out somethin' fu sho," she comforted although shaking her head skeptically.

"Who told you dis, Pet?" Jeremiah queried.

"I overheard Pat Chadwick tell old man Cuthbert that some white boys was fishin' down by de Big Mouth Crossin' and saw a body floatin' in de river that like to scared them half to death. They knowed it wuz a Negro boy, they said, 'cause they seed de head."

"Lord have mercy," Ella Mae murmured.

Pet Moore went on: "They wuz laughin' 'bout colored folks deservin' whatever they git 'cause them white men's lives got to be accounted for. Cuthbert asked Chadwick what de boys did wit de body, and Chadwick said they left it in de river."

"They didn't even have the decency to pull my baby outta de water?" Possum mumbled deliriously.

"Stop it, girl!" Enoch yelled. "Now jes stop it. We don't know if it wuz Clement or not. We'll jes have to wait and see."

"I came by to tell ya what I heard and to tell ya dat me and a couple o' otha boys is headed down to de river to see what we can find. I didn't know if y'all"—he meant Enoch or Jeremiah—"wanted to come. I sho didn't know you wuz here yet, Possum. I'm sorry 'bout what's done happened to Clement. I wish I—"

"Don't worry 'bout it, Pet," Jeremiah interrupted. "We sho thank ya for lookin' out fu de family." He turned toward Miss Mary and the others. "Y'all go on in de house and wait fu us to git back. We ain't gon be long. Enoch, let's go."

The three men squeezed into the small cab of the truck and bobbed away down the road.

"Come on in the house," Miss Mary instructed. "We gon pray and trust de Good Lawd to do His perfect will." She and Ella Mae escorted Possum slowly, and the children held the door open. "Lawd have murcy," Miss Mary repeated countless times.

Possum fell into the rocker. Ella Mae rested on her knees beside her, and whispered, "You stay strong, girl. You hear me? Everything's gon be all right. You jes gotta stay strong." She handed her a glass of water. "Drink it slow, Possum, and breathe deep. Everything's gon be all right. Jes take it easy." Ella Mae slapped her hand continuously as though trying to revive her.

The children were gathered at the kitchen table. Ray Ray admonished, "Don't cry, Sarah Jane. We don't even know nothin' fu sho yet."

"Who else could it be?" she whispered.

"I don't know, but ain't no need in gettin' all worked up 'til we know de truth. At least wait 'til Daddy nem come back."

"Is D-d-d-d-daddy nem gon b-b-bring de b-body ba-back here?" Chop asked.

"Shut up, boy!" the other two said. Chop lowered his head onto his folded arms, defeated.

"If it is Clement," Ray Ray directed toward Sarah Jane, "we gotta stay strong for Aunt Possum."

Sarah Jane looked at Possum's incapacitated form. "What chu think gon happen, Ray Ray, if—"

"I don't know," Ray Ray muttered. "But . . ."

"But what?"

"Never mind."

The women and children assumed a shield of silence while they waited. Somewhere in everybody's souls, they already knew the truth.

Fourteen

ET MOORE DROVE DOWN TALLEY LANE AND TURNED LEFT AT Old River Road. In the middle of the annual August drought, there was always a shallow crossing in the river where logs and debris gathered, so if the body made it that far, he assumed, it certainly wouldn't get any farther.

When they reached the river, they were surprised to see several other colored men ready and waiting with loaded shotguns.

"We heard de news," Tiny said, as they exited the truck. "We knowed y'all would be here sooner or later."

"I sho' 'preciate all o' y'all," Jeremiah announced sincerely. "Let's see what we can find."

Without instructions, the men formed a single-file line and walked into the river, shoes and all. They moved their feet back and forth with each step, some hoping to discover something, others praying not to. When the lead man was halfway across, he motioned for the others to spread out. Tiny bent and searched the riverbed with his hands as though feeling for something microscopic. At one point, he screeched, thinking he felt an arm or leg, but then he sighed and lifted a broken tree limb from the water.

Enoch, on the other hand, tiptoed through the muddy stream, having convinced his heart that Clement was still alive. Somehow. His head had a difficult time following his heart's resolve, though, especially with no proof, so Enoch examined the river cautiously, hoping not to find his nephew. While the others searched the expanse of the shallow waters, he kicked his right foot lazily within the same three square feet. He wanted nothing more than to return home and tell his sister that her fears were unfounded and that, in fact, they had found Clement tied up in a barn or next to a tree somewhere. At the very least he wanted to report that Clement wasn't in the river and, as of now, it looked as if he wasn't.

"We used to swim all up and down dis river," Jeremiah offered, disconnecting Enoch from his thoughts. "Back then, times wuz betta than they is now." He patted Enoch's shoulder.

"How's that?" Enoch asked, grateful for the distraction.

"'Cause Negroes did this all de time." He pointed at the other men.

"Did what?"

"Help one another out. We wuz always gatherin' hay for one another or pickin' peas together or diggin' up potatoes to put in each other's barn."

"We do dat now, Daddy, don't we?"

"Naw, son, not like we used to. I don't mean a few folks helpin' each other out. I mean"—he raised his voice for emphasis—"everybody. Sometimes it would be forty or fifty folks sittin' 'round shuckin' corn and laughin' and havin' a good ole time. Momma'd have a big pot 'o greens on de stove and fry two or three chickens in de big black pot in de front yard. Folks would sit and clown all night long."

Father and son looked around at the other men and dreamed of times when such a sight had been the norm.

Jeremiah reminisced further: "My granddaddy disappeared when I was seven. Just walked off one day and never did come back."

"Really?" Enoch said. "I never knew that."

"Lotta thangs Negro people don't talk about, but we oughta. Ain't no way de children gon know if de old folks don't teach 'em." Jeremiah continued: "Granddaddy was a li'l fella, maybe, five-five or so, but he could outrun anybody in dis county, young or old, all de way 'til he disappeared."

"He musta been pretty young when he disappeared," Enoch guessed.

"He left de day after his sixtieth birthday." Jeremiah turned to witness the disbelief sure to color Enoch's face. "Dat's right! Young fellas used to challenge him all de time, and he neva did lose. They'd git out in de middle o' Talley Lane and folks would gather all 'round 'em, waitin' on somebody to outrun Mr. Jessie. Dat's what everybody called him. But nobody neva did."

"Come on, Daddy!" Enoch said. "You mean to tell me dat twenty-year-old fellas couldn't outrun a sixty-year-old man?"

"Dat's right!" Jeremiah proclaimed. "Dat li'l man would take off like a lightnin' flash, and by de time de othas got to de finish line, he'd be standin' dere waitin."

"Git outta hyeah!"

"I'm tellin' you what I seen fu myself, boy! Couldn't nobody explain it. And, on top o' dat, he had arthritis."

"He musta been in tiptop shape to be runnin' like dat," Enoch asserted.

"Drank a glass a wine a day and ate chitlins every chance he got," Jeremiah teased. "One day, they say my daddy wuz caught under a wagon wheel and couldn't nobody move it. They went home to tell Granddaddy 'bout it, and he ran and moved de wagon and saved my daddy's life."

"I don't mean to sound rude," Enoch frowned, "but that don't sound like a big deal to me. Most wagons ain't very heavy."

"Well," Jeremiah chuckled, "they is if you first gotta run to Green-wood to lift 'em."

"What? Grandpa Jessie ran all de way to Greenwood?"

"In about fifteen minutes, they say."

"It takes forty-five minutes in a wagon!"

"I know how long it take. But that's what they say happened. Then, he lifted de wagon by hisself, and they pulled Daddy out."

"Wunnit nobody else around to help? I mean, surely there was some otha men who coulda helped lift de wagon and save him?"

"Plenty otha folks around, but none of 'em strong as Granddaddy. The wagon was loaded."

"You mean to tell me, Granddaddy Jessie lifted a loaded wagon by hisself when a whole group o' men couldn't move it?"

"Dat's what de tell me," Jeremiah affirmed. "And he neva did weigh over a hunnert fifty pounds."

"Daddy, some o' de thangs you tell me . . ."

"You ain't gotta believe it. It's gon be true even if—"

"Hey!" Tiny called. "I think I got something."

Jeremiah and Enoch froze. This was the moment they had strate-gically avoided. Knowing they couldn't any longer, they waltzed in the water, side by side until they stood before Tiny. Each glanced at the other's blank face and telepathically agreed to survive whatever truth they were about to encounter.

"What is it, Tiny?" Jeremiah murmured.

"Look," Tiny said, extending his right hand.

Some emitted sighs of sorrow; a few cursed freely.

"What is that?" Enoch asked, refusing to see what everyone else saw clearly.

"Hair," Tiny stated glumly. "It's somebody's hair."

Enoch felt his legs weaken beneath him. "It could be anybody's," he said, refusing to consider what the others had already concluded.

Jeremiah blinked tears away. "It's his."

"You don't know that, Daddy!" Enoch yelled. "Lot's o' boys swim in de river in de summer."

"They don't shave their heads in it, do they?" Jeremiah screamed.

Enoch wasn't prepared for such a direct response, but his heart couldn't submit without a fight. "Come on, Daddy!" He laughed uneasily. "Negro boys swim in de river all the time. Somebody's head brushed up against a tree limb—"

"Stop it, son."

". . . and the limb stratched a little hair off their heads like—"

"Stop, Enoch."

". . . when you jump in the river and accidentally scrape yo' head against a twig—"

"Enoch."

". . . I used to do that all the time! Every Negro boy in Money done experienced—"

"Enoch!"

". . . what happens when you jump in too quick and scrape yo' head against something then the hair floats on down the river—"

"Stop it!" Jeremiah finally screamed angrily. "We ain't gon do this!"

"Do what?" Enoch asked.

"Act like we don't know what this is."

"We don't know!" Enoch pressed on.

"Yes, we do, boy!" Jeremiah insisted. "Yes we do!"

"Daddy," Enoch cried quietly, "it really could be somebody else's, couldn't it?"

"No, son, it couldn't. Not this much." His palms were filled with wet, woolly hair.

Enoch sobbed as he called on the last bit of fight in him. "You still ain't one hundred percent sure," he lamented in his father's arms. "How you know the difference between one Negro boy's hair and another? Huh?" His words became unintelligible. Most of the men's eyes glazed over not from the thought of Clement, but from watching Enoch bleat like a sheep in a slaughter stall.

"Y'all go 'head on home now, boys," Jeremiah said casually. "I sho thanks ya. If we hear anything else, we'll let ya know."

The men hung their heads sadly and patted Jeremiah and Enoch on their backs. "Y'all take care," some whispered in passing.

Enoch was still crying when the procession disappeared. His head lay pressed against his daddy's chest, and Jeremiah rubbed it tenderly. They were still waist deep in the Tallahatchie River, only now they were alone.

"It's all right, son," Jeremiah said, rocking Enoch the best he could while standing in moving water.

"It ain't fair!" Enoch roared. "It just ain't fair!" His arms slid down to encircle his father's waist.

"I know, son. I know. But everythang's gon be all right."

Suddenly Enoch released Jeremiah and stepped back. "No, it ain't, Daddy! No it ain't!" Tears continued streaming down his cheeks. "It's always us. They always killin' us. Don't make no difference what we do, they try to destroy us!" he yelled.

"Take it easy now, boy," Jeremiah whispered.

"Take what easy, Daddy? I'm sick'o 'takin' it easy.'" he mocked vociferously. "I'm sick o' racist peckawoods killin' Negroes! Dat's what I'm sick of!" He kicked water angrily until both he and his father were drenched. "Don't ask me to take it easy no mo 'cause I ain't doin' it! Maybe that's Clement's hair and maybe it ain't. I ain't gon believe it 'til I see where they pulled it from his head. And if I see that"—Enoch trembled—"you'd better git somebody to hold me down 'cause jes like Jerry went and killed them white men for fuckin' wit Billie Faye, I swear 'fo God I'll kill all them muthafuckas!"

He turned and stomped out of the river. Although he was still crying, his gait exposed a clarity that frightened Jeremiah. That little tuft of spongy hair had transposed Enoch into a new man. Having never cursed before in his parents' earshot, Enoch's intemperate language scared his father more than all of his son's expressed frustration.

Jeremiah watched Enoch's body grow smaller as he walked away. Pet Moore begged to take them home, but both refused the offer initially, trying hard not to be rude but knowing simultaneously that they needed time alone in order to swallow what God had given them to chew. How arrogant it is, Jeremiah thought, for people to expect a Black man to remain humble when he's constantly being downtrodened. He would have to be Jesus to manage that kind of nonviolent forgiveness, and even then Jeremiah wasn't sure he admired such meekness. In the end, it always meant being trampled upon in the service of some higher principle in which, obviously, only the oppressed believe. Righteousness had not borne the fruit Jeremiah's ancestors promised it would, and, for the time being, he simply wanted to win. Just once. He wanted the thrill of victory, the recognition by his enemies that he had beaten them, and the life of his children to prove it. Others had warned that God's wrath would visit itself upon him if he exacted justice on his own terms, so, trying not to anger an all-powerful God, Jeremiah had surrendered to a nonconfrontational mode of resistance until the day Cecil and the Cuthbert boys tried to take his grandson away. After then, Jeremiah determined that God would have to do whatever God was going to do because apparently his people had never considered that righteousness and whippin' white folks' asses might be one and the same.

Jeremiah stood in the water defeated. He didn't want to go home, he didn't want to ride in the truck with Pet, he didn't want to have his grandson's hair balled up in his fists, he didn't want to forgive, he didn't want to forget, he didn't want to cry, and he didn't want to die. He wanted to skip death and confront God unannounced. Watching Enoch deteriorate, Jeremiah tried not to imagine what he would do if he had to bury his last son. He looked around at the contented river, the oblivious birds, and the unconcerned cotton stalks, and one bold tear escaped as loneliness teased him like a faint breeze on a hot summer night.

"I cain't do this no more," he mumbled. "What are we doin' wrong? What am I doin' wrong?" He looked puzzled and confused.

"You all right out there?" Pet hollered from the truck.

Jeremiah ignored him. "I know I work hard, so that cain't be it. I takes my family to church every Sunday. I only drinks on Saturday

nights, and when I do I don' neva git sloppy drunk. So I don't understand the problem." With outstretched arms and a head hung low,
Jeremiah's form resembled the crucifix.

Pet Moore exited the truck and stood on the bank of the Tallahatchie, watching his friend.

"Seem lak every time I ask something of You I cain't neva git it.
Why is that? Huh?" With every question Jeremiah became more
incensed. "Negroes is always beggin' God fu help! I'm tired o' that.
I wanna help myself now. I love God, always have and always will,
but I'm sick"—he screamed the word—"o' feelin' helpless. Somethin'
gotta change. I'm always waitin' on God or fate or time or somethin'
to keep my life in order, but why cain't I do it myself?" Jeremiah didn't
know to whom he spoke, but the speaking itself was too therapeutic
for him to stop. The flow of the river around him kept his adrenaline
pumping, providing him with just enough energy to purge his soul.

To Pet he looked like the picture of John the Baptist that hung on
his living room wall. The only thing missing, Pet thought, was a sub-
missive, willing Christ for him to baptize.

"You know what's funny?" Jeremiah chuckled and placed his hands
on his hips. "Negro peoples been good to white folks 'cause we scared
o' them. It ain't got nothin' to do wit bein' no Christian! You know
how I know? 'Cause we treat each other like shit!" he yelled. "We grin
and heehaw at whites 'cause we know they got de power to fuck our
lives up whenever they git ready. That's it! And since we ain't got no
power, we can treat each other any kind o' way 'cause it ain't gon
make no difference nohow. All this time I thought we wuz nice to
white folks 'cause we wuz tryin' to be good Christians. Bullshit! We
jes been nice 'cause we scared. We don't even believe in Jesus. What
we believe in is whatever will git us by. That's it!" he screamed and
pounded one fist into the other. "That's why we don't neva git ahead
'cause we always tryin' to figure out how to git ova instead o' gittin'
along. And white folks know it. So they keep fuckin' wit us 'cause
they learned years ago that, somehow, Negro people like them better
than they like themselves. This means they can do whatever they

want to us 'cause we love them too much to destroy them. That's why they did this to Clement! Killin' them white men suggested that I might love myself more than I love them, and they cain't neva have that 'cause if that ever happen, they whole way o' life is doomed. Oh shit!" Jeremiah danced in the river as his analysis became clearer. "They livin' good only because we love them! Damn! Why did it take me so long to figure this out? That's why Negroes cain't git ahead! We think de Bible and its teachin's is fu how we treat white folk—not each other. 'To hell wit a Negro man,' we tell ourselves. 'He ain't shit.' Yep, that's exactly what we say in our hearts. We might not say it out loud, but that's exactly what we think. That's why Clement's body is floatin' somewhere in dis river—'cause de rest o' de Negroes in this goddamn town don't think nothin' 'bout no Black boy dyin'. If it was a white boy, everybody would be out here tryin' to find him 'cause he mean somethin' to everybody. But that's all right," Jeremiah asserted, and began exiting the river. "My grandson mean somethin', too, and if it's de last thang I do on God's green earth, I'ma make somebody know exactly how much he do mean."

When he reached Pet, Jeremiah was smiling broadly. "Let's go, man," he said.

Pet stared at him, unable to understand what had just transpired. "You all right, Mi?"

"I'm just fine, Mr. Pet Moore. Just dandy!" Jeremiah retorted, and the two climbed into the cab of the truck.

"Who was you talkin' to?" Pet asked as they drove away.

Jeremiah burst into unconstrained laughter, a sign to Pet Moore that something in Money, Mississippi, was about to change forever.

When Enoch arrived home, he found Possum swinging her feet from the porch as they had done hours before, and now she was fanning mosquitoes with a stiff piece of cardboard.

"Didn't find nothin', huh?" she said, when her brother occupied the space next to her.

Enoch wasn't sure if Jeremiah had said anything, so he played it safe. "No, we didn't find nothin'. We walked de river pretty good, but didn't find no body. Thank God."

"Well, I'm glad"—Possum sighed—"'cause I don't know what I'd do if y'all came back here wit my boy in de back o' Mr. Pet's truck. I just don't know what I'd do."

"Clement's gon be all right," Enoch stated, then hated himself for saying it.

"Ain't nothin' in Mississippi all right," Possum corrected. "This whole damn state is fucked up wit racist crackers who cain't seem to come out o' de nineteenth century. And, on top o' dat, y'all Negroes cain't seem to do without 'em."

"Y'all?" Enoch defended.

"Yes, y'all. Why would anybody Black chose to stay in a place where people hate you and kill your children?"

"'Cause this place is our home, too! White folks don't own de goddamn ground in Mississippi. If anything, we own it 'cause we sho been de ones workin' it. Dat's why we still here," he argued. "We done worked far too hard to walk off and let somebody else reap our harvest. Shit, dis land right here?"—he waved his arms in every possible direction—"dis is *my* land. It was my great granddaddy's, my granddaddy's, then it was my daddy's, and now it's mine. No, we don't own no deed to it yet, but it's mine all de same 'cause I done gave my life for it. And quiet as it's kept, it's yours, too."

"Hell, naw!" Possum hollered, shaking her head fiercely. "I don't want no part of dis. You can have it if you want it, but don't save none fu me!"

"Well, hell, you ain't doin' no better up in Chicago! Don't you work fu white folks, too?"

"Yeah, but . . ."

"But what? White folks is white folks!" Enoch screamed. "They ain't payin' you shit up there, and they ain't payin us shit down here."

"But it's different," Possum said weakly.

"How?" Enoch bellowed.

"'Cause I ain't choppin' cotton all day long out in de hot sun!" Possum hollered back.

"But you washin' white folks' dirty draws from sunup to sundown! That makes you feel better?"

Possum paused. "No, it don't, but still."

"Still what!" Enoch was standing now.

"Still I'm not sharecroppin' and makin' some dirty old white man richer."

"Yes, you are! Do you own de place where you stayin'? Huh?"

"No, I don't," Possum confessed.

"Then you sharecroppin'! They jes got another name for it. They call it rent. But it's de same thang."

"How?"

"'Cause don't care how long you live there and pay, you don't never own it. You jes keep payin' and payin', month after month, and whenever you leave, you don't take nothin' but de same shit you brought with you. You done gave some white man thousands of dollars, and you don't git one dime of it back. Dat's de same thang we doin' down here. But at least we can eat if we git hongry."

Enoch's airtight argument couldn't be refuted.

"See, I'd rather be poor in Mississippi 'cause at least if I ain't got no money I can still eat. All I gotta do is raise a crop. In Chicago, if you ain't got no money, you been done starved to death 'cause you ain't got no land to grow nothin' on. And you callin' that better off?"

"Yes, I do," Possum suggested, "'cause at least I ain't got to bow and scratch when white folks walk by."

"OH! So you don't say 'yes ma'am' to dat white woman whose clothes you wash?" Enoch stared at Possum.

She confessed, "Yes, I do, but—"

"Oh, stop dis shit, girl! Negroes is strugglin' everywhere, and jes 'cause you a slave in de city don't make slavery in de country no worse."

"But, Enoch, there are a lotta Negroes who own their own businesses and live in neighborhoods with otha Negroes who doin' real good for theyselves. The whole time I lived down South I ain't neva seen no neighborhood of Black folks doin' good."

Enoch consented, and Possum seized the advantage.

"That's all I been lookin' for—the opportunity to do better. I ain't doin' so great right now, but I got the chance to do good. Down here, I didn't even have the chance. Where are the rich Negroes in Money? Huh? Show me even one! Most o' dese families been here for three and four generations, and they still doin' 'bout as good as the first generation did. At least in Chicago you got a chance to do better. It might happen, and it might not, but a chance is better than knowin' for sho you ain't neva gon git nothin' and nowhere.

"I might not ever make it big in Chicago, but I'm shonuff gon try like hell 'cause I done seen too many Negro people do it. And even if *I* don't, I get excited just watchin' other Black people do it. Down here, every Negro I know is in de same boat, and that boat is sinkin' fast." Possum regretted her last statement, but since she couldn't take it back, she simply fell quiet.

The two stared at each other for a long time. Neither wanted to admit the wisdom inherent in the other's position, but eventually they forsook their stubbornness and burst into laughter.

Possum said, "This is crazy, ain't it?"

"Real crazy. Two broke people arguin' about who's broker!" Enoch chuckled. "That's how they git us, sis. They make us fight each other instead of them."

"You right. God knows you right."

The lavender Mississippi sky caught Possum's attention. Clouds moved about nervously, unclear about their resting place, and, for the first time ever, Possum examined the night without hatred in her heart.

Enoch read her face. "It's beautiful, huh?"

"Wow. It's absolutely gorgeous. I don't ever remember seeing a night like this when we were kids."

"You didn't have the eyes to see it then," Enoch said.

"Did you?" Possum asked. "Did you always see the beauty of this place?"

Brief spouts of laughter punctuated Enoch's response: "Hell naw, girl. I wuz tryin' like hell to get outta here, too. You remember, don't you? I left here and went to Memphis . . ."

"Oh, yeah! You was tryin' to be a comedian," Possum cackled.

"I wunnit tryin' to be nothin'. I *was* a comedian," he joked. "The only problem was that Negro comedians wunnit makin' no money in Memphis. I didn't neva wanna come back here though. But after Jerry died and I moved back, I realized that a man gotta make happiness wherever he is, and home oughta be at least one place where he can always find it.

"So when I got back and realized I wunnit eva goin' nowhere, I stopped hatin' the place and started lookin' for its beauty. Many evenin's I sat out here by myself just lookin' at the sky and listenin' to frogs and crickets until one day I looked up and saw all these colors blended together, and I started cryin'. I cain't really explain why. I noticed birds dancing in the sky like just being there was a joy and I saw rabbits bouncing around in the garden and squirrels leaping from tree to tree, and when I put it all together, it hit me that I was sittin' in the middle of Paradise."

"I wouldn't say all that," Possum sneered.

"But think about it. Before humans came along and messed up the balance of the world, every place on earth was probably perfectly beautiful in its own way. You only hate this place because of how Negroes get treated. You don't hate the place itself."

Possum studied the magical sky again. "I guess you right, Enoch. I never considered anything beautiful about Money, Mississippi, or any place in Mississippi for that matter. I just wanted to get away."

"I understand," Enoch said, taking Possum's hand. "And now with everything that's done happened to Clement . . ."

"No! Let's not talk about that right now, Enoch. Let's just watch the sky."

Enoch rubbed Possum's hand soothingly as she basked in a wonder she had missed her entire life. Occasionally, she closed her eyes and rocked like an old church mother trying hard to follow a confusing sermon. The jade cotton plants across the field now registered in Possum's consciousness as majestic fruit of the soil instead of a sign of Negro subjugation. Chirping birds, which throughout her young life disturbed her sleep, now sounded like an ensemble of sopranos, altos, and tenors, all of whom sang in perfect, three-part harmony. Even the baby snake slithering beneath their feet contributed to the splendor of the moment, for instead of running in fear, Possum smiled slightly at the layers of brown, gold, and black that decorated its back.

"An artist could have a field day here," she murmured aloud.

"Uh-huh," Enoch mumbled. Then, suddenly, he laughed boisterously.

"What is it?"

"The other night I was sittin' out here jes like we doin' now and de Holy Ghost got all over me, and I started dancin' and shoutin' right here in de middle of de front yard."

"What!"

Enoch leaned on Possum laughing. "I ain't lyin'! Momma was sittin' on de porch in her rocker, and all of a sudden she heard me screamin' 'Hallelujah! Thank ya, Jesus!'" Enoch mocked himself.

Possum's body vibrated. "You gotta be kidding?"

"No, I ain't. It was the strangest thing, sis. You know how we used to make fun o' folks shoutin' and stuff? Well, dat's exactly what I started doin'."

"What got into you?"

"I don't know. I done thought about it a hundred times, and I still cain't figure it out. It's like . . . just for a moment I was at perfect peace with the world. And I got overwhelmed, I guess."

Possum was still snickering. "I woulda paid good money to see that, li'l brother."

"Yeah, I know," Enoch teased, "'cause then you could start makin' fun o' me jes like you used to make fun o' Miss Ophelia."

"I never laughed at Miss Ophelia!" Possum giggled. "That was you!"

"What?" Enoch protested. "You wuz de one who taught me how to shout like her!"

"No I didn't!"

"Yes you did! Everybody thought I wuz de one jes because I liked to joke and clown a lot, but it wuz you and Martha Mae—"

"Me and Martha Mae?" Possum screeched.

"Yep! Y'all would sit in de back o' de church and shout jes like Miss Ophelia. Don't act like you don't remember!"

"That Martha Mae was a fool!"

"You, too! Don't try to put it all on her!"

"She was worse than me. She could do somethin' real funny and look you straight in de eye like she ain't done nothin'. That's really what made me laugh. She was so good at acting innocent."

"She was crazy," Enoch corroborated.

"What happened to dat chile?"

"You didn't hear? She married Big Thang."

Possum screamed like she saw a ghost. "Big Thang? I know you lyin', Enoch."

"Yep, she married Big Thang and they got ten kids."

"That big ole boy? Get outta here! Ten children?"

"Dat's right. Now they call her Big Thang, too!"

Possum and Enoch hollered. Miss Mary ran to the front screen, wondering what in the world was wrong, and when she saw the two enjoying each other, she gave thanks for the reunion of her children, and returned to the rocker.

"Girl, Martha Mae bigger'n Momma."

"You a lie, boy!"

"Wait 'til you see her."

"She was always so skinny, Enoch! She couldn't have weighed more than a hundred pounds when we graduated from school."

"Well now her right leg weighs ninety pounds by itself."

Possum hit Enoch playfully. "Shut up!"

"I'm tellin' you! Wait 'til you see her."

"Oh my God! I used to be jealous of her 'cause she was so cute and had the cutest little figure."

"Well now she bigger'n a house, but she still cute."

"I gotta go see dat girl."

"She'd be glad to see you, Possum. Lotta folks would."

Enoch and Possum rose to enter the house for the evening. At the screen door, they paused.

"I ain't laughed like dat in years, Enoch." Possum smiled.

"Home has a way o' doin' dat to a person," Enoch said. Then he and Possum embraced for a very long time.

Fifteen

THE ALARM SOUNDED PROMPTLY AT SEVEN, AS IT HAD DONE
every morning since Rosenthal's return South.

"Good morning, Sutton," Rosenthal growled, studying
the eye, then returning it to the glass throne. "Did you sleep well?"

When his wife Marissa was living, she often rose at six, telling
Rosenthal that any man worth a dime was up and out by seven. Usually he just laughed and slept another hour. Yet since her death,
Rosenthal sometimes slept long after nine, simply because nothing
compelled him to rise. With Sutton around, however, he once again
felt motivated to live.

"Didn't sleep a wink, huh?" Rosenthal laughed at himself. "Well,
you're in a new place, and sometimes sleeping in a new place can be
difficult. Anything I can do to make your stay more comfortable?"

Again, Rosenthal sat naked on the edge of the bed. The bright sunshine glaring through the window invigorated him. "It's a great day, Sutton. What shall we do?" He stood and stretched. "I'm going to take good care of you. Don't you worry. I want us to be good friends, maybe even family." He touched Sutton gently, and said, "Now! Let's find some breakfast."

Rosenthal picked up the glass stand upon which Sutton rested and carried it carefully into the kitchen.

"Let's put you right here," he said sweetly, and placed the stand in the center of the table. Then he opened the white lace curtains and sunshine flooded the room. "That's better!" he noted as he looked around.

Rosenthal walked to the refrigerator, opened it, and bent slightly to see what breakfast food it contained. The sunlight accented his snow-white butt cheeks, which were pointed directly toward Sutton. When he stood, an accidental bumping of the table sent the eye toppling off its glass throne.

"Oh my God," he screeched. "Did I hurt you—again?"

Temporarily halting breakfast, he retrieved Sutton from the floor.

"Are you all right?" he asked, rolling the eye around in his hand. "I don't see any bruises or scrapes, so I guess you're okay."

He returned Sutton to the throne.

"I need to be more careful, huh? Since you're not like us—well, I mean, since you're not . . . a real . . . um . . . person . . . well, I mean you are a real person, Sutton, but since you don't have . . . um . . . ah, you know what I mean! I just need to be more careful with your kind."

Rosenthal turned and excavated a frying pan from a lower cabinet. The long, black hairs covering his buttocks, contrasted sharply with the whiteness of his cheeks.

"I hate to imagine how they separated you from the rest of your body," Rosenthal commented. "Some white men are sick, Sutton. There's no other way to explain it. I can't believe they beat you out of a human skull!" Rosenthal envisioned the act and his stomach churned, leaving a vile taste in his mouth. "Such ignorant fuckers!

Why couldn't they just beat . . . well, never mind. It's over now." He turned quickly. "I'm not saying they *should* have beat you or anything like that. I'm just saying it would have been better, you know, if they hadn't been so . . . so violent."

Staring at Sutton, Rosenthal recalled how, years ago, Sutton's eyes had pleaded with him for mercy he never showed.

"I'd like to bind Sheriff Cuthbert, Cecil, Larry Greer, and whoever else beat you and let your people beat them to death," he said, flipping bacon strips. "It would only be fair. If coloreds ever take vengeance on us, it's gonna be Armageddon." He cracked eggs into a small bowl and, covering them with salt and pepper, stirred vigorously. "It was probably a whole gang of them, huh? That's how they do it. In a group. Fuckin' cowards. They always need an audience. That's because it's not really about you. Not really. It's about proving their boldness to their friends. Your people just happen to be the means by which this . . . um . . ."—he snapped his fingers until the word came—"virility . . . gets established. It's pretty fuckin' sick, to tell you the truth, but it is what it is."

He poured the excess bacon grease into a tin container. "They usually taunt first. They probably called you all sorts of terrible names and then pushed you around for a while before they made you"—he didn't want to say it, but felt compelled to be honest—"suck them off. I could see Billy Cuthbert doing that. He's always been our resident rascal. They're white trash although they're rich. White trash can be wealthy, too, you know?"

Rosenthal placed bacon, eggs, and bread on the octagon-shaped kitchen table. He continued talking as he removed jelly and orange juice from the icebox.

"The real shame is that you couldn't have done anything so bad that it required your dismemberment. Y'all never do. You're such a nice people. I've known your folks for years. They work hard and never gripe about it. Those men should be ashamed of themselves."

When Rosenthal turned to sit, he bumped the table again, this time sending the throne crashing to the floor.

"Oh shit!" he screamed. "I'm sorry, Sutton!"

Rosenthal tiptoed through broken glass, and, with a spoon, scooped the eye from the floor, examining it anxiously. Relieved that it appeared to have suffered no physical damage, he said, "I'm glad you're resilient. All of your people are. That's what makes you people so strong. You survive regardless of how evil white people treat you. And you never become violent in return. That's pretty amazing. Well, sometimes you do, but usually you don't. I admire that quality about nig—coloreds."

Searching the cabinets for another throne, Rosenthal found a large punch bowl, and said, "This'll work," and placed it upside down on the table. "I'll try to be more careful this time. I'm 'bout as clumsy as they come!" he cackled. "You be careful, too, young man. You might not be so lucky next time."

Rosenthal swept the floor twice to assure that no microscopic pieces of glass escaped his broom. Then he resumed his seat and bowed. "Dear Lord, we give thanks for this food and this bountiful morning. I am grateful for the presence of Sutton and our newfound friendship, and I pray that more people find the joy we've found." He paused. "In forgiveness. Amen."

He fixed two plates. "I know you can't eat, but I thought you'd find the gesture pleasing." He smiled at his own consideration.

"I hope you like your eggs scrambled hard. I do. Come to think of it, I don't like soft foods. I'm a meat and potato kind of guy, know what I mean?"

He nodded as though expecting a response.

"You'd like my eggs. I know you would. My mother taught me how to make the perfect scrambled eggs. She always cracked them in a bowl first, to make sure they weren't defective, and then she'd add a little milk. That makes them fluffy and tasty."

Rosenthal chewed hard and fast, like one devouring his last supper.

"Then she'd sprinkle the eggs with salt. I've never been one for lots of salt, but I love pepper. I probably love it too much, but I can't eat eggs or anything else without it."

He smiled.

"Elijah used to cook for us sometimes, especially after Mom got sick. His pepper and garlic fried chicken was delicious! Make a man wanna die on the spot!" Rosenthal suddenly covered his mouth. "I'm sorry. That comment was thoughtless and insensitive of me. I didn't mean to make light of dying, especially in a time like this. It's just an old saying anyway. Think nothing of it."

He washed down a mouthful of bacon-egg mixture with a gulp of fresh-squeezed orange juice.

"You were really brilliant, you know? That's what made me and probably the sheriff so mad. We couldn't figure out how nig— coloreds! Damn! I keep doing that!—come out of the fields and man-ifest such extraordinary intelligence. It just isn't logical. But you stood up that day and put us white boys to shame. It wasn't supposed to be that way. At least that's what I had been taught. And you prob-ably said something to Catherine Cuthbert that made her feel small and insulted. I know it's not your fault, but I wish your people would be a little more careful in that regard. Sometimes we white folk are a little, let's say . . . insecure. Not that it's your job to pamper our inse-curities, but since y'all keep losing your lives when you try to embar-rass us, it might be wise to tone down that, shall we call it, unbridled display of intelligence? I'm probably not explaining this well." He wiped his mouth with the back of his hand.

"Oh Sutton! How did it ever come to this? We have to do better. I mean, we white folks." He chewed toast and reclined in the narrow kitchen chair. "Your people won't stay nice always, will they, Sutton? They can't. They'd be extinct if they did. Just like the Indians are now. It's a shame what white explorers did to all those Indians. And then sent them away on the Trail of Tears." He stared into space for a long while.

"But not coloreds!" he said. "Your people are stubborn, Sutton. I guess that can be a good thing. If it had been me, though, I would have left the South years ago when slavery ended. But to each his own!"

Rosenthal resumed eating. "Your granddaddy, Jeremiah, and the others are planning to fight back this time. I think that's great. I just hope it doesn't lead to bloodshed, you know what I mean?" He heard an automobile door slam.

"Shit! Who the hell . . . ," Rosenthal murmured, struggling to peek out of the window. "We're not prepared to receive visitors!"

He scurried to the bedroom and covered himself with a bathrobe. He had hardly reentered the kitchen when he heard the knock at the door.

"Just a moment," he cried out in panic. He stood before the kitchen door, trying to prepare himself to entertain an uninvited guest.

"Mr. Rosenthal!" a familiar voice called. "It's me, Patrick."

Rosenthal opened the door only slightly, hoping that, after a moment or two of general conversation, he could return to Sutton.

"Good morning, Patrick," Rosenthal whispered through a crack in the door.

"Did I trouble you, sir?" Patrick asked, sensing he had interrupted something.

"Oh no!" Rosenthal denied. "I . . . um . . . was eating my breakfast. But it's fine. Really."

The fake smile disturbed Patrick even more. "Maybe I should come back later," he suggested.

"Well, is there something I can help you with?"

Patrick hung his head and said, "I dropped by to see if you wanted some fish. You know I always bring you fish if I catch any."

"Well, I sure do thank ya, son. Just leave them on the porch here and I'll get them after I get dressed." Rosenthal stepped back to close the door.

"But," Patrick said abruptly, "I need to talk to you, too. It's real important."

Fuck, Rosenthal mumbled in his head. "Um . . . okay. Just give me a second." He closed the door and wiped the sweat from his brow. He almost forgot about Sutton, sitting atop the punch bowl bottom, but when he remembered, he grabbed it and slid it into the hip pocket of his bathrobe. He hated his disjointed behavior, but for now, he decided to do the best he could.

"Come on in," he told Patrick, and opened the kitchen door widely. "My house is a mess."

"Oh, don't worry about it, Mr. Rosenthal," Patrick smiled. "My folks ain't neva been ones to keep no clean house."

Just say what you want and get the hell out, Rosenthal thought, but instead he said, "Can I offer you some breakfast?"

Patrick saw the other plate sitting on the table. "Are you expecting someone?" he asked. "I didn't mean to barge in and—"

"No, no!" Rosenthal waved frantically. "I . . . um . . . just cooked too much and I put it on the table just in case someone came by. Sit down, sit down and help yourself." Rosenthal pushed Patrick's shoulder slightly toward the chair.

"Well, thank you, sir," Patrick said, and relaxed in the chair. "I don't mind if I do have a li'l breakfast."

Eat and get the fuck out, will ya? Rosenthal murmured inaudibly. He wrapped the robe around himself tighter, trying to make sure he kept his privates concealed.

"So what's on your mind?"

"Well, I don't quite know how to say this . . ."

"Just say it!" Rosenthal belted. "I mean . . . you know you can tell me anything. Don't be afraid."

"Well, okay, Mr. Rosenthal." Patrick swallowed the food in his mouth and blurted, "I wuz in de river checkin' my trot lines this mornin' and I found a body hangin' from one o' de hooks."

Rosenthal went pale. Patrick immediately saw the horror on his face.

"I'm sorry, Mr. Rosenthal. Maybe I shouldn't have come here." He began to rise from the chair.

"Oh no, son. It's fine. I . . . um . . . just hate to hear these kinds of things." His back moistened with sweat. *Stay calm*, he kept reminding himself. "Go on," he told Patrick.

"Well, like I said, I was checkin' my trot lines down by de old bridge when I felt somethin' real heavy at the end of the line. I wuz thinkin' a real big catfish or somethin' had done got hooked, but when I pulled de line up out o' de water, I saw a body. It like to scared me to death."

Patrick ate casually, expecting Rosenthal to respond any minute. "Well, what did you do?" Rosenthal asked.

"I tried to pull it out o' de water, but it wuz too heavy. An old gin fan was tied to the neck with some balin' rope, so I cut the fan loose and pulled de body out o' de water. Dat fan musta weighed seventy-five or eighty pounds." Patrick took a long gulp of orange juice. "I think it's dat colored boy, Mr. Rosenthal."

Rosenthal's head was swimming, but he couldn't let Patrick know. "Why . . . um do you think it's de colored boy, Patrick?"

"'Cause de lips are real big and de hair on its head—what's left of it—is like nigger hair. I can show you." He wiped his mouth with his sleeve and began to rise.

"Show me? How can you show me?" Rosenthal muttered.

"I got de body in de back o' my truck outside. Dat's why I come here, Mr. Rosenthal, to see if you could tell me for sure who it is."

"Me? Why me?" Rosenthal cried.

"'Cause you real smart, sir, and you know most o' de people in dis town. Momma say you talks to colored people, too, so I figured you might be able to tell me if de body is dat colored boy's or not."

"Why didn't you just take it to some colored people and ask?" Rosenthal felt urine trickle down his leg.

"I didn't want to upset them. Anyway, if the body is dat colored boy's, I'd like to know before I say anything. No need in upsettin' people for no good reason. They're probably nervous and all, you know?"

"Yes, I can understand."

Patrick motioned for Rosenthal to follow him. "Come look and tell me if you think this is de colored boy who's been missin'."

Rosenthal stumbled over a chair.

"You all right, Mr. Rosenthal?" Patrick frowned. "You look a little pale. Have you been gettin' enough rest?"

"I'm fine, son," Rosenthal said, collecting himself and retying his robe.

"Okay, well, come look and tell me what you think."

Patrick waltzed out of Rosenthal's kitchen door as carefree as a child going to hunt for blackberries. Rosenthal walked slowly, his vision blurred and his heart pounding like a hammer against a stubborn nail.

"I covered it with a old blanket I had layin' in de truck," Patrick said, "but that's the best I could do. I didn't wanna leave it in de river."

Rosenthal had not yet made it to the truck. He felt nauseous and feared he might faint when he laid eyes on whatever was under Patrick's covering. Knowing he couldn't stall forever, he took a deep breath and shuffled to the bed of the truck.

"The body's pretty bad-lookin'," Patrick warned, "and it smells something awful. I hope you got a strong stomach."

Rosenthal's belly went sour. He closed his eyes and tried to imagine the gory features of a mutilated, bloated body, but his imagination fell far short of what Patrick unveiled.

"Oh God!" Rosenthal yelled, and vomited. Had he not grabbed the truck's railing, he would have stumbled to the ground.

"I'm so sorry, Mr. Rosenthal!" Patrick cried helplessly. "I didn't know it would upset you like this."

"I'm"—breath—"okay." Rosenthal huffed and spit until he regained composure.

"Forgive me, Mr. Rosenthal. I'll ask someone else."

"No, no. It's okay." Rosenthal tried to smile but could not. "It's okay," he repeated and wiped vomitous residue from the sides of his mouth. "I was just a bit . . . unprepared."

Rosenthal raised his head and looked at the body again. The sick feeling returned, but this time he held it at bay.

"It's gotta be him," Rosenthal whispered, looking at Sutton's perfect match.

Patrick nodded. "I kinda thought it was. I mean, who else could it be? I knew you'd know, Mr. Rosenthal. I don't know what happened to the other eye, but it looks like somebody beat it out o' his head. You ever seen a head so bloated and bruised?"

To Rosenthal, Patrick's words were mere gibberish. He kept marveling that men, real human beings, could beat a child's eye right out of its socket. Even when he assaulted Sutton Griggs, Jr. at Harvard years earlier, he would never have dreamed, he convinced himself, of beating a human being that severely. Racist white men are monsters, he thought.

"Who you think did it?" Patrick asked.

"I can't imagine," Rosenthal lied. "But it's gotta be somebody really sick."

"Yeah, I know. Look at how big his head is! It looks like a black-and-blue balloon."

"Dear God," Rosenthal cried pitifully, with his left hand over his mouth. He thought about Sutton, resting peacefully in his pocket, and he decided to keep the secret to himself. He studied the corpse, this time noticing the excessively swollen lips and the wounded nose, crooked and flattened by some really heavy instrument. In his mind's eye, Rosenthal saw the sheriff and other half-drunk white men in overalls beating the boy like farmers threshing wheat.

"Stop it!" he shouted hastily. The voices in his head became louder and louder. "I said stop it!"

Patrick asked, "Mr. Rosenthal, are you okay?" He grabbed Rosenthal by both arms and shook him. "Mr. Rosenthal! Mr. Rosenthal!" he called firmly.

"Huh?" Rosenthal mumbled. If Patrick hadn't known better, he would have assumed the old man was inebriated.

"This was too much, Mr. Rosenthal," Patrick declared. "I shouldn't o' come here."

Rosenthal reestablished his balance by holding on to Patrick's arm. "It's okay, son," he breathed. "You did the right thing. It's just that"—Rosenthal struggled to regularize his breathing pattern—"I've never seen anything so . . . so . . . hideous. I can't imagine who could do this to a person."

"Me neither," Patrick agreed sadly. "But what am I supposed to do now?"

Rosenthal rubbed his head methodically and suggested, "There's only one thing to do really." He paused. "Take the boy's body to his folks."

"Oh I can't do that, Mr. Rosenthal," Patrick cried. "I don't know nothin' 'bout coloreds. I wouldn't know what to say."

"You say the same thing you'd say to a white family," Rosenthal said matter-of-factly. "Colored people hurt just like we do, Patrick."

Patrick nodded. "I'm sure you right, Mr. Rosenthal. Of course you'll go with me, won't you? I'd feel so much better if you did."

"Sure I'll go, son," Rosenthal agreed reluctantly. "Just let me get dressed."

"Oh sure," Patrick said, as Rosenthal turned to reenter the house. "Take yo' time, sir. He dead, so ain't no rush."

Rosenthal slammed shut every door he opened like one running from a phantom. Once confined to his bedroom, he placed Sutton on the nightstand, and said, "I'm so sorry, son. They should never have done this to you. Oh my God, I'm so sorry." His jittery nerves overwhelmed his ability to sit still, even for a second. "I'm going to take care of you. I promise. If I gave you back, it would be like abandoning you all over again. And what would they think of me? No one would understand. Plus, what difference would it make anyway? They've already destroyed you. One eye can't change that." Rosenthal retrieved his best black suit from the closet and began to dress himself. His trembling hands made buttoning the shirt practically impossible, and he resolved to ask Patrick to secure the tie around his fat, scarlet neck. Peering into the full-length mirror, Rosenthal protruded his chest proudly, and asked Sutton, "How do I look?"

"I understand," he moaned. "Those mean ole racist fuckers! But remember—everybody white ain't the same. You know that now, don't you?" Rosenthal sounded pitiful. "Of course you know it because you know the real me. And I'm going to take very good care of you." He made a bed of bathroom tissue in the palm of his left hand and placed Sutton upon it. Then he smiled at the eye as though having granted it a seat at the right hand of the Father. He folded the edges of the delicate paper until Sutton was completely concealed, all the while singing, "Rock of Ages, cleft for me! Let me hide myself in Thee." "That was my mother's favorite hymn," he noted, and slid Sutton into his pants pocket. "Oh, you would have loved her. She was kind to everyone and never would have participated in anything like what those men did to you. She would have left my father had he had anything to do with it. I'm certain of that. She would have loved you more than anyone ever could. That's why I have to keep you—to protect you from mean people who would rather destroy you. My mother would be so proud!"

Rosenthal patted his thigh pocket where Sutton rested and returned to the truck revived.

"You look so . . . refreshed now, Mr. Rosenthal." Patrick glared. "You musta had a little talk with Jesus." He chuckled. "That's what my mother always said to do whenever you troubled 'bout somethin'."

"Yes, I'm fine," Rosenthal said, more to himself than to Patrick. "Let's go."

The prince and pauper entered the truck and drove toward the colored section of Money.

"You think they'll take it hard?" Patrick queried.

"I don't know." Rosenthal sighed. "I've never seen colored people grieve, but I'm sure they do. Then again, these kinds of things happen to them all the time, so maybe they're used to it."

Patrick nodded. "Maybe so."

"These fields were once filled with colored people," Rosenthal said, looking across Chapman's estate. "From one end of the land to the other, colored folks toiled like workhorses. It was amazing how hard they worked and never complained about it."

"They were made for that," Patrick asserted. "You ever paid attention to their hands and feet? Bigger'n any white man's I ever seen!" He laughed freely. "Big eyes, too . . . like they always starin' at somethin'."

"I sorta like their eyes," Rosenthal said before he could tame his tongue.

"What? Why?" Patrick asked. "Oh I know why! It's 'cause they stare back at you like a treed coon, right?"

Rosenthal considered slapping Patrick across the face. Instead, he reached into his pocket and enclosed Sutton protectively. "My daddy would take me by these cotton fields and tell me how blessed I was not to have to pick cotton all day to make a living. Occasionally, he'd pull over and make me stare at the sea of black faces, glistening with sweat, and I'd thank God I was born white. But one day, I saw a little Black boy, about my own age, running up and down the cotton rows, delivering water to thirsty laborers, and he looked back at me desperately. I asked my daddy if I could go help him, but Daddy told me that white boys didn't have no business in no cotton field. I told him the Black boy needed help, but he assured me the boy could manage. I never forgot the look of yearning in that boy's beautiful, black eyes." Rosenthal caught himself and tried to temper his admiration. "I mean, they were beautiful because he was a child and"—Rosenthal hesitated—"because he was innocent. You know what I mean?" He stammered, "We're all . . . um . . . children of God."

"Now that's true, Mr. Rosenthal," Patrick agreed. "My mother always tells me that God made everybody, even the niggers."

Rosenthal now wished he hadn't come, but since they were half-way, he had no choice but to endure.

Patrick turned left onto Talley Lane, and asked, "Were you here when they had The Burnin'? I always hear people talk about it, but I don't really know any details."

Rosenthal hadn't thought about the event in years. "Yes, I was here. I was about fifteen then." He stared at a grove of trees in the distance. Knowing that he had once been more racist than Patrick made him ill. "Most people don't really understand what happened, but I know. I wish I didn't, but I do."

Patrick waited on Rosenthal to proceed.

"A white man named Greenlaw had a child by a colored woman."

"Were they married?"

"No. In fact, he had raped her. I heard him bragging about it to my daddy. The colored woman and her family lived on Greenlaw's property in a shack just east of the Sumner bridge. Well, they say she never told her husband about the assault until she had the baby."

"Why did she tell it then?"

Rosenthal chuckled. "Because she had to explain how two dark colored people could have a yellow baby with lime green eyes."

Patrick said, "Yep! That's a lot to explain."

"Apparently she told her husband the truth. I guess he was so angry he secured an old chopping axe, probably from Greenlaw's tool-shed, and went looking for him. When he found him, he hacked his body like one cuts up a chicken for frying. His wife had followed him, begging him to calm down, but he threatened to kill her, too, if she didn't let him have his way. So she watched as her husband dissected her rapist."

"Did they go back home after that?"

"There was no home to return to, because the colored man set the house ablaze before he ever went to find Greenlaw. I suppose he had no intention of returning. Anyway, he retreated into the woods and lived there for several weeks until, late one Saturday night, a posse of white men found him. What they did with him that night I do not know, but Sunday morning we dressed for church as usual and, after Sunday school, my dad, your grandpa, and a few other good deacons directed us to assemble on the front steps of the church. After a moment or two, a wagon approached from the distance with the colored man tied behind it. I asked Mother what was about to happen to him, but she silenced me by placing both her hands over my mouth. The Black man stumbled behind the wagon like a child just learning to walk but being forced to do so much too quickly.

"'Here he is, folks!' my daddy announced proudly like he did the time he hunted and killed a five-point buck for Thanksgiving dinner. I stared at the man, wishing he could set himself free, although knowing his fate had already been sealed."

This story, which Patrick had heard countless times, usually evoked laughter in him; however, Rosenthal's version dampened his Confederate pride.

"They asked the man if he had anything to say and when he raised his head slowly, blood was streaming from his eyes."

"Did you say blood?" Patrick asked in confusion.

"Yes, blood. I remember it because I had never seen anything like that before. What caused it I do not know; yet the event proceeded. Your granddaddy got a long two-by-four from the wagon and, with baling rope, they tied the colored man's arms horizontally to it. His head dropped so low that at first I thought he was dead, but since he maintained his upright position, I knew he was still alive. It amazed me that our women did not appear the least bit squeamish or even compassionate in the midst of what, at least to me as a child, seemed to be a very sad, sickening occasion."

Rosenthal studied Patrick's blank face for signs that the youngster was getting all that he implied, and then he returned his eyes to the green cotton fields rolling for miles on both sides of the old country road. "Several deacons unloaded bundles of sticks from the wagon and made a sizeable teepee, which they saturated with kerosene and set ablaze. Again, I looked at various faces, but none expressed the horror mine did. I tried to run away, but my mother's grip confined me, and my father's gaze assured me that to run away would have been a very bad idea for reasons I did not know. Suddenly, the congregation burst forth jubilantly with, 'When the roll is called up yonder! When the roll is called up yonder! When the roll is called up yonder, I'll be there!' Two men on each end of the two-by-four lifted the colored man's body and dangled it over the flames. Only when the soles of his feet blistered over, expelling yellow pus mingled with blood—which surprisingly sickened only a few of us children—did the colored man lift his head in unimaginable agony. Instantly our eyes met—the colored man's and mine—and his hypnotizing stare forced me to feel the entirety of his pain. Somewhere in the depths of my soul, I felt anguish unspeakable, and I discovered in that moment that colored people endure pain whites would find incomprehensible. I began to weep and my father struck me a heavy blow across the back of my neck. Upon recovery, I looked at the colored man again and, this time, denied him the balm he sought in me. My father must have noticed my refusal, for after returning to the colored man's side, he smiled at me approvingly. I guessed him to be saying that Black pain was something little white boys should leave alone.

"The deacons continued to lower the colored man into the flames as his charcoal black skin curled slowly, stubbornly away from his pink flesh, and fluids dripped into the fire and sizzled like drops of water in hot grease. The smell was wrenching. Before he took his final breath, he yelled his wife's name."

"What was her name?"

"Gabriel," Rosenthal offered slowly.

Once more, Patrick could not discern why Rosenthal's memory was not framed, like everyone else's, in joy and glee. A glance at Rosenthal convinced Patrick that, at any moment, the old man might deteriorate into tears.

"He held the final syllable of the name for at least thirty seconds before surrendering to the hungry fire. The crowd cheered in victory, and I cheered along, probably to please my father or to gain communal approval. Whatever the justification, I was inducted into the racist redneck hall of fame. I do hope God forgives me."

"There's nothing to forgive you for, Mr. Rosenthal," Patrick consoled. "He had to learn his lesson."

"And what lesson would that be?" Rosenthal snapped.

"Um, that niggers"—Patrick's smile dissolved—"shouldn't kill whites."

"I guess it doesn't matter that Greenlaw brutally raped his wife." Rosenthal smirked.

Patrick's eyebrows raised. For the life of him, he couldn't fathom the source of Rosenthal's agitation, and, for the moment, he decided to stop trying. "Do I turn here?" he asked after enduring several minutes of disconcerting silence. "I know lotta the nig—coloreds live south of the river."

"Yes, turn," Rosenthal relented, refraining from calling him a hillbilly bastard. Then he pointed, and said, "There it is. The little house over there."

"Somebody lives in that!" Patrick declared. "It looks like a old hay barn! Look at the rusty tin roof!"

Patrick never noticed Rosenthal's tightly clenched teeth; nor did he understand why the man chuckled at him.

"Let me do the talking," Rosenthal whispered fiercely.

"Fine with me," Patrick consented.

Sixteen

WHEN THE WHITE MEN ARRIVED, CHOP WAS PLAYING with a yo-yo he had found in a garbage dump behind the General Store. Enoch told him to take it back, but Miss Mary interceded insisting that he keep it since obviously some ungrateful, spoiled white child had thrown it away. If he couldn't have a new one, at least let him enjoy a used one, she said.

Chop looked up and saw the white men exiting the truck. Deep down inside, he knew their presence was bad news, yet to give his folks a few more precious moments of hope, he decided, against his grandfather's edict, to greet the visitors alone.

"Hi," he said nonchalantly when they approached him.

"Hello, young man," Rosenthal returned, and patted Chop on the head.

"Wh-wh-what y'all wwwwant?"

"Are your parents home?" Rosenthal tried to keep the exchange light and pleasant.

"YYYYYessir, they's here," he said slowly. "BBBBut we d-d-d-don't wwwwant no trrrrrrrrouble, sir." He was proud of himself for protecting the family's welfare.

"Oh, no son, we're not here to start any trouble," Rosenthal said. "We just have some business with your folks. I'd be much obliged if you'd get them for me."

Patrick almost called Chop a black ass monkey who had no business questioning a white man's motive, but since he had promised to let Rosenthal talk, he held his peace.

Chop ran into the house and summoned the others, who then burst through the front screen door, hoping against history to see a strong, vibrant Clement standing before them. When they saw only white men, their steps slowed.

"Good afternoon, Mr. Rosenthal," Jeremiah said, extending his right hand.

"Jeremiah, family." He nodded. "How is everyone?"

Their silence told him that they were absolutely in no mood for small talk, especially with white folks.

"How can we help you?" Jeremiah asked evenly.

"Well, um . . . I don't quite know how to say this, but . . . um . . ."

"Mr. Rosenthal, if you got somethin' to say, just say it," Enoch interjected.

"Okay, fine." Rosenthal sighed. "Clement's body was found in the river about a mile down from the old bridge."

"No!" Possum and Ella Mae screamed simultaneously. They held on to each other for strength neither had to give. "My baby!" Possum bellowed from her womb. "Not my baby!" She flung herself to the ground. "Oh God, Momma! They done killed my baby!" She beat the unyielding earth instead of the white men standing before her.

"I'm sorry to be the bearer of bad news, but I wanted to tell y'all personally. It's the least I could do since I promised to assist in any way possible. Patrick here found him when he was out fishing this morning." Rosenthal reached into his pocket and touched Sutton.

Patrick's emotionless expression only incited rage in Jeremiah, who refused to break while staring white men in the face. "Tell us exactly where you saw the body so me and my boy can go git it." Jeremiah's voice trembled.

Rosenthal's hands fidgeted. "Well, Jeremiah, um Patrick here saved you the trouble."

"What chu mean?" Jeremiah grimaced.

Sweat covered Rosenthal's face. "Um . . . Patrick brought the body back with him. That's why we're here."

"I don't understand, Mr. Rosenthal." Jeremiah's irritation was apparent.

"We have the body, Jeremiah, in the bed of the truck here."

Jeremiah's solid stance began to waver. Enoch grabbed his arm and whispered in his ear, "Slow, Daddy. Slow. It's gon be all right. Just take it easy." Miss Mary and Ella Mae comforted Possum while the children stood still, unable to decide what emotional response would be most appropriate.

"It's in really bad condition, Jeremiah," Rosenthal intoned, trying to brace the family for the unimaginable, "and I'm not sure you need to see it. Maybe Enoch here—"

Jeremiah had moved past Rosenthal and Patrick to stand before the bed of the truck. "Uncover it," he whispered.

"Jeremiah, listen," Rosenthal begged in a weeping voice. "I don't mean to be rude or to tell you your own family business, but I don't think you understand how horrific this whole ordeal might be."

Jeremiah stared at the covering without blinking, and Rosenthal pleaded further. "Let Patrick and your boy here carry the body in the house or the barn or wherever and send for the undertaker so he can get it presentable, then—"

"I said uncover it," Jeremiah said again without moving his eyes.

Possum now stood beside her father, waiting for the inevitable. "My baby, my baby," she kept murmuring.

Rosenthal placed his hand on the blanket but tried one last time. "Please, Jeremiah. Don't do this. Ma'am," he turned his attention to Possum, "you don't want to see your boy in this condition. I promise you you don't. Just let us carry it in the house—"

"Uncover it!" Jeremiah screamed.

So Rosenthal, against his heart's desire, snatched the cloth away and revealed the Johnsons' greatest fear.

Possum fainted into her mother's arms. Miss Mary rocked her awkwardly and recited, "The Lord is my Shepherd, I shall not want. He maketh me to lie down in green pastures. He leadeth me beside the still waters. He restoreth my soul. He leadeth me in the paths of righteousness for His name's sake." She began to holler angrily, "Yea, though I walk through the valley of the shadow of death, I shall fear no evil. For thou art with me!" Tears sprang forth unannounced onto her rounded cheeks. "Thy rod and thy staff they comfort me! Thou preparest a table before me in the presence of mine enemies! Thou anointest my head with oil. My cup runneth over. Surely!" She paused. "Surely!" she yelled, "goodness and mercy shall follow me all the days of my life and I shall dwell in the house of the Lord forever!"

Miss Mary's heavy breathing scared Patrick bleach white, and he leaned on the side of his truck, wishing he and Rosenthal had simply dumped the body and left.

Miss Mary improvised the same scripture more boisterously: "The Lord is *our* Shepherd!" she declared boldly, eloquently. "*We* shall not want!" She jabbed her finger between her voluptuous breasts. "He maketh *us* to lie down in green pastures! He leadeth *us* beside the still waters! He restoreth *our* soul!" Miss Mary peered into Patrick's pupils and spoke to his irascible heart. She released Possum to Ella Mae and walked slowly toward the young white boy. "He leadeth *us* in the paths of righteousness for His name's sake." Standing only inches from him, she proclaimed, "Yea though *we* walk through the valley of the shadow of death, *we* shall fear no evil! For thou God art with *us*! Thy rod and thy staff they comfort *us*!" She began to clap wildly. Patrick felt her spittle splatter on his pale cheeks, but he dared not move. "Thou preparest a table before *us* in the presence of *our* enemies!" Her eyes narrowed. "Thou anointest *our* head with oil! *Our* cup runneth over!" With hands lifted high, she shouted, "Surely! Surely! Surely! Goodness and Mercy shall follow *me and mine* all the days of *our* lives"—Miss Mary turned from Patrick and rejoined Possum—"And *we* shall dwell in the house of the Lord forever."

"Amen." Patrick smirked offensively.

Miss Mary swiveled, and exclaimed, "No! Awoman! And a colored one at that!"

She ushered Possum and Ella Mae toward the house. The two white men looked at each other in stark confusion, yet apparently Miss Mary didn't need their understanding in order to have her own. "It's gon be all right now," she repeated to her daughters. "God done declared it, and it's gone be all right." She was saying more than anyone understood.

Jeremiah had not flinched the entire time. He stared at his grandson's mangled body, contemplating how, when, and why someone had been so cruel. One solitary tear dropped from his left eye, and when Rosenthal reached to wipe it away, Jeremiah grabbed his wrist with strength Rosenthal assumed Jeremiah to have lost forty years earlier. Slowly Jeremiah loosened his grip, and Rosenthal returned his hand to his side, but Jeremiah never took his eyes off Clement's emaciated form. A million thoughts flooded his mind, but only one prevailed—how to even the score. He had to do something, he told himself. For all the Negro fathers and grandfathers who had buried children with no means of recourse, he had to do something. Clarity overshadowed Jeremiah's face as he realized God was waiting—again—on him to move.

"You all right, Daddy?" Enoch whispered, with his hand supporting his father's back.

Jeremiah didn't answer. He prayed for strength to do what he had decided. He wasn't sure who would stand with him or against him, but he knew he had to do it. When his tears broke free, Jeremiah didn't fight them, for he alone knew they would never come again. Not at the loss of one of his own. Rosenthal, Patrick, and even Enoch wrongly concluded that Clement's murder had overwhelmed the old sharecropper, and he simply couldn't hold his wailing any longer. Had they been telepathic, they would have known that Jeremiah cried that day for generations of Black lives unaccounted for. His eyes became the conduit for the weeping of thousands of mothers whose shackled lives never allowed them the room to grieve. All those Negro men who wanted to weep when their wives were raped and their children sold away and their bodies abused and their spirits demeaned . . . Jeremiah surrendered his eyes for the healing. When he doubled over in anguish and growled like a wounded bear, Enoch had no choice but to let him be. Falling to the earth heavily, Jeremiah submitted to the ancestors and bore the pain of people he never knew and abuses he never witnessed. He cried for children transitioned before their time—those who could have transformed the world had they lived on—and for love planted but unharvested. Balled in a fetal position with his mouth to the ground, Jeremiah moaned for the empty space in his heart where Jerry once dwelled, and called the names of others, like his friend Bull, whom no one had ever glorified. "Use me," he mumbled feebly while his body tossed to and fro in the dusty front yard.

"Daddy?" Enoch called repeatedly. He kept reaching for his father, but Jeremiah made it clear that he was not to be disturbed.

Patrick and Rosenthal didn't know what to do or think. Is the old man having a seizure? Patrick wondered. The unintelligible moans, accented by the snakelike body movements, convinced both men that Jeremiah was either crazy or spirit-possessed. Still, they didn't move. As if attending a performance, the men observed in mock silence and hoped they could recognize the conclusion. In some ways, Enoch's begging was more distressful to them than Jeremiah's writhing form. He kept pleading with his father, "Git up, Daddy! Please!" probably more embarrassed, they assumed, than worried. Had they not been there, Rosenthal thought, this whole metaphysical experience would surely have been even more intense. He wanted to turn and tell Patrick that he had witnessed, years ago, a Negro church service where people collapsed and screamed and shook violently under the power of what they called the Holy Ghost. He had never heard of the Holy Ghost before. In their Southern refined white church service, they spoke of the Holy Spirit, and clearly one had nothing to do with the other. Yet, in the moment, he couldn't explain this to Patrick for fear of interrupting what was obviously a private exchange between Jeremiah and something Invisible.

Twenty minutes later, the ghost—as Rosenthal thought of it—abandoned Jeremiah, and he lay exhausted in the front yard. The only sign of life in him was his ever-expanding and deflating stomach. He reached for Enoch now, who gladly assisted him from the earth.

"You all right, Daddy?"

Jeremiah brushed dust from his overalls and walked to where Rosenthal and Patrick were shifting uneasily.

"Jeremiah, I'm sorry," Rosenthal spoke prematurely. "I wish there were something more I could do." His hands motioned his perceived helplessness. "When Patrick arrived at the house this morning, I had no idea—"

Jeremiah cleared his throat, and said, "Tell them to get ready."

"Tell who?" Patrick asked rudely.

Dismissing him, Jeremiah told Enoch, "Git my boy outta this damn truck."

Enoch motioned for Ray Ray and, together, they carried Clement onto the back porch and laid him on a cooling board. Sarah Jane and Chop moved to stand next to their grandfather.

"I know this is hard on you, Jeremiah, but try not to be too bitter," Rosenthal said. "If there is anything I can do—"

"Yes." Jeremiah smiled broadly. "There's somethin' very impo'-tant you can do." He had one arm around Sarah Jane and the other encircling Chop. "Tell yo' people to git ready 'cause I'm comin'."

"What?" Rosenthal burbled in confusion. "Tell who what? What are you talking about, Jeremiah?"

He turned and walked toward the house with a peace and solitude at once unsettling and remarkable. Chop and Sarah Jane were left to bring the salutation.

"My granddaddy's very angry, sir," Sarah Jane announced.

"He ain't got no right to be angry at us!" Patrick declared. "Hell, we brought him de body!"

Rosenthal raised his right hand quickly and forced Patrick, once again, into the background. "Listen, children," he said paternalistically. "This is traumatic for all of us. For the whole town! I understand why Jeremiah is so upset—"

Sarah Jane didn't care, this time, that she was interrupting an elder. "No, you don't, sir!" she said boldly. "You wasn't here when my daddy killed hisself and my granddaddy had to bury him! You didn't see the look in his eyes as he rubbed the casket and cried!" She was crying now against her wishes. "And you didn't see my momma waste away after those white men raped her! And you don't know what it's like to bury one child after the other, Mr. Rosenthal, and you cain't never do nothin' 'bout it!" She paused and sobbed, but then proceeded a bit more controlled, "If I wuz rude, I apologize, Mr. Rosenthal, but I sho meant what I said." Sarah Jane wiped her eyes. "The family thanks y'all fu bringin' de body home and fu bein' nice enough not to leave it in de river. God bless you." With that, Sarah Jane and Chop turned and walked toward the house.

"Please tell Jeremiah I'm sorry!" Rosenthal called after them, but knew his words fell on deaf ears.

"Let's go, Mr. Rosenthal," Patrick said nonchalantly. "These niggers—"

"They're people, Patrick!" Rosenthal yelled. "They're people who feel and hurt just like you and me!"

"Okay! Whatever!" Patrick yielded.

"No, it's not okay!" Rosenthal screamed louder. "That's why these people are mad as hell right now. We keep treating them like they're nothing, and we expect them simply to go along with it. Well, I have news for you, young man! They're not going to do this forever. No, sir! One day, they're going to give us a taste of our own medicine!" Rosenthal entered the cab of the truck and slammed the door shut. He patted the eye lovingly through his pants pocket.

"Whatever," Patrick repeated carelessly, and drove away.

Possum didn't care to wipe the yellowy snot from her nose. Her facial expression had transformed from grief to uncontrollable fury. Ella Mae sat next to her on the old sofa and rubbed her back soothingly. "Bring me the body," she whispered.

"Oh no," Miss Mary muddled. "Don't do this to yourself, baby. Take thangs one step at a time."

"I need to know if that"—she shivered—"that . . . monster was once my boy, Momma. I need to know."

"Sweetie, just relax and take it easy—"

"I need to know, Momma! I need to know right now!"

Before Miss Mary could deny her further, Enoch and Ray Ray had retrieved the body and laid it on the floor in front of the sofa.

"Uncover it," Possum demanded, like God saying, "Let there be light!"

Enoch unveiled the body and, again, everybody gasped in horror. Clement's head, the size of a prizewinning pumpkin, carried bruises of every color: black, green, burnt orange, lavender, and piss yellow. The crater where his left eye once dwelled was deep and hollow as though a wood carver had been paid handsomely to burrow out a permanent reminder to Negro boys that white women, even in casual conversation, were not to be approached. With minstrel-size, purply blue lips, the face could have been a Halloween mask although no one—Black or white—would have offered sweets to such a horrendous sight. Actually, other children would have fled in terror, and parents would have asked what mother had approved of something so . . . so terrifying. Ridges of lumps and valleys, like a man-made cycle trail, evidenced the bat or crowbar or steel beam that had been used to flatten an otherwise beautifully round structure. The right eye, bucking and bulging in compensation for its missing other, stared at no one in particular yet all its viewers sensed its absolute attention. Possum knelt next to the unrecognizable form and, with her eyes closed, moved her right hand slowly and lovingly across the body, from head to foot. Everyone else awaited the verdict.

When she reached the corpse's bloated right hand, she stopped abruptly.

"Oh my God," she hummed sadly. "It's him, Momma. It's him!"

"How you know fu sho, baby? They done beat him so bad—" Miss Mary was praying against the odds that this monstrosity was not her grandson.

"It's him," Possum said confidently. "Look." She held up his hand and showed the family a ring. "It's his daddy's. Louis gave it to him on his twelfth birthday."

Jeremiah wasn't ready for absolute confirmation. "Look like any old ring to me," he said.

Possum struggled until she removed the ring from Clement's finger. She passed it to Ella Mae, who took it reluctantly. "Look on the inside," Possum murmured.

Ella Mae did so and covered her mouth to keep from screaming out loud.

"What is it?" Jeremiah asked.

"The initials L. T.," Ella Mae said.

"That stands for Louis Thompson," Possum explained. Then she wept bitterly. "Why did they do my baby like this? What kinda human bein' could beat a child's eye right out o' his head?"

"No kind," Jeremiah said. "Don't no human bein' do this to nobody."

Ella Mae and Miss Mary encouraged Possum not to waste energy on those "worthless crackers," but, somewhere deep within, she couldn't exonerate them as they had. Living next to human beings who ain't really human beings did not explain to Possum why white folks had annihilated her son. In fact, she took the explanation as Negroes' excuse simply not to confront the bastards. On Judgment Day, she thought, God won't exempt white folk from hell because of insufficient humanity. Rather, he'll send Negroes with them—for not holding their neighbors accountable and for convincing themselves that Negroes are more humane by nature.

Possum wailed, and hollered, "I can't handle this, Daddy!" Her expostulation frightened the children, who then excused themselves to the front porch. Enoch wrapped the body and returned it to the cooling board.

"Y'all th-th-think d-d-d-d-dat's Clement?" Chop asked.

"Of course it is," Ray Ray mumbled in agitation. "Didn't you see the ring? What other Negro boy you know 'round hyeah wit a daddy wit dem initials?"

Chop had no argument, so he asked, "Whwhwhwat ch'all th-th-think gone happen nnnnow?"

"I don't know," Sarah Jane whimpered. "But Granddaddy's actin' mighty funny."

"He sho is," Ray Ray agreed. "He keep bustin' out laughin' when ain't nothin' funny."

Sarah Jane studied the beautiful white clouds dancing against the blue backdrop. "Yeah, he up to somethin'," she said definitively. "I hope don't nobody git hurt."

Ray Ray frowned. "Somebody done already got hurt. In a way, I wish Negro people would take their guns and blow the peckerwoods' heads plumb off!"

"Thththat wwwwouldn't b-b-b-be t-t-too good, Ray Ray, 'cccc-cause ththththen ththey would git rrrrreal mad."

"So!" Ray Ray thundered. "Let 'em git mad! Why we always de ones gotta be mad? I wanna make *them* mad! I'm tired o' dem knowin' dey can make us mad and jes go on 'bout dey business. I hope Granddaddy do do somethin'. I really do."

Sarah Jane was a bit more cautious. "I got a bad feelin' 'bout all this," she said more to the wind than to her cousins. "Poor Clement!" she said melodiously, and shook her head.

"Naw, poor crackers!" Ray Ray said. "That's who you oughta be feelin' sorry for 'cause when they git theirs, it ain't gon be no joke. God ain't been lettin' this happen for no reason. Watch what I'm tellin' you. They gon git theirs, and they gon be sorry they ever messed with Negro people."

Sarah Jane scrutinized Ray Ray. She never knew he carried such enmity in his heart, and now she feared he might do something foolish. "Calm down, Ray Ray," she admonished, motherly. "Ain't no need in makin' things worse than they already is."

Ray Ray flung his hands into the air. "Thangs cain't git no worse, Sarah Jane! They done killed yo daddy, yo momma, and now Clement! We gon just keep watchin' 'til they kill de whole family? Huh?"

"No, we ain't gon jes keep watchin'"—Sarah Jane felt like she was being tried for racial disloyalty—"but we ain't gon be no fools neither."

"Then what we gon do? Huh? You tell me dat!"

Sarah Jane regretted her perfunctory response. "We gon keep prayin'! Dat's what we gon do 'til God tells us somethin' different."

Ray Ray smirked. "God ain't gon come down from heaven and tell us nothin' at all. We gon jes have to do somethin' and ask God to help us."

"How you know God ain't comin' down from heaven?" Sarah Jane posed desperately. "Grandma say He's comin' back."

"He ain't here yet!" Ray Ray challenged. "And it don't make no sense for us to keep waitin' on Him and buryin' Negroes, hopin' He comin'."

"God llllllloves everybody," Chop offered tangentially.

"Shut up, boy!" the other two yelled.

Chop pursed his lips and decided, as usual, to dwell in silence and yield the conversation to the articulate ones.

"We gotta be smart," Sarah Jane sighed, reigniting the exchange.

"Sarah Jane," Ray Ray huffed, "we done tried everything. We done talked to 'em, we done prayed for 'em, we done asked 'em to leave us be, we done worked for 'em like mules, and we done grinned in they face even after they killed our people. How much smarter can we be?"

"You right," Sarah Jane conceded. "You absolutely right." She didn't want to surrender to Ray Ray's tirade, but his points were too salient to argue. "Just don't do nothin' stupid, Ray," she pleaded.

Ray Ray stomped off the porch toward the barn. Chop began to follow.

"Leave him alone," Sarah Jane called. "He need time to cool down."

Chop swaggered around the front yard until an idea came to him. "I'll b-b-b-b-be rrrrrright b-b-back," he told Sarah Jane, and ran to the rear of the house.

Chop stepped onto the back porch where Clement's body lay. At first, he was afraid, but then he remembered Miss Mary telling him, "Dead folks can't hurt you. It's de live ones you'd better worry about!" so he relaxed and approached the corpse with uncanny boldness.

He frowned at the strong stench, comparing it to a thousand rotten, spoiled catfish, then unwrapped only enough cloth to see the head.

"Hey, Cllllllement," Chop said, standing next to the cooling board. He examined the evening, wondering if God were listening.

"Yo mmmmmmomma ssssay ain't g-g-g-gon b-b-be no fffffuneral in Mmmmississippi 'ccccause shshshe ain't lllllllleavin' her chchchild in d-d-dis rrracist plllace. Shshshe say shshe g-g-g-gon t-t-ttake you b-b-back to Chicag-go and lllllet de wwwwworld ssssseee what rrrracist wwwwwhite folks in Mmmmmississippi d-d-d-did to her b-b-b-baby."

He paused as though Clement might respond.

"B-b-b-b-but b-before you g-g-g-g-go, I g-g-gotta tttttalk to you 'b-b-b-b-bout sssssssssomethin'. It's rrrrreal important." He folded his arms. The single eye in Clement's bloated head stared back at him.

"I d-d-don't know wwwwwhat happened to yyyyyyyou, but it musta b-b-b-been real b-b-bad," he said. "And Grrrrrranddaddy rrrreal mad."

Chop looked away from the eye, which was beginning to disturb his solid resolve.

"Sssssomethin' gon' happen, Cllllement. I fffffeel it. Whhhhen Grrrrranddaddy lllooked at d-d-dem white mens today after thththey t-t-t-told him whwhwhat happened to yyyyou, I could t-t-tell he wwwwuz thththththinkin' somethin'. I d-d-d-didn't ask him wh-whwhat he wwwwuz thththinkin' 'c-c-c-cause he wwwwuz so mad, but I ain't nnnnneva ssssssseen G-g-granddaddy look llllllike d-d-d-dat b-b-befo'."

Chop breathed heavily again, like Jeremiah before he began to snore, then he stared at Clement.

"Granddaddy always ssssay d-d-dat when peoples d-d-d-die, they b-b-become spirits who c-c-c-can help us out whwhwhenever wwwwwe nnnnneed th-them to. Yyyyyou d-d-dead, ain't chu, Clement?"

Chop reached to touch Clement's warped nose, but decided against it.

"Well, sssssince yyyyyou d-d-dead, yyyyyou gotta help us out. I d-d-d-don't wwwwant nothin' happenin' to Grrrranddaddy or Daddy or nnnnnobody else, but I know thththey ththinkin' sssss-somethin'. Sssssarah Jane scared, too, Cccccccclement. Sssssshe feel whwhwhwhat I feel. D-d-d-did yyyyyyyou ssssssssee Grrrrrandma scrrrrreamin' to d-d-dem white mens? I ain't neva ssssssssseen no Nnnnnnegro scrrrrrream at nnnno whwhwhite man b-b-befo', and shshshe wunnit even scared!" Chop smiled pridefully.

"I gggget a ffffeelin' sssssssssomethin' real bad ffffixin' to happen, Cllllement. I-I-I wuz jjjes hopin' yyyyyyou could help iiif it d-d-do."

Chop felt a presence and chill bumps sprouted all over his little arms. He gazed at his unrecognizable cousin again and allowed himself to feel the anger he had tried to deny.

"Mmmmaybe ssssssomethin' need to happen," he murmured as vengeance crept into his heart. "Wwwwwe always d-d-dyin' 'cause o' sssssomethin' wwwwwe d-d-did thththat thththey d-d-don't llll-like, b-b-b-but whwhwhy d-d-d-don't thththey die whwhwhen ththey d-do stuff wwwwwe don't llllike?" Chop sniffled.

"Yyyyyyyyou knnnnnnnnow whwhwhwhwhwhat, Clllllllllement?" Chop said from an overflowing heart. "Jjjjes help us ooout iiif G-g-god llllet you. Ssssssince Grrrrrrrrrrrrrrrrranddaddy ain't sssssssscared and Grrrrrrrrrrandma ain't sssssssscared, I-I-I-I-I-I-I-I-I-I-I ain't sssscared neither!"

When Chop's voice broke, he knew he had said enough. He studied Clement's face, unable to discern how it had gotten so distorted. With the four fingers of his small, soft right hand, he caressed Clement's ruffled forehead, and closed his eyes, trying to remember what his cousin looked like only days earlier. The inundation of tears streaming down his cheeks didn't embarrass him like usual. When he leaned over and kissed Clement's enlarged cheek, he felt energy issue forth from his lips, and he smiled to know that Clement had understood.

"Whwhwhatever happen, Cllllement, jes help us out. Llllllike Grandma always ssssssay, 'We a fffffamily, wwwwwe always b-b-b-been a family, and we gon always b-b-b-be a fffffamily.'"

Chop replaced the covering over the corpse but did not leave. He thought about what Jeremiah and Miss Mary must have felt while Jerry was lying on this same board and now he wondered how they had been so kind to him and everyone else after having suffered so dearly. He prayed quickly that Aunt Possum had the staying power of his grandparents, and whispered, "Sssssseeya" as he walked into the house.

Seventeen

JEREMIAH REMAINED SILENT UNTIL EVERYONE ARRIVED. HE simply nodded his acknowledgments and smiled wryly in anticipation of the idea he was about to offer.

Some whispered, "What's wrong wit Mi? He actin' mighty strange," but no one could have guessed the contents of his heart.

The barn was full of colored people again, for the second time in a week. Actually, a few extra faces showed up, wondering what colored folks in Money could do about such heinous acts of violence against their children. Pet Moore interrupted the whispering with, "Let's get started, everybody. We need y'all to listen and pay 'tention to what you hear. This is a serious matter." He shook his head sadly and took a seat as Jeremiah rose.

Like that of a feared dictator, the old man's presence hushed the chatty audience. His smile transformed to one of hope, yet everyone sensed it more as warning than warmth. Before he spoke, Jeremiah looked at every attendee knowing that what he was about to say would either draw them near or drive them away, yet he was prepared to stand alone if necessary.

"Usually, in times like these, we pray first," he said, with a slight chuckle.

"Amen," the crowd responded.

"But not this time. We ain't prayin' 'bout nothin'!" Jeremiah slammed one fist into the other.

"Oh Lord!" Miss Mary murmured. Others frowned in fear.

"I ain't askin' God fu nothin'!" He reiterated, "'Cause God done told me what to do. He been tellin' us since we met these racist bastards, and they keep killin' our chillen 'cause we scared to do what we shoulda done years ago." Jeremiah's chuckle turned into a deep laughter. He was practically hollering.

"Yep!" he belted, "it's time. I'm sick o' prayin', I'm sick o' hopin', I'm sick o' grinnin', I'm sick o' turnin' de otha cheek, I'm sick o' bowin' down to white chillen half my age, I'm sick o' believin' they gon change, and I'm goddamn sick o' buryin' my own chillen!" His harsh language, which clearly troubled many, didn't disturb him in the least.

"Don't y'all git it?" He laughed heartily. "God ain't comin' to do nothin'! He ain't comin'!" Jeremiah snickered like one who finally gets the punch line of a joke. "White folks been laughin' for years, y'all! They been watchin' us pray and do nothin', and that's how they keep rulin' our lives. They know God don't do nothin' if you don't! We de stupid ones been sittin' round havin' prayer meetin's and then we go home like God is gon come down from the sky and change our situation. God's laughin' at this bullshit!"

"Jeremiah Johnson!" Miss Mary whispered. "Is you done lost yo' mind!"

"No, ma'am, I ain't!" he answered with a wide grin. "In fact, I done found it. I ain't neva been mo' sho' o' nothin' in all my seventy-odd years!"

Jeremiah trembled, and Miss Mary could do nothing but let him have his say. The fire in his eyes told her to leave him alone.

"Don't y'all git it?" Jeremiah repeated. "God waitin' on us! We ain't waitin' on Him! He done give us strength and power in numbers. All we gotta do is act. But we been so scared o' these bastards that we done convinced ourselves they cain't fall 'cause they so strong and mighty. Shit! They'll fall jes like any otha man! They blood is red, too! Y'all didn't know that, did ya?"

No one dared speak. Only Pet Moore affirmed Jeremiah's words with occasional "uh-huhs" and "amens."

Jeremiah began to pace between people's chairs. "This is really very simple," he said more calmly. "I ain't crazy, y'all. Everybody in dis room know me, been knowin' me all my life. I'm jes tellin' you what God told me yesterday after Mr. Rosenthal and Patrick brung my grandson's body back. I sat down and, for de first time in my life, I didn't ask God to do nothin'. I asked God why He hadn't done what I already asked Him, and He told me, plain as day, 'I been waitin' on you.' 'Waitin' on me to do what?' I asked confused, and God said, 'Waitin' on you to use yo' own strength to keep folks from killin' yo' own people. When yo' strength run out is where I come in.' That's when I finally got it. We been askin', but we ain't been fightin'. How we gon send God to fight a battle we ain't even in? Huh?"

Jeremiah was screaming again. Some people applauded his clarity as though they, too, had been needing it a lifetime. "Go 'head, prophet!" Pet Moore roared.

"So we ain't hyeah today to ask God fu nothin'! We don't need to ask God fu nothin', 'cause God done already gave us what we need! We hyeah today to see who bold enough to fight to save colored people's lives! It's dat simple. Long as we allow white folks to kill us and we don't do nothin' 'bout it, God ain't gon do nothin' either. And now I know why! And I don't blame Him 'cause if a people too scared to fight for theyselves, they ain't fit to live!

"Dat's right!" Aunt Sugar mumbled. "Dat ain't nothin' but right!"

"So what you sayin', Mi?" someone asked from deep in the crowd. "You sayin' we spose to go fight dese white folks now?"

"No!" Jeremiah said. "I ain't sayin' we oughta go fight dese white folks now! I'm sayin' we shoulda done it years ago! We late as hell, but late is better than neva 'cause it's plenty more young peoples 'round hyeah, and I'll be goddamn if they kill another one!"

"Amen!" several shouted.

Seeing that many were still skeptical, Jeremiah said, "Don't wait 'til you have to bury yo' own before you stand for what's right. That's how they git us, too. Don't nothin' really move us 'til it come directly befo' us. But by then, you buryin' yo' loved ones and cryin' 'cause ain't nothin' you can do. Let's do somethin' while we can."

"But what can we do?" Miss Gladys asked. "We sho cain't fight 'em."

"Why cain't we?" Jeremiah pondered. "We got fists, and we got guns, and we know how to use both of 'em. We fight each other! So why cain't we fight them?"

Pet Moore murmured, "Dat's a damn good point. I ain't neva thought about it that way."

"I ain't sayin' we go over there and start shootin'," Jeremiah explained with his hands. "I'm sayin' we go over there like a army, standin' tall and strong, and make them know that if they ever, and I mean *ever*, come in our community again like they gon take somebody out of it, they better prepare to die. Simple as that."

Enoch asked, "What if they attack us right then?"

"Then we commence to whippin' their white asses!" Jeremiah shouted. "We ain't goin' over there without our weapons! Come on! Let's not be foolish here. White folks in Mississippi don't respect nobody colored. We already know that. So it would be mighty stupid of us to confront them unarmed. We certainly hope we don't have to use no guns, but we sho gon take 'em with us just in case. If they would listen to sound reasoning and compassion, we wouldn't be in the situation we in right now."

"What if they start shootin'?" Miss Mary cried.

"We shoot back! Shit!" Jeremiah yelled. "That's the only way they'll respect us. Right now they know we too scared to shoot back, but if we ever show 'em we ain't, they'll think twice—or three times—about killin' a Negro. Right now, they kill us 'cause they know we ain't gon do nothin' 'bout it! I jes want us to teach them that there's a new Negro in town!"

"Amen!" people cheered.

"But don't git me wrong," Jeremiah warned. "I don't want blood-shed all over Money, Mississippi, any more than you do, but if blood is gon be shed, it ain't gon be no mo' colored chillen's blood. Not no mo'! Not if I can help it!"

Uneasy murmuring filled the barn. Jeremiah glanced around to see if anyone was prepared to stand with him. Their silence evoked another point.

"When these white bastards raped and killed my daughter years ago, I shoulda stood up then, but I was too scared. I let my boy go over there all by hisself, and they showed him what they do to a Nigga who stand alone. I ain't neva forgave myself for that. But when they brought Clement here yesterday, lookin' like somebody had done run over his face, I promised Jerry that I'd do somethin' differ-ent. All this Black life we jes keep givin' up like it don't mean nothin' to us"—he paused to see if others felt his sentiment—"gotta stop, y'all. Don't y'all see what they doin'? They kill de strong and leave the scared! The only way to change things is fu the scared to get strong. Then, the only way to destroy us is to kill every one o' us, and if they do that, shame on us!

"Tomorrow I'm goin' over there, and I'm gon stand proud, but I cain't go by myself 'cause that's what happened to my boy. I need y'all wit me. We gotta look like a army o' ants comin' down de road, and they gotta know they ain't dealin' wit de same colored people we used to be. So what y'all say?"

"Count me in!" Pet Moore threw his right arm high into the air.

No one else responded. Pet struggled to stand, and offered, "How did we git so scared?" He looked around. "All of us done buried some-body who was raped or hanged or shot or molested by these white folks. Is dat why y'all scared? Y'all think they'll come back for you if you say or do somethin'?"

The people sat like obedient children before a tyrannical teacher. Pet and Jeremiah gazed at each other and shook their heads.

Suddenly, Ray Ray screamed, "I'm goin'!" and ran to his grand-father's side.

"You ain't goin nowhere, boy!" Ella Mae corrected, reaching to-ward him.

"I gotta go, Momma," Ray Ray said. "Clement was my age, so that coulda been me. I ain't no little kid no more, Momma. I gotta—"

"No!" she demanded. "You ain't goin' nowhere, I said!" Miss Mary was holding her with all her might.

"He can go," Enoch said sternly, and stood beside Ray Ray.

"Are you crazy, man?" Ella Mae screeched. "You must be a fool if you think—"

"He goin' and dat's all to it. He fourteen, Ella Mae. He a young man now. He cain't be walkin' 'round hyeah scared o' white folks. I don't want him to be like I wuz." Enoch put his arm around Ray Ray's shoulder. "I love my boy jes like you do. I don't want nothin' to hap-pen to him neither, but I sho want these peckawoods to know that if they bother this boy, they gon have hell to pay. He'll be all right."

Ella Mae turned to Miss Mary and wept as though Ray Ray were already dead.

"I'm goin'!" Aunt Sugar announced freely. "Hell, I ain't scared o' no white folks! And what I got to lose? I was jes thinkin' 'bout how I would feel if somebody came and told me dat one o' mine had been killed and throwed in de river. I'd be a mad sista, Jeremiah, so, yeah, I'm goin' wit cha." She smiled and winked affectionately.

A few others announced their support, but the majority remained uncommitted.

"Y'all can go on home now," Jeremiah said kindly. "I ain't mad at nobody, and I ain't got no hard feelin's. Like I said, I been scared for seventy-odd years, so I know how hard it is to let go of fear. But I'm goin' to look these white folks in de face first thang in de mornin'. If de Good Lawd let me live to see it, I'm goin' over there, and I ain't gon be scared about it. If jes five or six of us go, so be it. Y'all might be buryin' me dis time tomorrow, but sho as de sun rise in de mornin' I'm goin.' "

Nobody moved.

"Y'all free to go," Jeremiah repeated. Folks stared at each other but didn't leave.

"It ain't that simple, Mi," Pet chuckled.

"Why ain't it?"

"'Cause folks obviously wanna go wit cha. If they didn't, they woulda left. They jes don't know how to believe in theyselves."

"What chu mean they don't know how? You make a decision, and you do it. That ain't hard to understand. I ain't tryin' to force nobody to do nothin'. I said my piece, and now I'm through."

"Mi, listen to me," Pet whispered, standing next to him. "Folks wanna go. They really do."

"So what they need to make 'em go?" Jeremiah asked.

Pet whispered even more softly, "They need somebody to show 'em how to let go o' fear."

"You jes let it go!" Jeremiah murmured loudly. "You make a decision, and you let it go."

Pet shook his head. "That's not what happened to you. I don't know what it was, but somethin' happened to you yesterday or last night that gave you a boldness you never had before. That's what they want, Mi. They want that boldness they see on you, but they don't know where to git it. What happened to you yesterday, Mi? Huh? Tell them that."

Jeremiah closed his eyes and tears came.

"It's all right," Pet said, rubbing Jeremiah's back. "It's all right."

Jeremiah took a deep breath and motioned for Enoch and Ray Ray to sit down. "I couldn't sleep last night, so I got up and walked down to The Sacred Place. It was probably 'bout midnight. I sat on dat big rock underneath the huge oak tree and I stared at the stars for 'bout thirty minutes. I started wondering if other people lived on those stars and what life must be like for them. Then I laughed 'cause I knew I'd never know. But all o' sudden I realized I didn't even know what was on this planet 'cause I was too scared to find out. I ain't neva been more than forty or fifty miles away 'cause I didn't think I had what it takes to live nowhere but here. God done made a whole planet called earth, I told myself, and you too scared to see it.

"So I started thinkin' 'bout fear and how it robs people, especially colored people, and I realized that we done gave up our God-given inheritance."

People stared at Jeremiah like witnesses must have stared at Jesus when Lazarus exited the tomb. Some wept.

"Since white folks brought us here, we been scared to live. They told us dat we wuz heathens who practiced witchcraft back in Africa and swung from trees like monkeys. Then they convinced us dat we needed this thang called Christianity in order fu God to like us. It don't take but ten minutes to see how crazy dat is, but dat's how scared we wuz o' dem folks, and dat's how bad we wanted what they had. So we adopted they beliefs and started callin' ourselves Christians, too. We never did believe everything they believed. We knowed dat deep down in our hearts God didn't like some people better than other ones. A child know dat's stupid! But out o' fear, we followed along, and white folks taught us dat God even look white like them. If we didn't believe it, we sho didn't say nothin'! And since they done convinced us dat they wuz made in de image o' God, we tremblin' anytime they come 'round.

"But when I looked up at de stars and saw how beautiful de night wuz, I finally realized that, in a lifetime, you git jes as much night as you git day. That told me that God is jes as black as he is white, and ain't nobody got no choice but to tolerate both of them. The moon wuz shinin' so bright I could see my hand in front o' my face clear as day, and the chirpin' of bullfrogs and crickets created a harmony I ain't never paid much 'tention to before. I said, 'The night is me and my people.' And I smiled when I pictured all o' y'all in my head, every shade of brown and black possible, and all together we wuz de still, dark night. If somebody didn't like it, it didn't matter 'cause de night is too big to fight. You jes gotta endure it 'til it goes away in its own sweet time.

"But what I liked most about de night is the guarantee that it'll be back tomorrow. You can hate it, you can dread it, but sho as de sun rise in de mornin', de night comin', too.

"See, we done worked fu white folks all our lives, so we ain't neva really noticed de beauty o' de night. We thank de nighttime is fu sleepin' in order to work ourselves to death durin' de day. But last night I sat in de middle of dat blackness and felt de presence o' God all 'round me." Jeremiah waved his hands in every direction. "I ain't lyin, y'all! I felt like I coulda stripped off all my clothes and jes been right at home!"

People laughed and encouraged Jeremiah to go on.

"So I started talkin' out loud. I wunnit talkin' to nobody in particular though. I wuz jes speakin' my heart. I started sayin', 'We missin' somethin'. I don't know what it is, but we missin' somethin'. I done buried a son, a daughter-in-law, and now I'm 'bout to bury a grandson. This don't make no sense. I know I ain't crazy. We missin' somethin'.' All o' sudden, a breeze blew real soft across my arm, and that's when the answer hit me."

"What answer?" Pet Moore asked anxiously.

"The answer to what we colored folks been missin'."

"And what is that?" people inquired.

"The fact that if we stand together, jes like de night, ain't nothin' white folks can do about it. They can complain and argue all they want, but they cain't move us. They'd have to get use to us jes like we use to them. See, when that breeze blew across my arm, I realized that that breeze woulda blowed whether I was standing there or not. It didn't need me to feel it! It wuz gon blow 'cause dat's what wind do! Since I felt it, dat wuz fine, but it didn't make no difference. Dat wind had a mission and a purpose, and it was bound to complete dat purpose whether I felt it or not. We think dat we cain't do nothin' 'less white folks okay it. Dat's how they control us! They make us think de wind cain't blow 'less they allow it and that the night cain't come 'til they say so. But I'm here to tell you dat de night comin' on its own terms, and de wind gon blow jes soon as it git ready. It don't need no permission. You can waste yo' time tryin' to stop either one o' 'em, but you'd be a fool 'cause God done gave them they task to do and dat's exactly what they gon do.

"Now it's time dat we colored people understand dat what God gave de wind and de waves, He gave us, too. Cain't nobody do nothin' to us if we clear 'bout who we is and why we here. All we gotta do is stand together! Let white folks huff and puff and cuss 'cause it don't make no difference. They cain't kill all o' us if we stand together 'cause it's more o' us than them."

"You sho, Jeremiah? How you know?" Miss Gladys asked.

Jeremiah smiled knowingly, and said, "'Cause we ain't de only ones I'm countin'."

People frowned, confused.

"See, while I was in The Sacred Place last night, I saw shadows everywhere. They wuz on de grass, de trees, de rocks . . . everywhere. Like to scared me to death! Then"—Jeremiah got choked up—"I saw my boy again."

Murmuring echoed throughout the barn.

"I wuz sittin' on de big rock, and a little way in de distance I saw Jerry. He started walkin' toward me, and I got up to run away, but he said, 'Daddy, it's me. Don't be afraid.'

"I reached my hand out to him, but he said, 'I cannot touch you until you become like me.' I didn't know exactly what he meant, but I knowed dat wuz fine wit me."

People laughed.

"He sat next to me on de big rock, jes like Pet sittin' here right now, and he confirmed what colored folks been missin'."

"What he say, Mi?" Pet begged.

"He said, 'Colored folks done lost they ways.' That's what he said," Jeremiah emphasized. "He said we ain't neva gon' have no peace o' mind in Mississippi 'til we stand together and let white folks know they cain't kill us whenever they git ready to. That's what he said."

People nodded approvingly. Jeremiah smiled to see that, finally, they understood what he was trying to say.

"If we stand together, ain't no way we can lose!" He was feeling good now. "All we gotta do is look bold and walk over there and say our piece. If they git rowdy, we protect ourselves, but if they don't, we thank God." He paused and surveyed the audience. "This is for our children, y'all. So they can be proud of us and love bein' colored. They'll remember the days when their folks used to shuffle 'round Money wit their heads bowed down 'cause we wuz scared to look white folks in de face, and they'll laugh at how ridiculous that musta been. Then we'll smile, either here or up in heaven, 'cause we gave our kids the greatest gift a people can ever give them."

"And what's that, Mi?" Pet smiled.

"Pride in theyselves!" Jeremiah shouted, with his head thrown back and his eyes closed. "They'll walk 'round Money"—Jeremiah began to strut like a proud rooster—"like they worth somethin'!"

"Yeah!" the crowd cheered.

"They'll say good mornin' to colored folks and whites with they head held up real high 'cause they glad to be alive in de land of de livin'!"

"Amen!"

"They'll buy they own land and plant they own crops and go to bed at night with the front door wide open if they want to 'cause ain't nobody crazy enough to bother colored people who'll fight!"

"Dat's right!"

"And colored children can start goin' to school year-'round, jes like anybody else so they can be whatever they wanna be!"

"Un-huh!"

"And these boys and girls will marry each other knowin' dat ain't nothin' like a strong colored man and a strong colored woman comin' together!"

"Dat's how de Lawd wanted it!"

"But ain't nona this gon happen if we don't stand together for the first time. Our job is to plant the seed, y'all. God gon bring de increase. Then all our children will eat the harvest."

"Tell it, Mi!" Pet reinforced.

"Listen, y'all." Jeremiah approached the audience like a healing evangelist. "Jes like they been killin' us, they gon keep on if we don't act like colored life mean somethin' to somebody. Ain't nobody gon protect us but us! Don't let it have to be yo' own grandson befo' you see how serious this is. Next time it *will* be yo' own!" Jeremiah paused. "That's why I called this gatherin', 'cause we don't want no next time. Amen?"

"Amen."

"We gotta stop white folks from treatin' us like dis, and de only way to do that is to stand like Joshua's army. Ain't that right?"

"You right about it."

"So all I'm askin' is that tomorrow mornin' we go together over to town and let folks know that the days of killin' Black folks is ova!"

"What if they laugh at us?" someone asked softly.

"They can laugh if they want to!" Jeremiah snickered. "But we'll make it clear to them that they'll pay dearly for not taking us seriously. All we gotta do is stand our ground, and they'll git the point. White folks ain't crazy."

"They sho ain't!" the crowd agreed.

"But we cain't go timid, y'all," Jeremiah warned. "We gotta look 'em dead in de eye and talk like God done gave us de authority to speak. They'll know we ain't playin'."

"Who gon do de talkin'?" an elderly man asked.

People murmured possibilities while making it clear that they were unwilling. Jeremiah hadn't thought that far ahead, but he knew he couldn't bring the people this far without leading them on.

"I'll speak!" he said boldly. "I ain't de best speaker 'round hyeah, but I'll do it if I have to."

"All right!" people affirmed.

"So once again I ask, who's comin' wit me?" Jeremiah peered deeply into the eyes of his neighbors and childhood friends.

"I'll go, Mi," one man said.

"Count me in," a high, soprano voice announced.

"I'll be here!"

"Wouldn't miss it!"

"Me!"

"I'm wit cha, Mi!"

"It's 'bout time!"

"No better time than de present!"

"Might as well!"

Jeremiah nodded his pleasure after each response and felt in his heart that something magical was happening to colored folks in Money. He looked at Miss Mary, whose wink solidified his resolve that, come what may, he was going to stand tomorrow like he had never stood before.

Possum had remained conspicuously silent. Her heart was too heavy to grieve and much too heavy to speak. She had no idea why her father had called the gathering, and now she had no idea what would happen to him the next morning. All she knew for sure was that her baby was dead, and somebody needed to pay.

"Git you a good night's sleep, Mi," Pet said as he rose to leave. "You gon need it."

"Oh, don't worry 'bout me none. I'll be all right. Tomorrow de beginnin' o' somethin' I done waited a lifetime to see, so I probably ain't gon sleep too much. Don't wanna die tonight!" Jeremiah and Pet leaned on one another and laughed.

"You ain't gotta worry 'bout dat!" Pet said. "God got somethin' fu you to do tomorrow, so you'll be there. I'll see ya in de mornin', bright and early," he said, and hobbled away.

Others gave their farewells, too, and walked home. The Johnson family retired to their living room and sat in silence like saints waiting on the Second Coming.

From the rocker, Possum whispered, "I'm goin with you in de mornin', Daddy. Somebody gotta 'splain to me why they did this to my boy." Her soft tone didn't hide her rage.

"I wanna go, too," Sarah Jane proclaimed out of nowhere. She was sitting on the floor next to the rocker, prepared for her grand-mother's objection.

"Then come on," Jeremiah said sweetly from the old sofa. "You's a young lady now. You oughta be dere."

Miss Mary stared at Jeremiah with uncertainty but remained silent.

"Thahhthen I'm goin', too," Chop added proudly. "'Cccccause I'm a bbbboy, and if girls can g-g-g-go, b-b-b-b-boys can, too."

"So my whole family's going, huh?" Ella Mae remarked. "Nobody cares that I might be sittin' here tomorrow evening wit no family at all. I guess dat ain't crossed nobody's mind, huh?" She smiled angrily. "Well, it crossed mine!" she screamed. "I'm spose to jes sit here and let my husband, both my sons, my niece, and the only father I ever had go out and tell white folks that we ain't gon let them bother us no more? And I spose to have peace about this?" She glanced from one person to the other. "Me and Momma spose to sit here as y'all—"

"I'm goin', too," Miss Mary said.

"What?" Ella Mae shouted.

"Girl, I ain't sittin' in dis ole house while everybody else out standin' fu somethin'. If we fall, all us fallin' together." She looked at Ella Mae kindly. "Dat's de way I see it."

"But Momma! We oughta let de menfolks handle that! It could git dangerous." Ella Mae was fighting a losing battle.

"It's been dangerous a long time, honey! And dat's where you young women go wrong. Y'all let de men handle de hard stuff while y'all hide behind their shirttail. Girl, my momma told me dat a col-ored woman oughta stand wherever standin' need to happen, whether a man there or not! You fight to protect him jes like he fight to protect you. If you let him do all de fightin', he gon do all de rulin', too."

Ella Mae shook her head despondently. "Fine. I give up." She rose to go to bed, then turned abruptly, and said, "Shit. Wake me up when it's time to go."

Everyone smiled.

Eighteen

BEFORE SUNRISE, THE JOHNSON FAMILY WAS UP AND PREPARED to go. The aroma of Miss Mary's homemade biscuits seeped through the front door and out the windowpanes, causing birds and squirrels to long for a place at the poor sharecroppers' table.

"Who dat in dere cookin' lik dat?" Pet Moore said when he stepped onto the front porch.

"Come on in!" Jeremiah hollered. "We got aplenty!"

Pet came through the front door dressed in his Sunday best.

"You sharp as a tack, man! I didn't know folks was gon dress up."

"Well, I wunnit sho what to put on"—Pet chuckled—"so I thought I better throw on dis ole suit o' mine."

"Hush up, man!" Miss Mary teased, placing biscuits and bacon on the table. "You know good and well dat suit ain't old! I ain't seen you wear it but one time."

"Mary Johnson, is you crazy? Dis suit older'n you is!"

The children giggled softly, especially Sarah Jane, who cherished elder interaction.

"Well, come on y'all, let's eat," Jeremiah insisted. "If we ain't neva needed strength, we needs it today. We gotta go change de world!"

Anxiety shrouded the family as they gathered at the table. Pet sat in Miss Mary's chair. "I cain't eat nothin', man," she told him. "Too much on my mind." She shook her head and made more biscuits.

"Well, I sho can!" Pet hollered. "Anybody turn down one o' Miss Mary's biscuits is either a fool or dead!"

Usually such a comment would have evoked widespread laughter, but remembering Clement, lying on the cooling board in the back room, subdued an otherwise exuberant family.

"Pet, you bless de food, man, since you de guest," Jeremiah instructed.

"I ain't no guest, man! But I'd be glad to turn de blessin'."

Everyone bowed.

"Well, Lawd," Pet began, "dis a great day! Don't none o' us know what 'bout to happen, but what we know fu sho is dat You hold de world in de palm o' Yo' hand. Bless us as we march dis mornin', Lawd, and keep Yo' angels camped all 'round us. And bless dis food we 'bout to eat, bless de preparer thereof, and make this physical nourishment enough to keep us standin' in de time o' trouble. Amen."

"Remember the Sabbath day to keep it holy," Miss Mary murmured.

"Jesus wwwwwwwwept," Chop said.

Ella Mae: "The Lord is my Shepherd, I shall not want."

Jeremiah: "Trust in de Lawd wit all thine heart, and lean not to thine own understandin'."

Ray Ray: "In the beginning, God created the heavens and the earth."

Enoch: "If God be for us, who can be against us?"

And Sarah Jane closed the scriptural litany with, "In all thy getting, get understanding."

With Jeremiah at one end of the table and Pet at the other, the family resembled Christ and his disciples at the last supper. Biscuits, bacon strips, and eggs vanished as quickly as Miss Mary placed them on the table. The angst in everyone's heart kept them silently shoveling food into their mouths, unsure of when or if another meal would come.

When the last lonely biscuit was embraced and devoured, Jeremiah belched long and deep, and said, "Time to go!" He rose and grabbed his old straw hat from the nail on the wall and tucked his shirt neatly into his good pair of overalls.

"You takin' yo' pocketbook, Momma?" Ella Mae asked.

"Naw, chile, I ain't carryin' no purse today. We goin' to handle business, but dis ain't got nothin' to do wit money."

Ella Mae stuffed a few bills into her right bra cup and left her pocketbook on the kitchen table. She pinned her long, black hair up into a bun and hid it under her white Sunday hat.

The children stood idle in the middle of the living room while the adults piddled around with miscellaneous details.

"Whwhwhwhwhat y'all thththtink g-g-g-gon happen?" Chop asked Sarah Jane and Ray Ray.

"Man, be quiet!" Ray Ray huffed.

Sarah Jane rubbed Chop's back. "Just wait and see," she said. "Everybody's a little nervous right now."

"I thththink it's gon bb-b-b-b-be all rrright. I jjjjjjes got a ffffffffeeelin'."

"Shut up, boy!" Ray Ray said more emphatically, balling both fists.

"Everybody ready?" Jeremiah called, and looked around.

"Guess so," Miss Mary answered for the family.

"Then let's go!"

When Pet Moore and the Johnsons stepped onto the front porch, they gasped in disbelief. In every direction, they saw black, brown, caramel, and dusky yellow faces looking back at them. Some were standing proudly in black dress clothes while others looked like farmers on their way to the fields. Jeremiah shook his head in awe.

"Oh my God . . . ," Pet Moore murmured.

Miss Mary started laughing hysterically. "I told you to look out fu de Lawd, didn't I?" Her mouth opened to full capacity, and she hollered, "Yessir! Don't chu never thank de Lawd don't know what He's doin'! Jes when you thank you done lost de battle, He'll pull a ram out de bush and remind you who sits on de throne! Oh praise His name!" She stepped off the porch and began to hug everyone.

Jeremiah looked at Pet, and said, slowly, "Never in a million years did I think—"

"Well, you ain't got to think no mo' 'cause here they is!" Pet's head rotated. "Good God from Zion! Look at all de folks!"

Jeremiah blinked back tears, and said, "I don't know what to say."

"You don't say nothin'," Pet answered. "You lead dese people where we need to be, and you thank de Good Lawd He heard yo' cry." Pet squeezed Jeremiah's shoulder.

Jeremiah descended the porch without greeting anyone and began to walk toward Money's white section. He strutted like an old peacock that knows others gawk in awe and reverence of its majestic gait. The crowd fell in line and mimicked his walk, proud to be part of a liberation movement they never dreamed would come to their neck of the woods.

"Chile, ain't it a great day!" Aunt Sugar declared, switching her rotund bottom like a rotating washing machine.

"Yes, ma'am, it is!" Miss Mary confirmed.

"I didn't have no idea so many folks wuz comin', Mary. Did you?"

"I didn't really think 'bout it. All I knowed fu sho was what de Lawd promised *me*." She pointed to herself.

"And what was that?"

Miss Mary lifted her flabby arms. "He told me that if I had the faith the size of a mustard seed, we could go over to dem white folks and they'd have no choice but to bow down."

"Sho nuff?" Aunt Sugar smiled.

"Jes pay attention and get your blessing!"

The Johnson children joined other children who followed their elders exultantly.

"You ain't nervous at all, Ray Ray?" another fourteen-year-old boy asked.

"Naw, not really," Ray Ray lied.

"I'm a little scared," the boy admitted. "I ain't neva seen no colored people look nobody white dead in de face."

"It's gon be all right," Ray Ray counseled. "We jes gotta stay strong and believe in ourselves. Dat's all."

The boy said nothing more, and Ray Ray was glad about it. He wondered why people kept talking and laughing like they were on their way to a celebration.

Sarah Jane walked next to Yolanda, Tiny's granddaughter.

"I like the yellow ribbon in your hair," she told Sarah Jane bashfully.

"Thank you." Sarah Jane smiled.

Yolanda smiled back. "My brother says you're the prettiest girl in LeFlore County."

Sarah Jane blushed. "I wouldn't say that."

"I would."

"I think you're pretty, too."

"Really?"

"Yep."

Each reached for the other's hand, and the two girls walked the rest of the way together, grateful to find the sister neither had.

When the mass of Black boldness crossed the bridge into Money, people immediately fell quiet. The truth of what they were about to do could no longer be disguised. Their steps slowed considerably, and the spaces between them closed like fingers preparing to make a fist.

Jeremiah stopped. He raised his head high and shouted unto the heavens, "Anybody who wanna turn 'round, now yo' last chance."

Nobody moved. People looked at each other for assurance no one alone could provide.

"'Fo we go any further," Jeremiah said, "I wanna ask my boy here to lead us in a word o' prayer."

"Amen!" the crowd agreed, grateful for a few more contemplative moments.

Relinquishing Possum's hand, Enoch knelt on one knee like a deacon during devotion, and the people followed suit. "To the great and merciful God our father!" Enoch declared. "We come to You as humble servants, dear Lawd, askin' You to be our shelter and our guide as we stand before these white folks today and proclaim what thus said de Lawd!"

The crowd said, "Amen!"

"We come as empty cups befo' a full fountain, Father, beggin' You to fill us up wit Yo' word and Yo' righteousness! We cain't do nothin' 'til You come, Oh God, and we ain't gon move from dis place 'less we know You guidin' our footsteps! Do us like You did de Hebrew children, Master, and deliver us if we git in a fiery furnace!"

"Yes, Lord!"

"Do us like You did Moses at de Red Sea, Hallelujah, and move every obstacle which dat ole devil done set up to make us fall!" Enoch clapped wildly. "We rebuke every imp, every mechanism, every power Satan done devised to bring against us, oh Lawd, and we claim victory in the name of Jesus!"

"That's right!"

"We don't always do what we spose to do, God, but we struggles to live like You want us to. Use us today, Master, and mold us 'til we look like You and sound like You and walk like You and talk jes like You told us to. Soften de hearts o' dese crazy white folks 'til they see Jesus in us and wanna know how they can have some o' dis God we got!"

"Hallelujah!"

"And, Lawd, if this be our dyin' day, comfort our souls in knowin' dat everything You do is good and perfect and right, and to be absent from de body is to be present wit de Lawd! Don't let us be scared o' nothin', oh God, and remind us like You did Jesus on de cross dat we is Yo' people in whom you are well pleased. Give us strength in our bodies and courage in our hearts to do what You done sent us to do. I ask these and all other blessings in Yo' precious son Jesus' name, Amen."

"Amen," people roared, and stood.

Before Jeremiah could speak, Billy Joe Henderson began singing, "I————love de Lawd, He heard my cry!"

And the crowd responded, "I————love————the———— Lawd! He————heard————my————cry."

"And pitied every groan!"

"And————————pi————————tied———— e————very————————groan."

"Long as I live and trouble rise! I'll hasten to His Throne!" Billy Joe bellowed.

"Long————————as————————I———— live————and————trou————ble ————————rise————————I'll———— hay————————sun————to———— His————throne."

Some cried, others shouted, a few lifted their hands in praise, and Enoch kept watch to make sure the devil didn't sneak up on them.

"It's time," Jeremiah said, and commenced walking again.

With each step the people took, their numbers multiplied. Folks glanced around without seeing the presences they felt, but they knew others were among them. Miss Mary shouted, "Un-huh, come on, come on!" as the children wondered to whom she was speaking. Aunt Sugar didn't wonder. She saw them, too, in their invisibility. Their long, graceful strides made her think of angels dancing around the throne of God. She imagined them cloaked in flowing white garments and marching to Zion like the songs prophesied. For now, their presence strengthened the people and made them feel like the Hebrew army preparing to face the Philistines. It was funny, Jeremiah thought, that as soon as he gathered the strength to stand alone, others came. And not just human others but spirit others who had the power and the authority to protect them from dangers seen and unseen. Sarah Jane felt them, but had not the eyes to see. The warm, tingling sensation in her arms felt like her mother's energy, and that was enough to convince her that they'd live to see another day. In one way or another, everybody knew that their original numbers were now exponentially greater and that God had sent the help they had prayed for. Only Miss Mary knew it would happen this way, having gotten used to God's moving when others weren't watching. She had seen the Invisible Ones before, in various places and moments, and prayed for the day when they and the living might unite. All those years of arguing and fussing with God had paid off, she concluded, and now, while others trembled, she sauntered confidently alongside those who'd seen God face-to-face. Meeting Aunt Sugar's eyes, they laughed knowingly, and Miss Mary declared aloud what both knew: "You can't always see yo' help, chile!"

Chop wanted to see what the women saw. "Wwwwhat is it, Gr-rrrrrandma?" he asked, tugging her dress.

Miss Mary wept and proclaimed, "De Good Lawd is here wit His angels, boy! Don't you see 'em?"

Looking throughout the crowd, Chop saw only familiar Black faces. "No mmmmma'am," he cried. "B-b-b-b-but I wwwwant to, Grrrrrand-ma! Cccccan you t-t-t-t-tell mmmme how to ssssssee 'em?"

Miss Mary said, "Look wit yo heart, baby. Don't look wit yo' eyes."

Chop didn't understand, but he determined to try. He closed his eyes and excavated the contents of his heart. He found Ray Ray there, and Sarah Jane, and they treated him kindly and asked his opinion on every subject. He saw Jeremiah and Old Man Cuthbert smoking pipes, laughing, and sharing stories about the old days. Aunt Sugar and Miss Mary made cakes and pies and fried enough chicken for everybody in Money, and people said, "Lawd have murcy! This de best food I ever tasted!" and the women smiled as Aunt Sugar declared, "Get on outta here, child! We jes throwed dat together!" and everybody laughed and everybody got full. And all the elders told all the children what life used to be like for colored people, and the children couldn't believe that hatred once held humans captive. And when Chop opened his eyes, he beheld the form of angels, hundreds of them, staring into heaven while standing guard among the believers. He gasped, "Grandma! I see 'em! I see 'em!" and reached to touch them, but Miss Mary blocked his hand, saying, "You feel 'em wit yo' heart, baby. You feel 'em on de inside. Anything you feel wit yo' hands ain't real."

Chop understood. He waved at beings who returned the gesture kindly. "Thank you," he told all of them. "Thank you. Thank you. Thank you," he repeated until his wet eyes could hold the tears no longer. "Thank you! Thank you! Thank you!" he shouted, then realized that when his grandma, over the years, had waved her hands, and said, "Thank ya!" she was actually talking to a host of Gods, to hundreds, maybe thousands of angels who had helped her or her people or somebody in the world survive something they couldn't handle alone. Chop concluded that God must be everybody and everything that ever lived all combined, working to teach earth folks how to love existence—not just physical life. With that knowledge, he counted the day a victory—whether they lived or not.

All the while, the people kept moving.

Billy Joe Henderson sang the call:

Go down, Moses,
Way down in Egyptland!
Tell old Pharaoh . . .

And the people answered:

Let my people go!

He continued:

No more shall they in bondage toil,

Let my people go
Let them come out with Egypt's spoil

And the people demanded:

Let my people go!
Let my people go!
Let my people go!

. . . until they knew, like Moses, that God had not brought them this far to leave them. Every colored citizen, buttressed by souls larger than themselves, borrowed strength from those Inexhaustible Ones and purposed in their hearts to tell their children and their children's children how, one dusty summer morning, God and the ancestors ushered them into victory.

By now, Miss Mary was laughing uproariously. A few thought she might have snuck into Jeremiah's moonshine earlier that morning, but, ignoring the spiritually indigent, she repeated, "Didn't I tell you? Huh? Didn't I tell you?" until her contagious joy caused others to chuckle without ever knowing why. Her rendition of "Woke up Dis Mornin' Wid My Mind Stayed on Jesus" comforted those who never understood the song's immediate relevance. Now they knew, and so they added their voices and created a trumpet call to battle that could be heard for miles. In fact, the people guessed that all those old Black church ballads were telling a story that would, one day, come to pass.

Ray Ray walked oblivious to the coexistence of spirit and flesh, for his heart's desire, in the midst of communal jubilee, was simply to get the ordeal over with. The façade of strength and resolve he wore made a perfect mask for an extremely insecure soul.

Chop told him, "Everything's gon be all right, Ray Ray. I just seen de angels!"

Ray Ray said nothing but appreciated—then borrowed—his little brother's courage. "I'm okay." He sighed.

"It's all right to be scared, Ray Ray. Everybody get scared sometime. I wuz scared, too, 'til I seen de angels."

"Wait a minute!" Ray Ray screamed, and grabbed Chop's shoulders. "Yo' voice! What happened to yo' voice? You ain't stutterin' no mo'!"

"That's right!" Chop said innocuously. Miss Mary winked at him. "I told you, I just seen de angels!"

Ray Ray snickered, "Well, good for you," without taking Chop seriously.

"No, I'm serious!" he cried. "De angels fixed my voice! I went in my heart and—"

"Don't worry 'bout it, baby," Miss Mary consoled. "You can't tell nobody 'bout God. They gotta see Him fu theyself jes like you had to. His turn'll come."

On the other side of the crowd, a voice whispered to Possum:

Hear you that shriek: It rose
So wildly on the air
It seem'd as if a burden'd heart
Was breaking in despair.

Saw you those hands so sadly clasped—
The bowed and feeble head—
The shuddering of that fragile form—
That look of grief and dread?

Saw you the sad, imploring eye?
Its every glance was pain,
As if a storm of agony
Were sweeping through the brain.

She is a mother pale with fear,
Her boy clings to her side,
And in her kyrtle vainly tries
His trembling form to hide.

They tear him from her circling arms,
Her last and fond embrace—
Oh! Never more may her sad eyes
Gaze on his mournful face.

"They killed my baby!" she began to wail. Possum had hoped to keep her agony contained, but the words of the poem insisted that she release. "Oh God! They killed my baby!"

"That's right!" the voice encouraged. "Tell the world! Let the world know!"

"He was my only chile!" Possum screamed. "Who would do a mother's baby that way? How could they jes beat him 'til his eye come right out o' his head?"

"Yes, purge it. Yes! Yes!"

"Clement!" she cried and stumbled. "I love you, baby! I don't know what I'm gon do without you!"

Ella Mae carried Possum's semilimp body as the grieving mother relinquished an unbearable weight.

"Oh God! I can't do this! I can't, Ella Mae! I can't!"

"We gon do it together, girl! You ain't by yo'self. That boy belonged to all o' us!"

"I can't do it, Ella Mae! Why can't I just die, too?"

"'Cause you cain't!" Ella Mae screamed. She couldn't explain her sudden burst of power and authority, although she could have had she seen the Invisible One standing next to her. "There are other chillen waiting on your love and your direction. Use Clement's life to teach, Possum! Stand up and tell Negroes everywhere that we shall never let this happen again. Declare to the world that your son was the last sacrifice of a people who ain't scared no mo! Prove to the world that, even when they kill some o' us, they make de rest o' us stronger! Live, girl! Live!"

Ella Mae surrendered to the spirit for Possum's sake.

"Yes, Clement is yo' son and you love him! But Clement ain't yo' only child! Do you see all dese chillen? These yo' chillen! And until we get clear 'bout that, ain't none o' us gon have no chillen 'cause our strength is divided, and once somethin' happen to our chillen, we don't commit to takin' care o' nobody else's. So, if we ain't careful, they gon kill every colored chile in America 'cause they don't neva have to fight nobody but de parents. You ain't in this alone!" Possum was in another zone. "We all lost a son in Clement! All of us! And dat's why we marchin' right now. To make sure white folks is clear that we ain't givin' up no mo Black chillen ever again! Unless they intend to kill *every single one o' us!*"

Possum felt her legs strengthen. She would still give anything, do anything, to have her son back, but thinking of Sarah Jane, Ray Ray, and Chop as her own, her *very* own, brought her healing within arm's reach.

Only a cotton field now separated the Black army from its white neighbors. None of them noticed Rosenthal in the distance, following clandestinely, hoping the sheriff and his racist crew wouldn't slaughter half the colored population of Money. As the Johnsons prayed over breakfast, Rosenthal had found a miniature jar into which he poured Sutton and the fluid, and had eased the jar into his pants pocket in preparation for a morning walk. When his walk and the march of the people converged, Rosenthal paused, thinking it inappropriate to interrupt what looked like a move of solid Black determination. Instead, he lingered behind trees and shrubs, trying to ascertain exactly where the people were going and what would be the impact of their actions on his life. His and Sutton's.

Without thinking twice, Jeremiah moved across the field, stomping cotton stalks boldly and daring anyone to stop him. Others did likewise. These poor, country soldiers never dreamed they'd do anything in a cotton field except pick it. That's why they waltzed and pranced like pompous royalty. Chop was grinning so broadly the corners of his mouth ached. He wanted to ask who had seen what he had seen, but he chose, rather, to bask in his own glory and, as Miss Mary advised, to let each person discover God for themselves. When he looked around one last time, only the original remained.

Jeremiah halted the crowd. "Y'all sure y'all ready?" he challenged.

"Yep! We ready!"

When they reached town, they stopped in front of the General Store. Whites began to gather and whisper about why their servants hadn't come to work that day and what they were doing bunched together in the center of Money.

"Shouldn't you nigras be in de fields workin'?" Catherine Cuthbert's Southern drawl screamed from the porch of the store. "You ain't done enough damage already?"

"Just be cool," Jeremiah mumbled, tight-lipped. "Don't nobody say nothin'."

Other whites surfaced and stared at the mass like observers at an exotic animal zoo.

"We wanna talk to de white citizens o' dis town," Jeremiah hollered. "All o' y'all."

"You wanna what?" the sheriff heralded. He approached Jeremiah, moving his tongue around in his mouth as though preparing to spit tobacco juice on him. "You must ain't found yo' boy yet"—he smiled—"'cause when you do, you'll know never to so much as look at a white man again."

Hold yo piece, ole man, Jeremiah told himself. "I got my grandboy," he said with deliberate intensity, "and dat's de reason we wants to talk to de white citizens o' dis town," Jeremiah repeated, staring into Billy's eyes for the first time.

"You killed my brothers, you fuckin' nigger bastard, and you think you can come over here demanding to talk to somebody?" he yelled. "Do I need to teach you another lesson?"

Jeremiah ignored the threat, and repeated, "We wanna talk to de white citizens o' dis town."

Billy mocked Jeremiah and laughed. "Y'all don't never learn. I thought takin' care o' dat boy would teach you once and for all, but niggers just don't never seem to learn." Billy's face was only inches from Jeremiah's. "And anyway, what ch'all gotta say to white folks, nigger boy?"

"We didn't come to start no trouble. We jes came to git a few thangs straight—today."

"Thangs like what?" the sheriff asked on behalf of the twenty bigots huddled behind him.

"We wants to talk to everybody—not jes you," Jeremiah said boldly.

"Oh, so you a bad nigger now?" Billy patronized. "You think you can talk to de whole white community like you a fuckin' nigger governor or somethin'?"

"We intend to be as peaceful as you let us be, but if you wanna make trouble, we can sho have some." Black folk lifted their rifles.

The sheriff's face flushed beet red. He raised his hand, and said, "I'll slap de fuckin' black off yo' face, nigger!"

". . . and if you do, you'll never do it again!" Enoch hollered, pointing his shotgun at the tip of Billy's narrow red nose.

"Dear Lord!" Miss Gladys mumbled.

"Do what my daddy asked, Sheriff, and won't be no trouble. Jes gather as many o' yo' folks out here as you can find so we can say our piece and be on our way."

Billy stared at the stoic Black faces in awe and wonder. He never dreamed a colored man would speak to him the way Jeremiah and Enoch had. "You'll die for this. You know that, don't chu? What *somebody* did to that nigger boy jes wasn't enough to convince you people to stay in your place? That's a mighty damn shame."

"Jes git the rest of your people," Enoch said again calmly.

Billy backed away, fearful and embarrassed. He hollered for other whites to come and look at all the niggers in Money, gathered together like they really meant something.

Other whites didn't take the scene quite so lightly. Most of them stood in the road quietly, unsure of exactly how bold the coloreds had become.

After several intense minutes, a sizeable mass of Southern whites had gathered and now stood directly in front of Jeremiah and the others.

"We don't mean no harm to any o' y'all," Jeremiah began kindly. "We jes come to talk to you 'bout how we been livin' in Money and to tell you how we gon live here from now on."

No whites responded.

"Somebody beat my grandbaby to death and throwed his body in de river. And dat somebody wasn't colored. Now I don't know which one o' y'all did it, but we here to tell you today that we ain't gon have this no mo'. Not never again."

A few whites chuckled.

"Laugh if you want to, but I promise you dat killin' anybody else colored in dis town is gon cost you more than you willin' to pay."

"What chu gon do, nigger boy?" Old Man Cuthbert asked.

"That's the last thing I'd like to show you," Jeremiah said with a broad smile. "But if you make me, I will."

"Are you threatenin' us?" the sheriff asked.

"You can call it what chu want to," Jeremiah offered, "but you'd be sorry fu tryin' us. I guarantee you that."

Silence consumed the white audience.

"Now let's get clear about a few things. We been buryin' Black folks fu years as y'all been killin' 'em, but we ain't doin' dat no more."

"Dat's right," a few brave, Black souls affirmed.

"For every Black funeral, it's gon be a white one," Jeremiah proclaimed. "Y'all gon stop comin'—"

Where the shot came from no one knew, but Ray Ray slumped to the ground, clutching his shoulder. Screams from both sides filled the air and ushered in the chaos Miss Mary had prayed wouldn't come.

"My baby!" was all Ella Mae could say, as drops of Ray Ray's burgundy blood stained her white Sunday dress.

"I'm okay, Momma," Ray Ray whispered. "It just brushed my shoulder. I ain't hurt bad. I'm okay."

The other shot came from Enoch's gun. He had prepared the target in case of such an emergency, and now stood proud that someone white in Money would finally know the feelings of intimidation and familial loss. When twelve-year-old Alvin Cuthbert Jr. fell, his mother collapsed along with him. "NO!" Catherine screamed, trembling and holding one she thought more precious than any Black child could ever be. "You shot my fuckin' son!" she announced, more in surprise than anger. "You killed my husband, and now my son?" In the sheriff's rage, he reached for his pistol, hoping to destroy Jeremiah, but the old sharecropper planted two shotgun shells in Billy's chest long before the white man ever touched his gun's trigger. Instead of inciting fear in Black people's hearts, Billy's tumble energized them. Whites never believed that Blacks would ever act in concert against them. Now they knew, and every Black citizen holding a gun sought to feel the pride Jeremiah and Enoch felt. So, before angry white men could hoist their rifles, angrier Black men and women pressed the butts of their own guns against their shoulders, closing one eye and aiming with the other. If they died that day, Blacks resolved in their hearts, whites were going down with them.

Rosalind had known this day would come. She used to tell Billy that coloreds weren't going to allow their own degradation forever, but she never guessed they'd kill him so soon. And so easily. Kneeling at his side, she wept—not for him or herself or her girls, but because, as always, her mother had been right. She had wanted nothing more in life than Billy Ray Cuthbert. And then she got him. At least now, she thought, the wounds and bruises on her face could heal before being made worse again.

Watching from the back of the crowd, Rosenthal had expected Jeremiah and the others to crumble in fear, yet, to his amazement, each stood resolute, one foot slightly ahead of the other, inviting the fullness of Chaos since it would not be denied. Had anyone white had the humility, he or she could have stepped forward slowly and seen the entire history of Black people in their red, translucent eyes, and they would have known why this day was inevitable. Yet whites in Money never considered the possibility that their own fate was somehow connected to their Black neighbors'.

Jeremiah's bottom lip quivered when he asked, "Y'all wanna talk now?"

Old Man Cuthbert yelled, "You fuckin' Black bastards! I hate you colored sons of bitches! You niggers are gonna pay!"

Jeremiah and Miss Mary cackled together.

"Pay?" Miss Mary shouted. "Did you say 'pay'? Chile, we been done paid!"

Catherine Cuthbert rose and screamed, "You ain't paid nothin' like what you 'bout to!"

Miss Mary sashayed forward, staring directly at the pale white woman. "Girl, I done buried half my family, and you think you 'bout to make me pay?" The fire in Miss Mary's eyes matched the vehemence in Catherine's. "Is you really serious? You think you can make me pay more than I done already paid?" Miss Mary stared beyond Catherine's pupils. Satisfied, now, that the woman knew she meant business, Miss Mary stepped back and blended once again into her people.

"Now, like I was sayin'," Jeremiah continued, "ain't no mo' Black life gon be sacrificed 'round here. Everybody in Money gon live in peace or ain't gon be no peace."

"That's right," Pet said.

"And if you think we scared to make good on dis promise, jes try us again." Jeremiah looked into the eyes of every white person present.

"Anythang y'all wanna say?" he asked lightly.

Jeremiah never dreamed he'd witness white silence in the midst of Black strength.

"Good!" he offered. "Now, one last thing."

Black folk lowered their weapons.

"I want somebody to 'pologize to my people for killin' so many o' us over de years." Whites lowered their eyes. "I'ma count to ten and somebody better start talkin' or more o' y'all gon start fallin'."

Jeremiah raised his shotgun again. "One," he said confidently.

Pet motioned for others to reassume warrior position.

"Two," Jeremiah said more loudly.

"Three."

"Ain't nobody 'pologizin' to you niggers!" Old Man Cuthbert declared. "You cain't come over here and shoot white folks and then make us say we sorry! You fuckin' niggers must be crazy!"

"Four." Jeremiah stared at Old Man Cuthbert.

Chop's nerves disintegrated, and he ran to his grandfather's side. "It's all right, Granddaddy," he whispered. "We can go now. I think they understand."

"We ain't goin' nowhere 'til somebody 'pologize for killin' my people. Somebody beat my grandson's eye right out o' his head, and somebody better 'pologize befo' I go to shootin' all o' y'all."

Rosenthal shivered. He thought of returning Sutton to his people, but now it was simply too late. No explanation would make sense, and the act might even cost him his life. "Everything's going to be all right, Sutton," he mouthed. "Everything's going to be all right."

"Five," Jeremiah said.

Rosenthal rushed forward. "We're sorry," he offered abruptly.

Whites grumbled their dissent.

"We're sorry for killing Black people over the years. It wasn't right. And what happened to your grandson should never have happened."

Rosenthal's right hand remained locked around the jar in his pocket.

Jeremiah looked confused. "I thought you wuz gon help us, Mr. Rosenthal? After all that talk, we never heard from you no mo'."

"I told y'all dat cracker wunnit shit!" Tiny yelled.

Rosenthal felt his reputation faltering. "I . . . um . . . meant what I said. I really did. But . . . um . . . things didn't turn out like I had hoped."

"Look where he's standin'," Tiny pointed, "and that'll tell you whose side he's on. Don't be no fool, Mi."

"I'm not one of . . . these," Rosenthal said awkwardly, looking behind him. "I'm on your side. Trust me. If you only knew—"

"If we only knew what, Mr. Rosenthal?" Jeremiah pressed.

He almost exposed the jarred Sutton, but was not yet convinced it would help one way or the other. "If you only knew . . . um . . . how I've changed."

"We thought we knew the other night," Pet chimed, "but now looks like we wuz wrong."

"But you weren't wrong!" Rosenthal protested. "You weren't. I just didn't get a chance to get back to you and—"

"You didn't get a chance to help me save my boy's life, Mr. Rosenthal? What wuz you doin' that wuz mo' impo'tant than that?"

"I was loving your boy!" Rosenthal belted regretfully.

"What?" Possum frowned. "How wuz you lovin' my son?"

Lost in a dark abyss, Rosenthal tried his last option. "I found this the other night." He removed the jar from his pocket and held it high for everyone to see.

"What the hell . . . ?" Jeremiah murmured, stepping toward Rosenthal.

"It's an eye. His eye. I found his eye in the woods." His hand trembled. "It's a beautiful eye. Just like the colored boy's at Harvard. I took it home and loved it. Its name is Sutton."

"What the hell are you talking about?" Possum screamed in disbelief. "You found my son's eye, and you took it home and put it in a jar?"

"Yes! That's it!" He hoped she was beginning to understand. "I took it home. And I loved it and surrounded it with liquid so it'd stay moist. We read aloud together and listened to music."

Tiny laughed. "Y'all gon listen to me next time!"

"You can hold it if you want to," Rosenthal offered, extending the jar to Jeremiah.

In slow motion, Jeremiah received it. He unscrewed the cap and looked into the jar like one fearful of beholding Satan face-to-face. "Mr. Rosenthal? You's a sick man," he said and resealed the top. He handed the jar to Possum.

"It's not what it seems," Rosenthal cackled. "I was doing my duty. I knew it was right because, although the eye belonged to your boy, it looked just like Sutton Griggs Jr., so I knew God was giving me one last chance to right my wrongs."

"What the fuck is this cracker talkin' 'bout?" Possum yelled in every direction.

Rosenthal knew his explanation wasn't going over very well. "It's very complicated, ma'am"—he smiled patronizingly—"so it's probably best if you don't even try to understand. You certainly have enough on your mind."

Enoch whispered, "Daddy, can I shoot him?"

Jeremiah raised his hand. "Let him be."

Possum enclosed the jar with both hands and stared at Rosenthal.

"I do need that back, though," he said. "That probably sounds pretty crazy to you, but our . . . um . . . relationship is just getting started."

Possum's silent stare burned a hole in Rosenthal's confidence. His hands fidgeted as though playing an invisible piano. "I need Sutton now," he said slowly, "to pay my debt."

"Y'all done killed my son," Possum intoned, "and now you say even his eye belongs to you? You a goddamn—"

"*I* didn't kill him!" Rosenthal boasted.

"You might as well have! You had his eye and didn't give it back!"

Rosenthal hesitated. "Yeah, but that's different." He sighed. "I knew you wouldn't understand. And it's okay. This whole thing is crazy. But please understand that I need Sutton—well, the eye— back. It actually belongs to me."

Possum squinted. "Well I'll be damned. Has this man lost his mind?"

"Just give me the eye back and I can explain more later. Right now, everybody's tense and probably should just go home and cool down."

Black folks snickered sporadically.

A white lady touched Rosenthal's shoulder tenderly, and asked, "Are you okay, Mr. Rosenthal?"

"Don't touch me!" he yelled, and jerked away. "I'm not crazy! I'm just trying to get back . . . um . . . something that I desperately need. Something that belongs to me."

"I don't know what chu talkin' 'bout, Mr. Rosenthal"—Jeremiah sighed, relinquishing the battle for clarity—"but this here eye's go-ing back where it belongs—in my grandson's head."

"Oh no!" Rosenthal pleaded. "You can't do that!" He realized the madness of his statement. "I mean . . . um . . . please don't do that. I have to have it. I have to. It's the only way I'll be forgiven."

Possum stared harder at Rosenthal. "There's no way you're get-ting my son's fuckin' eye, white man!" she bellowed. "Y'all ain't satis-fied with killin' Negroes? You want every little piece of us, too?"

"You don't understand!" Rosenthal shouted. "It's not that I want every piece of your boy! I just want . . . um . . . what I found, what be-longs to me."

"I cain't understand what chu talkin' 'bout, Mr. Rosenthal, but like I said, this here eye's goin' back where it belongs. At least then we can bury my grandson whole."

"Okay! Fine!" Rosenthal waved frivolously, "but can't I just hold it once more? I mean, what harm would that do?" His yearning eyes evoked no sympathy.

Jeremiah said, "We ain't gon talk about this no mo', Mr. Rosen-thal. We'll be goin' now."

"No!" Rosenthal cried, and fell to his knees. "I just need to hold it a few seconds. That's all. I promise! I'll give it right back. I will!"

"Let's go, Daddy," Enoch suggested, touching his father's elbow. "We done had our say, and you got yo' apology."

Jeremiah nodded, and said, "Let's go, y'all. We got one mo' piece o' business to handle."

The Black mass turned to leave.

"Please don't take Sutton away from me again!" Rosenthal groaned to the people's backs. "I know this sounds crazy, but I found it, and it's mine!"

His wrinkled white body contracted into a fetal position upon the ground. Tears issued forth freely, but no one really understood all that Rosenthal was trying, though failing, to articulate. The farther the Black mass retreated, the harder he sobbed, having no choice now but to recognize how and when he had failed.

Throughout the ordeal, Rose Love, Cecil's wife, studied her maid's countenance. She feared the Negroes' stark defiance might mean Inez wasn't coming to work the next day. If she did come, Rose surmised, Inez would probably insist that she stop calling her "gal" and start calling her by her name. Such a demand would be a meager price to pay, Rose admitted, for a woman whose hands and knees had never touched her own floors. She just hoped Inez hadn't become drunk with self-righteousness. Had Rose known that Inez would never set foot in the Love home again—much less clean it—she might have run after the Black recessional and promised Inez all sorts of perks, like having some weekends off or even being called "Miss Inez." But Rose's inability to read her maid's mind or to understand the finality of the moment just passed left her praying for the impossible while, down the road, Inez chuckled at the prospect of sleeping in her own bed long after sunrise.

When the bold ones reached The Sacred Place, Miss Mary began singing, "I know it was the blood!" Her hands shot into the air like one under arrest. "I know it was the blood! I know it was the blood, for me! Oh yes! One day when I was lost, he died upon the cross! I know it was the blood for me!" Twisting and jerking convulsively, she screamed, "Thank ya, Lawd! You been so good!" Her huge palms created thunder each time they met, and others began to weep simply watching Miss Mary surrender to the Holy Ghost. Then, slowly, she moved throughout The Sacred Place, touching trees, flowers, butterflies, birds, deer, rabbits, and squirrels, all of whom accepted her anointing willingly, lovingly and nodded as she continued, "One day when I was lost, he died upon the cross. I know it was the blood for me!" Others joined her, creating a collective voice that reverberated throughout The Sacred Place like the voice of God. "He never said a mumbling word!" the people sang, releasing the angst of the day. Together, they looked possessed, marching from tree to bush, singing to the animate and the inanimate about the power of sacrifice and giving. Their slow motion and unrestrained weeping made Rosenthal, standing at the edge of the clearing, wonder if, indeed, they all had consumed the same drug. They seemed to have lost their consciousness, he noted, for none of them had the least concern for onlookers or the backlash of earlier insulted whites. Instead, they floated throughout The Sacred Place, wailing and moaning a song Rosenthal didn't know and therefore couldn't sing.

Having always been reserved, Miss Gladys didn't know what to do when the fire hit her. She clutched her arms tightly, trying to deny the spirit's overflow, but her soul cried out "Hallelujah!" anyway. She grabbed Pet's arm to steady her step, yet her feet started shuffling a dance only her ancestors would have recognized. "They whipped him all night long!" she sang out and flung her head in every direction. Images of Billy Cuthbert—or whoever—beating Clement crowded her consciousness and caused her to scream, "They whipped him all night long for me!"

"Oh yeah!" the crowd supported.

"They whipped him all night long for me!" Miss Gladys declared without shame. "For me! For me! For me!" Her hands joined Miss Mary's in thunderous applause of a God who, though never punctual, was always right on time. Pet tried to constrain her, saying, "It's all right, honey, it's all right" while rubbing her back gently, but Miss Gladys was glad to be free of the bonds of propriety that governed genteel, educated Black women. Her jerks and subsequent strides looked choreographed as she made her way to the middle of The Sacred Place, proclaiming all the while, "For me! For me! He did it for me!"

"They beat him 'til he died!" Miss Mary resumed the lead.

"Oh yeah!" the people returned.

"They beat him 'til he died, for me!" Together, the people sang, "One day when I was lost, he died upon the cross! I know it was the blood for me!"

Like an electric current, the Holy Ghost moved across the crowd and filled everyone's spirit to overflowing. Screaming, shouting, and dancing, they conjured Clement's spirit and thanked him for being the bridge that took them over.

Sarah Jane marveled at the sight. She wanted to feel that invisible power rush all over her, too, but, for some reason, she couldn't. Then she closed her moist eyes and visualized Billy and others beating Clement mercilessly. She heard, in her soul, the hollow sound of the hammer bludgeoning against Clement's skull, and that's when she began to tremble. The men's hyena-like laughter crushed her microscopic dream that whites might, one day, honor Black life. Each time they slapped Clement, Sarah Jane shuddered, feeling the pain as though it rested upon her own face. Even the kicking, which made his thick brown body coil like a snail, left Sarah Jane doubled over in agony as she wondered who could treat a child that way. Yet the sound of the crowbar cracking Clement's crown was more than she could bear. Each hollow thump, like an axe against a stubborn log, churned bile in her stomach and made her sure that, at any moment, she'd vomit her entire insides. She tried to abort the imagining, but each time her grandmother cried, "They whipped him all night long!" the imagery strengthened in her mind's eye and she saw Clement's blood mingle with the red clay near the banks of the Tallahatchie. Why he wasn't protesting she didn't understand. He just stood there, it seemed, leaning against an old oak tree, as though he owed the price they extracted from him. Eventually the blows cut him down. The final strike sent his left eye hurling into the darkness—"No!" Sarah Jane shrieked—and the men dragged his body away. So when Miss Mary announced, "He never said a mumblin' word!" Sarah Jane understood, finally, that she and her grandmother were in the same spiritual moment, and she gave thanks for her inclusion.

"He never said a mumblin' word!" Miss Mary repeated melodiously. "He never said a mumblin' word, oh me!" With eyes closed and arms stretched wide, she declared, "My baby! They done killed my baby!" The crowd finished the chorus: "One day when I was lost, he died on the cross! I know it was the blood for me!" Dust rose and created a brown cloud around the people's feet. The pandemonium inspired even an ant community to pause its busyness and watch Money's Black elders dance the cosmic merger of spirit and flesh.

From a distance, the people's bodies appeared elevated, like angels preparing to ascend into midair.

"Thank ya, Jesus! Oh, Glory to your name! Hallelujah!" voices declared to the heavens. Even the children shared the ecstasy, crying quietly as their elders connected with a spiritual tradition found only in the people's epic memory. The spirit became contagious that day. A young cypress sapling, desiring desperately to contribute unto the praise, fanned its leaves vigorously and bent its branches until they touched the earth. An observer might have screamed in horror, for the tree moved as though it had come to life. Yet the Black participants simply danced along.

When Miss Mary sang richly, "He's comin' back again!" and the people confirmed, "Sho nuff!" Jeremiah released a lifetime of pain. His entire body shook as he cried "I love ya, Lawd!" and fell to his knees. No one understood the fullness of Jeremiah's purging, for most had never seen an old Black man sob that way. Ray Ray almost ran to his grandfather, thinking the old man needed some help in restoring his usual resolve, but Sarah Jane told him, "He's all right. Leave him alone. This is between him and God now."

And suddenly, those ancient beings, the once Invisible Ones, came again. Yet this time, they arrived in radiant splendor. Draped in flowing, snow-white garments with matching headwraps and accompanying staffs, they looked like gigantic African spirits on their way to a river baptism. As Revelation foretold, they descended from the sky like majestic clouds of glory. One by one, single file, they marched to an earthly Zion, humming "I Know It Was the Blood," crying congratulatory exultations to a people who had finally converted prayer into power. And they kept coming by the thousands. Chop gawked at the legions, processing like a Black Baptist church choir, who then filled The Sacred Place and encircled their children in a Jericho wall of pure white. "Wow," he mumbled, and noted that their faces were midnight black. The eyes, however, were solid white, lacking irises and pupils, but their warm smiles kept the boy from fearing them. One with Billie Faye's robust shape and confident swagger winked at Sarah

Jane and bowed slightly before her. She bowed in return and waved excitedly, far too overwhelmed to speak. Her soul was satisfied. The Sacred Place was indeed heaven, she thought, complete with all the people she loved and those beautiful, colossal, Black spirits singing, along with her elders, about how somebody's blood had set them free.

Though miniature next to the ancestors, Miss Mary walked among them, shaking hands and speaking as though knowing them personally. She then constructed her own verse: "They threw him in de river!"

"Oh, yes!" the spirits bellowed in response.

"They threw him in de river!" Miss Mary was beside herself now. "They threw him in de river . . . for me!"

"Hallelujah!" the spirits sang in chorus. Then they belted, "One day when I was lost, he died upon the cross! I know it was the blood for me!"

Enoch and Jeremiah each held one of Possum's arms as she shouted and kicked away her agony. Snot rested on her upper lip and dried tear streaks, like warrior marks, painted her face. Her torn dress hung limp across her left shoulder, exposing a full, right breast, but no one bothered to cover her. She was in the land of the free, and her only desire was to understand why Clement, her only begotten son, had been the sacrifice required to save the people. So she danced and wept, screaming "Why? Why? Why my chile?"

In the next improvised verse, her mother explained, "Trials come to make you strong!"

"Oh yes!" the spirits confirmed.

"Trials come to make you strong!"

"Sho nuff!"

"Trials come to make you strong . . . oh me!" Miss Mary's arms oscillated like helicopter propellers.

Other elders ad libbed, "My Lord!" and "Good God!" until the moment echoed with a thousand tongues contributing unto a spiritual ritual none had ever experienced before.

Unable to get her fullest deliverance, Possum escaped the patriarchal clasp and ran to her mother.

"Momma!" she yelled. "It hurts so bad!" Clutching her sides, her torso bent to a ninety-degree angle with her legs. All she knew to do was cry out, "Ahhhhhhhhhhhhhhhhh!" The ancestors wept streams of living water for Possum, thanking God for the fruit of her blessed womb. Their tears fell upon her like waterfalls rushing to cleanse and heal one whose entire life had been composed of nothing but struggle, heartache, and loss.

"Sing de song, chile!" Miss Mary declared. "Sing de song! You gotta sing de song!"

"It hurts too bad, Momma! Why did dey have to kill my baby?" Possum ripped the remainder of the dress from her flesh and flung her arms wide in surrender to anyone willing to help her. Naked and unashamed, she yelped, "Help me, Lord!"

"Sing de song, chile!" Miss Mary repeated. "Sing de song!"

With eyes aglow, the ancestors stared at Possum their hope that she would follow her mother's directive. They hummed the chorus line incessantly, waiting for her to assume the lead, and suddenly Possum felt a small, familiar hand pat her shoulder, and she knew her child was safe among the angels. She rejoiced, "They beat my baby down!"

"Oh, yes!" the ancestors answered, waving the sleeves of their white gowns frantically.

"They beat my baby down!" Possum sang sadly.

"Hallelujah!" Miss Mary cried.

"They beat my baby down . . . and he did it for me!" Possum's feet stomped the earth.

The ancestors finished the chorus, "One day when I was lost, he died upon the cross. I know it was the blood for me!"

Possum wasn't finished. The smiles of her mother and her people erased what would have been the shame of her nudity, so with embarrassment unencountered, she sang, "They gouged out his eye!"

"Oh Lord!" the ancestral chorus declared.

"They gouged out his eye!"

"Uh-huh!"

"They gouged out his eye . . . for me! One day when I was lost," they sang together, "He died upon the cross! I know it was the blood for me!"

"Dat's right baby!" Miss Mary heralded. "Sing yo' song!"

Everyone, spirit and flesh alike, gathered around Possum and contributed to the healing of her soul.

"He's comin' back again!" Possum sang, with head held high and breasts standing at attention.

"That's right!" the chorus belted.

"He's comin' back again!" Possum began to walk among her people, like her mother had done, shaking hands and hugging necks while spirits rejoiced above them.

"Oh praise his name!" they declared.

"He's comin' back again . . . for me!" she poked her chest proudly. Jeremiah, Enoch, Ella Mae, and the children cried, "Thank ya, Jesus!" and others murmured, "Get what cha need, baby. Get what cha need!" One lone spirit stepped forth and ended the melody in Jerry's silky smooth bass, "One day when I was lost, he died upon the cross. I know it was the blood for me!" The spirit nodded to all who had risked their lives earlier, then, standing before the Johnson family, bowed slowly and held the bowed position as though wanting each family member never to forget the beauty of what they had initiated. There were no tears this time. Pride, clarity, and determination shone on Johnson faces as they bowed in return, thankful for the reunion each had dreamed of. Now Sarah Jane was free to love and Jeremiah would never again carry the guilt of inactivity. Enoch and Ella Mae thought they heard the words "thank you" and their response was simply to enshroud Sarah Jane between them. Had they spoken, they would have said, "No, thank you. All of you." Bursting with joy, Miss Mary grinned and nodded, grateful that years of hoping, praying, and believing had not been in vain. Chop and Ray Ray understood now why their grandmother stayed on her knees and hummed incessantly. They smiled as they decided to join her next time. Two other spirits joined hands with the first and the Johnson family was made whole again.

Then, one by one, like they came, the spirits marched into the sky until each being merged with the clouds. Chop waved vigorously as they returned to glory. Sensing closure of the moment, the animals retreated into the safety of the forest, and the trees stood themselves upright again.

When the spirits were no more, the people calmed to a deafening silence. They joined hands tightly, all of them, and formed a circle as Possum covered herself with shreds of her mangled dress. Each set of eyes confirmed in the others that colored people in Money had become one—one people, one strength, one fortress—and they knew they'd meet in this place again. Until then, they gloried in what they had witnessed and, after shaking hands and embracing, each bent and touched the earth of The Sacred Place in celebration of the union of flesh and spirit on holy ground. Upon exiting, they waltzed slowly through the woods, single file, strutting like Billie Faye used to, clear that the war was not over, but clear also, now, that they could win.